ASSASSIN OF THE GODS

Rebekah Sinclair

BEFORE YOU DIVE IN

Welcome to Avalon, the second installment in a vast fantasy multiverse.

While *Assassin of the Gods* begins a new journey, it picks up after the events of *Awakening the Forgotten Goddess*, book two of *The Forgotten Goddess* series.

You don't *have* to read *The Forgotten Goddess* first—but if you want a deeper understanding of the world, its history, and the forces at play, it's highly recommended.

Either way, prepare for a tale of gods, destiny, and the price of power.

REBEKAH SINCLAIR
THE FORGOTTEN GODDESS
AWAKENING
THE FORGOTTEN GODDESS
RECLAIMING
THE FORGOTTEN GODDESS
VENGEANCE
OF THE FORGOTTEN GODDESS
YOU ARE HERE
ASSASSIN OF THE GODS
REBEKAH SINCLAIR

CONTENT WARNING

Assassin of the Gods is a **dark fantasy romance** that contains mature themes, violence, and explicit content. While this story is crafted with care, readers should be aware of the following potential triggers before diving in:

Content Warnings:

! **Violence & Gore** – Includes combat, battle scenes, assassinations, and graphic depictions of injury.

! **Death & Murder** – Features on-page deaths, execution, war-related casualties, and past traumatic losses.

! **Explicit Romance Scenes & Strong Language** – High-heat sexual content and frequent use of profanity.

! **Mild Torture / Punishment / Threat of Sexual Assault** – Includes descriptions of suffering, captiv-

ity, physical violence, and implied or attempted
sexual coercion.

This book is intended for **mature audiences (18+)** and
includes **dark, high-stakes themes** intertwined with
romance, court intrigue, and supernatural forces.

Reader discretion is advised.

AVALON
FROSTHAVEN
EVERSHADE
CAIRNVAIL
ASTRALANA
VAILSEA
LEDORIA
THORNSPIRE
CASTLE STARFALL
MOONSHADOW COVE
GLOAMREACH
UMBRANOR
SYLVADORA
MIREVALE
WASTELANDS
UMBRAL TIDES

THE COURTS & RULERS OF AVALON

1. Eldoria (The Shimmering Court)

- **Ruler**: Lady Liora
- Eldoria represents the light Fae and stands in contrast to the dark Fae of Avalon. They are known for their radiant beauty and illusion magic.

2. Gloamreach (The Twilight Court)

- **Ruler: King Eryndor**
- This court exists in a perpetual state of dusk. They are the arbiters of balance, often mediating between the light and dark Fae realms.

3. Cairnvail (The Stone Court)

- **Ruler: Lord Granite**
- Located in a vast mountain range, Cairnvail is a kingdom of earth and stone, ruled by powerful Fae warriors. Their magic is tied to the earth, making them nearly indestructible.

4. Sylvadora (The Enchanted Forest)

- **Ruler: Lady Thalassa**
- A kingdom deeply connected to nature, where ancient trees and spirits dwell. The Fae of Sylvadora are protectors of the natural world and wield powerful elemental magic.

5. Umbranor (The Shadowed Court)

- **Ruler: Shade**
- A realm of darkness and shadows, Umbranor is even more mysterious and dangerous than Avalon. The Fae here are masters of shadow

magic and deception, often acting as assassins or spies.

6. Astralana (The Celestial Court)

- **Ruler: High Seer Astrael**
- This court is tied to the stars and celestial bodies. The Fae of the floating islands of Astralana are scholars and seers, with the ability to predict future events and manipulate cosmic forces.

7. Mirevalis (The Swamp Court)

- **Ruler: Duchess Morwen**
- A kingdom of marshlands and mist, Mirevalis is home to Fae who are deeply connected to water and poison. They are often seen as outcasts, but their knowledge of the arcane is unparalleled.

8. Frosthaven (The Winter Court)

- **Ruler: Queen Eira**
- **Role**: A cold and harsh realm ruled by ice and snow. The Fae here are known for their stoicism and ability to endure extreme conditions.

9. Evershade (The Eternal Night Court)

- **Ruler**: Lord Umbriel

- It is unclear if Evershade is a close ally to Avalon but certainly harbors its own ambitions. The Fae here are deeply tied to death and the afterlife.

10. Thornspire (The Briar Court)

- **Ruler**: King Thorne
- A wild and dangerous realm where thorn-covered forests and treacherous landscapes dominate. The Fae of Thornspire are fierce and untamed, with a reputation for cruelty.

Times of Night:

- **Morning:** First Shade
- **Afternoon:** Mid-Shade
- **Night:** Evenfall

Salutations:

- **"Bright moon to you."** – A formal greeting, akin to "Good morning,".
- **"Steady stars."** – A well-wishing phrase, suggesting stability and clarity, much like "Have a good day."
- **"Darkness guide you."** – A respectful farewell, akin to "Safe travels,".

For Kristen,

*A warrior whose story deserves to be
written among the stars.*

*May your courage shine like the brightest constellations,
your laughter echo in the wind, and your spirit dance in
realms where time holds no power.*

*Some souls are too brilliant for this world
—they belong to eternity.*

CHAPTER 1

Tana

"You'll be lucky to make it to forty."

The sharp scent of antiseptic stung my nose, but it was the doctor's words that left the real burn as he removed the needle from my arm.

The cool rush of whatever he had just injected me with made my arm cold.

"Forty."

The word feels heavier than it should, like lead in my mouth. I force a chuckle, though it tastes bitter.

Somewhere in my mind, the doctor's voice rattles things off—likely condolences and the usual advice to keep a positive attitude. But I can't hear any of it.

All I hear is the cynical beep of the machine, reminding me that I am awake and this is not a dream.

The steady buzz of the fluorescent light overhead mimics the static that had filled my mind for the last several minutes. Its buzzing increases, as if I can feel the energy of it, demanding my attention and forcing me to focus.

Looking up at the light, I give in, letting the intensity of it burn my eyes and bring me back into the moment.

My chin meets my chest, and I blink as the white spot

covering my vision turn black. The unfocused room comes back into clarity, and with it, the doctor's voice.

His black foam clogs serve as the anchor that hold me here, ensnaring my gaze and refusing to let it go.

"Hold on, I gotta put my shoes in sports mode."

I snorted a disheartened laugh, hearing my dad's voice from last year's memory.

Never did I think I would see the ever-rigid Brigadier General wearing Crocs, but there was a first time for every-thing—like hearing that you're going to die soon.

I realize the doctor has been quiet for a moment now.

I feel his sympathetic stare on me, expectant. With a few final blinks, I finally meet his dark brown eyes.

His thin-lipped smile tells me he is sorry he had to be the one delivering the news, but really, I bet he is just hoping I won't break down in tears.

"Well," my voice cracks, and I clear my throat, "that's thirteen years to live it up. Could be worse, right?"

"I know this is overwhelming. You're young, healthy, but—"

Here it goes—the pep talk.

"But dying. Just say it, Doc." I cut him off, my tone sharp as a blade. "I'm dying."

I lean back against the hospital bed, rubbing the IV stuck into the top of my hand. The white tape holding it in place pulls at the fine hairs, bugging the shit out of me.

Almost as much as the damn buzz of the lights.

"This isn't about giving up, Tana." Dr. Williams's voice is soft but firm, like he actually believes in this mind-over-matter bullshit.

"It's about managing risk, staying proactive. You've accomplished so much—you could still have years ahead of you."

I can't help but snort. "Oh, good. I'll pencil in 'don't die' right between cardio and filing my discharge papers."

My eyes squint, betraying the faintest crack in my armor, and it forces me to look away.

"And what? Pamphlets? Support groups? Tell me, Doc, do they cover 'how not to fall apart while planning your funeral'?"

Steeling myself, I look back at him.

The compassion in Dr. Williams's eyes softens, and he reminds me of my dad's favorite actor, Denzel Washington. Eyes that have seen it all.

Patience that has lasted through everything.

Short, curly salt-and-pepper hair and practical pale-green scrubs beneath his white doctor's coat complete the image of a man who could probably survive any catastrophe.

Dad would probably like Dr. Williams.

I should introduce them—maybe he can have a friend after my funeral. Dr. Williams lives here, close to base.

I bet he sees a lot of soldiers.

Dad could use someone looking out for his high blood sugar, someone to smack treats out of his hands since I won't be here to do it.

"It's not about the pamphlets, Tana. It's about what you choose to do with the time you have."

That is laughable, given my line of work. I suppose I've

been trying to get myself killed since I turned eighteen and Mom died.

"My mom... she was thirty-eight. You think she had this too?" My voice is so quiet it is nearly a whisper.

Dr. Williams exhales slowly. He probably knew this question was coming. Most of his questions in the last forty-eight hours have been about her.

"It's possible. I can't say for sure without her records, but..."

I hold up my hand, shaking my head. "Doesn't matter. She didn't make it past forty either."

"I'm sorry, Tana."

I guess I should get used to that.

I heard it a million times after my mother died.

From the first responders in the ambulance. The nurses who watched me waiting in the emergency room until my dad could get there.

A million people over the next few days at her wake and funeral.

I was sick of hearing it then. I was already sick of hearing it now.

Discharged from the hospital and riding the bus back to my apartment, I pretend to look outside, but really, I am watching myself in the reflection of the window.

The haunted look in my eyes reminds me of how she looked.

Wide-eyed and unblinking, like she was seeing a ghost.

She hadn't moved as the strained breath crawled out of her throat and she clutched her chest, lying on the kitchen floor and staring at me.

It had probably been half a minute that I just stood there looking at her while my brain caught up to what was happening. She was having a heart attack. She was dying.

The ambulance came, and it was such a high step up, climbing into the back and riding by her side to the hospital. The paramedics moved around me; their muddled voices couldn't penetrate the static in my head.

She died there in the ambulance. I remember hearing that final, long-drawn-out beep of the monitor registering the last pulse of her heart.

The bus jostles around the potholes, and I brace my grip on the seat in front of me. I wonder if I will know when the final beat of my heart happens.

I wonder if Mom had known—if she had felt it.

She was only thirty-eight when a massive heart attack stole her from us.

She had never been sick before. Never shown signs of having problems.

But I have been ignoring this for a year now.

The irregular beats of my heart that seemed to slow, then race forward. The tightening in my chest that feels like my breath is being wrung from my lungs.

Something told me she had known.

Perhaps not how short her time would be, but she must have known something wasn't right.

The bus slams on its brakes to avoid hitting a cyclist crossing the street, and I lurch forward—just like when the ambulance arrived at the hospital.

They flung the doors open, and her stretcher was pulled out in an instant, rolling toward the wide double doors.

I had just realized we'd stopped moving. I hadn't even gotten out of the ambulance myself yet.

It felt like the ground had disappeared from under me, and I was still moving fifty miles an hour.

I watched through the windows while they rushed her inside and down a hallway.

The same paramedic who had been doing CPR in the ambulance was riding the stretcher with her. Straddling her torso, he kept pumping his hands, his entire upper body pressing down as he tried to save her life.

"Goodbye, Mom," I whispered as someone slammed their hand against a button on the wall. The hallway doors opened. She disappeared behind them.

I never saw her again.

Stepping off the bus, the loud burst from the air brakes blows my hair. I shove my hands into the pockets of my jacket and walk toward my apartment complex.

I'll have to discharge from the military.

The thought I've been avoiding since the doc talked about pamphlets.

What else would I be if not a military brat?

I had been only eighteen for a few days when Mom had her heart attack, but even before that, I knew I was going to be a soldier for life—just like Daddy.

He had enlisted as soon as he could and ran straight to boot camp. Lived on base and sent nearly all his money to his mother those first few years.

Nanny had raised him all by herself, and there was no one in this world he respected more than her.

They had a small home, and she worked in the cafeteria

at his school during the day and did laundry at night. She cooked for all the kids at the school and still made a fresh dinner when they got home.

Every weekend she made some kind of dessert, but Dad's favorite was always Nanny's pies.

That was because he got two desserts whenever she made pie.

Nanny told me the story once when I helped her make the lattice crust for the top of her cherry pie.

She would take the leftover crust and flatten it on a tray. Brushing it with melted butter and a generous layer of cinnamon and sugar, she would bake it.

It was only to keep from wasting anything since they were so poor, but Dad only knew he was getting two treats. He and Nanny would sit at their small table and eat it fresh out of the oven.

One day he brought a friend over and asked her to make it for them, only to realize he never knew what the dessert was called.

Sugar Crisp.

She made it up right there on the spot, and it forever rooted itself in our family.

Stepping into my apartment and tossing the pamphlets and medical folders onto the counter, I roll my shoulders back and stretch my neck.

The air-conditioning vent blows one of the leaves on my pothos plant, and it waves at me. It is the only thing in this empty apartment that greets me.

Rounding the corner, I open the fridge and pantry, fetching the ingredients for Sugar Crisp.

It had become Nanny's remedy for everything, and maybe it will fix me now.

Anytime Dad was upset as a child, she made some up for him. When he got a bad grade in school or came home with a broken arm, he knew the sweet scent of Sugar Crisp was going to fill their small home soon.

Within a few minutes, it was filling mine as I changed my clothes.

Standing in the bathroom, I give myself a thorough inspection.

I don't look like someone who is dying.

But I suppose we all are.

Everyone is marching toward death from the moment we are born—we just never know when we are going to meet up with the Reaper.

I think that's what I'm stuck on. The end of my road is ahead, but I have no idea where it drops off.

I'm curious if I'll see the end before it gets here or if it'll sneak up on me like it did Mom.

Eighteen years.

That's all she had with our little family. It always felt like she got the short end of the stick.

She and Dad got married when she was twenty, and I was born a few months later. Their only child—and a girl. Just like her mother before her. And her mother before that.

For as many generations as we know, there has only ever been one child born to a family, and it is always a girl.

Nearly eighteen years after carrying on the legacy of our maternal bloodline, her road came to a dead end.

I snort at the morbid pun and work my unruly hair into an elastic band.

My hair always has a mind of its own—a wild, curly crown that does exactly what it wants.

Big, bold, and unapologetic, like it is made for another world altogether.

It's thick and lush, a tangle of curls reaching out in every direction. Softer than they look, but still fierce. Most days, I love it.

Other days, it's a battle just to keep it in line.

I guess that's what I get for being stubborn and strong—my hair's just a mirror.

Sitting on my balcony with a plate of steaming Sugar Crisp, I look over the military discharge process, even though I've already reviewed it a dozen times.

I knew this was coming when the tests took so long.

I'll have to submit Dr. Williams's assessments and my heart scans for medical evaluation. They'll determine I am no longer fit for service. I'll get my discharge papers.

I'll no longer be a Ranger.

Fucking bullshit.

They should just let me fight until I die—or until it kills me. Either way, it won't change the outcome. It just feels like such a low blow against all my hard work.

I was the first goddamn woman to earn the Ranger tab, and now I'll be the first to give it up.

I chew on the same piece of Sugar Crisp for several minutes as it turns to ash in my mouth.

When the Army finally opened all combat roles to

women in 2015, two of my friends and I were the first women to take the RASP at Fort Benning, Georgia.

Eight weeks later, when we were passing Victory Pond, I was the first of us to earn the distinctive black-and-gold shoulder tab of the Rangers.

I was the first to graduate Ranger School.

The first woman to lead Rangers in combat, serving in the Army's most elite unit, the Seventy-fifth Ranger Regiment.

Only the best from the Brigadier General's daughter.

And I am the best.

There is a reason my callsign is Valkyrie: *Chooser of the Slain.*

Out in the field, I decide who lives and who dies.

Rangers line up to join my lead. They even wait years for a spot because I've never lost a Ranger. I've never failed a mission.

But it seem that in less than fifteen years, I won't get that choice.

One day in my not-so-distant future, the Valkyrie will be choosing me to join the warriors of the afterlife, and I'll have no choice but to go.

There is no point wasting time reinventing myself or crying over what couldn't be changed.

The end of the road is waiting, sure—but I'll be damned if I don't kick up a storm on my way there.

I brush the crumbs from my hands and stand, gazing out over the quiet city below.

The lights blur like stars caught in motion, and for a brief moment, I feel untouchable. Infinite.

But even stars burn out.

"Well then," I mutter, my voice swallowed by the night. "If I'm on borrowed time, I might as well make every second count."

And just like that, a new kind of clarity settles over me—sharp, electric, and untamed.

I'm not going to wait for death to find me.

If the bastard wants me, he'll have to come and find me.

CHAPTER 2
orion

She's calling me to her sanctum. I can feel it—sense the tug of her magic around my abdomen.

The lasso she has cast into the atmosphere of Avalon waits, knowing I'll answer it.

I do. Every time.

I have to; there is no other choice.

Not simply because one does not ignore the call of the Lady of the Lake, but because I *have* to know.

I have to know how to stop this.

I have to know *who* stops this.

I drain the rest of the wine in my glass, the rich red coating my tongue with the faint taste of smoke. Placing it back on the ancient round table, I rap my knuckles twice on its dark surface.

"I will return soon," I call out to Hypnos as I turn for the door, not waiting for his answer. He knows who calls to me. He feels the power of the one who hails the Prince of Avalon.

Each step I take down the spiraling stairs is a descent into the marrow of our realm, where whispers of the past cling to the damp stone like ivy.

The Sanctum of Echoes is older than Avalon itself—or so the stories claim.

It is said the first threads of magic were spun here, in the heart of the realm, where the Lady first wove her veil of visions.

Only she can draw back that veil and peer into the beyond, seeing not just what Avalon is today but what fate may hold in its future.

The air thickens as I near the bottom, heavy with the weight of ages—of choices made and futures abandoned.

A cool breeze off the lake stirs. My long white hair dances with it, as if this were a joyful reunion of friends.

Once, this place was a sanctuary for the first seers of Avalon—the keepers of prophecy—who came to commune with the Lady and glimpse the threads of fate.

Now, it is little more than a hollow echo of what it once was, its power as faded as the thousands of stars that no longer shine brightly in our sky.

Yet even now, the cave seems to whisper faintly with the remnants of that ancient magic, as if the Lady herself breathes life into the stone, waiting for the day the threads of destiny might be rewoven.

Dread knots within my stomach when I reach the base of the stairs.

Staring back at me from the cave's open mouth is the judgmental moon of the realm—our sentient guardian, always watching, always glowing in our ever-night sky.

She looks down on me, and I feel the weight of her stare. It has not changed. I fear she will show me nothing new tonight.

I'll be tormented once again, forced to watch this destructive fate and walk away with the mockery of knowing there is nothing to be done to stop it.

I pause, bowing to her, then unbutton my coat and shove my hands into my pockets. The soft clink of my sword in its scabbard follows me as I straighten.

Like the sanctum, the moon is older than magic, older than the Fae. These ancient deities—this prophetic cave, its attending Lady, and the watchful moon—have earned our divine worship until the last star burns in the sky.

Which may come much sooner than I would like.

Waves crash against the rocks, sending a burst of fine mist against me as I turn the corner, walking deeper into the cave. The torches lining the walls ignite as I pass, lighting my path to the basin.

Each torch that flares to life casts long, flickering shadows that stretch across the jagged walls like clawed hands reaching for me.

The crash of waves echoes off the cavern walls, a rhythmic reminder of Avalon's restless heart, still beating— if only barely.

The walls pulse with the magic of the Lady, a low hum that resonates in the atmosphere anytime she surfaces.

Of course, she is here, waiting. Again, she knew I would come.

I always do.

The stone floor beneath my boots is slick with a fine layer of mist, as though the Lady herself is leaving traces of her presence behind.

A ridiculous notion, of course. She never leaves the lake.

If ever she did step foot on land, the lake would join her, ensuring its majestic waters are the only surface she steps upon.

However, in this ancient grotto, the Lady will be waiting deep within the cavern, within the sanctum and its rich pool of whispers.

The basin has already risen out of the water that is its eternal home.

The Lady waits with it, her webbed hands holding the sides of the Silvermere, her blue skin catching some of the silver light that dances off its surface.

Her black eyes seem impossibly deep, reflecting nothing yet revealing everything, as though she sees not just my actions but my intentions.

Assessing whether the time is right to finally let me know—to finally let me see.

The faint ripple of her energy brushes against my magic, testing it, prodding it, as if to remind me that her power dwarfs even mine.

Or perhaps she is seeing how my power has waned since my last visit here. Either is probable, and both give me cause for irritation.

I assess her in return, but she gives nothing away. Like the guardian moon, she only observes me and lets my torment continue. The only way I'll find out is by peering into the Silvermere.

She doesn't speak. I'm not even sure she has the ability to, though I feel her voice within my mind, stirring the Fae magic inside me.

I understand her command: *Look into the basin.*

We've done this a thousand times. And each time, the vision is the same, unchanged through the ages.

I run a hand through my hair, the motion slow, almost mechanical, and exhale deeply. The ache beneath my ribs sharpens, a cruel reminder of the starlight within me fading inch by inch.

There was a time when I believed my strength was limitless, when the light in my veins burned brighter than the stars.

Now that light is a flickering candle, and I am powerless to stop it from going out.

I press my fingers into the edge of the basin, steadying myself against the weight of what I'm about to see—what I've already seen a thousand times.

The silence of the grotto presses in on me, broken only by the faint drip of water from the stalactites overhead.

"Show me again," I whisper, my voice rough, low.

The basin's light flares as the vision takes hold, its tendrils of silver magic pulling me in, dragging me toward the inevitable collapse.

The Lady shifts to the cavern wall behind her to watch me from the opposite side of the pool.

Avalon unravels before me, as it always does.

The hills wither, flowers fading to ash. Rivers dry into cracked beds. The sky darkens, clouds swallowing the constellations that once painted the night.

The land dies in stages, an unrelenting march of decay that chokes the magic from the realm. The hills blacken faster this time, the flowers dissolving into ash as though Avalon itself is eager to show me its end.

And at its center—at the very heart of the collapse—I see myself.

I hate this part.

I brace as the shadow of my future self comes into focus: the familiar hollow eyes and crumbling form that haunt my every step.

My hair, once silver-white and gleaming with the light of the stars, is dull and lifeless. My veins, which once pulsed with the magic of Avalon itself, are blackened and dry.

My body crumbles to ash, carried away on a bitter wind.

As I fall, so does Avalon.

This is the end.

It's the only end I've ever seen.

My jaw tightens as I watch the scene play out for what feels like the millionth time. My hands clench into fists, and my shadows wrap around me, but I don't look away.

I can't.

There has to be something—anything—I've missed.

A clue.

A sign.

A reason to believe there's a way to stop this.

I lean closer to the basin, my breath ghosting over the surface of the water.

Nothing changes.

The Lady's presence brushes against my thoughts, her silence filled with a quiet curiosity. She doesn't need to speak for me to understand her question: *Why do you keep watching this?*

"Because I have to," I reply, my voice harsh and low. "If I stop looking, if I stop trying, then Avalon is already lost."

And so am I.

Her black eyes glint, a faint ripple of power washing over me like a cold tide.

"And yet you find no answers."

The words pricks at my patience, and I release a sharp breath, shadows curling tighter around my shoulders.

"What choice do I have? You show me nothing but the same end, over and over again. If there is another way, then why won't you show it to me?"

The Lady tilts her head, her stillness unnerving. When she speaks, her voice presses into my mind, low and unyielding.

"You have seen what lies ahead because it is the fate you believe in most. This ruin is all you allow yourself to see. How could I show you another path when you do not believe it exists?"

Her words strike deeper than I want to admit. My lips press into a thin line, and I look away, my gaze fixed on the flickering light within the basin.

"You think I want this?" I snap, the frustration spilling out of me. "You think I haven't tried to find another way? Avalon is dying. The magic is dying. I–am dying. If there is another way, then why won't you show it to me?"

The Lady tilts her head, her gaze cutting deep as though she sees the cracks in my resolve.

"Because you have never believed there is another way."

The words echo in the cavern, pressing against the walls of my mind. I don't want to hear them, yet they take root.

I have never believed there is another way.

I grip the edge of the basin, my shadows writhing around me like restless serpents.

The thought dies in my mind as I realize what she is waiting for.

She's not showing me another road because I've never let myself believe one exists.

My breath catches, the weight of the truth pressing into my chest like a stone.

"If this road is traveled, it ends with Avalon's end. With my end. But if another road exists—if fate can shift—if I choose to believe..."

My voice trails off as the thought takes hold, unraveling centuries of despair in its wake. My grip tightens as my shadows twist and recoil.

Lightning dances across my knuckles.

I glance at the Lady, her silence unsettling. But in her stillness, I find an answer—a permission of sorts.

It's not her choice to make.

It's mine.

It has always been mine.

And in this moment, I understand the truth she has been waiting for me to see.

"There is more than one road," I say, the words feeling foreign on my tongue. "More than one fate. One of them leads to Avalon's end, but another..." I falter, the weight of hope almost too much to bear. "Another might lead to its beginning."

The Lady's gaze remains steady, unflinching, as though willing me to cross the threshold of doubt. My chest tightens, my pulse pounding in my ears.

I force myself to meet her eyes and let out a slow, trembling breath.

"Show me," I say, my voice breaking as I surrender to the possibility. "Show me how Avalon begins again."

The Lady's eyes narrow, her silence stretching for a moment as though she is weighing my sincerity.

Then, slowly, she wades back, her gaze never leaving mine as she walks across the water's surface.

The air shifts.

A thunderous crack splits the silence, and light erupts from her like a supernova, casting brilliant white radiance in all directions. Her black eyes blaze silver, the glow so intense it sears away the shadows that cling to the cavern walls.

Her mouth gapes in a silent cry, and her hands grip the basin's edge as if anchoring herself to its power.

I stagger back, shielding my eyes from the blinding light. The ground trembles beneath my feet, and the basin's surface begins to churn violently. My shadows recoil as a burst of power ripples outward, slicing through the air.

Her form stiffens, her back arching as an unearthly energy surges through the grotto.

The Lady doesn't move, her form locked in this state of raw, crackling energy.

Her presence surges, electric and sharp, bending the very fabric of the grotto as she reweaves the threads of destiny.

The light flares brighter, and then—

The vision changes.

The sudden surge of light slices through the gloom, drawing me back to the Silvermere.

A new vision fills the basin, and a voice resounds around

the grotto, its tone and tenor sinking into my soul: *"If the bastard wants me, he'll have to come and find me."*

My breath catches as I see her.

A woman.

Mortal.

Walking through Avalon's ruins with quiet determination.

Her presence cuts through the darkness like a ray of moonlight in a clouded sky, pushing back the shadows that cling to her path.

My heart pounds in my chest—not from the vision itself, but from the way she moves—effortless, certain, as though the ruin around her is only a temporary obstacle.

I can't see her face—not fully—but something about her sets my pulse racing.

Something deep inside me stirs, a feeling I thought I'd buried long ago.

Hope.

The vision shifts again, showing me the serene Caves of Pandora.

Just a stone's throw from here—a short walk down the shoreline—and within, the portal, long dormant and lifeless, blazes to life. Its edges swirl with radiant blue starlight, alive, pulsing.

The portal's light spills outward, bathing the barren landscape in a glow so intense I can feel it warming my face.

It takes my breath away, and I clutch my chest.

Or perhaps it is her that causes me to gasp—the rebellion in her gaze, the promise of resistance.

Her presence doesn't just disrupt the darkness.

It reshapes it.

Bending the shadows to her will, as though they've been waiting for her all along.

As though *I've* been waiting for her all along.

The vision flickers, alternating between the two scenes—the mortal woman and the portal—demanding I interpret its message correctly.

Again and again, they draw closer to me.

With every step she takes, life is left in her wake. Flowers bloom. Lush grass races across the rolling hills once more.

I blink—and suddenly, she is standing before me.

So close.

Something within me is drawn to her.

My fingers twitch at my sides, my instincts betraying me, desperate to reach out.

I lift my hand, wanting to touch her.

Of course. She is not here.

I exhale, my curiosity rippling the surface of the Silver-mere, and the vision fades.

It leaves me gasping, my hand tightening on the basin's edge as I try to reconcile what I've seen with what I know.

The Lady lingers, her gaze heavy, unyielding, as though daring me to accept the truth she has already embraced: Avalon has a savior.

My chest tightens.

The savior the realm has been crying out for is real.

She is real.

And she is coming.

Somehow the dormant realm portal in the Caves of

Pandora will come to life once again and through it, Avalon's hope will emerge.

A mortal.

Hope is not a luxury I have allowed myself for centuries. But it rises within me, unbidden and unrelenting, refusing to be silenced.

For the first time, the basin does not feel like a tool of despair but a promise—a portal to a future I never dared to believe in.

I straighten, squaring my shoulders as the echoes of the vision fade, the mortal woman's words still ringing in my ears:

"If the bastard wants me, he'll have to come and find me."

A slow, sly smile tugs at the corner of my mouth, almost unfamiliar.

There's fire in her voice—a defiance that cuts through the ruin and despair.

She isn't cowed by the darkness; she challenges it.

Dares it to rise against her.

That challenge hums in my veins like a long-forgotten melody.

"So, you'd make me chase you, would you?"

I murmur the words to the empty air, the question lingering between us like a whispered promise.

There's no bitterness in it.

Only intrigue.

A mortal with such resolve, such tenacity, is a rarity. It's not just her words that linger—it's the weight behind them.

Her resistance is a spark against the shadows threatening to swallow Avalon.

And I find myself eager, even hungry, to see how brightly she can burn.

"Very well," I say softly, the words laced with quiet promise.

"If it's a game you want, mortal, I'll play. But when I find you..."

My fingers trace the hilt of my sword, a subtle spark of lightning flickering across my knuckles.

"...you'll have to decide if you're ready for what comes next."

The thought settles in my mind, steady and sure.

Let her defy the bastard, whoever he is.

Let her run.

Let her fight.

I will meet her at the edge of light and shadow.

And together, we will see if her fire is enough to set Avalon ablaze once more.

CHAPTER 3
Tana

"I feel like we're in the butthole of South America," Ghost whispers as we sit high in a tree, surrounded by nothing but lush forest.

Rolling my eyes, I stifle a chuckle as a bead of sweat races down my back.

"Ironclad, is this why you smell like shit all the time?"

The former British SAS operative is only trying to goad our task force into a pissing contest.

"I'm from Brazil, you fucktwat. We're in Peru."

Ironclad, a former Brazilian Marine, is my go-to soldier for heavy weaponry and tactical defense.

He's not just a big, burly motherfucker; he's unyielding on the front line. Ironclad—just like his callsign.

"Blaze, can you blow his mouth off so he'll shut the hell up?"

"No. The noise will alert the pack to our presence."

Blaze, always practical, came from Argentina's special forces and specializes in demolitions.

She's also our combat medic, so she probably doesn't

want to be the one to tend to his dumb ass after blowing his mouth off.

We've been hunting a terrorist group of wolf-shifters for three days, and we're currently sitting in the rainforest of Peru.

It's the dry season, but that doesn't mean it's any less humid. The suffocatingly warm moisture in the air, lack of sleep, and our upcoming leave time are making the task force act like toddlers.

A rare cool breeze ushers gently through the leaves, and something uneasy settles over me—a chill that meanders up my spine, as if someone is assessing me from afar.

It makes the fine hairs at the nape of my neck bristle, and I shiver.

Turning behind me, it seems as if the shadows of the forest deepen. The lush green turns richer, like darkness is spreading its claws and reaching for us.

I narrow my eyes, not trusting the stillness, and brush off the oily sensation.

Loading my gun with thaumium bullets and checking my oleander-venom darts, I remind myself that tomorrow I'll be sunbathing in Hawaii as I holster my weapon.

I won't be dealing with twenty- and thirty-something-year-old toddlers, shifter terrorists, or rainforests.

I'll be wrestling the waves on sandy beaches, and my biggest decision of the day will be which fruity cocktail to order next.

The mic crackles as Sentinel joins the shit-talking.

"Ghost, how do you manage to be so fucking quiet when

you're on the ground hunting but can't shut up any other second of the day?"

Sentinel is recon and surveillance. I can tell by the way he's speaking that he must be squinting into the scope of his rifle, likely scanning the vegetation for movement.

"I also shut up when your mom is choking on my dick, Sen," Ghost retorts.

"I imagine it's difficult to keep small objects in one's mouth," Sentinel responds quickly in his usual dry, carefree tone. "I can see why it would take concentration."

Ghost takes a breath to defend himself when the task force's hacker joins the line.

"The shifters are thirty seconds out from range. Linking your feeds to the drone thermals."

The feverish clicking of Wildcard's keyboard comes through the comms as she monitors the team from our control room in Area 51.

"Aww, so sorry, Push Pop," Sentinel chides Ghost with one more dig. "Time for you to go stealth, which means I get a few minutes of peace and quiet."

"Button up, everyone. The fun is over."

I silence my soldiers, and the team tenses under my order.

The atmosphere becomes heavy, almost as if the team is evoking the warriors within themselves as we ready for the pack heading toward us.

Days ago, tragedy struck the world as a coordinated attack was carried out across the globe.

Two dozen world leaders were assassinated—no, executed—all at once.

Many of them died live on TV as they addressed their nations.

President Sims had been gathering on the White House veranda, ready to inform the world that immortals exist.

Monsters are real, and civilians were finally going to know.

My soldiers and I were guests of honor—Task Force 777 standing at attention by the president's side.

It was during Sims's first term as president that he fortified Umbra, the secret division of the U.S. military that fights the gods.

He backed it with funding and tech, rebranded the branch, and got serious about protecting mortals from the gods who live in secret beside us.

They pulled the best of the best from around the world, including me and every member of my team.

Except Wildcard, that is.

Our resident hacker found Umbra on her own.

She broke past their defenses, walked right into Area 51 with a laptop in hand, disabled security footage as she roamed the halls, fried the keypads, and let herself into the debriefing room.

I'll never forget the look on Colonel Stone's face.

"I'd like a job here," she said.

One look at Sentinel, and I knew we agreed.

"She's with me."

I claimed her on the spot and didn't even wait for Stone's answer before I got up, my task force following me, Wildcard making her introductions on the way to our next mission.

For five years, we've been policing the immortals, and the world was finally going to know.

Then, the shot blasted through Sims's skull.

The fucking blood splatter got all over my face.

I spent hours getting chunks of brain out of my hair.

There was no sound of a bullet, no trace of an attack, and we immediately knew:

The gods were starting a war.

The past forty-eight hours have been hell, and shit's about to hit the fan.

My team needs a break before the world ends, because we won't see a moment of peace for a long time—I expect.

Stone wanted to deny our leave, but I told him we would walk.

What the hell else could he do?

Task Force 777 is the best in Umbra. If I walk, so does my team, and he'd be up shit creek without a paddle—with immortals on his ass.

This is our last mission before ten days of leave, and we're all trying to contain the building eagerness.

For now, we focus on capturing this pack of shifters so we can get the fuck out of Dodge.

"Going to Morse."

Wildcard switches our earpieces from audio to Morse code.

The shifters have impeccable hearing, so now that they are within range, it's radio silence and hand signals.

The silent drones flying overhead provide us with a thermal view of the approaching pack.

"Fuck, that alpha is big," Hawkeye taps out.

We all interpret the clicks.

The packs always move in the same formation. The weaker members are at the front and rear of the pack's line. The stronger guards surround the mated alpha pair that leads from the center.

That means we need to make the alphas move from the center to the front.

My team has dispersed into a semicircle, strategically poised around this small clearing where the line of shifters must travel.

Blaze rigged pheromone canisters along the trail, and Sentinel watches the thermal cams.

Raising his arm with his hand open, he holds until most of the pack has passed—then he closes his fist.

With his signal, Blaze activates the first of the canisters.

The pheromones work to entrance several wolves at the rear of the pack, who begin diverting off course from the others.

Ironclad is waiting to receive the stray wolves with oleander darts and thaumium bindings.

Ahead of us, Wildcard is ready with a drone fitted with a speaker. It plays a recording of Ghost whispering, as if attempting to be quiet.

These wolves know we're hunting them, so making them think we're ahead of them will force them into defensive positions.

Another canister is released, and Ghost's scent is carried downwind.

As the sound of whispers reaches the pack, we watch

their ears shift, locating the noise as they raise their snouts, sniffing the new scent on the wind.

They speak telepathically, so there are no commands or noises that we can hear.

We only know our plan is working when we watch the thermals and see the mated alpha pair disengage from the center and trot to the front of the pack.

"This is going to be too easy," Ghost taps out.

"Don't bring us bad luck," Hawkeye answers.

Another signal from Sentinel tells us he has visuals. The pack is nearing, and our ambush is only moments away.

Hawkeye, Ironclad, and Sentinel lock targets on the wolves at the rear of the pack. I can practically feel Ghost buzzing with anticipation on the ground. Those wolves are walking right past him, and they have no idea.

He'll be on top of the female alpha before she realizes what's going on. *"The male is mine."*

Blaze has more canisters at the ready for detonation. These are filled with silver-laced smoke and will disrupt their senses, slowing their reaction time.

Wildcard has drones in position, ready with thaumium nets.

I'm palming my favorite blade. Oleander toxin is stored in the handle, slowly lacing the sharp edge of the knife, ready to root the venom into my victim with each slice.

"Show-off," Sentinel taps out, glancing at my choice of weapon. Figures. *"The largest pack and biggest alpha we've seen in weeks, and you pick a cheese knife to fight with."*

"I prefer a hands-on approach," I type back with a wink. *"I have to remind you why I'm captain."*

"Oh, I don't need reminders."

During training, he thought he had team lead in the bag, especially when it was just down to the two of us at the end.

He figured the hand-to-hand fight would be over in seconds, and he'd be taking the position at the top of the Victors' Climb.

I showed that asshole he was dead wrong when I broke his femur. There were no rules during Umbra basic that said cadets couldn't kill each other, and several did.

A few even tried to kill me, but each attempt was pointless.

They were heavy-footed and too eager—gave themselves away before they even got close.

But you don't build a team by killing your soldiers. And you don't pass Umbra basic if you don't stand at the top of Victory Hill.

So I let him live. I even braced his leg and helped him climb the hill. He stood on one foot and watched while I took the top spot.

As I became the first Assassin of the Gods. And he's been my loyal second ever since.

"Okay, Valkyrie, who lives today?" Sentinel taps out.

It's become a tradition before our attacks. Our talisman of good fortune as we battle the unstoppable.

"We do."

The pack reaches the center of the clearing, and we unleash hell.

Hawkeye, Ironclad, and Sentinel take down six wolves in the time it takes Ghost and me to launch ourselves at the mated alphas.

Silver-laced smoke fills the ground, rushing up the great beasts as thaumium nets fall from the sky.

I sling my body around the alpha's neck and use my momentum to bring him down. He quickly recovers, but I never stop moving into my next attack.

Pushing off the tree trunk, I soar into him, my blade slicing deep into the shoulder tissue as he snaps his large jaw at me.

Tucking and rolling under him, my knife cuts along his abdomen as I emerge from the other side.

With all my strength, I fling my blade to the ground, pinning his paw to the forest floor.

Snatching another blade from my uniform, I hurl it through the air. It strikes the female alpha, driving deep into her eye socket.

Her wide jaws, poised to bite Ghost's neck, go slack.

The soft tissue gives way to my instrument of death, and the oleander poison seeps into her brain.

The male alpha roars in pain, but a greater cry of agony echoes through the forest when he feels his mate die.

As their bond severs, I use the moment to drive another thaumium blade into his neck, ripping through arteries and tendons as the wolf's blood paints the forest red.

The ground trembles when his massive body thuds into the earth.

Under the cover of our nets, the remaining pack whimpers as they sense the connection to their alphas fade away with the breeze.

"We've got company." Hawkeye's voice breaks the silent comms. "Another line of wolves is approaching."

"What the fuck?" Sentinel growls. "A counterattack?"

"*Defensive positions,*" I command through our silent comms.

The team converges to the center of the clearing. Backs together, we watch the perimeter for the second attack, but it never comes.

We hear the gentle steps of the wolves as they creep forward. My heart pounds—several beats erratic—before it gallops at a steady pace as I level my breathing.

The pain in my chest constricts, but I know it won't last long.

Emerging from the thick greenery, we see the first muzzle. Teeth bared, a low snarl warns us. Another snout appears, followed by more.

But it's the center of the pack that gives us pause.

Younglings.

Likely twelve of them.

"*Were they just transporting fucking children, and we killed them?*" Ironclad taps out his question, his anger evident with each heavy pound in our ears. "*This can't be the wrong pack, can it?*"

Something doesn't feel right. Task Force 777 doesn't make mistakes.

Taking in the children, I notice one small wolf shift its gaze to the comrade next to it.

They seem skittish, huddling close together, but that would be a natural response to walking into a clearing of dead wolves.

Narrowing my eyes, I catch the faint glint of dull metal around the wolf's neck.

They are collared. All of them.

"They're prisoners," I tap out, my body heating with anger.

This pack of wolves was sentenced to death for their part in running a shifter breeding facility.

My stomach still curdles at the memory of what we saw in those dark rooms as we swept through, killing every man and immortal we found.

And now, they have children.

"None of them live."

With no warning, the dozen wolves we had just taken down rise up from the forest floor. Seeing their rejuvenated packmates, the newly arrived wolves lunge for us, abandoning the younglings they are supposed to be guarding.

My team doesn't flinch, never moving a muscle. We know we don't have to.

There are no rejuvenated wolves. They are still on the forest floor, dead or trapped under our metal nets. This is a projection—a three-dimensional image cast by the silent drones.

Each of those drones also has targets locked on the remaining adult wolves.

Now that they are clear of the younglings, Wildcard takes the rest of the pack down with a single push of a button. The small wolves whimper as their captors fall around them.

We hold for a moment, and I raise my hand, warning the younglings to remain still. Sentinel and Wildcard ensure the area is clear and give us the signal to stand down.

"Comms are back up." Wildcard's voice cracks again over our earpieces.

"And just like that, ladies and gentledicks, it's another great day of saving the world."

"Ghost," Ironclad mutters, rolling his eyes, "shut the fuck up."

Despite the victorious mission, that eerie sense of looming dread surrounds me again.

Either five years of killing immortals is getting to me, or we're being hunted.

CHAPTER 4
Tana

The hum of the teleportation pad fades into the echo of boots on concrete.

The air is sterile, cool, tinged with the metallic tang of thaumium—the alloy that keeps gods and monsters locked in Area 51.

Topside, conspiracy theories about UFOs mask the truth: this is a prison for immortals.

I step off the platform, adjusting my duffel bag as Sentinel scans his ID.

A chime, a mechanical groan, and the steel doors slide open, revealing the same spotless corridors, artificial lighting, and recycled air.

Home sweet hell.

We dropped the juvenile wolves on an upper level and debriefed with Wildcard. She rarely joins us in the field and is eager to head home to South Korea, so she's handling the reports.

The team follows behind. Ghost mutters about needing a drink, Blaze slings her duffel over her shoulder, and Sentinel strides ahead like he's still on duty.

Me?

I'm heading for the showers. Twelve days of hunting shifters and vamps, and I still feel the blood on my skin.

I push into the locker room, the scent of industrial-strength soap hitting me as I strip down.

Steam billows as I twist the shower knob, the first blast of heat burning against my chilled skin.

I groan in relief, leaning into the water.

A towel snaps, a curse follows. *Fucking children.* Ghost and Ironclad's shit-talking hasn't stopped since the mission ended.

"Just fuck already," Blaze calls out.

Ghost is quick to redirect his attention to Blaze. "I'd be more than happy to tangle with you, Firecracker."

I nearly gag. Hawkeye pretends to retch.

Blaze shuts off her shower, wrapping a towel around her head. "I don't shit where I sleep, baby," she says with a wink, strutting out as Ghost watches.

I can't blame him. I've drowned in that sweet pussy before. She is delicious.

We all know they've been fucking for two years. Ghost wants more. Blaze won't give it to him.

None of us expect to leave Umbra in anything but a body bag. What's the point of love when death is inevitable?

The team is quieter than usual. Normally, we're rowdy after a mission—mocking Ghost's screw-ups, trying to make Sentinel crack a smile.

Tonight, everyone just wants out.

I section my curls, working in cream, letting the tight coils spring to life. Our time outside brought out caramel highlights, and I'm not mad about it.

"I can taste the fruity umbrella drinks already," I murmur, drying my hair.

It's still damp, but good enough. I want one night in my own bed before two weeks in paradise.

I've spared no expense on the resort, but there's nothing like being home. It's been months.

And I need to say hi to Daddy.

Propping one foot on the thin wooden bench that runs down the center of the lockers, I lace up my black Doc Martens.

Ghost lies down, lacing his fingers behind his head, pretending he's just killing time. He's really waiting on Blaze, who is taking a curling wand to her chestnut hair.

"Are you going to get some R&R in, Cap?" Ghost asks as I finish lacing my other boot.

"I'm going to get fucked, get darker, and get drunk," I answer, zipping up my duffel bag. "And not necessarily in that order."

Ghost raises his hand for a fist bump as I pass by. Tossing my duffel bag over my shoulder, I put on my sunglasses.

"Anyone who bothers me gets latrine duty for a year. See you in two weeks."

Another step onto a teleportation pad, a blaze of light, and within a second, the chirping of birds fills my ears as I inhale the crisp Montana air.

My cabin is the only thing here for miles, and my smile widens as I turn to it.

This was Daddy's old hunting cabin, and I moved in full-time after my diagnosis. I have such fond memories of pulling up here, seeing the trees open up, and an endless blue sky above me.

Somehow, it's freeing.

It's my sanctuary—a place to release the stress of my job, the pain that shoots through my heart, and the fear that every irregular beat might be my last.

Sometimes it helps, knowing the end of the road is coming; other times, it terrifies me. I've kept to myself more and more, even when Daddy was still alive.

He passed away two years ago, and I was secretly grateful for it. He watched so many soldiers die over his long career. He didn't need to see his daughter die too.

I never told him.

Sentinel's the only one who knows about my condition. He says I push too hard, like I'm racing my heart, daring it to keep up. And maybe I am.

Maybe I want to force that last beat to show itself—because if I'm the one who coaxes it out, maybe I'll fear it less when it finally comes.

Shutting the cabin door behind me, I kiss two fingers and place them on Daddy's picture, which sits on my entry table. "Hey, Daddy." I put my keys down, then unlace my boots.

After checking my email and bills, I neatly pack two suitcases of bikinis and short dresses guaranteed to barely cover my ass.

I plug in my vibrators and choose between a few small bottles of lube while I check my stash of condoms.

I need a few things from town, and of course, I have

nothing to eat here but a stale pack of saltines and one bottle of beer.

Rolling my eyes, I grab my gun, my leather jacket, and the keys to my bike for a trip into town.

I'll definitely need to get a few more boxes of condoms because I plan on having a cock in my pussy and a cunt on my face no less than twice a day my entire vacation.

Town is about a fifteen-minute ride on my bike, and with condoms and toiletries in my leather bookbag, my growling stomach eventually won.

"Hey, Mike, turn this shit down," I call to the bartender, the dive bar's blown-out speakers wailing twangy country.

Dammit if he doesn't make the best cheeseburger known to womankind. It's worth the suffering, but I'll never admit it.

"You can stay on that barstool all night as long as you don't insult Willie," he fires back, retreating to the back just as a body drops onto the stool next to me.

Fucking great.

"Well, I know every angel in town, but I don't know you, sweetheart." Cigarettes and cheap beer hit my nose as I glance him over—faded jeans, worn-out boots, and a sun-bleached flannel.

His trucker hat probably hasn't left his head since Garth Brooks sang about thunder.

"That's because I'm not an angel. I'm just a bitch." I toss back the last of my whiskey, shove my plate closer to where Mike will find it, and stand.

So does Mr. Ash-Breath. I'm six feet without my Docs. He's several inches shorter.

"Aw, don't run off, sweetheart. I was hoping to buy you a beer."

Not only is this asshole missing every context clue, but he's also too dense to notice what I've been drinking.

These guys act like every woman is just waiting to hand out a charity fuck.

Or maybe he's looking to be pegged and thinks he's ready to climb this tree.

Not in a million fucking years.

"I'm not looking for a little spoon tonight, so no thanks." I catch Mike's eye as he returns. "My tab?"

He waves me off, like always. "Your daddy's money was no good here, and neither is yours. See you when you get back."

"Maybe you're looking for a daddy tonight, then, huh, sugar?"

I squint at him. *The audacity.*

If the sex gods of Hawaii are listening, I just want a giant man with a massive cock to rail me into next week and leave me begging for more. Is that so much to ask?

I don't waste a response. Instead, Sentinel's "Push Pop" comment about Ghost comes to mind, and a smirk tugs at my lips as I push in my barstool.

"Something funny—" His face reddens. "—skank?"

"Aw, what happened to 'angel'?" I bare my teeth in a smile. "Talk to me again, and those words will be the last you say for a few days."

Without waiting for an answer, I swing on my jacket and head for the door, throwing up a hand at Mike, who nods in return.

The parking lot has one blinking streetlight, its glow barely cutting through the darkness. Crumbling asphalt and gravel-filled potholes crunch beneath my boots.

The buzzing bulb flickers, humming like an omen. That oppressive weight settles over me—the feeling of being watched.

I almost convince myself it's just Little Spoon sulking inside.

But no. This is different.

Supernatural.

Immortal.

That instinct has kept me alive more times than I can count. And when I feel it, I never ignore it.

Like in the rainforest.

I turn, scanning the edges of my vision, watching for the telltale ripple in reality—the distortion that betrays the presence of something *other*.

There.

The shadows shift, too fluid, too alive. The air cools, and a single word forms in my mind.

Vampires.

A chill crawls down my spine, chased by heat. Vamps are prideful bastards. It wouldn't surprise me if one followed me home, looking to turn me into a blood bag.

Not tonight, motherfucker.

My hand moves to my gun, tucked under my waistband. No metallic scent of vamps in the air, but the feeling won't leave.

Something is here. Watching.

I back toward the bar, eyes locked on the shifting darkness. Then—bang. The bar door slams open, music crashing through the silence. The tension snaps like a wire pulled too tight and the air warms again.

Little Spoon stumbles out with his drunk friends, making eye contact like he has a death wish.

I roll my eyes, turn on my heel, and head for my bike.

"Oh, don't get shy now, baby." He follows after me, and I hear the boots of several others trailing behind him. This bitch actually wants to die tonight.

"We're a whole lot of fucking fun if you'd just stop being a prude."

It's when he grabs my arm to turn me around that I give him a reminder of my earlier warning.

In a single step, I spin.

He doesn't even see my fist flying toward his face, but as my knuckles connect perfectly with his jaw and cheek, his head snaps to the side with the force of the hit.

His eyes roll back in his head, and he crumples to the ground like a sack of potatoes.

The man closest to me becomes my new focus as I pull my gun from its hidden holster and press it against his forehead.

My gaze is harsh, and his is terrified. My grip is solid, and my arm is steady as the tension becomes palpable.

I don't go anywhere without my gun.

I'm a fucking shifter and vampire hunter, for god's sake.

Of course, I'm always armed.

While my bullets would kill these motherfuckers, they're made to kill immortals, and I'm not wasting good ammo.

But these pissants don't need to know that.

Speaking of pissants, the man at the end of my gun is trembling, and while I don't hear splashing urine, I certainly smell it.

Looking down, it's clear: yup, this guy is absolutely pissing his pants.

The dark spot spreads at his crotch, making a line down one pant leg. His urine trickles out, running along the cracks in the pavement... right into his unconscious buddy's face.

You can't make this shit up.

I look back at him and cock an eyebrow. After a short pause for dramatic effect, I walk away, holstering my gun as I climb onto my bike.

The ride home is quiet—too quiet. The steady hum of my bike beneath me does nothing to drown out the oppressive silence of the Montana night.

It feels as though the stars themselves are holding their breath.

That creeping sense of dread—the one I thought I'd left back in the parking lot—has returned. Stronger this time. Heavier.

Something is following me.

The air grows colder the closer I get to the cabin, each breath sharp and crisp in my lungs.

This doesn't feel like any vampire I've encountered, and a cold realization grips me tightly.

This is either the most powerful entity I've ever faced— or it's an entire coven of vampires.

Either way, I'm fucked.

My grip tightens on the handlebars as I fight the urge to

look over my shoulder. I know better than to give it the satisfaction of my fear. Whatever this is, it's patient.

Waiting.

Stalking.

It was in the jungle, watching us. It was there when I left the bar, and now it's here, following me back to my cabin. What the fuck it's waiting for, I have no idea.

By the time the trees open up and the cabin comes into view, my pulse is hammering against my ribs like a warning bell.

I don't slow my bike until I'm right up against the porch steps, the engine growling in defiance as I cut it off.

The silence that follows is deafening.

I climb off the bike, boots crunching against the gravel path. The shadows around the cabin are too deep, too still. My fingers twitch toward the gun in my waistband, but I leave it there.

I don't want to move and alert my hunter that I have a weapon. Or weapons, I should say. Adjusting my jacket, I scan the tree line. Nothing moves.

Not yet.

The sense of dread sharpens, pressing against my chest like a physical weight. Whatever's out there is close. I can feel it.

Good. Let's get this over with, asshole.

I take a few deliberate steps toward the cabin door, letting my boots echo against the ground, my ears straining to hear anything—everything.

If it's watching me—and I know it is—I want it to know

I'm not running. My jacket hides a knife in each of my sleeves, secured with holsters stitched to the fabric.

I trigger the releases, and the knives drop silently to my palms. The hilts of both blades are cool and reassuring as I reach the porch, my pulse a steady drumbeat in my ears.

The shadows shift, and I sense the setup instantly.

It's the same fucking move we pulled on the wolves in the jungle.

Distract your prey, let it think you're ahead, when in reality, you're right fucking next to it.

It's too close to pull my gun. Knives it is. I do prefer a hands-on approach.

It's subtle—a ripple at the edge of my vision—but enough to make my muscles coil for the attack. My hands grip the hilts of my blades, and I fling one knife to the side where the entity is really hiding.

The blade whistles as it bites through the air before sinking into something solid. A low hiss cuts through the stillness.

Got you, bitch.

But before I can spin around to face my attacker with my second knife, the world tilts violently. My heart surges, a series of rapid, uneven beats stealing the breath from my lungs.

Pain lances through my ribs, sharp and unforgiving.

No. Not now.

I stumble back, one hand clutching my chest as the other grips my weapon, slashing it in front of me without aim. The shadows seem to stay where they are, their edges wavering as my vision blurs.

White spots dance across my sightline, and the ground beneath me feels impossibly unsteady.

A heaviness surrounds me, and my knees buckle.

Sleep.

It's a thought in my mind but not my own. More like a command.

The knife slips from my hand, hitting the ground with a dull thud as I collapse.

The last thing I see is the faint gleam of my first blade in the grasp of a shadow and a pair of glowing yellow eyes before darkness claims me.

CHAPTER 5
Tana

My head is pounding, and it feels like an elephant is sitting on my chest. I can't explain it, but everything around me feels—off. It's like the atmosphere isn't as heavy as it should be. It feels gentler... lighter.

My mind is strangely at peace, and I lie still for a moment while my thoughts wake up along with my body. I can't quite remember what I was doing before I fell asleep, but I feel like I'm supposed to be somewhere.

Taking a deep breath, I notice an unfamiliar but pleasant scent of leather and smoke surrounding me, mingled with something else—something faint and sweet, like honeysuckle after a gentle rain.

It's soothing and comforting until I realize it's a distinctly masculine scent, one that informs me I'm not in my room. I'm in someone else's.

My eyes shoot open as everything rushes back to me like a flash of lightning.

I was attacked outside my cabin. My chest pain had started, and I passed out. The entity... the vampire... whatever it was wouldn't have just left me.

I should be dead.

I shoot up too quickly, crouching in the bed, steadying myself with one hand on the mattress while the other holds the side of my throbbing head.

The room spins, and black spots dot my vision. I blink, forcing my eyes wide and willing myself to regain control.

I'm indoors, and it's still nighttime, but... am I in a fucking castle? I release a breath, and my heart beats frantically as I set my feet on the stone floor.

Patting my body, I blow out a deep sigh of relief. I'm still in my clothes, and my gun is in its holster—though I don't have my cell phone. It must have fallen out of my pocket, or maybe the being took it.

Thank fucking God I didn't pull my gun on that motherfucker.

I check that the bullets are still in the clip and chamber a round.

The circular room is vast, and the ceiling is incredibly tall. Stone blocks make up the walls, and a cool breeze, smelling of sweet flowers, wafts in from several open lattice windows.

The moon is especially bright, allowing me to see clearly, even though only a few candles fixed to brass holders illuminate the room.

The furniture is lavish—the canopy bed dressed in luxurious black sheets, furs, and blankets. Tapestries with detailed hunting scenes and a lake hang from several walls.

A fire burns in a large fireplace, making the space comfortable despite its stony vastness.

Scrolls and papers cover a simple writing desk while

books sit haphazardly on shelves behind it. Over the fire-place is an odd-looking coat of arms.

On either side, portraits of a decorative chalice and a sword driven into a boulder hang on the walls.

Am I in fucking Camelot? Is King Arthur himself about to roll up in this bitch?

No, this screams vampires. Fucking dramatic-ass bitches that have ever existed.

Walking around the room, I'm careful to keep my steps quiet as I search for more of my belongings—or anything to tell me where I am. Even vampires have technology, but I see nothing—not a plug in the wall, nor a tablet.

This place seems oddly medieval and rustic, but somehow less dramatic and gothic than other vampire lairs I've seen.

The papers on the desk are in no language I'm familiar with, though my profession doesn't require I learn the languages of the immortal races.

My team is more of a *kill first and collect shit for smart people to research after* kind of team.

An intricate silver dagger on the desk reflects the moonlight from the adjacent window, drawing my gaze outside.

The moon is enormous—so close, I feel like I could reach up and touch it as it hangs in the sky.

Nearing the window but staying off to one side, I look across the landscape. Yup. A castle, complete with a moat, a drawbridge, and a fucking forest that even Robin Hood would envy.

Now I realize vampires may be the least of my worries.

"Toto, I've a feeling we're not in Kansas anymore," I

mutter to myself as I holster my gun and tighten my grip on the letter opener.

I can't identify the metal, so it's not thaumium or Stygian iron–metals that kill Immortals.

It's a bit larger than I'm used to and heavy, but it will be better for silent combat than my gun.

I can't exactly fire my weapon without knowing where I am, who has taken me, or how the fuck to get out.

Looking outside again, I search for an escape route. I could scale the wall, but I would stick out like a sore thumb, hanging here like a goddamn bat.

About ten yards down, there's a break in the wall—a door leading to the forest beyond. My eyes scan above the trees. Nothing but dense foliage, then darkness swallows everything beyond the horizon.

Getting the fuck out of here through that gate is my first plan. I'll figure the rest out after.

With a deep breath, I stretch my neck to each side and head to the closed wooden door.

Okay, Valkyrie, who lives today? I think to myself. "I fucking do."

Surprisingly, the door isn't locked, and it opens quietly enough. Immortals have incredible hearing, and while a human wouldn't pick up the faint sound of me easing the metal latch closed again, a vampire certainly would.

Looking down each side of the long hallway, all is quiet —which doesn't sit well with me.

Why was no one guarding the room? Why was it even unlocked? This smells fishy, and my senses skyrocket on high alert.

This is certainly not how my team would operate with a captive, and I'm not naïve enough to think for one second that I'm safe.

Gray stones surround me, marred periodically with scorch marks from the burning torches fixed to the walls. A faint draft drifts from my left, so I head that way.

Doc Martens are suitable for any event and terrain... even traipsing through enemy castles.

My steps are silent as I hurry forward, heart pounding, breaths controlled. At the hall's end, I pause, straining to listen. Whispers grow louder. Shadows stretch toward me.

Fuck.

Too far to double back. I turn left, chasing the cool current of air that feels like my way out.

The shadows move. I glance back, paranoia crawling up my spine. Dark fingers reach, hungry to pull me in.

Left. Right. Four steps down. Another left.

I keep running, whispers at my back, the sentient dark watching. Firelight flickers, making the shadows turn with every step, as if tracking me.

Voices drift from the halls I just cleared. I pick up speed.

Right. Right. Up six stairs. Across a landing. Down ten stairs. Left.

The voices close in.

I need cover. *Now.*

Pressing my ear to a door—nothing. I try the handle. Locked.

Of course this fucking door is locked, but my room wasn't?

Another door. Locked. Another. No luck.

Sweat slides down my back as I sprint.

Left. Left. Left. Right. Down the long-ass hallway. Faster, Tana.

Move your fucking ass.

Right. Spiral stairs. Right again.

How big is this goddamn castle?

I sense his presence before my mind or eyes catch up to what's happening.

The moment I turn the corner, he's there—a towering figure whose presence seems to displace the very air around him.

Without hesitation, I react. Pushing off the wall with all my strength, I launch myself at him. My leg wraps around the throat of—what must be a fucking giant because, damn, he's a big bitch.

Using the momentum, I twist my body and take him down, the impact reverberating through us both.

Before he can recover, I pin him to the ground. My knee digs into his chest, and my blade presses firmly against his throat.

I've heard stories of time standing still—of moments so profound that the universe itself holds its breath, pausing in reverence before surging forward once more.

That's exactly what happens as I meet a pair of silver eyes, swirling with the fury of a rolling thunderstorm.

Creamy-white skin seems to glimmer unnaturally in the delicate moonlight, and straight hair, white as snow, fans out across the stone floor.

A deep scar of three gashes starts just above his left eye and runs into his scalp. The sides of his hair are shaved, but the scar prevents anything from trespassing on the skin it seems to have claimed.

The man beneath me doesn't fight back. His massive chest rises and falls steadily, as though having a blade pressed to his throat is just another mundane annoyance.

His piercing gaze locks onto mine, unnervingly calm for someone in his position, but I couldn't look away even if I wanted to.

When my eyes drift to his lips—full and soft—it's the quick smirk that is my only warning before the universe comes screaming back to life.

I take a breath, intending to grill this asshole, but all the air rushes from my body.

It takes me a second to realize why.

I'm suspended from the fucking wall, my wrists bound together above my head. My boots hit against the stones as my body stills from the unexpected change in position.

The bindings are tight—uncomfortably so—and as I glance up, my stomach twists.

"What the fuck?" I whisper the words, staring at the restraints holding me.

They're not ropes.

They're shadows.

Dark, translucent ribbons wrap around my wrists, never stopping their slow, undulating movements. It's as if they're alive, constantly battling the flickering light of the torches.

I file this observation away for later. Right now, I have more pressing matters—like getting the hell out of this situation.

It happened faster than a lightning strike, and the

mysterious man doesn't even seem to have strained one bit. He's not winded.

His long hair moving back into place is the only indicator he has moved. Otherwise, you would think him a stone carving decorating the castle hall.

He takes me in. A chill moves down my body, following the path of his gaze. *Assessing, contemplating—judging, perhaps?*

It pisses me the fuck off.

A small glimmer of salvation is the faint cut on his neck where the point of my weapon pierced his skin. A thin red line gives way to a single dot of blood.

This bitch bleeds.

Good.

I'll be spilling the rest of his blood and getting the fuck out of here.

My gaze moves from the small cut on his neck, and I meet his eyes. With a cock of one eyebrow, I hope he understands my message: One point for me, motherfucker.

Perhaps he does, because that arrogant smirk is back briefly as he raises his own eyebrow.

Then, without a word, he turns his back to me and struts away.

And yes, it's a goddamn strut.

Fuck me, he's tall.

Swinging my legs up once, then twice, I gather momentum. On the third swing, I haul my legs higher, planting my feet on the wall just above my hands. With a grunt, I push off, straining against the bindings.

The shadows snap with an audible crack, and I land on

the ground in a low crouch, boots firmly planted on the stone floor.

Empty-handed.

Dammit.

The oversized letter opener is still embedded in the stone wall, glinting mockingly in the flickering torchlight.

There's no time to retrieve it.

I flick my gaze back to the retreating man, who has stopped just short of a set of massive double doors at the end of the hallway.

He turns his head slightly, as though checking on me out of the corner of his eye.

With a push, he opens the doors, stepping into what appears to be a dining hall. The doors remain open—a deliberate invitation.

Well, fuck you, asshole. If he thinks I'll follow–

I spin on my heel and sprint in the opposite direction.

The halls blur as I run, the slap of my boots echoing against the stone walls. My breaths come fast and hard, my pulse hammering in my ears as I weave through the labyrinth of the castle.

Left. Right. Straight. Another hallway.

The castle seems endless, a maze designed to disorient.

The doors that lead outside must be nearby, and I pick up my pace when I spot a pair of double doors at the end of a corridor.

Pushing through them, I slide to a halt when I realize—

I've entered that same fucking dining hall.

And the smirking oaf from before is sitting at the head of the table as if he has no worries in the world.

A split-second glance around, and I see a woman—short, wearing all black—with a mound of food in front of her. A man with a shining bald head and skin much darker than mine stands behind her like a guard.

But his eyes... he must be blind because there seems to be no color in them at all, as if the iris and pupil are both white.

Another giant of a man—like a redheaded fucking Santa Claus—is sitting across from the woman, a mound of food nearly as large as hers in front of him.

FUCK!

Well, so much for laying low on my escape.

I need to distract them so I can make it out of this room.

Pulling my gun from my holster, I aim for the white-haired mega-hottie and pull the trigger.

The bang of the gun flashes, and he's in my face.

That bruising grip from my imagination is wrapped around my wrist, pointing my gun toward the ceiling as he flexes his jaw.

The thunderstorm in his eyes is now a raging typhoon, his chest rising dramatically, matching my own breathing.

Finally... the stone statue reacts.

I hear my bullet ricochet twice, then see the fast movement of the woman.

She just caught the bullet.

With. Her. Bare. Hand.

And she didn't even pause her bite to do it.

She sniffs the bullet, inspecting it with curiosity, then sets it on the table next to her—completely unbothered by anything happening in this room.

I keep my eyes locked hard on the man holding me. It's now that I see pointed ears jutting out from his hair.

No vampire I know has ears like that.

So what the fuck kind of immortal is this guy?

A fairy? Are those even real?

At this point, I wouldn't question anything.

The jolly Santa takes a breath of awe, and I hear his wooden chair slide across the stone floor.

"What is tha' beauty?" Jolly Santa sounds Scottish and in utter amazement as he keeps hobbling toward us as if in a daze. The clank of wood is an artificial peg-leg and I upgrade him to a Jolly Pirate Santa.

"This," my captor says, his lips curving into a full, dimpled grin, "is our new queen."

CHAPTER 6

orion

"N o' her, ye daft eejit," Hephaestus nearly barks at my response. "The contraption she's holdin'."

The end of her weapon, so close to my ear, smokes. The sharp tang of the burnt substance fills the air between us—biting and bitter.

It reminds me of smoldering wyrmroot, used in the old wars to create smoke screens and ward off beasts. The scent stirs memories of battlefields, chaos, and survival.

"New queen, my ass." Her voice is sharp, a blade aimed directly at me, though the weapon in her hand is far more literal.

"I'm going the fuck home," she says, turning her wrist—still firm in my grasp—so her weapon points toward my head. "And you'll be taking me—now."

I raise an eyebrow, suppressing a smirk. The bravado she exudes is... entertaining.

For a mortal.

"Careful, starling. You are in Avalon now, and threats like that are only amusing for so long."

Her glare doesn't waver. *Impressive.*

Of course, she is not queen yet.

Our current queen and traitor, Demeter is locked in the dungeons.

The realm will call for her trial and execution. Then, the path will be clear for our new mortal friend to ascend her throne.

All this she will learn in due time.

Letting go of her wrist, I give her my back and return to the table, glancing at Mor with a look that conveys my disappointment. She and Hypnos should have checked our guest for weapons before taking her from Gaea.

Hypnos has the decency to give me an apologetic and understanding nod, accepting the weight of the oversight. Mor only shrugs in indifference, exacerbating my thinning patience.

This must go well. *It is imperative.*

"Yer Majesty," I hear Hephaestus' voice carry to the stone ground as he bends at his waist for our new queen. "Name's Hephaestus—blacksmith an' weapons master, loyal tae the crown o' Avalon."

"I don't know what that is," she grits between her teeth, though I know her attention is still on me—the burn of her stare at my back, the heaviness of her weapon as she keeps it fixed on me. "I want my things, and I want to leave."

"Your request was heard the first time, starling." I finally look back at her as I reach my seat.

"Don't call me that."

The chosen queen of Avalon stands within the dining hall, a creature unlike anything the realm has ever known.

Her skin gleams in the dim light like polished caramel—

warm, smooth, an earthy richness that reminds me of the lands of Gaea: untamed, fierce, and resolute.

It has been ages since the Fae traversed to our sister realm, home of the mortals, but I remember it well.

Her dark brown eyes hold mine with an intensity that both dares and defies, the kind of fire that refuses to be tamed. There's a depth to them, a challenge that makes it impossible to look away.

Her hair is a storm in its own right, cascading in wild curls that seem to defy order and confinement. It's as if the winds of Gaea decided to take permanent residence atop her head.

And though she stands smaller than many Fae, she commands the space around her with a quiet, unwavering authority.

The simplicity of her attire betrays her earthly origins— a crisp white shirt clinging to her frame, dark rugged pants that mold to her legs, and those boots.

Black, scuffed, and sturdy, they speak of someone prepared to walk through darkness and back.

There's no flourish or finery, no delicate ornaments to distract. Just her, standing there, ready for a fight.

The lack of pretense is almost... *refreshing.*

Mortals of her kind are supposed to be fragile, fleeting things. But this woman, with her fierce gaze and battle-ready posture, is anything but. She is iron wrapped in silk, mortal yet unyielding.

I can't help but admire her boldness, even as she points that damned weapon at me.

A human threatening the prince of Avalon.

By the gods, I can't decide whether I should be insulted or impressed.

I summon the staff from the kitchens.

They have worked long and hard to prepare a banquet for their new queen. Waiting until they round the corner with platters of food, I direct her to the table, pulling out a chair and gesturing for her to sit with my hand.

I stand on the other side of my own chair, ensuring it is between our new mortal and myself, hopefully giving her some sense of peace that she is in no danger from us.

The Lesser Fae are eager for a glimpse of the queen but remain respectful as they place platters of food on the table.

As many ages as we have spent away from Gaea, it has been just as long since we have entertained a mortal here.

It's easy to forget their fragility.

Giving our visitor a brief curtsy, several of the staff cast their eyes up quickly, unable to suppress their curiosity.

Mor sits up, pulling a fresh platter of roasted stag with crimson glaze. Several glowing root vegetables are quickly consumed before she spears a large piece of meat.

"The Morrigan." I gesture to my darkness-wielding friend, her cheeks puffed to the brim with food, hunger always beckoning her.

With great effort, she swallows most of her food and nods at our guest.

"Mor," she says, taking a long pull of her elven mead. "Call us Mor." Her voice is as smooth and unhurried as ever, the vastness of dark power she wields resonating in the space she takes up.

The mortal should feel small next to her, next to *us*—but she doesn't. Not an ounce of fear rolls off her.

If anything, there's a challenge in her eyes, a sharpness I don't expect from someone so fragile.

The mortal lifts her chin and replies, "Tana."

It's such a small word, simple, but the way it lands... gods. It's like the sound ripples through me, sharp and resonant. I feel it settle in my chest, low and deep, lingering like embers.

What in the hells was that?

For a heartbeat, I'm tempted to look around, to see if Mor or the others noticed it too. *Did they feel it? Did they hear it the way I did?* But no one stirs, and that alone tells me enough.

Whatever that was—it is mine to bear.

Tana, I repeat silently in my mind, testing the sound as I would the balance of a blade. It doesn't cut the same way twice.

My imagination, as I suspected.

I school my features, drawing up the mask of the cold prince.

"A trusted advisor to the crown, Hypnos." I indicate my old friend, who stands next to Mor, guarding her as if she requires the protection.

But he did not trust the new guest to react well to being captured, stolen away to a new realm against her will.

It seems, once again, he was correct.

Tana finally lowers the weapon in her hand, though she keeps a finger close to a small lever near its center.

This must be how she activated the device before.

"Could I hae a wee look at yer weapon, yer grace?" Hephaestus holds his breath, trying to contain his excitement.

"No."

She pulls up her shirt, and the armament disappears beneath the waistband of her pants.

Ah, the last piece of the puzzle is revealed. That must be how Mor and Hypnos missed the artifact previously.

I make a mental note: *our new queen likes to store weapons within her clothes.*

I will not underestimate that fact a second time.

Hephaestus towers over most like a mountain giant, a head taller than even me. But his form shrinks into that of a child in his chair, disappointment pulling him down at her rejection.

Flicking her crimson eyes to our bearded friend, Mor tosses the metal wisp discarded by Tana's weapon.

It is as if Hephaestus is watching the only sunrise that graces the night realm, the joy alighting his face. He catches the small object, which nearly disappears in his large hands.

A quick inspection, and, like most weapons, it seems to speak to our master of arms.

"No' deadly tae a Fae, mind ye." He takes in the metals and shape. "But I'd wager it still bites like iron in the veins."

"Someone needs to speak up and tell me what the fuck is going on before everyone gets iron in the veins."

Our fierce little mortal casts her sharp gaze at each of us gathered while one of the kitchen attendants places a trencher of food before her.

"Thank you."

She nods and gives the Lesser Fae her gratitude with much softer eyes than she has given me.

My kin's eyes widen in shock, traitor Queen Demeter's kind never having known gratitude from a Lesser Fae.

Tana's *thank you* drops into the room like a stone in still water, sending ripples she doesn't see.

Mor's expression flickers—intrigue sparking in her dark eyes, a smirk tugging at her lips. She's already calculating how this mortal's kindness could be used in the courts.

She says nothing, but her gaze sharpens like a hawk about to dive.

Hypnos leans back against the stone wall, one brow arching in lazy amusement. Though blind, I know he feels the shift in the air, already filing it away for later.

"Well, isn't she full of surprises," he murmurs, just loud enough for me to hear.

Hephaestus breaks the tension with a booming laugh, startling an attendant.

"A mortal wi' manners! Now there's a sight worth forgin' a tale aboot."

His massive frame shakes with mirth, arms crossing over his chest, a grin splitting his bearded face.

The stunned Fae attendant blinks up at Tana, disbelief giving way to a shy smile. Her voice wavers, filled with wonder.

"You're... welcome, Your Grace."

She dips her head quickly, as if afraid the moment might be taken back.

I find my own reaction simmering beneath the surface—a strange mix of pride and apprehension.

This mortal is unlike any ruler Avalon has ever seen.

She moves with the blunt, earnest grace of someone who doesn't know the weight her words can carry here.

And yet, that is what makes her so dangerously compelling.

She does not play the games we do, does not guard her heart behind centuries of politics and power.

She is not Fae, I remind myself, the thought settling like a cold touch on my spine.

This is what makes her different, why I felt that pull when she said her own name.

And now, here she is, acknowledging a Lesser Fae in front of us as if it were *nothing*.

But it is not nothing.

It is a promise, however unintentional, that she will be a different kind of queen.

And in this realm of schemes and shadows, choking on darkness, that could either save us or unravel everything.

Tana stands, both hands planted firmly on the table, and casts me a cutting glare.

"You have three seconds to tell m—"

"As I stated, you are the chosen queen of Avalon," I interrupt, only to be cut off by our sharp-tongued sovereign in return.

"And what is Avalon?"

I stretch my neck to the side, taking a calming breath.

From this angle, I watch the pulse in Tana's neck, beating rapidly under her skin, and I count the beats.

She is nervous. The quick flutter betrays the calm façade in her eyes.

"Please sit. Eat. I will explain."

"Fuck you. Tell me what I want to know, or I'll shoot you again and leave."

Clearing my throat, I offer a hand in surrender. "Try."

She narrows her eyes at me, as if disbelieving what she's hearing. "Excuse me?"

"*Try*—to shoot me again." I place my hands on the table, leaning closer, mimicking her position. "You didn't succeed the first time."

The grin that slides across her face is nothing short of beautiful, but I do not miss the promise she hides within it.

"My bullet may not have found you," she begins, her eyes flicking quickly down to my neck, "but my blade did."

I raise my fingers to the spot where she held the edge of my scroll opener against me.

The cool touch of the metal still kisses my flesh like a lingering embrace.

Pulling them away, I find no blood, but I feel the distant sting of pain from a small cut.

Satisfaction blankets our new queen's face, a victory won.

She rights her position, pulling the ends of her shirt down and finally sitting.

With her spine intentionally straight, she clasps her hands in front of her.

The celebratory sneer morphs into one of feigned politeness.

"I am ready now. You may begin."

"*This is going to be a long fucking coronation, isn't it?*" Mor asks, her voice a dry echo in our minds, our guest unaware of the silent conversation around her.

"*Language, Morrigan.*"

"*You're not our father.*"

I stretch my neck to the other side, taking two calming breaths as I sit.

Mor is right.

This is destined to be a long coronation.

CHAPTER 7
orion

The dungeons of Avalon are carved deep into the rock, where the walls seem to drink in the faint torchlight, leaving the air cold and thick with the scent of damp stone and ancient dust.

Shadows writhe across the jagged surfaces, twisting as if alive, echoing the torment of those imprisoned here.

I step through the threshold, the silence broken only by the drip of unseen water and the low crackle of flames clinging to their torches.

Before entering deeper, I weave a subtle glamour around myself, masking any trace of Tana's scent—any lingering whispers of her presence.

Demeter must not know.

Allies can be scarce, and enemies many. I am no fool to presume Demeter has only an abundance of enemies. As darkness consumes the realm, it also clouds one's judgment.

None of the Fae are beyond a bargain, and once struck, an agreement is binding forever.

There is no telling the manner of corruption Demeter may have inflicted before she left—the Fae she could have made promises to upon her return.

Glory, wealth, position—all things the fickle hearts of the High Fae lust after.

It's pathetic, their loyalty to such fleeting things, and precautions are required in all aspects of Tana's ascension to Avalon's throne.

The castle has been cleared of High Fae, leaving only the Lesser Fae most loyal to Starfall Castle. The usual roster of guests has been upset by the order of the traitor queen's trial.

In truth, this keeps Tana secure and out of sight from the prejudicial High Fae. Her introduction into Fae society will need to be carefully planned and executed once she has become a Fae herself.

But for now, I must focus on the traitor I have come to speak with.

Demeter sits chained to the wall at the end of her cell, bound by bands of iron that pulse with enchanted runes, dull against her skin.

The once-powerful Fae queen is a ghost of herself—her dark hair matted and streaked with dirt, her eyes that once blazed now sunken and hollow.

But even caged, she holds her chin high, a twisted defiance glimmering there.

"Come to gloat, have you?" Her voice cuts through the silence, cold and sharp. The metal chains rattle as she shifts, the only betrayal of her discomfort.

"No," I say, my voice steady as I step into the torchlight, letting it cast long, cruel shadows over the stones. "I came for answers."

Most of the story I know.

My grandmother fell. Than my mother.

Aunt Demeter ascended the throne in their absence.

She was not chosen by the realm. Not a true queen like my grandmother, Pandora. Her magic was not tied to the realm, yet I felt it when she left.

Abandoning the seat of power she claimed. For what—that is the mystery.

Why take a crown that is not truly yours, then leave it behind for ages?

Demeter's eyes narrow, calculating, and a smirk tugs at her cracked lips.

"You already know the answers, boy. My mother's blood is on my hands, my sister—your mother—her screams echo in my ears. What more could I give you?"

My fists clench at my sides, the shadows around me thickening, vibrating with barely contained rage.

"You betrayed your realm, your bloodline—for what? Power?" I step closer, the glimmer of iron catching in my periphery.

"Greed may have driven you, but it was not that alone, and I want to hear it from your lips."

Her silence mocks me, the stillness between us tightening like a vise.

Then, slowly, she leans forward, the chains straining as she does, her eyes gleaming with dark amusement. "It doesn't matter what I say. The trial will reveal everything, and the realm's judgment is absolute."

I lean in, close enough to see the faint rise and fall of her chest. "It won't matter, no. And I will see justice done, whether by your confession or by the will of Avalon."

Demeter's smirk fades into something bitter, her eyes narrowing.

"Justice? Is that what you think this is, Orion? You bring–a mortal–into this realm, believing she can rule? The Fae will never bow to one born of Gaea."

The taunt lands deeper than I'd like, and before I can mask it, she sees the way my jaw tightens, the way my eyes flicker with doubt.

She knows.

The realization lances through me, my breath catching in my chest.

"How do you know?"

The question slips out before I can stop it, my guard fractured just enough to betray a weakness I cannot afford.

Her laughter breaks the silence, a hollow, bitter sound that rings against the stone walls.

"Your secrets are not as well kept as you think," she whispers, her eyes glinting with triumph.

"The realm is bleeding, Orion. The Fae are restless. Even your shadows, your glamour, can't cover the scent of your desperation."

I take a step back, the rage that had simmered now boiling over.

The shadows around me twitch and coil, ready to strike, ready to silence her once and for all.

Her gaze dares me, her eyes wide and expectant.

"Did you never wonder why your mother gave birth to a son? Why not a daughter?"

I hold my ground, the stones beneath my boots colder than ever, anchoring me as her words strike like a dagger.

My shadows coil tighter, vibrating with the desire to answer her taunt with force, but I keep them in check. Barely.

"Enough," I bite out, the word slicing through the silence.

But she steps forward, chains clinking, her eyes narrowing with the satisfaction of a predator tasting blood.

"Oh, but it's not enough, is it? Not for you. You've felt it, haven't you? The way the realm shifts beneath your feet, restless and searching. It knows, Orion. It knows that the women of Pandora's line were meant to carry the mantle—not a son born of misplaced hope."

Her words dig into old scars, wounds I thought long buried.

I swallow the bitter taste of anger, focusing on the flicker of torchlight, on anything but her gleaming eyes.

"Your mother knew it too," she continues, her voice a whisper laced with venom.

"Perhaps that's why she couldn't bring herself to fight me as I took her life. But did you ever wonder, even in your moments of fevered doubt, whether she carried another child?

A daughter, maybe?

One that could have been the realm's salvation."

My shadows hiss, snapping against the stone walls, and I feel my heart stutter, a painful lurch that leaves me breathless.

The idea seeps through me like poison.

Could my mother have been with child?

Could there have been a chance, however small, that the line of succession wasn't broken after all?

My eyes narrow, but she tilts her head, lips curling into a knowing smile.

"You don't know, do you? You'll never know if I snuffed out Avalon's true queen that night."

The urge to let my shadows loose is almost unbearable as my power calls upon the thunder outside.

Lightning sparks across my skin, flickering within my gaze.

Coiling and uncoiling, my darkness tastes the air, straining to close the distance between us and snuff out her immortal life.

She sees it and lets out a laugh that is more a rasp than a sound, empty and cold.

"Do it," she goads, her eyes wild with the anticipation of a release I won't give her.

"Kill me now and spare me the realm's judgment. Show Avalon that even the mighty Orion can't control himself.

Let them see you for what you truly are—a desperate guardian clinging to a legacy already crumbling."

The lingering doubt of my mother's bloodline is exploited by the traitor queen. It is true, why my mother had a son–not a daughter–has been a lingering question in my mind for ages.

Only a women sits upon the throne of the Fae.

And my grandmother served as the first queen chosen by the realm. Those that came before her were appointed or took claim of their own.

But a darkness threatened the Fae. And the realm responded.

Pandora was chosen as the warrior to bring starlight back to the night sky. And she did. For a long time.

Until she was murdered by her own daughter, and the darkness was free to consume the realm once more.

Now, that murdering daughter is back. Another self-appointed queen without true power, waiting to face the realms judgement for her crimes against it.

And she wants me to give her a graceful death. Taunting me until I snap and end her Immortality.

"Kill me, Orion. Your queen commands it."

The erratic beat of my heart thrums in my ears, but I force the shadows back, letting them melt into the corners of the room like oil on water.

No.

I won't give her the satisfaction.

She'll face the realm's judgment, and it will be far worse than my wrath.

"You're queen for now," I say, turning my back to her, each step a battle to keep my composure intact. "But that is a title you will not hold much longer."

Her laughter follows me, echoing down the cold stone halls, mingling with the sound of my own ragged breath as I walk away.

The thumping against my head matches the erratic pound of my unsteady heart as my chest squeezes tight. A pain I push against until I am out of her sight.

The dungeon doors close behind me, and I press my

back against the cold stone, my heart still stuttering in my chest from Demeter's words.

Each beat sends a dull throb of pain radiating through me—a cruel reminder of my condition, one I cannot afford to let show.

I take a deep breath, holding it until the discomfort ebbs, and the shadows I control slither back into place, resting at the edge of my vision.

Damn this affliction.

If I could but cut out my heart and live without it, I would.

This weak muscle will eventually be my demise, and I resent it for its fragility.

As if I carry the organ of a mere mortal.

It's infuriating.

It is what makes Demeter's chiding all the more painful.

My mother should have delivered a daughter. Instead, a prince graced the cradle within the nursery meant for a princess. Me.

It is no wonder the realm punishes me with a faulty heart that has a limited number of beats.

A penance for stealing the place by my mother's side where a daughter was meant to stand.

The corridor is dim, but a soft ruby glow catches my eye.

Mor sits perched on a window ledge, one knee drawn up, biting into a segment of Crimson Solfruit. The juice glistens on her lips, deep as blood, and her eyes, ever watchful, flicker with curiosity as she observes me.

There is no need for me to hide from Mor or Hypnos.

They are the only souls in this realm who know of my ailment—my waning strength and depleting power.

The Morrigan and I share a kindred bond, one forged at the mouth of a cave over the course of three millennia.

Truth hides in the darkness, but she *is* darkness.

There was never any ability for me to hide that truth from something so profoundly her.

She knew my secret in an instant.

She could feel the pulse of my dark power weaken slightly with every thrum.

My life is draining out of me with each beat of my heart, and I am powerless to stop it.

Hypnos is a god over the power of emotion.

Feelings fall from us like a discarded force field—our excitement, our fear, everything we experience thrumming off our bodies in constant motion.

Like a second aura, one made of our truths, he can see it.

While Hypnos has no physical sight, he does not need it.

The lingering contamination of our emotions covers the ground, allowing him to see.

Every weakness you try to hide with lies is laid bare before him.

He could see the fear, the insecurity rolling off me in torrents.

No, there was no hiding the truth of my fate from them.

And so, as The Morrigan's crimson eyes cut into me, I let my pulse calm and the pain in my chest ease, knowing there is no judgment—only patience.

"Done rattling the chains of ghosts, are we?" she says, her tone playful but edged with knowing.

I force my breathing to steady, the ragged pace finally slowing. "I needed answers."

"And did you find any worth the trouble?"

She breaks off another piece of the fruit and holds it out to me.

The air between us is thick with unspoken questions, but I cross the corridor and take it from her fingers, the bittersweet taste flooding my mouth, grounding me.

"None that will help."

I glance at her, the shadows on her face shifting as she studies me.

"The trial will be a spectacle to remember."

Mor wipes a stray droplet from her chin, her eyes gleaming with a flicker of amusement.

"Do you think she should watch?"

My jaw tenses, and Mor sees it.

"No. Tana will be kept away until her transformation. She needs to remain hidden from the Fae, protected from what they might do if they discover a mortal in our midst."

The words come out sharper than I intend, but the vision of her wide eyes filled with fear at the sight of Demeter's punishment makes my stomach twist.

"And the trial... it would only terrify her. She might reject the realm's call."

Mor's eyes narrow, her amusement shifting to something more serious. "The realm chose her, Orion. She must learn that fear is not a luxury she can afford."

I say nothing, the silence stretching as the implications settle over us.

If Tana were to refuse the calling, to turn her back on Avalon, the realm would wither.

We would fall into an age darker than any before.

And then we would cease to exist.

The vision played out within the Sanctum over and over again will be our fate.

Mor leans back on the window ledge, finishing the last segment of her Crimson Solfruit, her gaze fixed somewhere beyond the horizon as if peering into a distant past.

The silence holds, heavy and suffocating, until I finally break it.

"Mor," I say, keeping my voice steady, testing the waters, "Tana could use someone who understands what it is to be thrust into a fate not of her choosing."

"Well, good for her."

"Someone who was perhaps once a mortal as well. Who was also meant to carry the mantle of queen."

I continue, peeling another solfruit.

"We hope she finds that person."

Mor's tone is as dry as the empty riverbeds in the wastelands.

"Why don't you speak to her? Befriend her?"

I lay it out there, knowing the likelihood of Mor skipping off to spark a friendship with the mortal is as likely as the moon turning into a sun.

"Why in the hells would we do that?"

She finally turns her eyes to me, and they are flat, dark pools, unreadable.

"You think we care about some mortal who stumbled into a destiny she neither wanted nor deserves?"

"Not care," I counter, a hint of a smile playing at my lips.

"But you know better than anyone what it's like to be raised to lead, as well as what it is like to resign your mortal life for another. You could show her what it means to navigate her new future—to survive it."

Mor's expression doesn't shift, but the temperature in the corridor feels colder.

"We didn't survive to play tutor to a mortal queen," she says, her voice flat, each word heavy with finality. "This realm is not ours. This fate is not ours."

I hold her gaze, searching for something beneath the steel in her eyes. She means it, at least in part. But there is something else there—something I recognize all too well.

Denial.

She doesn't want to care, but she already does.

I let the silence stretch between us, unspoken truths settling like dust on the cold stone floor.

Then I take a measured breath. "Maybe not. But you're here, Mor."

Her eyes flicker, but she says nothing.

"You've stayed by my side when you had no reason to. You know what happens if Tana fails."

She leans back against the window ledge, her gaze shifting toward the sky.

"And so it comes to this. You want us to shepherd her, to make sure she binds herself to this realm so your precious Avalon doesn't crumble. Don't pretend it's about her, Orion."

I don't.

"You're right. I'm not pretending. This is about Avalon.

It's about ensuring she understands what's at stake and doesn't run."

Mor's lips press into a thin line, but she doesn't interrupt.

"If that means appealing to your grudging sense of loyalty or your buried compassion, so be it."

A muscle in her jaw flexes, and she looks away, her fingers idly tracing the hilt of the dagger at her waist.

Then, after a long pause, she speaks. "We've buried our compassion, Orion."

Her voice is quiet, but there's an edge to it, a finality that warns me against pressing further.

I step closer, my shadows whispering against the stone as they reach for hers, drawn to the void within her just as I am.

"You forget, Mor. I know where you buried it."

She doesn't flinch, doesn't acknowledge the truth between us, but she doesn't refute it either.

"Find someone else to mind your queen."

I take a breath, preparing to unleash a fresh argument, when Mor turns on me suddenly. The shift in her gaze from irritation to calculation is abrupt, and I brace myself for what's to come.

"Speaking of Tana, how curious it is that she managed to escape a locked room.

And even more curious that shadows—shadows so like yours—guided her through the halls, this way and that, until, oddly enough, she ran right into... you."

She arches an eyebrow, the playful accusation unmistakable.

I shrug, feigning innocence. "Strange things happen in Avalon, don't they?"

She raises an eyebrow higher. "Don't play coy with us, Orion. You knew exactly where she was the entire time."

One side of my mouth quirks up in a grin. "I was merely testing her," I say, as though it were the simplest explanation in the world.

"I only wanted to know if the mortal the realm has chosen is capable of surviving on her own."

"Ah, yes, always so practical," Mor replies, her tone dripping with sarcasm. "Testing the mortal for the good of Avalon, nothing more. Certainly not because you find her… intriguing."

"I don't—" I begin, but she cuts me off with a wave of her hand.

"Keep telling yourself those excuses, Orion. They're very convincing."

She turns away, her casual pace carrying her farther down the corridor.

"I was only testing her," I call after her, my words echoing faintly in the empty hall.

"Of course you were," Mor replies without turning back, her voice laced with exaggerated agreement. "A noble effort, indeed."

I watch her retreat, the silence settling back in around me, heavy and suffocating.

The pain in my heart pulses again, but it's not just the physical ache. The shadows flicker around me, restless like my thoughts.

I whisper to them, to myself.

"She has to be ready. We all do."

CHAPTER 8

Hypnos walks in silence, leading me through the castle. After Dickhead left, Hypnos tortured me with a history lesson and offered a tour, but I just need space.

And a shower.

And an escape plan.

We retrace the halls I ran through earlier. My silver-dull dagger is still lodged in the wall, and I snort softly.

Up several flights of stairs, I realize I'd been running in circles. All those twists and turns—I must have wasted minutes looping around each floor.

It pisses me off.

Those fucking shadows played tricks on my mind. Without them, I'd have been out of here in minutes. Son of a bitch.

We stop in the middle of a hall, doors on either side.

"Whose room is that?" I ask, pointing to where I woke up.

"The Prince's," Hypnos replies smoothly, gesturing to the open door across the hall.

My eyes narrow. Orion had me put in his room when there was a perfectly empty one right here?

I step inside cautiously, scanning every corner. The room is grand, like something from an old fairy tale, but there's a ruggedness that makes it feel lived-in.

Dark stone walls, cool to the touch, are draped with woven tapestries—winged figures, sprawling forests, all glinting with silvery thread. A large fireplace crackles, throwing warm shadows across the wooden floor.

I take in the carved bed, piled with deep-green and midnight-blue covers, the writing desk beneath a tall window, sheer curtains shifting in the breeze, carrying the scent of night-blooming flowers.

But my focus locks on the three Fae women near the hearth.

Pointed ears mark them as Orion's kin, yet they lack his imposing presence. One, with silvery hair in a long braid, meets my gaze and dips her head slightly.

The others are just as striking. One has hair black as ink, her eyes glinting like stars. The third has fiery auburn curls and a freckled, impish face. Their pale, flowing dresses shift as if stirred by an invisible breeze.

They exchange glances—curious, apprehensive, waiting to see what I'll do next.

"Welcome, my lady," the silver-haired one says, her voice melodic.

Is everyone here gorgeous as hell?

"Hello." I dip my head. Their eyes widen slightly, a ripple of surprise passing between them.

Hypnos steps forward, amusement flickering in his pale

eyes. "My lady, these are your handmaids—Elowen, Thalindra, and Brynja."

The three dip their heads in graceful unison.

I shake my head. "That's not necessary. I don't need—"

Hypnos lifts a hand, cutting me off with a hint of a smile. "It is necessary. Refusing them would offend the Fae. They uphold the queen's comfort and Avalon's customs."

I glance at them, noting their carefully neutral expressions. He's right. The subtle shift in their posture tells me rejecting them would be a mistake.

"And more practically," Hypnos adds, "this castle is vast and . . . unpredictable. They will help you navigate, answer your questions, and ensure your needs are met."

The weight of his words settles in. And he's right—I won't be here long enough to figure this place out myself.

Elowen steps forward, voice gentle. "It is both our duty and honor."

I meet her gaze, finding nothing but sincerity. With a sigh, I nod. "Thank you. I appreciate the help."

Hypnos inclines his head, satisfied. "Accepting help in Avalon is often wiser than refusing it." His tone carries an unspoken warning.

The door closes behind him with a heavy thud, leaving me alone with the handmaids. Their keen but unreadable eyes hold a quiet expectation. I clear my throat.

"Right. Let's start with—were any of my belongings brought here?"

Elowen shakes her head. "No, my lady. Just yourself."

"And how exactly did I arrive?"

They exchange glances. I already know the answer—they aren't allowed to tell me.

Elowen steers the conversation elsewhere. "May I suggest a bath to refresh after your travels?"

I scoff at *travels*, but a bath isn't a bad idea. Still, I'd prefer a shower.

"Do you have . . . showers?"

Thalindra tilts her head, puzzled. "Showers?"

Brynja perks up. "A mortal custom?"

I sigh, shaking my head. "Never mind. A bath is fine."

Elowen smiles approvingly. "This way, my lady."

They guide me into a bathing chamber fit for a dream. The air is warm, scented with lavender.

A massive sunken tub, carved from dark stone, shimmers like starlight. Water flows from unseen sources, tinted with subtle shades of blue and green.

Thalindra pours a fragrant essence into the water. "Moonblossom. It eases tension."

I nod, more out of politeness than understanding. As Elowen moves to help remove my outer layers, I stop her with a look. "I can manage."

She hesitates, then bows. "As you wish, my lady."

They curtsy and exit, leaving me alone.

I sit at the edge of the bath, trailing my fingers through the warm water, but it does little to ease the ache of confusion in my chest.

Pressing two fingers to my pulse, I count the beats—an old habit, a tether to something familiar.

Waking up here feels like stepping into a story that isn't

mine. And with my team on leave, no one will even start looking for me for two weeks.

I rest my head against the cool stone. "Fuck."

The word alone carries an impossible weight. Here, they speak it as though the crown is already mine. Does that mean they expect I become one of them?

Are the Fae immortal?

The thought unsettles me. If they are, would I have to be?

Can someone *become* immortal?

The question lingers, twisting unease in my stomach. What does that entail? A ritual? Magic? Something darker?

I shake my head. It doesn't matter.

I will play their game for now, learn what I must, but escape is my only promise.

The door creaks open, breaking my thoughts. The hand-maids return, their movements fluid and precise as they approach with towels, their eyes downcast.

"It's okay. I'm not modest," I say, standing as water streams from my skin.

Thalindra's gaze flicks to mine, then down my body, her eyes darkening. She avoids looking too long, but I catch her glance darting toward me more than once.

Mmm, interesting.

Elowen steps forward with a sheer black robe, draping it over my arms. The fabric feels like cool silk against my damp skin.

Its bell sleeves are edged with a soft feathered fringe, and the slit up the center reveals flashes of my thighs as I walk.

The moment shatters when I reenter the bedroom and spot Orion.

He stands near a rack filled with ostentatious dresses, his expression hard as stone. He leans casually against the rack, inspecting his nails, but the tension in his posture betrays him.

"Get dressed," he barks without looking at me.

Cocking a hip, I cross my arms over my chest. "Get fucked," I snap back, drawing a quiet gasp from the hand-maids behind me.

Orion's molten eyes shift slowly to meet mine. His gaze doesn't linger on the robe clinging to my body; instead, it locks on my eyes, unwavering and cold.

"I don't do dresses," I say easily.

"You do now," he replies sharply, "and this is not up for argument."

"Look, you may be used to dictating whatever you want to *your* people, but I don't belong to you. Where I come from, I give the orders. I don't take them."

I step closer, my pulse rising with irritation. "I. Don't. Do. Dresses."

"You. Do. Now." He punctuates his words, standing inches away from me.

The tension crackles between us like a live wire.

"It is not my choice to have you attend the trial of our current queen. A traitor." he adds, his voice dropping to a low growl.

"If it were up to me, you'd sit out of sight, where you couldn't open your mouth and cause chaos among the High Fae. But–the realm demands it."

"Well, looks like you'll get your way, because I'm not going anywhere but home."

The words barely leave my mouth before Orion is pacing toward me, forcing my steps back until I hit the stone wall behind me, his molten gaze burning into mine.

His voice is low, rough with warning. "This is not a game. You cannot go home. You are stuck here. And while you are here, you will keep yourself alive."

I push against his chest, my palms flat against the heat of his body. He doesn't budge—not even an inch. The weight of his presence presses against me, a suffocating reminder of his power.

"Back off," I snap, shoving him again, harder this time.

His jaw tightens, and the muscle there ticks, but he doesn't retreat.

"You think this is about orders?" His voice is sharp, cutting, like a blade sliding across stone.

"This is about survival, *starling*. You're in a realm where your stubborn pride will get you killed."

"And what's that to you?" I spit back, feeling the heat of anger flush my face. "What do you care if I live or die? I'm just a mortal inconvenience, aren't I? So send me back home."

For a moment, his grip on my hip tightens, and his gaze flickers with something unreadable. He pulls back just enough for the cold air to slip between us.

"You think I asked for this?" His voice is low, laden with sarcasm.

"Do you think I wanted the realm's will to drag you into this mess and put me at the center of it with you?

You, with your defiance and blind ignorance? No, *starling*, this isn't about what I want—it's about what has to be done."

"Then you'd better get comfortable with disappointment," I say, refusing to let the tremor in my voice show.

"Because I'm not dressing up in one of your ridiculous gowns and playing the part of some captive queen. I'm finding my way home, and you can watch as I walk out of this nightmare you call a castle."

His expression sharpens, anger shifting into something darker, something more dangerous. He leans in again, and the air around us seems to shift, heavy with his power.

"If you step out of this room, if you even so much as breathe wrong while the High Fae are here, you'll be more than a captive—you'll be dead before you reach the gate. And that, *starling*," he says, his voice dropping into a near-growl, "is not a fight you can win."

I clench my fists, his words pressing against the stubborn defiance in my chest.

"I've faced worse," I bite back, my voice cold.

"No," he replies, his tone harsh and absolute. "You haven't."

Silence stretches between us, heavy and suffocating. I can hear the unsteady beat of my pulse in my ears, but I don't dare break eye contact.

Orion steps back abruptly, his presence retreating like a receding storm. He gestures sharply toward the rack of dresses.

"You may hate me. You may hate this. But none of that

matters. The realm has spoken, and you will attend Demeter's trial."

I let out a bitter laugh, the sound sharp in the quiet room. "And if I refuse?"

He turns to face me fully, his broad shoulders silhouetted against the warm light of the fireplace. The air around him seems to hum with restrained energy.

"Then the realm will force you," he says, his voice carrying an edge of finality. "And you do not want to find out how merciless it can be when crossed."

The threat isn't just in his words—it's in the way the room seems to grow colder, shadows shifting as if the castle itself is alive and listening. The grumble of distant thunder underscores his warning, a reminder of the unseen forces at play.

My defiance twists under the weight of his words, but I refuse to let it crumble entirely.

"Fine," I say, my voice steady despite the chill that lingers in my veins. "But don't expect me to play your obedient little queen."

His jaw tightens, and for a fleeting moment, I think I see a flicker of something softer—relief, perhaps—but it's gone before I can be sure.

Without another word, he turns on his heel, his movements precise and calculated, leaving the room with the tension crackling like a storm about to break.

CHAPTER 9
Tana

Avalon's eternal night streams through the windows, casting a silvery haze over the dark stone walls.

Elowen holds out a gown that shimmers in midnight blue and silver, embroidered with starlit vines and sheer gossamer sleeves—stunning, otherworldly, and completely outside my comfort zone.

"I still prefer pants," I mutter, eyeing my reflection. The dress drapes over me like a stranger's skin, and the headache I woke up with hasn't faded, each pulse a reminder that I'm not home, not safe, and definitely not in control.

Brynja chuckles, smoothing the fabric at my shoulders. "Your preference is noted, my lady," she says, wry enough to border on sarcasm. "But tonight, blending in is more valuable than comfort."

I sigh, watching them through the mirror's warped glass. They're trying, I'll give them that.

Thalindra adjusts the fit at my waist, Elowen fusses with the hem, their movements precise, deliberate. Their words about tonight's trial have been carefully chosen, rehearsed. There's a script I'm not allowed to read.

They've sworn an oath to protect me, bound to Orion himself. Breaking it won't just cost them their roles—it'll cost their lives. Ashes to dust.

All of that for me, the reluctant queen of a realm I never asked to rule.

The thought would be touching if it weren't terrifying.

Brynja steps back, arms crossed, assessing me. "Hold your chin high, my lady," she says, her tone firm.

"And if they speak to you, do not show fear. Silence can be as sharp a weapon as any blade."

I nearly laugh. Me? Silent? "Noted," I say, ignoring the irony.

This isn't a gown. It's armor. A disguise. A mask they've stitched together to make me something I'm not.

But for tonight, I'll wear it.

I'll play the part.

If nothing else, I'll learn the rules of their game—so I can break them later.

I turn, squaring my shoulders. "Thank you."

Elowen's expression softens, a hint of a smile ghosting her lips. "We serve you, my lady. Always."

Not always.

Only until I find a way out of here. Until I'm free.

I glance back at the mirror one last time as the door swings open, and Orion strides in, the room seeming to darken around him as if it knows to bow to his presence.

"Oh, goody, you're back," I deadpan as I let my eyes take in his new clothes. "Avalon's administrative assistant."

Black leather garments hug his tall, muscular frame, each line and curve accentuated with polished silver accents that catch the glow of the moonlight streaming through the window.

His silver hair flows around his face, catching the light like a halo made of frost.

And that cape—billowing behind him like a shroud of the night—makes him look as if he's been carved from the shadows.

I force myself to look away, focusing on digging my nails into my palm, my hands clenched at my sides.

He casts an unimpressed look over me, his piercing eyes taking in every detail with a critical sweep. "This is adequate," he says, the deep timbre of his voice laced with cold detachment.

Before I can respond, he steps closer, hand outstretched. I grab his wrist in an attempt to put him in a hold.

A move I've done a hundred times, but only with humans of my own strength apparently. Because this motherfucker doesn't even flinch.

"What the hell do you think you're doing?" I snap, my eyes narrowing as the defensive edge in my voice cuts through the room.

He pauses, his expression unyielding, but the faintest smirk betrays the burning irritation. "Putting a glamour on you," he replies, his voice clipped but steady.

"Fae magic that will mask your mortal scent and disguise your appearance. It will make you appear as one of us."

I keep my gaze locked on his, searching for a sign of deceit, but all I find is a hard resolve that matches my own.

The room feels smaller with him in it, charged with an electric tension that pricks at my skin. His hands hover in the space between us, waiting. A silent request for permission.

Reluctantly, I nod, unable to keep the defiance from my expression as I let go of his hand. "Fine. Just get it over with."

He steps forward, close enough that the subtle scent of cedar and smoke reaches me, mingling with the cool night air.

His fingers brush my temples, and I brace myself, expecting pain or discomfort. Instead, there's a strange warmth that spreads across my skin, sinking into my bones. A tingling sensation follows, like a thousand tiny pinpricks tracing the outline of my face and ears.

My breath shudders as the magic unfurls, cascading over me in waves.

I glance at the mirror and catch my breath. My reflection stares back with subtle, pointed ears, blending seamlessly with the hairstyle the handmaids have arranged.

The mortal traces in my eyes seem dulled, replaced by a cool, unearthly gleam. It's still me, but it isn't. The illusion is flawless, unsettlingly so.

Orion steps back, his gaze unreadable. "You'll pass as one of us now," he says, a shadow of something unspoken crossing his features before vanishing.

I touch the edge of my newly pointed ear, the unfamiliarity of it gnawing at me. "Why do I feel like this is just another cage?" I mutter, half to myself.

His eyes harden, and he tilts his head slightly. "Better this cage than the alternative," he says, the warning clear in his voice.

I don't respond, the weight of his words settling over me like a cloak of my own.

Orion's gaze sharpens, the molten silver of his eyes seeming to darken as he speaks. "You will be overseen by Hephaestus and his mate during the trial. You are to follow their instructions and remain silent unless spoken to. I expect you to—"

"Expect?" I cut in, my voice taut with defiance. "I'm not a dog that needs to be trained, dickhead."

The tension snaps like a bowstring between us. His jaw clenches, and he leans in, just close enough that I can feel the chill of his power threading the air.

"You will learn, starling, that your defiance holds no shield here. Test me, and you'll find out just how thin the line is between protection and danger."

Oh, I don't plan on testing that line. I'll blow it into next fucking year.

His words hang between us, charged with warning.

When it's clear I'm not going to back down, he turns on his heel, the black cape billowing out behind him as he strides from the room.

"See you 'round, Professor Snape," I call out as the door closes with a firm finality, and the silence that follows is heavy and cold.

Elowen steps forward, breaking the stillness. "My lady, it is time."

I take a steadying breath and follow the handmaids out.

We descend through winding halls, stone steps echoing beneath us as I memorize narrow passages for possible exits.

Passing through the bustling kitchens, I catch the scent of fresh bread and spiced fruit, the warmth briefly cutting through my unease. But as we step outside, the tightness in my chest eases entirely.

Cool air fills my lungs, the vast openness clearing my mind like a release from an unseen vice.

Above, the sky stretches in an endless expanse of velvet, brilliant stars scattered like shards of colored glass. The oversized moon, pale and watchful, looms as it had when I first woke here—unchanged, unmoving.

"When does the sun rise?" I ask, my gaze locked on it.

"We have only one dawn, Your Grace," Brynja murmurs. "The Night Court lives in eternal moonlight."

Damn. I like nighttime, but forever?

Brynja leans closer, voice hushed. "Stay close, my lady. Speak only when necessary."

I nod, nerves humming beneath my skin. For all its beauty, this place is a battlefield.

Ahead, Hephaestus's towering frame casts a long shadow over the stone path.

Even taller than Orion, his broad-shouldered form radiates raw power, the silver accents on his dark attire highlighting the deep auburn of his beard and hair—like a Scottish warrior stretched to eight feet tall.

Beside him, a woman glides into view, and my breath catches. I understand why they were chosen to guard me.

Unlike Hephaestus, whose sheer size makes him imposing, his mate exudes an eerie, otherworldly grace.

Her blush-pink skin shimmers under the moonlight, a delicate fin tracing the crown of her head. Patches of iridescent scales glow faintly along her arms, collarbone, and cheeks.

Large, reflective eyes—suited for the depths of the ocean—study me with quiet curiosity. She is serene, beautiful... and undeniably powerful.

A soothing warmth wraps around me, easing my headache, steadying my pulse. It feels deliberate, intentional. Magic.

Hephaestus's voice rumbles like distant thunder. "Lady Tana," he greets, warmth softening his rough edges. "This is my mate, Hestia. We'll be your company during the trial. Stick close, and you'll be fine."

Hestia steps forward, offering a small, knowing smile. "Welcome, Lady Tana," she says, her voice as gentle as waves against the shore.

"I know this must feel overwhelming, but we'll ensure you're comfortable in the presence of the High Fae tonight."

Her sincerity stirs something I can't name. I glance between her and Hephaestus—one an immovable force, the other a quiet, steady current.

"Thank you," I murmur, hoping the gratitude is evident.

As we walk down the stone path, the cool night air carries the scent of honeysuckle.

A misting lake stretches ahead, its surface glowing

under the moon, wisps of vapor curling like slow, steady breaths.

I steal a glance at Hestia. She moves like the water itself, fluid and effortless. What stories lie beneath that calm exterior?

"May I ask something?" I keep my voice low, knowing how keenly the Fae can hear.

"Of course, Your Grace," Hestia says with a small bow.

"Where I come from, trials are for criminals. Nothing here resembles home. What should I expect?"

She hesitates before answering. "The trial may be difficult to witness, but even in darkness, there is light. You are here for a reason, Lady Tana. Never forget that, no matter what you see today."

"Well, that's not ominous at all," I mutter, but she doesn't elaborate.

We cross a literal drawbridge—because of course there's a drawbridge—and beyond it, the Fae gather.

As I suspect, they aren't uniform in appearance. Some have antlers sprouting from long, silken hair. Others bear bark-like skin, their limbs resembling gnarled branches.

Some have hair that moves like living vines, rustling in an unseen wind.

I inhale sharply, steeling myself. "So," I mutter, glancing at my escorts, "is this where I act totally unbothered and not terrified?"

Hephaestus lets out a booming laugh. "Aye, lass. Maybe just pretend ye've seen a drawbridge before."

"Won't they find my presence suspicious? Do they come here often?"

Hestia's lips curve faintly, her iridescent scales catching the moonlight. "Some will be curious, but they will see what we show them. Strength. Composure."

I eye the gathering skeptically. "Right. But if one of those tree people starts sprouting vines at me, I can't make any promises."

Hestia's soft laugh ripples like a gentle tide. Even Hephaestus chuckles. "Ye'll be fine. Keep that sharp tongue, but not too sharp, aye?"

I smirk. "Noted."

As we near the courtyard, Hephaestus's tone shifts, growing somber. "Trials here aren't what ye may know from Gaea. They're a spectacle. Families bring their younglings, wagers are placed. It's part justice, part theater."

"They bring their kids?" I frown.

"Aye. It teaches them about consequence and court politics. But don't mistake this for one of those trials." His expression darkens.

"This is the trial of a queen. There will be no laughter or casual bets—only sharp eyes and heavy hearts."

I hesitate before asking, "Do you have children?"

"Aye, lass. Fourteen bairns." His eyes twinkle with amusement.

I gape. "Fourteen?! My god, stay off her!"

Hephaestus roars with laughter. "Nay, lass, it's her tha' needs to stay off me. I can't go two steps without her demandin' a kiss or patting my arse."

Hestia smacks his arm playfully, her musical laugh filling the space between them.

Hephaestus's teasing fades into something softer as he

looks at her. "But how could I deny her? When the stars themselves envy the way she makes me feel, I'd give anything to see her smile."

The sincerity in his voice makes me clutch my chest dramatically. For a moment, the weight of Avalon's shadows lifts under the simple joy between them.

"Men on Earth?" I scoff. "Or Gaea, I guess. They could never. No, they want you to split the bill, then have the audacity to ask, 'You came too, right?'"

Hestia and Hephaestus exchange baffled looks. The sight of two powerful Fae—one a mythic giant, the other an ethereal water being—staring at me like I've spoken in riddles nearly makes me laugh.

Hephaestus shakes his head. "I dinnae ken what that means, but it sounds like the males of Gaea are sorely lacking."

"You have no idea," I sigh.

Hestia watches me for a long moment, something unreadable in her gaze. It isn't pity—something else.

The courtyard opens before us, a vast space lit by floating orbs of pale light. Fae of all kinds mill about, their voices blending in a symphony of languages, each different from the next.

Some are humanoid, others beastlike or utterly alien in form.

At the center, an obsidian platform rises from the ground, runes pulsing along its edges.

A hush seems to settle over the space as the crowd shifts, making way for us.

"This is where Demeter will stand," Hestia murmurs.

My gaze locks onto the platform, unease curling in my gut.

Hephaestus's voice drops to a low murmur. "Strength and calmness."

I exhale slowly. "Strength and calmness," I repeat.

But as my eyes drift back to the platform, a dark weight settles over me.

Whatever happens next will be anything but calm.

CHAPTER 10
orion

I stare at the crack between the two massive doors of the castle, my mind wandering down the path that has led us here.

It began with my grandmother, Avalon's first-chosen queen, taking her place on the throne and binding herself to the realm.

From that step, a sequence of decisions twisted through time, with Demeter veering sharply away, embracing shadows over moonlight.

Now, that path ends with her facing immortal death.

Behind me, what remains of Demeter is more creature than queen. Bound in two sets of shadow-forged chains, the Morrigan and I hold her within our power.

Her hands are shackled before her, and a clasp over her mouth ensures silence.

Her pallid-gray skin, once a mark of her formidable presence, now appears ghostly, stretched tight over bones that jut out beneath skin as thin as parchment.

She looks as if she has been starved for many ages, though it has been only two nocturns since she was returned to Avalon.

She will walk before the Fae she betrayed, face the realm's judgment, and bear its punishment.

The moon's glow intensifies as the clouds retreat, casting a silver light that sharpens the edges of the scene.

I feel the pulse of the realm—gentle yet undeniable—like a heartbeat beneath my feet. Demeter senses it too.

Her spine straightens, shoulders set back, and her sunken, dark eyes focus forward, masking her dread with a stoic front.

But I see it—the slight tremor in her hands.

Her talon-like nails and long, bony fingers are the color of charcoal. Fading midway up her arms, it is the telltale sign of the darkness she embraced.

It changes you, marks you in ways that can never be undone.

The links of chains formed by our shadows are soundless as we walk to the dais near the shores of Avalon's great Misting Lake.

According to legend, the lake is where the realm's magic began and where the first Fae emerged.

No one can be certain, but it is agreed that the lake is alive, breathing mist into the air that carries whispers of enchantment, the past, and sometimes the future for a few who gaze into the surface.

The Misting Lake is thus a place of trials, where judgment is passed not just by Fae lords but by Avalon itself.

It is where rulers are tested, traitors are punished, and the realm's will becomes manifest. Demeter will not just face the eyes of her peers but the judgment of the realm's very soul.

Walking the path to the dais, I resist the pull to glance at Tana, to make sure the glamour I cast holds. I know it does —every thread of magic woven precisely—but the urge gnaws at the edge of my thoughts.

The crowd, a sea of High Fae draped in silks and adorned with ethereal jewels, watches with a mix of curiosity and hunger. Their whispers trail after us like the wind, sharp and cutting.

"Traitor queen," one voice hisses, venom lacing the words.

Another murmurs, "When will the realm choose? Will we see the crown claimed today?"

Speculation ripples through those gathered like a restless tide.

"It must be Queen Liora," an eager voice proposes. "The realm deserves the radiance of Eldoria, the Shimmering Court."

I suppress a sneer at the mention. Liora and her court of stars—the self-proclaimed superior court.

Their vanity is as vast as the constellations they drape themselves in, starlight spun into silks and crowns that gleam as though their light could outshine Avalon itself.

Their arrogance blinds them to the deeper truths of this realm, content only when others bask in their supposed glory.

Another Fae, with eyes glistening like frost, leans forward, voice edged with daring.

"No queen. A king this time. King Thorn of Thornspire, the Briar Court, would rule as the realm demands—rooted, unyielding. Exactly what the realm needs in times of such darkness."

I push their voices to the periphery, focusing on the steps before me. The dais looms, carved of dark stone and etched with patterns that seem to pulse under the moon's silver light.

The whispers grow louder as I guide her to the center of the dais and turn to face the gathered Fae.

The sea of faces reflects a myriad of emotions: eagerness, suspicion, anticipation. It is a scene I have witnessed countless times, yet never with stakes so high.

My gaze sweeps over them—controlled, cold—until it lands on her.

Tana.

She is hidden among them, appearing as one of our own, yet the tension in my chest tightens as if it can sense her heartbeat.

Our eyes meet for only a moment before I force myself to look away, lest the connection betray more than intended.

I step forward, raising my arm as my voice cuts through the whispers and murmurs—deep and commanding.

"Order."

The single word resonates, echoing through the gathering and sending a shiver down the spine of every Fae present.

The air thickens with an ancient energy, as if the realm itself is holding its breath, and a dense mist rolls in from the lake, creeping across the dais.

Demeter stands bound in shadowed chains, her gray skin pallid, yet her eyes blaze with a fierce light.

As I monitor the realm's prisoner, I catch sight of Demeter glaring harshly at Tana.

To my surprise, Tana holds the stare—not with the ignorance of someone who doesn't know better but with determination that says she will not be intimidated.

The corner of my mouth twitches, a sliver of pride threatening to break through, but I bite it back, keeping my face as impassive as stone.

Perhaps the realm has chosen our new queen well.

The mist thickens, swirling and pulsing with a silvery sheen, and the Lady of the Lake steps from the fog as though born from it.

Her blue skin shimmers under the moonlight and is dotted with scales that glisten like tiny jewels.

Her black hair falls like liquid ink down her back, and her webbed fingers stay ever so slightly dipped in the water that follows her.

Wherever she steps, a thin, glistening layer of water remains beneath her feet, connecting her to the lake she guards so fiercely.

A hush falls over the gathered Fae, reverence rippling through the crowd like an unseen wave.

The Lady's eyes—wide and ancient—shift to the dais, seeing all but speaking nothing. Though her lips remain sealed, her intent is understood by all.

The Fae in attendance exchange glances, their thoughts running wild with speculation, as they always do when she appears.

Some believe her to be the first Fae of Avalon, born with

the realm's first heartbeat. Others think her the physical form of Avalon itself.

Some—a goddess exiled from a forgotten pantheon, now bound to the lake by powers no one dares to name.

But one thing is agreed upon: all will bow in her presence—in awe, in respect of the magic she carries within her.

As the Lady raises her webbed hand, the mist around the dais shifts, drawing the waters up in elegant, liquid tendrils.

The lake answers her silent call, rising and weaving together until it forms a mirror before Demeter.

The surface shimmers—opaque yet mesmerizing—charged with magic so old it defies time.

Gasps rise from the Fae as they see the Mirror of Sins, its surface rippling with secrets that are about to be revealed.

The reflection seems to pulse, and a tremor runs through the crowd—anticipation, fear, and morbid curiosity mingling as one.

Demeter's defiant gaze flickers, and her fingers tense against the chains.

The mirror shimmers, ready to expose every treachery, every dark choice that brought us all to this moment.

The Lady of the Lake, still standing upon the thin water beneath her feet, remains expressionless, yet the weight of her presence presses down on us all, demanding the truth.

The trial has begun.

CHAPTER II
Tana

I'm as restless as the crowd of waiting Fae.

If you had asked me forty-eight hours ago where I would be at this very moment—witnessing the trial of a queen who betrayed her throne, her people... on a realm I never knew existed—would not have been on my bingo card.

Hephaestus leans in, whispering, his voice low and steady, as he fills me in on the types of Fae around us. "See those antlers? That's one of the Stagkin.

And there—those twisted-bark limbs—Dryads, from Gloamreach."

His gaze scans the crowd again, his lips curling into a half smirk. "Though I'm not surprised the Sprites haven't turned up. Lil' buggers, they are. Never were ones fer order."

A silence falls across the land. The wind stills. The surface of the lake lies flat, undisturbed. Even the misting fog that's been swirling endlessly has paused its journey.

Cresting the hill, Orion and Mor walk side by side, and my eyes lock on the creature behind them.

When I imagined what a queen of fantastical creatures might look like, I thought of elegance—long, shimmering hair, oversized eyes that could peer straight into your soul, and wings so magnificent they could blot out the sky.

The thing paraded through the crowd of gathered Fae is anything but that.

She looks more like the withered thing that guided Frodo through Mount Doom—a hollow figure trudging toward her end.

I don't know much about ancient mythology, but the name Demeter is familiar enough. I'd envisioned someone mighty, regal—but what I see now is no queen. This is a creature, not a ruler.

Her gray skin hangs loosely on her frame, sallow and lifeless. Patches of her disheveled, thinning hair have fallen away entirely, exposing a pale, uneven scalp.

She wears what looks like a long, dirty nightdress, clinging to her frail body. The sight is grotesque and pitiful all at once.

Orion and Mor walk ahead of her, their expressions carved from stone, unyielding and impassive. My breath catches when I see the chains.

Shadows.

The same cool, whispering shadows that wrapped around my wrists when I first met Orion—when he pinned me to the wall with nothing but his power.

My wrists tingle at the memory, and I find myself rubbing them as if to chase away the phantom cold.

The chains should clank with every step, but they are eerily silent as they move with her, securing her wrists, encircling her waist, and trailing down to connect with her ankles.

She shuffles forward under the weight of sneers from the gathered Fae, her back hunched, her movements slow and labored.

I can't tell if her posture is because of her captivity or the crimes she bears.

I don't know what she's done—what horrors brought her to this moment—but seeing her like this, starving, her body broken, I feel a pang of something that surprises me: pity.

She looks as though her soul is being devoured by something I can't understand.

Her sunken eyes scan the crowd, darting from face to face as if searching for someone. A kindred spirit, perhaps. Or maybe she's looking for something far simpler—someone who isn't cursing her name.

My gaze drifts to her hands, and at first, I think the dark lines snaking up her forearms are faded tattoos. But then I hear Hestia's sharp hiss.

"Dark magic," she whispers, her voice like a ripple of unease.

"Aye," Hephaestus mutters beside me, his brogue thick with quiet disdain. "It's eatin' her alive now that she's stopped feedin' it." His eyes flick to me, his expression grave. "Tha' darkness—it must always feed."

My stomach churns, and my eyes instinctively find Mor. The small woman, cloaked in black, her red eyes sharp and all-seeing, moves with a confidence that borders on defiance.

After what I saw in the dining hall—the way she

devoured the platters of food with an unrelenting appetite —I wonder if she feeds something more than just herself.

I watch as Orion and Mor flank Demeter on the dais, their power palpable even from where I stand. The crowd quiets, the sea of Fae shifting like restless shadows beneath the glow of the oversized moon.

My heart pounds, and I'm not sure if it's from the charged atmosphere or the sight of Orion's commanding presence as he turns to face the gathering. His silver eyes scan the crowd briefly before locking with mine.

It's only a second, maybe less, but it's enough.

A rush of something sharp and unsteady floods through me, stealing my breath.

It's not fear, exactly, though it unsettles me all the same —like standing too close to the edge of a cliff and feeling the pull of the drop.

His gaze is a storm, all heat and cold at once, and then it's gone.

I force my focus away, back to Demeter.

Then I feel that rush of the cliff's fall when her hollow, dark eyes are focused intently on mine.

A chill races down my spine, and the weight of her gaze sinks into my bones. There's something in those eyes—something that twists and writhes, ancient and malevolent.

It's not desperation or sorrow but something darker. Something that claws at the edges of my mind and makes my skin crawl.

Evil.

Pure and unfiltered, lurking just beneath the surface like a shadowed monster waiting to pounce.

My throat tightens, and I force myself to stand straighter, to hold her stare even though every instinct tells me to look away.

The crowd fades into the background, their murmurs distant and unimportant.

It's just her and me, locked in this silent battle of wills.

She doesn't blink, doesn't waver.

Those black, soulless pits bore into me as if trying to unearth something buried deep inside.

For the first time since I woke in this strange, endless night, I feel the weight of true danger—not from the Fae around me, not even from the power of the realm itself, but from her.

A monster wearing a crown.

Whatever she is, whatever she's done, the evil in her eyes is enough to make me question whether pity is what she deserves.

So focused on this standoff, I don't notice the chill in the atmosphere shifting until cool fog dances around my ankles, ruffling the long ends of my dress.

Ribbons of water begin moving of their own accord up the hill, swirling around the dais.

The gathered Fae fall silent, and the monster that had been attempting to rip into my soul visibly shakes with fear.

A woman, so majestic she seems more legend than reality, emerges from the fog.

Her long, dark hair blows in currents that swirl just for her.

She has blue skin and large black voids for eyes, and she

glides forward like a ghost, her presence both ethereal and commanding.

There's an otherworldly grace to her—a quiet sovereignty that feels as though it could flatten mountains if she so desired.

She doesn't walk so much as float, her feet never touching the ground, and where she passes, water remains, glistening like an offering to the earth.

Beside me, Hestia drops to one knee, her head bowed low.

The motion is quick, fluid, and filled with reverence, as if it's an instinct embedded deep in her bones.

She rises a moment later, her expression awed.

The gathered Fae are silent now, their faces a mix of wonder, fear, and devotion.

Even Demeter—the creature who moments ago seemed intent on boring into my soul with her malevolent stare—trembles.

Her gaunt form shrinks under the weight of the woman's presence, and for the first time, I see fear ripple across her sunken features.

It's a stark contrast to the monstrous defiance she had been exuding, and the sight sends a chill down my spine.

A thin mirror of water takes shape, weaving itself into a delicate sheet before Demeter.

The surface shimmers, and a beam of light from the oversized moon makes the reflection in the mirror glow.

And then I hear it.

A voice—not a voice exactly, more like a thread of

thought that doesn't belong to me, slipping uninvited into the corners of my mind.

"Shadows remember what the moonlight forgets."

The words are faint, like the whisper of a breeze brushing through the mist.

My throat tightens, and I glance around, expecting to see someone next to me, but it's only my two chaperones, their attention fixed on the mirror.

I follow movement within the crowd and watch as the woman from the water weaves between the witnesses.

They don't move or seem to notice her, and it makes me think they're frozen.

Or perhaps they can't see what I'm seeing.

"Do you see, little one?" the voice murmurs again, softer this time, almost mocking as she stops her slow path and turns, looking into me with the deep abyss of her gaze.

"What was, what is, or what will be? The mirror knows."

I grip the fabric of my skirt, trying to steady myself as the surface of the mirror ripples.

The first images appear—Demeter's crimes, as seen through the eyes of the crowd.

Betrayal. Blood.

Her hands, stained with darkness, pour shadows into her veins like ink spilled across a page.

Gasps ripple through the audience as the vision unfolds, each detail exposing her treachery with painful clarity.

She killed an older woman.

Then another, who looks so much like herself, writhes in pain, clutching her head as she screams in agony.

But what I see is different.

The mirror shifts, and suddenly, it isn't showing Demeter's sins.

It's showing something else entirely.

A realm, vast and magnificent, consumed by a living shadow.

The skies are blackened, and what little light remains struggles against the encroaching darkness.

The trees wither, their branches twisting into skeletal fingers, and the ground cracks, veins of shadow crawling like a plague.

Screams pierce the air, desperate and unending, rising in a cacophony that tears through me like the flashes of lightning bursting within the nightmare of the mirror's reflection.

I can't tell if the screams are within the mirror or within my mind, but they claw at my ears, sharp and relentless.

My breath quickens as the darkness spreads, devouring everything in its path.

I try to look away, to close my eyes, but I can't.

I'm frozen, forced to watch as the mirror pulls me deeper, showing me a future—or perhaps a past—I can't understand.

"Tana..." the voice whispers again, right behind my ear and more insistent now. *"Beware what you see."*

My chest tightens, the air thick and unyielding, as if the vision itself has reached out and wrapped its cold, suffocating fingers around me.

The images flicker—ruin, despair, death—

And then, for a split second, I see myself.

Standing in the heart of the darkness, alone, a shadow curling around my feet as if claiming me.

"Choose."

The Lady's voice barrels through me, and the vision ends abruptly.

The screams stop, leaving only the sound of my ragged breathing as the trial continues around me.

The vision is gone, replaced by Demeter's crimes once more, but the weight of what I saw lingers.

I feel sick, my legs trembling as if they might give out beneath me.

I glance at the Fae around me, their attention still locked on the mirror, unaware of what I've seen.

Unaware of what the darkness whispered to me.

My heart hammers in my chest, and a hammer pounds within my head.

I know, deep down, that this wasn't just a warning of the past or a glimpse of the future.

It was both.

And I need to get out of here as quickly as I can.

CHAPTER 12
orion

The visions fade in and out of the mirror, each revelation hitting me like a blow.

My jaw tightens, and I force myself to stand rigid, the weight of my fury pressing into the still air around me.

The crimes against Avalon are abhorrent enough, but it is the betrayals against my family—against my grandmother and my mother—that threaten to splinter my control.

The mirror ripples, and the first vision takes form. It shows the moment Demeter forged her secret bargain. The bargain with a god-killer.

The figure of the hidden deity emerges in the vision, veiled in shadows that pulse with an emerald light. Its whispers are like claws, and I can almost feel the malice in the air as Demeter bows before it.

She offered herself in exchange for a throne she was never meant to claim, betraying her realm for promises forged in destruction.

The scene shifts, and I see a pergola, once a sanctuary of moonlight, now draped in shadows.

Artemis—the ancient Titan protector of Avalon—steps forward, her golden glow meeting Demeter's cold gaze.

I know what's coming before it happens, yet it still twists my stomach.

Demeter's deceitful words, her betrayal laced with honey, lure Artemis into the deity's trap.

The Titan falls, her light extinguished in an instant.

The impact is devastating.

Raging battles follow, sweeping across the Fae lands like a storm—burning, breaking, and bleeding into our history.

Avalon alone is spared, but only because Demeter sold it at the cost of the other realms.

My fists clench at my sides as the veil ripples again.

Gasps rise from the crowd.

The scene unfolding before us is one I hoped we would not see.

My mother, Elaine, and my grandmother, Pandora.

The mirror reflects Demeter's poisoned hand, her fingers tipped with deceit as she delivers their deaths.

Pandora's face is the first to fade, regal even as pain takes her, her bond to Avalon severing in a flash of light that dims the realm itself.

And then my mother.

Her final moments linger in the water longer than I can bear.

Her eyes meet mine—or perhaps it's a trick of the mirror—but it feels like she's staring straight through me.

I don't breathe.

I can't.

The image lingers like a specter, her pain seared into my

mind before the mirror ripples once more, pulling me out of the moment.

The final vision begins: Demeter's reign as queen.

A slow unraveling of everything Avalon once was.

It shows her weaving lies and promises, her words twisting through the courts like poisoned vines.

She played them all against one another, deepening rifts that had once been shallow divides. The courts grew restless, mistrustful, while the realm itself suffered under her touch.

Her reign is like a creeping blight.

Flowers wilt and turn black, their brittle petals crumbling to ash under a tainted wind.

Creatures of Avalon, once vibrant and magnificent, become twisted echoes of their former selves—horns bent unnaturally, fur matted with shadow.

This is what she has done—to Avalon, to my family, to me.

I glance at Demeter, bound in shadowed chains, her face gaunt, her hollow eyes locked on the mirror as it betrays every moment of her treachery.

Her hands tremble, but it isn't fear.

No, it's rage.

Even now, she refuses remorse.

The fury inside me surges, darker than the shadows I command.

My grandmother's death. My mother's death. The lies. The destruction.

She has taken so much—too much.

And for what?

A throne she never deserved and will now never hold again.

The Mirror of Sins trembles, its surface rippling violently as if struggling to contain the weight of Demeter's crimes.

Then, with a sound like the splitting of ice, it shatters.

Countless shards of water crystallize in midair, each holding frozen images of her betrayals:

Pandora. Artemis. The Fae lands. The abandoned throne of Avalon.

My mother.

The shards hover in the air, spinning and glinting under the glow of the oversized moon, their jagged edges sharp as truth itself.

The crowd gasps—a collective, sharp intake of breath—as the shards begin to move.

Slowly, deliberately, they converge above Demeter's head, forming a crown of guilt.

Her hollow eyes widen in panic, and she thrashes weakly against the shadows that bind her.

It's futile.

The shards press into her scalp, embedding themselves deep.

Black ichor drips down her temples like a grotesque mockery of blood, and she lets out a strangled cry, the sound chilling and hollow.

The Lady of the Lake remains still and silent through it all.

Her verdict, impossibly clear and resonant, echoes through the minds of all who witness, racing across the realm of the Fae.

"By the breath of the mists, by the blood of the waters, your crimes are known, Demeter. Avalon's pain is yours to bear."

Demeter collapses to her knees, her body wracked with tremors.

Her crown glows faintly, the images of her sins flickering like a haunting reminder of all she has wrought.

Without a word, the Lady of the Lake turns and begins her descent back to the waters.

Her movements are graceful, unhurried, each step trailing a thin layer of water beneath her.

The mists rise and swirl around her, as if clinging to their source, reluctant to let her go.

She disappears into the lake's surface without a ripple, vanishing as if she were never there.

Nothing but the mists remain.

They linger over the dais, heavy and charged, before shifting, slowly creeping up the path that leads toward the castle.

The gathered Fae part instinctively, murmuring in hushed tones as the mist travels with purpose.

I know where it's going—to the sacred Grove of the Queens.

The mists coil through the grove, moving like sentient wisps of silver, twisting between the ancient trees.

I know where they lead.

To Demeter's final judgment.

The Grove of the Queens has long been a sacred place. It is home to the orchards of the golden apples, the fruit of Avalon's blessings.

These apples, once vibrant and lustrous, were the

embodiment of fated unions, prosperous partnerships, and the fertile blessings of children—if desired.

But without the seed of a rightful queen to nurture the realm, the orchard has withered.

The once-brilliant fruit is now pale and tasteless.

Like the Fae, many of the ancient trees stand barren, their branches drooping as if mourning their loss.

The realm's will has spoken, and the mists carry its command.

Avalon's judgment demands Demeter's life, and she will give it in the grove that dies under her rule.

The mist coils around Demeter, guiding her forward with an unseen force.

Freed from their purpose, the shadows that once bound her dissolve.

Her gaunt frame trembles as the silent crowd watches, whispers of disbelief rippling through them.

In the grove's center, the mist thickens, twisting into thorned vines that writhe like living creatures.

They reach for her, burrowing deep the moment they touch skin.

She flinches, jerking as the thorns pierce her flesh.

Black veins spider from the wounds, dark magic spreading through her like rot.

Above, the crown of shards glows faintly, thick tar seeping from its edges.

It drips down her chest, hardening into an iron seed that glows like embers.

A strangled gasp escapes her as it burrows into her

heart, its tendrils sinking into her veins, entwining with her life force.

Her body bows in agony, the invasion consuming her from within.

The vines pulse, thickening grotesquely, binding her in place.

Roots explode from the iron seed, jagged and writhing, forcing her upright like a ghoulish effigy.

They burrow deep into the earth, and from them, twisted flowers bloom—blackened things shaped like screaming skulls, their vines contorting into grotesque, anguished faces.

The seed devours her power, stripping away her connection to life and fertility, inch by inch.

Around her, nature warps—flowers bloom only to crumble into ash, fruit swells grotesquely before bursting into decay.

The grove transforms into a landscape of rot, mirroring the corruption overtaking its queen.

Demeter's body withers, her gray skin pulling taut over fragile bones.

Her breaths turn shallow, rattling with pain as the roots siphon every ounce of her remaining magic.

The agony stretches unbearably long until, at last, her form begins to crumble.

Inch by inch, she disintegrates, black ash scattering into the wind.

The grove falls silent, save for the whisper of mist retreating toward the lake.

Where Demeter stood, a single twisted tree now grows.

Its bark is blackened, its branches gnarled and bare.

No leaves adorn it, no blossoms or fruit hang from its limbs.

It is a monument to her crimes, a scar on the Grove of the Queens, and a warning of what happens to those who betray Avalon.

The gathered Fae watch in stunned silence, and I stand unmoving, the weight of the moment pressing down on me like a mountain.

Avalon's judgment has been delivered.

The realm has taken back what was stolen.

But as the mist coils away, I can't help but feel the burden that remains.

The grove is not healed.

The apples are not golden.

The darkness has not lifted.

The realm still waits for its queen. *For her.*

The realization hits me a moment too late. The seed. This is why the realm demanded Tana join.

I spin on my heel, my dark cape a whirl with my movement.

The second my eyes find her, so does the moonlight.

A beam of silvery light pierces through the mist-laden air, encasing Tana in a soft, ethereal glow.

The veil of glamour I placed over her dissolves, fading like darkness under a rising sun.

"Damn it," I curse under my breath, my gaze darting to Mor and Hypnos.

Their faces betray no surprise, though Mor's sharp eyes narrow in silent understanding, and Hypnos tilts his head, a faint trace of intrigue crossing his otherwise impassive face.

Tana's back arches as her body is lifted effortlessly into the air.

Her eyes are unfocused, unseeing, her expression serene in its detachment.

The silken glow wraps around her, like threads of starlight, weaving her into the moon's embrace.

Gasps ripple through the crowd, quickly followed by sneers and sharp murmurs.

Every Fae eye locks onto her as the glamour is stripped away, exposing the truth.

"A mortal."

"The realm has chosen a mortal to be our queen."

The realization spreads like wildfire among the spectators.

The disbelief is palpable, a mix of shock and disdain etched into the faces of the gathered Fae.

Whispers rise, carrying words like impossible and blasphemy, but none dare speak above the wailing cry that echoes through the grove.

It's Demeter.

Her howl twists and distorts, a mournful, agonized sound that pierces the heavy silence.

The crowd recoils as a seed of pure moonlight emerges from Tana's chest, floating with radiant purpose.

It drifts through the air, glowing brighter as it approaches the charred, gnarled tree that now stands as Demeter's eternal prison.

The seed presses into the bark with a soft hiss, and a

blazing symbol burns itself into the blackened wood—the crest of Avalon.

The tree groans as if in protest, its branches twisting, but the mark holds firm.

The wailing from within grows louder, a spectral scream of despair and torment.

Demeter's spirit, forever bound to the tree, will remain aware.

She will exist within the very darkness she nurtured, trapped forever in the corrupted land she helped create.

Her torment is fitting, but there is no satisfaction in it.

She will remain an eternal reminder to those who would tip the scales of the realm's balance.

A rolling wave of moonlight rushes out of the crest burned into the tree's bark.

As the moonlight flows outward in all directions, so does life once again flow throughout the orchard.

Around us, the grove's trees stand taller, firmer, their roots stretching deep into fertile, moist soil.

Branches unfurl as thousands of leaves sprout in an instant.

And dropping heavy, weighing down the strong branches, the rich apples of Avalon almost glow in the pearlescent light of the moon.

The grove falls silent again, save for the faint creak of the twisted branches, now full of life and fruit once more.

The crowd stares at Tana, their disbelief replaced with a tense, almost reverent stillness.

The realm has spoken, and its choice is clear: Tana.

My gaze returns to her, suspended in the moonlight, her

mortal fragility a stark contrast to the power surrounding her.

The silence of the crowd begins to crack as whispers and quiet protests rise.

This is unheard of.

Unacceptable to many.

A mortal? A queen?

And yet, here she is.

The beam of moonlight fades, and Tana's body lowers gently back to the ground.

She sways, her legs unsteady as Hestia moves quickly to catch her arm, keeping her upright as her hand instinctively clutches her chest where the seed emerged.

She looks dazed, unaware of the storm of reactions her presence has ignited.

The whispers grow louder, rippling with doubt and outrage.

But through it all, one truth remains undeniable:

The realm has chosen her.

I step forward, fury simmering beneath my calm facade.

Without hesitation, I pull my belt of shadows from my waist.

The inky strands lengthen into a whip, and with a sharp snap, it cracks through the air, cutting across the rising voices like a bolt of lightning.

My power rolls thunderous in the distant clouds.

"Enough!"

My voice booms, silencing the chaos.

The grove falls quiet, the murmurs strangled mid-breath.

Eyes widen, and all attention shifts to me, the command in my tone leaving no room for argument.

Mor and Hypnos close ranks around Tana, their movements fluid, precise, protective.

Mor's crimson eyes sweep the crowd, sharp and predatory, ready for a fight.

Hypnos tilts his head, his blank, white eyes narrowing slightly, as if reading the emotions of each Fae present, cataloging their fears and defiance.

Together, they are an unbreakable barrier, a clear warning that no one will touch the mortal the realm has chosen.

I take my place beside her and drop to one knee.

The motion is deliberate, purposeful, a signal that cannot be ignored.

From the corner of my eye, I see Hypnos follow, his descent fluid, almost reverent.

Around us, the crowd hesitates.

It's as if the weight of my action ripples through them, pulling them toward submission.

Slowly, one by one, most of the Fae bow, their heads lowering reluctantly, grudgingly acknowledging what the realm has decreed.

But not all.

My eyes find those who remain standing.

A handful, stiff-backed and defiant, their expressions etched with disdain and disbelief.

Fools.

My gaze hardens, cold and sharp, and I lock eyes with one.

The male Fae is unmistakably from Thornspire, the Briar Court.

His sharp, angular face is framed by bramble-like hair that shifts unnaturally, as if alive.

His blackened armor, etched with thorned patterns, bears the mark of his court: a crimson rose encircled by barbed thorns.

The air chills.

Fog thickens, dark and sluggish, slithering through the trees to coil at his feet.

Overhead, a cloud swallows the moonlight, casting the grove in gloom.

The wind carries faint, venomous whispers, their meaning elusive but laced with doubt and malice.

Ruvan Kael does not bow.

His stance is rigid, rooted like the gnarled trees of his homeland, amber eyes gleaming coldly as they lock onto me.

The whispers around him rise, almost conspiratorial.

He tilts his head slightly, listening, then nods, as though conferring with unseen voices.

Mor's crimson gaze narrows.

"Ah, the Thorn Warden himself," she muses, disdain curling her tone. "A briar-hearted bastard if ever there was one. The Briar Court doesn't kneel easily—seems he intends to make that clear."

Ruvan's smirk is faint but pointed, his cloak of thorns shifting as the fog curls higher.

The quiet defiance in his expression is not reckless—it's

measured, the kind of resistance bred from surviving treacherous terrain, both literal and political.

"Ruvan Kael," I call, my voice cutting through the wind.

Shadows hiss at my sides, lightning flickering across my knuckles.

"You will kneel before your queen."

The whispers around him swell, seething with approval.

He lifts his chin, standing tall.

"Avalon may have chosen," he says evenly, "but the Briar Court does not bend to mortals. Not now. Not ever."

"Careful, Kael," Hypnos warns, stepping forward. "You speak boldly. Can you be certain King Thorne will stand by your defiance?"

Ruvan doesn't flinch.

Instead, he takes a slow step forward, fingers brushing the hilt of his sword.

My own hand twitches in response, shadows twisting down my arm, crackling with restrained power.

The whispers grow sharper, still indistinct but charged with dark approval.

Ruvan hesitates at the grove's edge, then releases his weapon.

His bramble cloak sways in the wind, the whispers twisting with it.

"The Briar Court rejects this chosen queen," he declares, his voice carrying like the toll of a warning bell.

"If my lord and king does not challenge her—I will challenge her myself. To the death."

CHAPTER 13
Tana

I will challenge her myself. To the death.

Just fucking perfect.

Not only do I not want to be stuck in this fucking realm, but now I'm receiving death threats. Fuck this place.

The cool draft that meanders through the castle carries the wail of Demeter, her soul bound to the twisted tree for eternity, and these Fae sit around the dinner table like it's just another day in Avalon.

Orion sits at the head of the table, speaking in low tones to a Fae lord about politics and the treachery of the Briar Court's "insurrection."

Mor sits across from me, just as she did when I first awakened. A seemingly endless supply of platters is placed in front of her, and she eats just as urgently with the fifth platter as she did the first.

It seems her appetite is endless, and I'm not sure if the kitchen can keep enough cooked to sustain her.

With my fork, I shepherd a piece of roasted potato around my charger as I stare at the map over the massive fireplace.

No one speaks to me, and it's a good thing.

I keep myself busy burning the image of the map into my memory—where the castle sits, each court marked clearly, and the winding paths that connect them.

The threat of the Briar Court's warden cuts through my mind like the cool wind that seeps through the drafty castle halls. Orion is determined to make me queen, and that man is equally determined to see me dead. But perhaps there's another solution to this problem.

Maybe, with the right leverage, this warden of the Briar Court will be my ticket out of here. I don't know how long it will take to get there on foot or what I could possibly use as a bargaining chip. But it doesn't matter.

As far as I have to go, whatever I have to do, I won't stop until I find a way home.

Excusing myself to my room, I bring a small satchel of cheeses and dried meats from the kitchens.

Using the excuse of a poor appetite and needing a snack later, no one thinks twice about my request. Adding some fruit, I sling it over my shoulder and walk at a casual pace to my room.

I don't have to act like my mind is elsewhere because it's stuck, playing out Demeter's execution on repeat.

The moonlight's touch felt invasive, peeling away Orion's glamour like it was nothing, baring me to the eyes of every Fae in the realm.

A mortal, glowing as if I were some chosen savior. A shiver runs through me—not at the memory, but at the understanding that the power didn't feel foreign.

It felt like it came from me, like I commanded it.

My hand drifts to my chest, brushing over the spot

where the seed emerged. Golden, alive, pulsing with an energy that felt like a fragment of my soul had been lying dormant, waiting for the moon to coax it free.

And when it did, when that golden seed was born from me, I swear I felt the pulse of three hearts beating as one. My heart, the heart of the realm, and something else.

The magic, perhaps.

Reaching my room, I tear loose the stifling dress and let it fall to the ground. I squeeze my eyes shut, rubbing my temples as the pounding headache I've been trying to ignore surges back.

"This is insane," I mutter, walking to the window and throwing open the glass shutters.

The night air whispers faintly, carrying with it a strange stillness. Somewhere in the distance, I hear the faint, ghostly echo of laughter—or maybe I imagine it, but it almost seems to mock my presence here.

I grip the stone ledge of the window, my gaze dropping to the jagged rock face below. I cement my plan to leave in my mind. This castle wall is intimidating but climbable. If I've scaled mountains into vampire dens, surely I can handle this.

I just need to figure out a way down.

My eyes land on the gaudy dress, and a sly smile creeps across my face. "Guess this can be useful after all."

Rummaging through the cabinet, I find fitted black pants and a dark tunic. With my Docs laced, gun and holster secured, I turn back to the dress.

Long strips of the dress are torn and braided tight. Two more dresses follow, and soon I have a rope thick and long enough to hold me. Tying it to the bedpost, I test the knot, tugging hard.

The fire poker catches my eye. Its iron weight feels good in my grip, steadying my nerves as I tuck it into my belt. I gather the satchel of food, and I'm ready.

Perched on the windowsill, I swing my legs over, the chill of the night air rushing up to meet me. The ground below looks impossibly far, but there's no turning back now.

"This is the stupidest thing I've done in years," I mutter, gripping the rope tightly. "Which is saying something."

The descent starts smoothly, the braided fabric holding firm under my grip. The jagged rock scrapes against my boots as I search for footholds, moving deliberately, step by step.

Then the wind picks up, yanking at my hair and pressing me hard against the wall. My heart pounds in my chest as I cling to the rope.

"Focus, Valkyrie," I hiss through clenched teeth. "One step at a time."

Halfway down, a sudden gust slams into me. I freeze, gripping the rope with trembling hands.

"Okay. Not dying here. Not like this."

My breath comes in sharp bursts, but I force myself to keep going. Finally, my feet touch solid ground. Relief floods me as I flick the rope free and coil it over my shoulder.

My scraped palms sting, but it's a small price for freedom.

"All right, Tana," I mutter under my breath, brushing dirt off my hands. "You're out. Now, where the hell do you go from here?"

Pressing myself against the castle wall, I scan the open lawn stretched out before me. Beyond the cyan-colored grass, a small wooden bridge arches over the moat, leading to a heavy wooden door in the outer wall.

Past that lies the forest—dark and foreboding—but the first part of the trip to the Briar Court.

The bridge creaks faintly under my boots as I cross the moat, each sound sending a spike of adrenaline through me.

Once I reach the shadowed wall, I flatten myself against the cold stone, my pulse racing but steady. I test the door. It doesn't budge.

Locked. Or stuck.

I twist the handle harder, putting more force behind it. Still nothing.

"Figures," I mutter, rolling my eyes as I look to the top of the wall, searching for a good location to scale it.

The air shifts suddenly. It feels heavier, colder, as tension coils around me like a tightening noose.

I tug harder at the handle when a low, guttural snarl freezes me in place.

It's coming from the other side of the door.

The sound reverberates through the wood, deep and menacing.

A large beast, judging by the weight of its breath, presses its snout against the door. The exhale is powerful, rattling the wood beneath my fingertips.

My fingers slip from the handle as I take a cautious step back, my breath catching in my throat.

The darkness around me thickens unnaturally, pooling

and twisting like a living thing. A figure emerges. For a moment, my eyes and mind can't make sense of it.

I can't tell who—or what—it is. It's a woman, cloaked in dripping, tar-like shadows, her eyes glowing a predatory yellow.

I pull the fire poker from my belt, wielding it like a sword. "Stay back!" I command.

The figure steps forward, her movements fluid and unsettling. The moonlight finally catches her face, and my stomach twists with recognition.

"Mor?" My voice cracks, betraying my nerves.

She steps closer, her shadowy form dissolving slightly as her familiar features come into view. But this isn't the sharp, grumpy woman I met before.

This is something else entirely.

Something dark. Something dangerous.

"I said back!" I swat at the air between us.

Mor doesn't stop.

Her shadows flicker, curling around her like sentient tendrils. One coils around the iron rod mid-swing, yanking it from my grip with unnerving ease.

The inky darkness peels away, revealing Mor's usual form. Her crimson eyes are sharp, unamused, and all too familiar.

But the air around her hums with an energy I've felt before—the oppressive, suffocating force that had stalked me in the jungle and chased me home from Mike's Dive Bar.

"So that was you?" I snap, anger and fear sharpening my voice. "Following me to my house?"

Her crimson gaze narrows, unreadable. "Of course, it was us. How else do you think you got here?"

She flips the poker in her hand and extends it toward me, hilt first. I snatch it back, realizing just how useless it is against her. My mind flashes to the knife I'd hurled at her before my abduction.

"Sorry about the knife," I quip, raising an eyebrow. "Hope I didn't cut you too badly."

Mor doesn't react, but I catch the faintest flicker of something beneath her stony exterior. "You didn't hit us."

Us? Who the fuck else was there?

"But you have impressive aim, striking without looking at your target."

"Great. So, how about you tell me how I get back home?"

Her expression hardens as she steps closer, her small frame radiating an overwhelming presence. Though I'm nearly a foot taller, I instinctively step back.

This isn't fear—it's survival instinct. Whatever power she wields is like nothing I've ever encountered before.

"Tana," she says, her voice low and sharp. "Tell me something. Once you made it beyond the wall, what was your plan to survive the dark forest?"

The question throws me for a second. "I'm resourceful. I'll figure it out," I reply defensively.

Her sharp huff cuts through the air, mocking and biting. "Figure it out? Do you have any idea what waits for you in those woods?"

She steps closer, her shadows curling at her feet. "How exactly were you planning to get past the beasts of Avalon?

Past the Cŵn Annwn*? Poke them to death? Or perhaps you were going to gripe them into submission?"

I narrow my eyes. "The…"

Her lips curl into a dark smirk. "The Cŵn Annwn. Shadow hounds of the Unseelie. Ten feet tall. Teeth sharp enough to shred bone. And they always roam near the forest's edge for the easy prey."

A cold knot forms in my stomach.

"Still think the woods are a good idea?" she asks, her tone dripping with mockery. "Be our guest."

I glare at her underestimation of me. "So what? You're here to scare me into staying? I kill shifters for a living. I can handle a few puppies."

"Hmm. So brave. So ignorant." Her smirk fades, replaced by a scowl.

"We're here because your selfishness puts more than just your life at risk. You think this is just about you? There's a blight sweeping the land, a pestilence turning living beings into dark, twisted specters of what they once were. Every move you make has consequences, *Your Grace*."

She spits the title at me. "And running into the woods to make a deal with the Briar Court will only make things worse."

I hold back my reaction that she knew of my plan.

"Worse for who?" I snap. "You? Orion? The realm? Because I don't see how any of this is my problem!"

Her shadows lash out, snapping toward my feet. In an

---

* Cŵn Annwn: (pronounced coon 'anun) spectral hell hounds

instant, she's inches from my face, her crimson eyes burning into mine. Her voice drops to a deadly whisper.

"You don't have to see it. But the realm does. And whether you like it or not, it's chosen you. Stop acting like you can outrun it like a common coward. You can't."

I don't respond. My jaw tightens as her words settle over me like a weight I can't shake.

The silence between us stretches, thick and suffocating. Finally, she steps back, her shadows retreating. I swallow hard, my irritation bubbling under the surface. "I don't trust you."

"You don't have to trust us," she says, her voice quieter now but no less firm. "But you'd better trust that you won't survive more than a few steps in that forest."

With that, she turns and disappears into the darkness, leaving me standing at the door, cold and uncertain.

My grip tightens on the poker as I glance toward the door separating me from my freedom. The iron rod suddenly feels so small in my hand.

The snarling is gone, but the weight of Mor's words lingers, heavy and impossible to ignore.

For now, my escape will have to wait. But only for now.

CHAPTER 14

The early shade feels heavy today, making Starfall Castle feel more like a dungeon, than my home.

For a place so vast and full of history, it should hum with life: servants shuffling through the corridors, guards patrolling the walls, the faint murmur of conversations echoing from the courtyards.

Instead, the silence presses against me—heavy and unrelenting.

Tana tried to run last evenfall, just as I predicted she would. The kitchens informed me immediately of her request for food, practical to eat in one's chambers, which was her excuse. But more so, practical to carry on a trip.

She didn't even wait until the rest of us returned to our chambers to sleep before she scaled the walls. Mor watched it all from within the protective shadows of her darkness.

"She really is quite remarkable," Mor spoke into my mind, keeping me apprised of our small human. *"–for a mortal, of course."*

Of course.

I should enchant the wall to keep her away, a subtle

nudge steering her elsewhere. But Hypnos insists she must choose this role on her own. For now, I refrain.

My footsteps are soft against the stone as I wander, hands in my pockets, mind restless. The weight of the realm, Tana's defiance, and Demeter's trial press down with every step.

This place, a labyrinth of duty and expectation, feels more prison than sanctuary. With no set destination, my feet seem to know where I want to go.

It doesn't take long to find her.

I step into a room near the western wing, drawn by the quiet rustle of movement. She stands in the center, back to me, studying the tapestries that line the walls.

Moonlight from the narrow windows casts silver across her dark curls, making them shimmer.

Leaning against the doorframe, I watch. She doesn't notice, too absorbed in the woven histories of Avalon. There's curiosity in her stance—frustration, too. Amusement tugs at me.

"What the hell is this?" she mutters, arms crossing as she studies a tapestry.

"I believe the term is 'history,'" I say, breaking the silence.

She whirls, eyes narrowing. "Ever heard of knocking?"

"This is a public room," I reply smoothly, stepping inside. "But please, don't let my presence interrupt your scholarly pursuits."

She rolls her eyes, exaggerated enough to be theatrical. "Don't you have princely duties to attend to? Brooding? Scowling? Being insufferable?"

A smirk tugs at my lips. "No. I find your interpretations of Avalon's past far more entertaining."

"I think it's overrated," she mutters, turning back to the tapestry.

I step beside her, my gaze following hers. "Ah, the White Stag," I muse, nodding toward the luminous figure in the woven forest. "I've never seen one myself, but my grandmother did, once."

"Mmm." Her gaze shifts to the center of the room, to the circular table. She traces the carved surface with her fingers. "And this?"

"The council table," I explain. "Each section represents a court of Avalon."

She frowns, counting. "Ten," she mutters, more to herself than to me. Her gaze lands on the uncarved void near the edge, where Avalon's crest is seared into the wood like a brand.

I watch as realization flickers across her features. She looks to the tapestries again, scanning the symbols, her mind piecing something together.

Her brown eyes snap back to the table. "But... what happened to these two courts?" She points to the empty space.

I blink, caught off guard.

"What do you mean?"

She gestures at the tapestries. "Twelve beasts. Twelve symbols. But there are only ten sections here. And this blank spot? The size of two courts. So, what happened to them?"

Her words hit like a cold wind. I stare at the table as if seeing it for the first time. Had I truly never noticed?

"The table has always been this way," I say, though the words feel hollow.

"Uh-huh," she replies, crossing her arms. "So what? Someone forgot to pay their HOA dues and got kicked out of the realm club?"

I glance at her, brow furrowing. "I do not follow."

She smirks, clearly enjoying my confusion. "Never mind."

Her casual dismissal irks me more than I care to admit, but I let it pass. "You're more observant than I expected."

She snorts. "Someone has to be. You clearly missed it."

Rather than reward her with a response, I study the void in the table, unease gnawing at me. "The past holds many secrets," I say, more to myself than to her. "Some are better left undisturbed."

"Yeah, well," she mutters, turning away. "Secrets don't stay buried forever."

Her words linger as she moves, the weight of her observation pressing against my thoughts.

Perhaps the mortal sees more than she should.

Or perhaps she's here to make us see what we've chosen to ignore.

Either way, I'll have Hypnos look into this.

"Come," I command, striding toward the massive doors of the throne room.

Behind me, Tana scoffs. "Would some manners kill you?"

I don't respond. Indulging her sarcasm would only derail the moment. Instead, I push open the doors and step inside. She follows, curiosity leading her forward despite her irritation.

No matter how many ages I've spent here, the splendor of the throne room never fails to strike me. Moonlight streams through stained-glass windows, casting shifting patterns over the polished obsidian floor.

My gaze flickers briefly to the one depicting my grand-mother's coronation, the moon shining down as her crown was placed upon her head.

"This," I say, breaking the silence, "is the throne of Avalon."

Tana blinks, mouth slightly agape as she takes it in. "Yeah, I gathered that," she mutters.

I nod toward the large portrait beside the throne. "My grandmother, Queen Pandora." My voice softens despite myself.

She approaches, curiosity flickering in her expression. "She doesn't look much older than a college student."

The term means little to me, but I understand. "She was young when the realm chose her. Barely more than a girl, though she proved herself quickly."

Tana folds her arms, studying Pandora's face. Her usual defiance fades, replaced by something quieter.

"She didn't look ready for this either," she murmurs.

"She wasn't," I admit, then add, "But the trials prepared her. As they will prepare you."

Her head snaps toward me, eyes sharp. "Excuse me? Trials?"

"You are not queen yet." I hold her gaze as the shadows

at my feet stir, restless in the silence. "The realm may have chosen you, but that is only the first step. You must pass the trials to prove your worthiness."

Her reaction is immediate—fire in her eyes, her jaw tightening. "You have got to be fucking kidding me."

I don't flinch, though the weight of her anger rolls off her like a gathering storm. "I am not. And no one knows when the trials will occur. Avalon decides when the time is right."

She lets out a sharp, bitter laugh. "Let me get this straight. You—Avalon—drag me here, parade me in front of the whole realm, turn me into some glowing mortal sideshow, and now I'm supposed to just sit around and wait for the Hunger Games?"

Her voice rises with each word. "When exactly does Avalon 'feel the time is right?'"

"That is not for me to answer," I say evenly, though her frustration stings more than I care to admit.

She stops pacing, turning to me with a glare that could cut glass. "And what happens when the Warden of Thornspire returns, and I'm still just the glowing mortal sideshow? What then, Orion?"

I let the silence stretch before I answer. "Then I will kill him."

Her mouth opens, but no words come. For a moment, she just stares, caught between disbelief and something sharper. "You'll kill him," she repeats.

"That's your solution? Just keep swinging your sword and hope the realm fixes itself?"

"It will not come to that," I say, though the weight of the truth lingers. "You will be queen by then."

She exhales sharply, anger radiating from her. "You don't get it, do you? I don't want this. I never asked to be here, Orion. I had a life—imperfect, sure, but it was mine.

And you dragged me into this chaos, and now you expect me to just—what? Wait around while a magic realm decides my fate?"

Her words strike like a lash. Shadows stir around me, unbidden, responding to the tension crackling between us. "The realm chose you for a reason," I say, my voice measured but firm. "If you believe I had any say in this—"

"I don't care about the realm's reason!" she cuts me off, voice ringing through the chamber.

Her fists clench, breath sharp and ragged, as if she's ready to lash out. But instead, she meets my gaze with unwavering defiance.

"Take me home, Orion. Now."

I hold her stare, letting the silence weigh on her. She doesn't flinch, doesn't waver, but the storm in her eyes betrays her. She's scared, though she'd probably rather eat glass than admit it.

She has to face the reality of her situation: There is no going home. The sooner she understands that, the sooner we can get on with this.

Finally, I step back, snapping my composure into place like armor. "Fine," I say, my tone icy and clipped.

Her reaction is immediate, confusion flickering across her face.

"Fine? That's it?"

I turn away, striding toward the door without sparing her another glance. She can think what she likes, but she won't find the resolution she's looking for in defiance. Not here.

The castle's massive double doors loom ahead. I push them open without ceremony, letting the cool night air rush in. "After you," I say, gesturing toward the path beyond.

She hesitates, eyes narrowing as if expecting a trap. Even as she steps forward, her gaze never leaves me. A flicker of amusement stirs within me—she doesn't trust me, and perhaps she shouldn't.

The drawbridge creaks beneath our feet, its sound swallowed by the stillness of the night. The path winds through familiar terrain, not far from where Demeter met her end.

The air is cooler here, the lake's mist curling around us like ghosts, clinging to the trail as we move further from the castle.

Tana walks in silence, her focus fixed forward, but I catch the subtle flick of her eyes—always calculating, always watching.

The trail narrows along the lake's edge, its still, foggy surface reflecting the oversized moon. A faint ripple disturbs the water, and for a split second, her steps falter.

The pulse of Avalon's magic presses around us, watchful and heavy. Perhaps she feels it too.

Ahead, jagged rock juts from the earth, its dark mouths yawning like secrets waiting to be unearthed. Without hesitation, I step into the largest cave, letting the shadows swallow me whole.

"What is this place?" she asks, voice barely above a whisper.

"The caves of Pandora." I don't slow as I move deeper inside.

Silver veins snake through the stone walls, casting faint glimmers of light. The air is cool and damp, thick with the weight of centuries.

I glance back. She lingers at the entrance, fingertips brushing the stone, her gaze shifting toward the lake. Her expression tightens, as if she's seen something.

"Keep up," I call, my voice echoing against the cavern walls.

She mutters something under her breath—undoubtedly a curse at my expense—but steps inside, moving carefully but following nonetheless.

"This way."

The chamber ahead is vast, its walls shimmering faintly with Avalon's magic. At its center, a raised stone platform stands, its carvings pulsing with a faint silver glow.

The air here is thicker, charged with the remnants of something ancient.

She eyes the platform warily. "What is this?"

"A portal," I answer, my voice softer now. "One of the

few that once connected Avalon to the other realms. It was destroyed during the Titan Wars and hasn't worked since."

Her eyes narrow, suspicion flashing across her face. "You're lying," she accuses, her voice tight with anger. "You just don't want me to leave."

I exhale slowly, the weight of her mistrust settling deep. "Believe what you want," I say, meeting her gaze. "But don't insult my integrity. The truth doesn't change.

You cannot leave, Tana."

Her expression hardens, anger flashing in her eyes. She moves before I register it.

A silver glint slashes across my arm. Pain sears through me as blood wells, dark against my skin.

"Dammit!" I bark, but before I can react, she shoves me.

Cold water engulfs me as I stumble into the shallow pool. She doesn't hesitate, sprinting toward the platform.

Instinct takes over. Shadows coil around her legs, yanking her back. She crashes to the stone, dragged toward me as I rise, soaking wet and furious.

In a blink, I'm on her, gripping her throat, pinning her against the cavern wall. "You think you can run from me?" I growl, my knee pressing between her legs, keeping her in place.

She glares up at me, chest heaving, defiance still burning. My shadows pluck the weapon from her hand, sending it clattering to the ground.

A fucking fork.

I inhale slowly, pushing past my irritation. I should've remembered she hides weapons in her clothes. That oversight is mine.

I lean closer, my voice sharp. "I'm not opposed to keeping you tied up in my shadows until your ascension—if you insist on behaving like a child."

Her breathing quickens, a flicker of something in her gaze. Fear. Or anger. Maybe both.

"Let me go," she demands.

I study her, my thumb brushing against the pulse in her throat. A strange jolt courses through me. Reluctantly, I step back.

"You don't have to like it," I say quietly. "But you do have to accept it."

She doesn't answer right away. Instead, her gaze drifts to the platform, the weight of realization settling over her.

"Is it really broken?" she asks, voice softer now.

I nod. "The Titans' war severed the connection to Gaea long ago. This was one of the casualties."

Silence stretches. I see the doubt in the clench of her fists, the set of her jaw.

"Then how did I get here?"

"Fate provided a one-way door," I admit. "I took it. Blame no one else for your being here but me."

The cave feels smaller, heavier. Her chest rises and falls in sharp, quick breaths, her frustration palpable.

"So, I'm stuck here?" she demands.

"You were never meant to leave."

Our eyes lock, the air between us charged. Tenacity burns in her, and I wonder if it will carry her through the trials or break her first.

I turn, breaking the tension.

"Where the fuck are you going now, asshole?" she snaps, voice low, almost a warning.

I don't look back, wringing excess water from my sleeve as I stride toward the entrance. "To get you some gods-blessed weapons."

Her stare follows me, but I don't slow. My boots squelch with each step, echoing through the cavern.

Over my shoulder, I add, "You can't defend yourself against a High Fae with a dinner fork."

CHAPTER 15
tana

"*You were never meant to leave.*"

The quiet tone of his voice haunts my mind as I trail behind Orion. A one-way door opened, and he used it to bring me here, knowing I'd never be able to leave?

The truth in that—the cruelty of it—has a vice grip around my throat.

"*Blame no one else for your being here but me.*"

It wasn't just him. I know I felt Mor, her immense darkness stalking me that entire day. And last night, Mor very clearly said "us."

Someone else was there at my house, and it's likely Hypnos. It's rare that I've seen Mor and he's not been close by.

I blame them all—Orion, Mor, this realm, the very moonlight—for ripping me away from my home, the only family I had left.

Not even giving me a warning or time to say goodbye.

Hell, we all know I wouldn't have gone willingly without a fight. But not even being given a chance—it feels like being bound and thrown off a cliff, helpless to watch as the ground rushes to meet you.

It only hardens my resolve to find the warden and make a deal with him.

The path we follow should lead back to the castle—or so I assume—but instead of climbing the hill toward the drawbridge, Orion veers sharply to the left.

"Where are we going now?" I snap, my boots crunching against the gravel path.

He doesn't answer, of course. His silence is maddening, and I briefly entertain the idea of shoving him off the cliffside path we're now descending.

Castle Starfall looms above us, its spires stabbing into the night sky like jagged teeth, glowing faintly under the oversized moon.

The path slopes downward, winding along the cliffside until it curves sharply.

That's when I see a small village nestled at the base of the cliffs, its warm glow a stark contrast to the cold, imposing grandeur of the castle above.

The air shifts, carrying the scent of fresh bread and something sweet. There's movement everywhere—figures flitting between stone cottages and wooden stalls, the soft hum of life filling the town.

My stomach growls, and I realize I haven't eaten since breakfast. It's difficult to tell how much time passes without the movement of a sun and moon crossing the sky.

I blink, taking it all in. The Fae here aren't like the ones I saw at Demeter's trial. There's no gleaming armor, no haughty grace.

These Fae are dressed plainly, their appearances more akin to my handmaids, with delicate features and understated elegance.

As we pass through, heads bow in reverence to Orion. Every single Fae stops what they're doing to incline their heads, murmuring quiet greetings of respect.

He acknowledges them with a quick nod, his expression unreadable, but there's a lightness in his posture now, as if the weight of their gazes does not press upon him like the High Fae's.

It's not just him they're looking at, though.

Their eyes linger on me, speculative and calculating. Some are wide with curiosity; most are narrowed with thinly veiled mistrust.

I keep my chin high, matching their stares with one of my own.

I've faced worse than prying eyes as I paved paths in the military where few women had been before. Still, the scrutiny makes my skin crawl.

Among the crowd, I spot creatures that remind me of pets back on Earth, though they're stranger, more fantastical.

One Fae holds a birdlike creature with shimmering scales instead of feathers, its long tail coiled around their arm. Another leads something resembling a fox, except its fur glows faintly, like embers in the dark.

"Do they all work for you?" I ask, my voice low as I step closer to Orion, not wanting to give the villagers the satisfaction of overhearing me.

He glances at me briefly. "Not me directly. Most serve the castle in some capacity."

The farther we walk, the quieter the villagers become. I feel their gazes trailing behind us long after we've passed, their curiosity prickling at the back of my neck.

"Why are they staring?" I finally ask, unable to keep the irritation out of my voice.

He doesn't stop walking, his strides purposeful and unwavering. "Most have never seen a mortal before. It has been a long time since our races have mingled."

I swallow the lump forming in my throat, forcing myself to keep my expression neutral. If they've never seen a mortal, then I'm not just an oddity—I'm an anomaly.

And in Avalon, I'm learning, what isn't understood is something to be feared.

I glance at Orion's back, his broad shoulders cutting an imposing figure against the backdrop of the village.

He seems unbothered by the stares, but I can't shake the feeling that he's as much of a barrier between me and them as he is a target of their whispers.

For now, I stay close. Not because I trust him, but because I don't trust anyone else.

Hestia emerges from what must be a bakery, balancing a tray of steaming buns high above her head as a group of Fae children dance around her, their little arms reaching up.

She laughs—a genuine sound—and passes one to each eager hand. Her blush-pink skin practically glows under the moonlight, and her smile is radiant when she catches sight of us.

"Lady Tana!" she calls warmly, her red hair cascading

over her shoulders as she raises a hand in greeting. "Bright moon to you."

I blink, momentarily taken aback by the cheer in her tone. It's a far cry from the calculating stares of the villagers.

Orion, ever the stoic, strides forward without pause. But as we pass, he plucks a warm bun from the tray with ease, turning to press it into my hands.

I look at the steaming bread, then back at him, arching a brow. His expression is unreadable, save for the faintest flicker of something that might be amusement—or annoyance.

"Eat," he says flatly, his tone brooking no argument.

I scowl, hating how easily he seems to read me, but my stomach betrays me with a low, rumbling growl.

With a resigned sigh, I tear off a piece of the bun and pop it into my mouth. It's soft and buttery, with just the right amount of sweetness. Damn it.

Next to the bakery, a wide wooden building looms, its chimney puffing a stream of smoke into the night sky.

Orion leads us beneath a covered awning, the faint scent of metal and oil mingling with the sweeter aromas of the bakery.

Inside, my steps falter.

Bindings. Chains. Cuffs. They line the walls in neat, polished displays, gleaming under the soft light of a few scattered lanterns.

My chest tightens, and I glance at Orion warily. "What is this?" I ask, my voice sharp.

He doesn't answer immediately, his silver eyes scanning the room with a detached air.

A thought crosses my mind, and I hate the chill it sends down my spine. Is this where he plans to keep me tied up, as he threatened in the caves?

My fingers itch to reach for the silver fork, but it's still lying on the floor of the caves.

Orion finally turns to me, his expression cold and distant. "Walk inside," he orders, his irritation palpable.

I narrow my eyes at him, standing my ground. "For what?" I ask, suspicion thick in my tone.

He exhales sharply, the sound laced with exasperation. "For the love of the gods, starling, no one is chaining you," he snaps, brushing past me toward the door.

Inside, the heat hits me first—a blazing, dry warmth that makes me wince as I step over the threshold.

The room is vast, with a high, vaulted ceiling that seems to stretch endlessly upward, the space clearly designed to accommodate its equally massive occupant.

A roaring fire blazes within a circular hearth at the center of the shop, the flames crackling and casting dancing shadows across the walls.

The rhythmic clang of metal-on-metal echoes through the space, but it's the odd twinkling of bells mixed with sharp, brash voices that makes me pause mid-step.

My eyes dart toward the source of the commotion.

At first, I think I'm hallucinating.

Tiny figures—no larger than six inches tall—flit around the towering, broad-shouldered Hephaestus.

They're fiery. Literally. Their skin glows in shades of oranges, yellows, and deep reds, their hair like flickering flames or plumes of smoke.

Their eyes are like molten embers, glowing white and intense, and their wings shimmer, catching the light like the iridescence of dragonflies.

They're yelling—well, squeaking—at Hephaestus, their small hands waving furiously as they flit in erratic, angry patterns around his head. It's like watching a swarm of pissed-off fireflies, and it's both mesmerizing and utterly absurd.

"You're barmy, the lot of you!" Hephaestus bellows, his voice booming enough to rattle the tools hanging on the walls. "A little hotter? You'll melt the damn anvil, ye wee sparks!"

My jaw drops as I watch one particularly daring fairy, its hair billowing like smoke, dart forward to wag a tiny fist at him.

Another, its wings a brilliant orange, crosses its arms and pouts, its glare fiery enough to ignite the room if looks could kill.

"I can't believe this," I mutter, half to myself, my eyes glued to the chaos.

Orion chuckles softly beside me, the sound catching me off guard. I glance at him, noting how the sharp lines of irritation that have been etched into his face all morning seem to soften.

"Flame Sprites," he says, his tone lighter than usual. "Always dramatic."

Hephaestus doesn't seem fazed by any of it. His booming laugh fills the space as he waves a massive hand dismissively at the Sprites.

"Off with ye! Go cause mischief elsewhere, ye flaming gobshites!"

The fiery fairies scatter, though not without a show of defiance. One sticks its tongue out before zipping away, and another actually throws a tiny fireball that forms in its hand.

Hephaestus blows it out with a huff of breath, as though extinguishing a birthday candle, shaking his head in mock exasperation.

He turns toward us, his face breaking into a wide grin as soon as his eyes land on Orion.

"Prince Orion!" he booms, his thick Scottish brogue even more pronounced in his excitement. "Look who's finally come to see me! What brings ye down from yer perch on high?"

The warmth in his tone is infectious, and I find myself momentarily disarmed.

Orion steps forward, nodding in greeting. "I was just here yesternight."

"Aye, beggin' an escort for our beautiful queen to the trial." Hephaestus takes my hand gently in his large one and feigns a kiss on the back of it.

Orion rolls his eyes, and I get the sense Hephaestus is only goading him into irritation.

"When was the last time ye came tah sit an' fire the irons with me?"

"Hephaestus," Orion says smoothly, his tone dry. "I've come for weapons—for her."

He gestures toward me, and Hephaestus's grin widens. I swear I see a spark of mischief light up his eyes. Pirate Santa, as I immediately dub him, may be one of the few people here I can trust.

"Well, well, well," he says, crossing his arms and looking me over. "Let's see what we can do fer ye, lass."

Hephaestus's shop is a maze of gleaming metal and worn leather, weapons of all shapes and sizes displayed on panels, racks, and hooks.

It smells like smoke, oil, and something earthy—like stone warmed by a fire. The forge at the center roars constantly, its heat pushing back the chill of the perpetual Avalon night.

I trail behind Hephaestus as he gestures proudly at his wares. "Take a look around, lass," he says, his voice booming yet oddly inviting. "See if anything catches yer eye."

I nod, scanning the walls lined with swords, daggers, axes, and weapons I don't even recognize. Some are elegantly crafted; others look brutish and practical, all of them whispering their promise of destruction.

Just as I'm about to step closer, Hypnos walks in, his pale, sightless eyes landing on Orion. He doesn't say a word, but the weight of his look is enough. Orion stiffens, then exhales sharply, clearly reluctant.

"Please excuse me. I will return soon," he says, his silver gaze flicking to me before he strides out of the shop. Hypnos follows him silently.

"Now," Hephaestus says, turning back to me with a grin and rubbing his hands together conspiratorially, "let's talk about that weapon ye discharged at our prince the first time ye met him."

I freeze, confused for a second, before realization dawns. "You mean my gun?"

"Aye, is tha' its name?" he says, his tone laced with curiosity. "I've never seen the like of it. Mind if I take a closer look?"

I hesitate, but there's nothing in his expression but genuine interest—and maybe a bit of reverence. With a shrug, I pull the gun from its holster and remove the bullets before handing it to him. "Knock yourself out."

He takes it with a mixture of awe and care, holding it up to the light and turning it over in his massive hands. "By the gods..." he mutters, his fingers tracing the contours of the weapon. "This... this is somethin' else entirely."

I glance around while he examines it, catching sight of a few Flame Sprites working off to the sides.

They're watching me, whispering to each other, and giggling behind tiny, glowing hands.

I raise an eyebrow at them, and they scatter with exaggerated squeals of laughter, flitting to the forge like fiery streaks.

Turning back to Hephaestus, I notice something dangling around his neck—a small charm made of polished metal. It takes me a second to recognize it, but when I do, my brows shoot up.

"Is that... my bullet?"

Hephaestus follows my gaze, then rubs the back of his neck sheepishly. "Aye," he admits, his voice uncharacteristically quiet. "Thought it'd make a fine token of my queen."

I blink, stunned. "Your queen?"

"You," he says simply, his tone warm but matter-of-fact.

I open my mouth to respond, but he barrels on, his enthusiasm returning.

"I've studied the metal, ye know. It's not harmful to Fae or any creatures here in Avalon. Fascinatin' stuff. If ye'd let me keep this weapon a while longer—inspect it, along with the projectiles it holds—I could create somethin' special for ye."

I hesitate, then decide it might be worth making a friend of a weapons master. It could come in handy if I am to escape and seek passage home from the Briar Court.

I don't care what Orion claims—I don't think my passage here was as one-way as he says.

"Keep it. I don't think I'll have much use for it anyway, given how Orion barely lets me out of his sight."

His eyes widen, and for a moment, he looks genuinely emotional. His large hand clenches around the gun like it's a sacred relic, his lips parting as if to speak before he closes them again.

Twinkling laughter from the direction of the Flame Sprites grows louder, their tiny voices high-pitched and almost mocking toward Hephaestus.

He bristles instantly, his booming voice shaking the walls. "I am not cryin', ye little pests! Now get back to yer work before I dunk ye in the water trough!"

The Sprites scatter again, their laughter echoing faintly as they disappear into the corners of the shop.

Rolling my eyes, I turn my attention back to the weapons.

My gaze lands on a set of small swords, then a particularly sharp-looking dagger, but it's the throwing knives that catch my eye. Compact, deadly, and precise. I grab a few, testing their weight in my hand.

"Good choice," Hephaestus says, his voice returning to its usual hearty tone. "How's yer aim, lass?"

The door creaks open, and I glance up to see Orion stepping back inside, his expression unreadable as his silver eyes land on me.

Without missing a beat, I whirl and throw the knife. It slices through the air with a soft hiss, embedding itself perfectly in the center of a target painted on the post Orion leans against.

The blade lands mere inches from his head.

"My aim is okay," I say, smirking as I cross my arms.

Orion doesn't flinch. He doesn't even blink. Instead, he tilts his head slightly, folding his arms over his chest.

"When are you going to stop trying to kill me?"

"When you're dead," I bark back.

He snorts softly, a hint of amusement flickering in his eyes. "Well then, I hope I live long enough to see the day."

CHAPTER 16
Tana

Four days. That's how long I've been here, though it feels like a month.

Four rotations of this eternal night—no sunrises, no sunsets, just the oversized moon looming above Avalon, glowing like a pearl and eclipsing the sun behind it.

The sky shifts through shades of darkness: deep indigo at First Shade—their version of "morning"—before plunging into the blackness of High Shade, their afternoon.

Then, without fail, Evenfall swallows the moon, an ink-black void stretching over the realm.

According to Hypnos, it is alive. The darkness isn't just a metaphor—it's sentient.

A shadow circling Avalon, hungry for the light in everything living. I keep my windows shut when true night falls.

I don't remember drifting off, but I feel myself waking, the dream already slipping away like smoke. Yet the sensations remain—vivid, inescapable.

My skin burns, every nerve alight. Cool air does nothing to temper the ache between my legs, an ache I try to ease with my fingers. I'm close.

I grasp for the dream, trying to sink back into it—rough

hands roaming my body, lips hot and insistent, a voice deep and commanding.

Even now, the memory makes me shiver.

A whimper escapes as my fingers circle my clit, thighs clenching involuntarily. I hold my breath, chasing the release just out of reach. Instead, the longing sharpens, raw and overwhelming.

A breeze ghosts over my bare breasts, making my nipples tighten. My free hand slides up, teasing the soft mound, pinching the sensitive peak.

The other moves faster, but I'm too slick, too desperate for friction.

Frustration builds. With a sigh, I stop.

Rolling onto my side, I stare at the pale glow of Avalon's "morning" seeping through the window.

I know who it was.

I didn't see a face, but I know. Long white hair. An insufferable smirk.

A bitter huff leaves my lips.

I sit up abruptly, dragging my hands through my tangled hair. The polished floor is cool beneath my feet, grounding me through the haze of frustration.

"Get it together, Valkyrie," I mutter. "Now is not the time to lose your head over some—some prince of shadows or whatever the hell he thinks he is."

It's not real. It's this place—its magic, its moonlight, its suffocating pull.

That has to be it. Avalon has been creeping under my skin, whispering things I don't want to hear, tempting me with promises I know better than to believe.

Still, as I stretch, I can't shake the ghost of his touch—the phantom hands on my skin, the lips brushing my neck.

I tell myself it's exhaustion, stress, the strain of being thrust into this world I barely understand.

But I don't believe it.

Since my arrival, I've tried to escape this place three times. Three spectacular failures.

The last time, I nearly made it over the castle walls before Orion pulled me down, his shadows coiling around my legs like snakes. I even tried to kill him—twice. Once with his own dagger.

The bastard only laughed.

My treacherous body is making things worse.

Every time I'm near him, there's an overbearing pull—like he's my gravity. My eyes find him in every room, my ears catch even the softest sound of his voice.

I tell myself it's only to learn my enemy's weaknesses.

But deep down, I know I'm lying. My pulse still races. My body still aches for someone I shouldn't want.

Still standing by my bed, wearing nothing but the denim haze of Avalon's moonlight, I barely have time to gather myself before the door opens.

Elowen and Thalindra step inside.

"Good morning, Your Grace," Elowen greets with a curtsy. "We've come to prepare you for Beltane."

My brows knit. "Beltane?"

Thalindra's lips curve into a knowing smile, her gaze sweeping down my body, tugging at the frayed edges of my restraint. "The start of our Bloomrise celebration," she explains, voice smooth as silk. "Avalon's season of fertility."

Hypnos mentioned Bloomrise in his endless lectures on this realm's seasons and trials.

I recall something about wine and revelry, followed two weeks later by the sunrise—Avalon's only one for an entire *turn*. Their version of a year, I suppose.

But none of that matters right now.

Not when my body is still thrumming from last night. Not when Elowen is looking at me like she wants to taste me.

Her pale cheeks flush, her breath quickening as if even breathing requires effort. My nipples tighten under her stare, the air crackling between us, thick with something unspoken.

It's suffocating. Charged.

Ever since last night, sex is everywhere—in my dreams, in the air I breathe, wrapping around me like a whisper.

They feel it too.

My chambermaids have been giving me lingering glances since my first night here.

I'd be lying if I said I haven't imagined taking them to my bed—how they'd feel beneath me, how they'd taste as they unraveled on my tongue, how beautifully I could make them sing.

But those fantasies are overshadowed by another.

Orion. Watching. Joining.

Pulling every drop of pleasure from me as my mouth claims one of them.

Thalindra watches Elowen, as if reaching a decision. Sliding an arm around her waist, she pulls her closer.

"Come," she murmurs against Elowen's ear—loud enough for me to hear.

Their eyes find mine.

Heat surges through me, pooling low, impossible to ignore. I press my thighs together, breath catching as they step closer, as the air between us demands surrender.

Thalindra lifts Elowen's hand, pressing a slow, deliberate kiss to her knuckles. She lingers, savoring the moment, before turning to me.

"You feel it, don't you, Your Grace?" Her voice is a purr. "Desire is heavy in the air this morning."

Understatement of the gods.

"Yes," I whisper, barely recognizing my own voice. My hands glide over my thighs, uselessly trying to smother the wildfire inside me.

"Elowen would like to enjoy the celebration," Thalindra muses, amusement dripping from her tone, "but she's never known the touch of a female. Only her male mate."

My eyes flick to Elowen. Her cheeks are crimson as she avoids my gaze.

"She and her mate wish to explore with Brynja tonight, but our shy handmaid is... hesitant."

Thalindra grins, trailing one of Elowen's fingers across her lips before flicking her tongue along the length of it. A soft moan escapes Elowen as Thalindra kisses the tip.

I'm drenched.

"She wants to feel a woman's lips... here." Thalindra tilts Elowen's chin toward her, their mouths a breath apart, teasing the inevitable. "And here." She guides Elowen's hand between her own thighs, the thick folds of her dress the only barrier.

Elowen's head falls back, lashes fluttering as a moan slips free. My breath catches, my tongue instinctively brushing my bottom lip.

Rooted in place, I feel my feet unstick from the floor, drawn toward them.

Slowly, I close the distance, drinking in Elowen's delicate features.

With a gentle knuckle, I trace the curve of her chin, inching closer to her mouth.

"Will you show her, Your Grace?" Thalindra's voice is silk, but her question slices through the charged air.

Thalindra has never hidden her interest in me, and even Brynja's glances have grown bold. But this request surprises me. Elowen has a mate—one she plans to share Brynja with tonight.

Perhaps that's why Brynja isn't here. To let Elowen... *practice.*

My attention shifts to Elowen, her chest rising and falling rapidly. "Would you like me to show you, Elowen?" My voice is low, each word a caress.

"Yes, my Queen," she whispers, trembling, as if already on the brink.

Thalindra releases Elowen's hand and moves behind her, fingers tracing her skin, drawing another whimper.

My knuckle skims down Elowen's chin, her throat, the neckline of her dress. Goosebumps rise in its wake.

"So needy," I murmur, lowering my lips to her exposed skin. The taste of her makes my breath hitch. "Aren't you?"

"Yes," she pants, the word a plea.

Thalindra's fingers work the straps of Elowen's dress, and the tight bodice loosens, sliding to the floor. Pale skin, kissed by moonlight, is revealed. My eyes drink her in.

"Beautiful," I whisper.

Thalindra lets her own dress fall, stepping closer, brushing a kiss over Elowen's shoulder. I trace a hand down Elowen's hip. "Have you touched a woman before?"

"N-no. I'd like to know... for tonight. For my mate and me to enjoy another. It's common to share pleasure here."

Hm. Avalon might not be so bad after all.

I brush my thumb over her bottom lip before pulling her flush against me.

Thalindra presses soft kisses to her shoulder as I nuzzle against Elowen, our mouths sharing a breath.

"Please, Your Grace," she whispers, heavy-lidded with need.

I take her lips, tasting her sweetness as my hands grip her waist.

She's shy at first, but as my tongue sweeps into her mouth, she melts into me, her hands seeking purchase on my hips.

"Yes, Elowen," Thalindra hums, pressing kisses along her throat and shoulder.

Breaking the kiss, I turn Elowen to face Thalindra, guiding her hand to my lips.

I suck two of her fingers into my mouth, swirling my tongue around them. She moans softly.

Thalindra meets my gaze, eyes gleaming as she takes

one of Elowen's nipples into her mouth. Her siren-like stare never leaves mine.

"Your mate touches you?" I murmur against Elowen's ear. "Licks you? Fucks you?"

"Yes," she breathes.

"Then you know what to do."

I guide her hand between Thalindra's thighs, pressing her fingers to the damp heat beneath. The feel of her slickness draws groans from all of us.

"Rub her here first—soft, then harder. Slow, then faster."

One hand stays on Elowen's breast, teasing her as I lead her movements with the other.

Thalindra's hips begin to roll, breathy pleas filling the air as she chases the release we're building.

"Tell her what you want," I whisper against Elowen's ear, nipping her lobe gently. "Do you want her to come for you? Say it."

Elowen swallows, her voice trembling. "Come for me, Lindra."

Thalindra's head tilts back as her hips stutter, her cries echoing around us. Elowen licks a slow line up her throat before their foreheads press together, lost in the moment.

As Thalindra's orgasm fades, I ease Elowen's hand away, brushing my lips over her neck. The air still hums with lingering tension, the spell of desire unbroken.

I raise Elowen's fingers to her lips. "Suck them clean for us, beautiful. Get your first taste of her."

A moan slips from her throat as she slides her fingers into her mouth, her wet tongue tracing between them.

Thalindra tilts her chin with a fistful of her hair. "Give

our queen a taste, Wen," she purrs. "She looks starved for you."

And I *am*.

Elowen turns to me, her shyness fading into something darker, something hungrier. I don't wait. My hand finds her waist, pulling her flush against me as I claim her mouth.

The kiss is softer this time, exploratory, but the taste of her is intoxicating.

I deepen it, sliding my tongue against hers, savoring the sweet, breathy whimper she exhales. Her hands clutch my shoulders like she might fall without my anchor.

"Come here," I murmur, guiding her toward the bed.

She hesitates, uncertain, but Thalindra presses a teasing kiss to her neck, coaxing her forward. Elowen climbs onto the mattress, straddling my waist, her warmth pressing against me.

A soft groan rumbles in my chest as her hips shift, instinctively grinding down.

"You can fuck her like this," I murmur, gripping her thighs as I tilt my head up, capturing her lips again.

"And your mate can fuck you *here*."

Behind her, Thalindra's lips trail lower, ghosting over the curve of Elowen's ass. She gasps, her back arching as Thalindra caresses her.

"Hold on to the headboard," I command, voice husky.

Elowen obeys without hesitation, shifting her knees as she braces herself. The scent of her arousal thickens the air as she lowers herself to meet my mouth.

I waste no time. My tongue slides up her slit, tasting her—divine, like honeyed moonlight.

I press a kiss to her clit, swirling my tongue before sucking gently.

Her cries grow louder, echoing through the room as she rolls her hips, desperate for more.

"Good girl, Wen."

Thalindra doesn't hesitate. Her hands slide along my thighs, her touch seeking approval.

Silken strands of her hair graze my skin as she leans down, pressing kisses along my inner thighs.

I spread my legs for her, moaning into Elowen as her tongue finally finds me.

Thank the gods.

The rhythm between us builds, urgent and consuming. Thalindra's expert tongue and teasing fingers push me higher, while I work Elowen with everything I have, holding her steady as she rides the pleasure spiraling through her.

"Yes, Your Grace," she whimpers, voice shaking. "Please—don't stop."

As if I would.

Thalindra moves faster, her fingers sliding inside me, curling perfectly.

A cry tears from my lips against Elowen's clit, the vibration sending her over the edge. She screams, her release spilling onto my tongue as her body trembles.

Thalindra doesn't relent. Her touch drives me higher, and I fist her hair, grinding into her mouth as pleasure surges through me.

I shatter, my climax sharp and raw, my cries mixing with Elowen's as I come apart beneath her.

When the last waves ebb, Elowen laughs softly, cheeks

flushed as she climbs off me, her shyness creeping back in—but her smile is brighter now.

"Thank you, Your Grace." She fucking curtsies while I sit up, leaning on my elbows. The evidence of her orgasms, still on my face.

"It's my pleasure Elowen." I answer, sitting up further. She giggles as she bounces back to her dress, retrieving it from the floor.

Thalindra and her siren eyes pull my gaze to her. She crawls to me, offering me a taste of her fingers. I knew she played with herself, and I have to have another small taste of her before she leaves.

She straddles me, pushing her chest into mine as she rubs her nipples against mine.

"I hope you enjoy Beltane, Your Grace." She whispers against my lips before she opens them for me. Our tongues meet, as my hand rubs up her smooth thigh and I squeeze a handful of her plump ass.

I think there is a collective understanding that we could fuck each other for hours but we also know they have duties to attend to.

And I'm expected for breakfast and more lessons. Lucky me.

Thalindra is a fucking tease. Crossing her feet at the ankles, she bends down for her clothes, giving me a perfect view of her pretty pussy, still wet and wanting.

She looks back at me with a smirk.

Bootsteps just outside the hall approach the door and I watch as a shadow darkens the stone on the other side.

"See you later, Lindra." I lean against the bedpost with my hand on my hip giving her a slow shake of my head.

Elowen is only holding her dress onto herself and Thalindra is still naked, dress in hand as they open the door.

With a startle, they find Orion leaning against the stone blocks that frame the doorway.

He gives them a knowing smirk as they giggle past him. "Ladies."

"Your Grace."

"Your Grace." They curtsey quickly and rush off as Orion gives me his quicksilver stare.

I remain leaning against my bedpost wearing nothing but the moonlight of Avalon on my skin. "Good morning."

"Sounded like it." He runs his eyes down the view of my body that I'm giving him before I push off, swaying my hips as I walk toward the door.

"You are expected at breakfast." He runs his tongue across his bottom lip. "If you still have an appetite this morning, that is."

He rights himself, taking up most of the doorway with his large frame.

He reaches above him, holding onto the stones above the door and giving me a show of his muscled arms.

I may try to kill him again, but I can appreciate how good he looks in the meantime. Even if his mouth does piss me the fuck off half the time.

"Oh, don't you fret over my appetite, big boy. I'm famished."

Grabbing the door, I slam it in his smug face just as he cocks a grin.

I need a bath.

And a fucking vibrator.

CHAPTER 17
tana

The sky above Starfall is painted in hues of cobalt and violet, the colors hinting at a change in the constant darkness.

I'm looking forward to the sun, even if only for a single moment.

Mor swept me away after breakfast, leading me up a never-ending spiral staircase. She finally opens a wooden door, and we are released from the castle's interior, standing on its topmost level.

From the turret, the view stretches far, and I see a convoy of carriages heading toward the castle.

The first of the court's dignitaries are arriving, and the sight fills me with equal parts awe and apprehension.

Mor sits on the stone ledge, a plate of honeycakes balanced precariously on her lap.

She bites into one with a quiet hum of approval, her dark-crimson eyes fixed on the distant carriages. Her presence is strangely grounding, even as I feel the tension in the air building.

We've not interacted much beyond my first night, when she caught me trying to escape.

But I see her watching and assessing me. At times, I earn a rare nod of approval—mostly when I'm mouthing off to Orion.

I pick at a honeycake, tearing off a small piece and popping it into my mouth. "So, the court leaders are going to stay until the day they can watch the sunrise?"

I ask, my voice casual but tinged with curiosity.

She waves a hand dismissively. "Don't be fooled by the grandeur. It's a spectacle wrapped in politics."

My gaze returns to the convoy, the carriages gleaming as they emerge from the forest.

The leaders' entourages are as extravagant as I expected, with banners and crests denoting each court.

I keep an eye out for the Briar Court.

"You think it'll go smoothly?" I ask, popping another piece of cake into my mouth. I've heard some of the High Fae will stay until Starfall, which marks the end of a mooncycle.

I suppose it's the equivalent of a month on Earth. And it's what the castle is named for.

At the end of each mooncycle, a cascade of shooting stars streaks across the sky. The ancient Fae once considered them omens, reading their patterns for guidance.

The reflection of the stars falling over the Misting Lake is apparently a wondrous sight, as they appear to fall right into the water.

I can't say I'm especially excited to be on my best behavior at all times.

The extra guests will mean more guards, making my attempts to escape more difficult.

But if I play my cards right tonight, I may be heading to the Briar Court before the realm's only sunrise.

Mor snorts softly. "It never does."

I watch as the first carriage halts at the gates, its passengers descending in a flurry of silks and shimmering fabrics.

High Fae—beautiful, cold, and otherworldly.

Their movements are graceful, their expressions neutral masks.

"Which court is that?" I ask, nudging Mor and nodding toward the gates.

"Evershade," she says, not bothering to glance. "Umbriel always insists on arriving first. It's his way of asserting dominance. Even though he's not attending, he expects his court to represent him accordingly."

"Charming," I mutter. "And the others?" I press, curious despite myself.

Mor points lazily with a honeycake. "That'll be Frosthaven behind him, followed by Gloamreach. And, ah—there's Mirevalis, bringing the stench of the swamps with them."

I wrinkle my nose as the carriages she mentioned roll into view. "Sounds like a fun crowd."

Mor sighs, but I think it's because she's nearly out of honeycakes. "Just wait until they're all in one room. It's a delicate dance. One wrong step, and it'll turn into a bloodbath."

The weight of her words settles over me. No pressure at all.

Mor looks at me, her crimson eyes seeing much more

than I realize. "You'll manage. Just don't stab anyone unless absolutely necessary."

Her dry humor eases some of the tension in my chest, and I allow myself a small smile. "Noted." But her expression doesn't change, and I'm not sure if that was a joke.

We sit in silence for a moment, watching as more carriages approach, the procession growing larger with each passing minute.

The Courts of Avalon are here, and a knot forms in my stomach.

Another convoy appears on the horizon, sparkling so brightly it's as if the sun itself decided to tag along.

The procession gleams with a kind of ostentation that makes my stomach turn—every carriage encrusted with glittering jewels that catch even the faintest moonlight.

The guards are decked out in polished armor, their movements exaggerated and theatrical, as though they're on a stage.

"What the hell is that?" I mutter, narrowing my eyes.

Mor doesn't even look up. "Eldoria," she says flatly, her tone dripping with disdain. "The Shimmering Court—and the reason we are out here."

"Shimmering is one way to describe it." I snort, watching as the leading carriage—a monstrosity of crystal and mirrored panels—rolls to a halt at the gates.

The doors open, and a Fae woman steps out, nude save for the gilded sheen of her skin. She moves with deliberate grace, her every step calculated to draw attention.

Her golden hair flows in soft waves, catching the light as

though spun from threads of sunlight. Even her eyes gleam like molten gold, radiating arrogance with every glance.

"She's... uh... really into gold," I say, trying to find the right words for the walking monument to vanity.

Mor's lip curls, her crimson eyes narrowing as she watches the spectacle unfold. "Liora," she says, her voice so sharp it could cut glass. "High Lady of Eldoria. The Shimmering Court's self-proclaimed gift to Avalon."

I raise an eyebrow, watching as Liora pauses at the gates, her head tilted back as if she's waiting for the world to applaud her mere existence.

She's flanked by male courtiers, all vying for her attention like moths to a flame.

A few of the other court leaders nearby seem to be quietly arguing over who gets to fawn over her first.

"She's naked," I point out, deadpan.

Mor's gaze flicks to me, her expression unimpressed. "She considers herself above such trivialities as clothing."

"Right. Of course she does." I roll my eyes, my irritation bubbling over. "I'm sure she's a real delight at parties."

Mor actually smirks, but it's predatory. "We avoid her as much as possible." I wonder who *we* is in that statement.

The golden Fae continues her exaggerated strut, her entourage trailing behind her like starstruck puppies.

"She's unbearable," Mor mutters, her fingers tightening around the edge of the stone wall. "If you were to stab just one Fae tonight, we would not blame you if it was her."

I laugh despite myself, the tension from earlier lifting for a moment. "Tempting. Very tempting."

"You'd be doing Avalon a favor," Mor adds, her tone lighter now, though her eyes never leave Liora.

"Make no mistake, Liora will not hesitate to kill you if she can. She longs to be queen of the realm, and you will be in her way."

I study her. Nothing about her *looks* lethal, but I've learned the Fae are deceiving. There's no doubt she could break my neck with a single squeeze of her hand.

"Noted, again," I reply with a grin, my gaze fixed on the golden spectacle below.

Mor hops down from her spot on the wall, the empty platter of honeycake crumbs tucked under one arm. Without another word, she makes her way into the castle, her stride as languid as ever.

I remain still, watching the live soap opera unfold. I should have fucking gone inside.

The golden newcomer stands in the center of the courtyard, her posture painstakingly deliberate.

One hip juts out, her hands resting just so, drawing attention to her curves.

Her expression is one of practiced seduction, her gilded eyes scanning the scene as though she's already claimed ownership of everything and everyone.

My stomach twists uncomfortably when I see Orion striding toward her. He's dressed in his formal princely attire, his cape sweeping the ground behind him. Even from this distance, he's a vision of regal authority, commanding attention with every step.

Liora's smug expression softens into something far more

calculated. She extends her hand, and Orion takes it without hesitation.

I hold my breath as he raises it to his lips, pressing a brief, princely kiss to her knuckles.

It's a diplomatic gesture, I'm sure, and I try to ignore the flare of heat in my chest as I wonder what their relationship is.

Jesus Christ, Tana, stop being ridiculous.

I don't give a shit what this walking bath bomb is to Orion. I'm leaving here. I can't even stand him.

I've tried to kill him several times. I should be *glad* there will be someone else here to distract him tonight so I can try to talk to the Warden from the Briar Court.

Just as I think of that, I realize the gates to the castle are closing. There are no more travelers arriving. The Shimmering Court must have been the last.

Does that mean Ruvan isn't coming? Is my plan falling apart before I can even enact it?

My face heats with irritation as I watch the scene below, hoping Ruvan will be arriving later.

Orion turns, standing next to Liora, and she slides her hand into the crook of his elbow as she glances up—directly at me.

My hands clench into fists. Her golden eyes lock onto mine, and her radiant smile morphs into something far smugger. She's *trying* to rile me up.

What a bitch.

As if to hammer the point home, Liora leans into Orion's side, her bare breasts brushing against his arm as he escorts her inside the castle—a gesture he hasn't extended to any other dignitary tonight.

So why *her*?

No, stop. *It doesn't matter to me.*

I tell myself it's political. Eldoria's High Lady is clearly accustomed to being treated like royalty, and Orion is just playing the part of the diplomatic prince.

But the image of her pressed against him burns in my mind, and a sour taste refuses to leave my mouth.

I exhale sharply, forcing my gaze away from the courtyard. This isn't my problem.

And it doesn't matter.

I toss the remaining honeycake over the wall with a dismissive flick and turn to the door, releasing a slow breath.

The fire still burning in my chest tells me I'm full of shit.

It *does* matter.

And I don't know what to do with that.

CHAPTER 18

orion

The air in Starfall Castle feels heavier with the anticipation of the Beltane celebration humming through the halls.

Servants rush to and fro, arranging every detail to perfection, while the faint strains of music and laughter drift up from the lower levels.

It's a day of promise, of renewal—a reminder that soon we will experience a single, fleeting moment when Avalon will be bathed in the soft golden light of its only sunrise.

And yet, the darkness lingers at the edges. I feel it more keenly than usual.

Striding through the main corridor, my boots thump against the polished obsidian floors.

The moonlight filtering through the stained-glass windows casts fractured rainbows across the walls, a pale echo of the light we will soon witness.

My destination isn't far—the small dining hall where I know Hypnos has Tana cornered, subjecting her to a final course in Fae etiquette.

The door is ajar, and I hear her voice before I see her, sharp and dripping with sarcasm.

"So let me get this straight. If someone offers me a drink, I don't take it unless they specifically say it's safe? But the phrasing matters because they could be disguising the offering as a bargain? This sounds like a fun party. I can't fucking wait."

"You jest," Hypnos replies, his tone calm but with a distinct note of warning, "but such an oversight could cost you dearly. Fae politicking is no less dangerous than combat."

"I'll keep that in mind while I'm dodging magical cocktails." Her voice carries that distinct mix of humor and defiance that seems to cling to her no matter the situation.

I step into the room, and both heads turn toward me. Hypnos sits at the far end of the table, his blind eyes unseeing but his awareness as keen as ever.

Tana leans back in her chair, arms crossed, and regards me with a look that could cut stone.

"Are you here to critique my table manners too, Your Highness?" she quips, raising an eyebrow.

"No," I say evenly. "Hypnos seems to have that well in hand. I'm here to ensure everything is progressing as it should."

Her eyes narrow slightly, but she doesn't reply.

Instead, she picks up her fork and stabs at what's left of her lunch, clearly dismissing me from her thoughts—or perhaps reminding me that dining utensils are her primary choice of weapon.

"Are you threatening me with more cutlery?" I bite back.

She ignores me, turning instead to her meal. Her dismissiveness is not unusual, but today, her anger seems to accompany it.

Hypnos tilts his head, a ghost of a smirk playing on his lips before he glances behind me.

Mor is waiting just beyond the hall, her arms crossed and her red eyes glowing faintly in the dim light.

"You're late," she says flatly, falling into step beside me as we walk toward the courtyard.

"I had other priorities," I reply, brushing off her tone. "What did your patrols find?"

"Nothing good," she mutters, her voice low and gruff. "The darkness is shifting—growing. It's not like before. It's almost as if it's learning, finding new ways to spread."

I glance at her sharply. "How?"

She shakes her head, her expression grim. "I don't know yet. But it feels stronger. Hungrier. We've never seen it move like this."

The unease in her voice is enough to make my chest tighten. I rub at my sternum as my heart beats erratically before settling into tempo. If the darkness is adapting, it could pose a threat we aren't prepared for.

"Keep watching," I tell her, my voice hard. "And double the patrols. If it shows any sign of encroaching further, I want to know immediately."

As we part ways, I find myself glancing back toward the dining hall, where Tana and Hypnos are still locked in conversation. The weight of what lies ahead settles over me like a shroud.

Tonight will bring more than just celebration.

It will bring questions, challenges, and dangers we can only begin to predict.

And somehow, I have to make sure Tana survives it all.

The kitchens are alive with bustling energy, the warm, rich scents of baking bread and roasting meats curling through the air like an embrace.

Fae of all shapes and sizes move with practiced efficiency, their hands deftly working over pastries, stews, and intricately garnished platters that gleam under the soft glow of enchanted lanterns.

I step inside, and the noise dulls slightly as heads turn to acknowledge me.

A wave of bows and nods ripples through the room, but I wave it off with a flick of my hand. "Carry on," I say, my tone firm but warm.

The head cook, Ylsa, is a stout Terra Fae from Cairnvail. With tawny, stone-like skin and eyes that glint like veins of amber running through her hardened form, she runs this kitchen without mercy.

"Your Highness," she says, her voice brisk but proud. "The preparations are nearly complete. We'll be ready by Evenfall."

I nod, glancing over the array of dishes laid out on long stone counters.

It's an impressive spread, even by Starfall standards. The Feast of Beltane is meant to honor the realm's fleeting light, and they've more than risen to the occasion.

"Excellent work," I tell Ylsa, letting a rare smile tug at my lips. "You have outdone yourselves, as always."

Her chest swells with pride, and she dips her head. "Thank you, my prince. I will verify every dish offered by the attending courts tonight to ensure the queen's safety."

I give a final approving nod and step back, letting the hum of activity swallow me as I turn toward the side exit.

The cold air hits me as soon as I step outside, the faint mist curling around my boots. I take a steadying breath, the weight of the night pressing against my shoulders like a boulder.

The pulse of Avalon beats harshly with my footsteps.

A sharp, blinding pain lances through my chest, sudden and unforgiving. It steals the air from my lungs, buckling my knees as I grab for the wall, my other hand bracing against my thigh.

I grit my teeth, willing the agony to pass, but it lingers like an iron claw tearing through my ribcage.

I close my eyes, the cold stone beneath my palm grounding me as my thoughts spiral.

The darkness is growing.

Mor felt it.

I feel it.

The pulse of Avalon echoes faintly in the back of my mind, like the fading heartbeat of a dying animal. Its pain is my pain; its weakness, my own.

Ever since I was a youngling, I've known that my life is bound to the realm's fate, as much a part of it as the mist and the moon.

And now, that bond feels more fragile than ever.

A bitter laugh escapes me, rough and hollow.

Selfish—that's what this is. Pushing Tana to embrace a destiny she never asked for, all because I cling to the faint hope that saving the realm might save me.

It's cruel, and I know it.

But the alternative—the thought of Avalon falling, its light snuffed out forever—is unbearable.

The pain finally begins to ebb, leaving me breathless and trembling. I straighten slowly, leaning back against the castle wall and dragging a hand through my hair.

The cool air bites at my skin, sharp and bracing, and I let it anchor me.

If the realm can be saved, perhaps... perhaps there's a chance for me too.

A sliver of hope I dare not voice aloud.

For now, though, there is work to be done.

Descending the narrow stairway carved into the cliff-side, I keep my pace brisk despite the nagging ache that lingers in my chest.

The village below comes into view, its rooftops clustered like children huddled beneath the looming shadow of Star-fall Castle.

The faint hum of daily life reaches my ears—laughter, the clang of tools, the rhythmic pounding of a distant loom.

The blacksmith's shop is alive with its own music: the

roar of the forge, the hiss of cooling metal, and the occasional crackling of Flame Sprites chittering in their fiery tongues.

I push open the heavy wooden door, the familiar scent of molten iron and charred wood hitting me immediately.

Hephaestus stands near the forge, a blade raised to the light of the fire as he inspects its edge with a keen eye.

The glow from the flames dances across his face, highlighting the rough-hewn planes of his features. He turns at the sound of my footsteps, his expression breaking into a broad grin.

"Ah, just in time, yer grace," he says, his voice rich with its lilt. He lowers the blade and steps toward me, his towering frame as imposing as ever. "I've got somethin' special for ye."

He holds out the knife, its handle crafted from polished ebony wood inlaid with faintly glowing silver veins, reminiscent of Avalon's own mystic energy.

The blade itself is slender, deadly, and gleams like the surface of the Misting Lake under moonlight.

Etched along its surface are faint runes that shimmer, their meaning known only to those versed in ancient scripts.

"A blade for the queen," he declares proudly, presenting it like an offering to the realm itself.

I take it from him, weighing it in my hand. It's perfectly balanced, light yet sturdy, the edge sharp enough to slice through armor. I twist it in my grasp, inspecting the runes and feeling the faint pulse of enchantment coursing through the blade.

It's not just a weapon; it's a promise of protection.

"She'll appreciate this," I say, nodding in approval. "Good work, Hephaestus."

He beams, clearly pleased with the praise. "Aye, it's got the right edge for a fighter like her. And the runes'll give her a bit of an advantage if she's facin' anythin' from our realm."

I nod, satisfied. "Will you and Hestia be attending the celebration tonight?"

He chuckles, a gleam of mischief in his eyes. "Not a chance, lad. Hestia's lined someone up to watch tha' younglings, and we've got a rare night to ourselves."

I smirk, shaking my head. "Then enjoy it. Just don't add too many more little ones to your brood."

He lets out a hearty laugh, the sound booming through the shop. "No promises, yer grace. A man's got his limits, but I'm not complainin'."

With a final nod, I hand the blade back to him, gesturing for it to be readied for delivery to Tana. "Finish your polish. I'll make sure she gets it before the evening begins."

"Of course," he says, carefully placing the knife back on its display rack, his expression softening for a moment. "She'll be safe with this, I promise."

I take my leave, stepping out into the cool air that clings to Avalon's perpetual moonlit sky. The faint glow of the Misting Lake in the distance catches my eye as I climb the path back toward the castle.

Tonight will be a celebration, a night of revelry and promises renewed.

But beneath the surface of Avalon's festive facade, the darkness stirs, hungry and waiting.

My steps quicken as I ascend toward the towering spires of Starfall.

I have preparations to make—both for the festivities and for the inevitable scuffle the High Fae will bring to our new queen.

For tonight, Tana must be safe.

The realm's future depends on it.

CHAPTER 19
Tana

I pace the archives like a caged animal, my boots thudding against the stone floor in rhythm with the pounding in my skull.

The room reeks of old paper and musty regret, neither of which does me any favors. Books tower on every side, their spines etched with Fae symbols I can't begin to decipher.

Hypnos told me this was the best place to "ground myself."

Honestly, I think he just wanted me out of the way. Either that, or we have very different ideas about relaxation.

The arrival of the dignitaries adds more pressure to the castle, which is starting to grate on me. Each new face feels like another weight pressing on my chest, forcing me into a role I never asked for.

Queen. Of fucking Avalon.

The title tastes like a bad joke, one I'm tired of hearing.

And the fucking Briar Warden is a no-show. The one Fae who might actually help me find my way home is not coming tonight, and I've been counting on him.

Everything is wearing thin—my patience, my composure. Thoughts of my task force, who surely know I'm missing by now.

The endless maps and books I can't read, all useless in the search for a way back. Even the air around me is grating.

It's thick, buzzing like static electricity on steroids. I feel it crawling under my skin, humming in my veins. It's doing *something* to me.

My body feels too aware—every touch of fabric, every movement, *everything*. My irritation is sharper, rawer.

And the headaches.

God, the headaches.

A drumbeat of pain behind my eyes that refuses to quit.

I pull a small vial of relief drops from my pocket, twisting the cap off with shaky fingers before tipping the liquid onto my tongue.

Bitter.

Sharp.

But within moments, the pain begins to fade, leaving a faint buzz at the edge of my awareness.

Leaning back against a shelf, I close my eyes and exhale a long breath. For all its grandeur, this castle feels like it's closing in on me.

No sunlight. No breeze. Just endless stone and endless demands.

"Tana, don't accept drinks from anyone."

"Tana, bow like this, not like that."

"Tana, stop threatening Orion with cutlery."

That last one was probably fair, but still.

I need out. Air. Space.

Pushing off the shelf, I leave the archives. I pass the pair of guards stationed by the door.

One keeps his beady black eyes on me too long for comfort before blinking and returning to his stoic position.

I weave through the castle's labyrinthine halls, the ornate tapestries and carved stone blurring together.

When I reach the main gates, the fresh air hits me like a slap—crisp and cool. Mist from the cliffs below curls upward like ghostly fingers.

The castle looms behind me, its spires clawing at the night sky.

I glance back, half-expecting someone to come running, but the guards don't move.

Maybe the day's excitement is enough of a distraction. Or maybe my babysitter is preoccupied with his newest guest.

I ignore the way the thought of Orion and Liora together pisses me off.

It's none of my business.

The path down the cliffs is steep, winding along the rocky edge. The village below glows faintly, warm light spilling from its scattered cottages.

I descend, my boots kicking up gravel, the distant hum of life growing louder with each step.

I need to find Hestia and tell her my headaches are getting worse—she'll know what to do. Or at least she'll have more of those drops.

That's good enough for me.

I've never had headaches like this. I wonder if it's related to my heart condition.

Not that it would matter back on Earth—no doctor could tell me anything about such a rare affliction.

For now, I'll blame the constant pain in my ass.

A certain prince.

Each step away from the castle lets me breathe a little easier, the weight pressing on my chest finally lifting.

By the time I reach the village, my headache has dulled to a low throb. Manageable, but still annoying. I almost think of turning back.

The streets are alive with the quiet hum of Fae life.

Vendors close their stalls, children dart along cobblestone paths chasing glowing creatures, and the faint scent of bread and spices lingers in the air.

I head straight for Hestia's bakery at the village's edge. Planters under the dark windows hold a chaotic blend of herbs, flowers, and something that looks like it might bite.

I knock, the sound echoing in the stillness, but there's no answer.

"Hestia?" I call, cupping my hands over my eyes to peer into the windows.

The fires at Hephaestus' blacksmith shop seem to be cooling, and I resign myself to the fact they've gone home— likely to prepare for Beltane.

I step back, glancing around.

I should return to the castle.

Much longer, and Orion will likely storm down here with his ridiculous cape to drag me back to my prison.

Each Fae I pass gives me the same calculating look—a mixture of curiosity and mistrust, as if they're waiting for me to sprout wings or declare myself unfit to rule.

The air shifts, cool and sharp.

My stomach tightens.

It's not unpleasant, but unsettling—like a whisper brushing the back of my mind.

My feet stop, and I find myself standing at the edge of the village, staring down a path leading to the cliffs below.

There it is again—a pull, faint but undeniable. The dark caves at the base of the cliffs yawn open, moonlight casting jagged shadows like an invitation.

"Nope," I mutter, shaking my head. "Not happening. Creepy caves? Classic horror movie setup."

I turn back toward the castle, but the pull doesn't go away.

If anything, it grows stronger, tugging at something deep and primal.

My pulse quickens.

The air around me feels alive, whispering things I can't understand.

"Just go back to the castle, Tana," I mutter.

But my feet don't move.

The caves are a beacon, calling to me.

What if it's the one-way door, opening again to offer me a way home?

I'll never forgive myself if I walk away without knowing.

"Damn it," I say through gritted teeth, my hands balling into fists.

Fine.

Just a quick look, and then I'll head back before I do something stupid.

Like get eaten by a giant cave beast.

The path down the cliffs is narrow, winding sharply along jagged rocks. The sound of waves crashing below grows louder with each step, the spray of saltwater misting the air.

The pull intensifies—less a whisper now and more a voice, urging me forward.

At the bottom, the air thickens with something I can't name. It presses against my skin, humming just beneath the surface.

Could this be magic?

The caves loom ahead, their shadows twisting and shifting in the moonlight.

I hesitate at the entrance. Cold air spills out, sharp and biting, like a breath from the earth itself.

"This is a terrible idea," I mutter but step inside anyway.

The cave's interior is damp and cool, the stillness oppressive, as if time itself has stopped. My footsteps echo against the stone walls, each sound amplified in the silence.

A headache that had dulled to a faint thrum now flares, sharp and insistent, like a warning I can't decipher.

I press my palm to the cold stone wall for balance, its rough texture grounding me. But when I glance down at my hand, my breath catches.

The hand touching the wall isn't mine.

The skin is pale, weathered—like that of an old woman.

My heart lurches, and I yank my hand back. I stare at it—it's my hand again.

"What the hell," I whisper.

Another step. Another flash of pain.

My boot disappears, replaced by a bare, gnarled foot.

I stumble back, but the image vanishes, my own boots firmly on the ground.

This fucking cave is playing tricks on me.

Bracing myself against the wall, I force my legs to move deeper into the shadows.

My phantom hand flashes again—younger this time, its skin smooth and unblemished.

The sensation isn't fear.

If anything, it's familiar. Kindred.

"Get a grip, Tana," I mutter, ignoring the visions and pressing onward.

Torches embedded in the walls flare to life as I pass, each igniting in a burst of golden light. The flickering shadows they cast seem unnervingly alive, rippling like water caught in a breeze.

My headache sharpens with every step, dizziness coiling in my stomach.

I grip the wall, fingers digging into the stone.

A flicker of silver catches my eye deeper within the cave. Subtle at first, like a distant star, it grows stronger as I approach.

My instincts scream at me to turn back, but the pull is impossible to resist.

"Sure, Tana," I mutter, my voice strained. "Follow the creepy glowing light. Nothing bad ever happens when you do that."

The path opens into a wide chamber.

At its center lies a pool of water, impossibly still, its glassy surface reflecting the torchlight like a black mirror.

The air here is heavier, charged with the same pressure pulling me forward.

I kneel, running my fingers over deep grooves carved into the stone floor. Runes.

They hum faintly, an energy vibrating beneath my skin.

In the pool's center is a basin carved from the same dark stone as the walls. Its polished surface gleams, torchlight dancing across it.

My fingers hover above it, drawn to the smooth, cool stone.

Before I can touch it, pain lances through my skull—sharp and blinding.

I stagger back, clutching my head as the runes begin to glow, their light growing brighter with every passing second.

The pool's surface ripples—subtle at first, then violently, as though boiling.

My breath catches as a figure begins to rise from the depths.

Dark, wide eyes. Blue skin.

I step back, pressing myself against the wall. The image reminds me of a horror movie—a cryptic figure with long, dark hair climbing out of a television.

But this isn't a movie.

This is the Lady of the Lake.

My chest tightens, and each breath feels like a struggle. Panic claws at me, but I force myself to stay still. The runes blaze to life, casting the chamber in an eerie glow.

My headache spikes so violently I clutch the wall for support, my knees threatening to buckle.

I force myself to straighten, meeting her gaze. Her presence is commanding—more so than the day of Demeter's trial.

Here, in this confined space, it's suffocating.

"You've been in my head," I say, my voice raw and unsteady. "You showed me things—things I don't understand. Avalon falling to darkness. What does it mean?"

The Lady tilts her head, her expression unreadable.

Shimmering water clings to her form, shifting like a living veil.

"What does it mean?" I demand, my voice trembling. "If you're going to keep dragging me into your cave, the least you can do is explain these visions."

Her lips part as if to speak, but the air hums with energy, crawling over my skin.

My headache surges again, and this time it's not just pain—it's pressure, an overwhelming force pressing against my skull.

The runes flare brighter, and the pool churns violently.

I clutch my head as images flash before my eyes—a sword driven into stone, a dark cloud choking me, a fiery forest.

They're disjointed, chaotic, fragments of a dream I can't piece together.

Through the chaos, one image repeats—a sword buried in a cracked boulder, the hilt gleaming with ancient light, at the center of a gazebo-like structure.

The pressure in my head peaks, then abruptly releases, leaving me gasping.

I stumble back, my fingers brushing against the cold

stone wall for support as the images fade, leaving only the echo of the sword burned into my mind.

"What is this?" I demand, my voice hoarse. "Why are you showing me this?"

The Lady of the Lake remains silent, her gaze piercing, as though she's peeling away layers of my soul.

Her presence presses down on me like a physical weight—heavy and suffocating.

She doesn't speak, but I feel the answer stirring deep within me—not in words, but in instinct. She won't hand me explanations.

Whatever the sword means, whatever these visions are, it's up to me to figure it out.

Her gaze softens—not warmth, exactly, but something less distant. Approval, maybe.

Then, slowly, she begins to sink back into the pool.

The water rises to meet her, rippling and shimmering, until she disappears beneath the surface.

"Wait!" I shout, taking a shaky step forward. "You can't just—"

She's gone.

The pool stills, the runes dimming until the chamber is cast in nothing but the faint flicker of torchlight.

The silence is deafening, broken only by my labored breathing and the occasional drip of water somewhere in the cave.

My head feels hollow, the ache dulled but still lingering—a phantom reminder of what I've seen.

I stare at the pool for a long moment, frustration bubbling in my chest.

She wanted me to see the sword, that much is clear.

The image was vivid, almost seared into my mind. The cracked boulder, the gleaming hilt, the gazebo-like structure —it's not just a clue. It's a command.

I exhale sharply, running a hand through my hair.

"Fine," I mutter, my voice thick with irritation and resolve. "If you want me to play this game, Lady, then I'll play it."

This could be the first trial, the first opportunity to reopen that one-way door and get home.

Once the realm sees I'm not the right mortal for this job, I can leave.

I turn from the pool, my steps unsteady but purposeful. I need to find that sword.

Wherever it is, it's close.

I can feel it.

CHAPTER 20

The fresh air isn't helping anymore. It feels like Avalon itself is laughing at me, like some cosmic joke I'm too dense to understand.

My boots crunch against the uneven ground, the tug within me pulling me back to the vast castle.

The vision of the sword and the cracked boulder keeps replaying in my head, clearer than anything else I've seen since I arrived here.

A sword in a stone. Really.

Am I in some medieval movie? They've even got a round table in there—fucking King Arthur's castle.

All I need now is a pack of knights and the Sheriff of Nottingham.

Or is that Robin Hood?

I don't know what's worse—the fact that I'm chasing this wild vision like some desperate lunatic or the fact that it's starting to feel like this is the first thing that makes any damned sense in this fucking place.

I pause in the center of the courtyard, catching my breath, looking around like a neon sign will be pointing out the boulder.

My legs ache from the climb, my head is still pounding from whatever the Lady of the Lake did to me, and my nerves are frayed enough to snap.

But I can't stop.

Something is pulling me forward, an invisible thread that tugs at my gut every time I think about turning back.

"You're not getting the best of me," I mutter, glaring up at the oversized moon like it's responsible for all of this. "I'll find your stupid sword and shove it up your ass."

Orion catches my eye, looking down at me from one of the parapets.

I give him my middle finger and keep walking.

"I'll shove it up *his* ass too," I mutter to myself.

The castle grounds are vast, and two rows of trees form a sort of tunnel. The path narrows, winding through trees that seem older than time itself.

Their gnarled branches twist above me, forming a canopy so dense that even Avalon's eerie moonlight struggles to filter through.

The air grows cooler, damp with the smell of moss and earth. I ignore the shiver crawling up my spine as I wonder how long it's been since anyone last visited here.

The farther I walk, the quieter it gets.

No rustling leaves, no chirping insects—just the sound of my boots scuffing against stone and dirt.

It's unnerving, like the world is holding its breath, waiting for something to happen.

Finally, the trees give way to a clearing, hidden so well by the overgrowth that I don't think you can see this from the castle.

From up there, it would look like nothing more than the forest that surrounds two sides of this enormous place.

Vines hang like curtains over what looks like the ruins of an old gazebo.

Its columns are cracked and covered in moss, and the stone floor is barely visible beneath a thick layer of dirt and dried leaves.

It's ancient. Forgotten. Like something straight out of a fairy tale.

My heart thuds in my chest as I step closer, my boots crunching softly against the undergrowth.

The vision of the sword flashes in my mind again, stronger this time.

It's here.

It has to be.

The gazebo is large—though smaller than it looked in the vision—its roof partially caved in, its once-intricate carvings eroded by time.

The vines have claimed most of it, weaving around the columns and draping over the edges like a shroud.

But in the center, where the floor is still intact, a large boulder sits, jagged and cracked. My breath catches when I see the faint outline of a sword. It's not glowing or majestic like it was in the vision.

If anything, it looks artificial. Like a prop left behind after the set of a bad medieval drama was dismantled.

But it's *there*.

I step closer, my pulse quickening. The air feels heavier here, charged with the memory of something terrible. The closer I get, the more my headache starts to return, a dull throb at the base of my skull.

It's the magic.

The realm around me—beating against me, trying to get in.

That *has* to be it.

As I think about the moments when my head pounds hardest, it's near the lake, around the Lady, and *here*. Places where the magic of the realm could be more potent.

I lock this away for later—I'll talk to Hestia about it.

Stopping just shy of the boulder, I stare at the sword's hilt.

It's partially embedded in the stone, tilted at an angle like it's *mocking* me, daring me to pull it out. My palms tingle, wanting to touch it.

This could be a bad idea.

The silence around me seems to deepen, as if the forest itself is waiting for what I'll do next.

I glance around, half-expecting someone—maybe Orion or Mor—to pop out from the trees and tell me this is a bad idea.

But there's no one.

Just me and this ridiculous, overgrown monument.

"Well, no time like the present," I say, rolling my shoulders. I step up to the boulder, gripping the hilt with both hands. "Here goes nothing."

I pull and the sword doesn't budge. Not even a fraction of an inch.

It's like trying to lift a mountain with my bare hands.

I let out a frustrated growl, planting my foot against the

boulder for leverage. "Come on, you stubborn piece of—" I pull harder, straining against the weight of the thing, but it's no use.

The sword remains as immovable as the stone itself.

My arms ache, my palms sting, and my pride takes a nosedive. Admittedly, this would have been too easy—but a girl's *gotta* try. Finally, I step back, glaring at the sword like it personally insulted me.

"Seriously? What's the point of showing me this fucking thing if you're not going to let me take it?"

The moon doesn't answer, and the forest remains silent. Unhelpful as ever.

I run a hand through my hair, pacing around the boulder as my mind races. There *has* to be a reason I was led here— some clue I'm missing.

But no matter how hard I think, no matter where I look for runes or something to dislodge the sword, the only answer that comes to mind is the same infuriating thought I've had since the moment I arrived in Avalon.

I hate this fucking place.

CHAPTER 21

Tana

The dressing chamber hums with an energy that matches the knot of tension coiling in my chest.

Fae attendants flit around me, their hands deftly adjusting fabrics that gleam like starlight, dotting my skin with shimmering powder, and fastening intricate jewelry onto me as if I were some prized statue on display.

The air reeks of lavender and musk, the intoxicating mix thick enough to make my already dizzy head spin.

I don't want to think about the sword I found earlier.

Or the fact that it didn't budge an inch when I pulled on it.

Or the weird pull in my chest that wouldn't go away, even after I left that overgrown gazebo.

Or that Orion might have *known* it was there.

"Hold still, Your Grace," an attendant mutters, dragging me back to the present as she adjusts the neckline of my gown—a feat of fashion and engineering that might as well be made of liquid midnight.

"This is what we're wearing to the ball?" I quip, though the sarcasm falls flat.

My thoughts keep circling back to the sword.

And Orion.

But the gown is gorgeous—little more than two panels of nearly sheer silk, fashioned with a sort of leather harness.

From the side, the entire length of my long legs is on display, and I can't say that I'm mad about it.

"This is nothing," Thalindra purrs from across the room, her voice rich with amusement. "Wait until you see what we wear to the Solarium."

Her very voice is a caress across my skin, and the arousal that has lingered through the day begins to stir again.

As I take her in, I try not to gape.

Draped in silver so sheer it's invisible, with polished discs barely covering her nipples, she looks like a goddess on her way to seduce the moon.

"You look incredible," I say, the words slipping out before I can stop them.

There's no hiding the awe in my voice.

Not that I want to.

"Thank you, my queen."

Her tone is sweet, but the flicker in her eyes—playful and dangerous—makes my pulse jump.

"I hope you will make time to visit the Solarium this Beltane."

"You're not staying by my side tonight?" I ask, trying to ignore the thread of disappointment winding through me.

Hypnos's lectures on Fae politics and manipulation had left me with the impression I'd need all the support I could get tonight.

I trust my handmaids.

They know the gossip on everyone.

They've helped me during this past week, and I would feel more at ease navigating the trickery that will surely play out tonight.

"We will join you for the first presentations," Brynja answers from across the room, where she's being dressed in something equally breathtaking.

Her silver-adorned outfit leaves little to the imagination, her long legs accentuated by flowing sheer skirts and high slits.

"But at the time of dinner, the Lesser Fae will be excused until the Bloomrise sun."

"Well, that's fucked up," I mutter.

A Fae attendant mutters a soft curse in response to my movement.

I shoot her an apologetic glance, trying to remain still as she carefully lines my eyes with shimmering silver.

Thalindra chuckles softly.

"The Solarium will be far more enjoyable than any High Fae dinner, Your Grace."

Elowen whispers as she steps closer, her hands brushing over my bare shoulders.

The gentle touch sends a shiver down my spine, the memory of her hands from earlier this morning still vivid.

I smirk, arching a brow at her.

"Someone's feeling bolder than they were this morning."

Elowen's lips curve into a shy smile, but Thalindra cuts in smoothly.

"She's a fast learner, Your Grace."

Her fingers slide over Elowen's thigh, higher and higher—until Elowen swats her hand away, laughing softly.

"Let's just say, my queen," Brynja joins them, her voice teasing as she trails a slow lick up Elowen's neck, "we are very excited for this Beltane."

I glance at them, warmth blooming in my chest despite myself.

"I didn't expect the Fae to be so... open, sexually," I admit.

A few attendants exchange quiet chuckles and amused glances, their hands busy fastening the final touches of my gown.

"The Seelie Fae of Hel are much more reserved," Thalindra says, her voice laced with disdain.

"They believe their bright Day Courts make them superior, but they are as selfish as they are arrogant."

"Much like the Shimmering Court here in Avalon," Elowen whispers conspiratorially.

"They think they placed the stars in the sky."

Several attendants roll their eyes, muttering quiet agreements as the final piece of my outfit is secured.

I join them—not looking forward to interacting with Liora tonight.

The show she put on for her arrival will likely be only an appetizer compared to whatever she may have planned for the celebration.

My bodice is a masterpiece—deep midnight blue and black, threaded with veins of silver that shimmer like constellations.

The flowing skirt cascades in layers of iridescent fabric, catching the light with every move.

Jewels adorn my hair, matching the faint shimmer dusted over my exposed shoulders and collarbone.

Brynja kneels to secure a black-leather holster around my thigh.

Her touch lingers, sending another wave of heat through me.

"What is this?" I ask, curiously looking for the blade this holster should be securing.

"His Grace, the Prince, has a gift for you this Beltane."

Her tone is soft but serious.

The knot in my stomach tightens.

I place my hand over my abdomen, feeling like every touch, every word spoken, is meant to bring me closer to pulling these clothes off and giving in to my needs.

Glancing at the mirror, as the attendants step back, I take in the woman staring back at me.

She is powerful.

Untouchable.

That part is familiar.

It is the elegance flowing off me that feels out of place.

The draping fabrics demand a certain poise that seems to rest comfortably on my body.

Thalindra opens the door, one knee bent, showing off her pearly skin.

"If you are ready, Your Grace, it is time to put the other courts to shame."

The hall buzzes with quiet energy as my handmaids

glide ahead, their movements an intoxicating melody of grace and sensuality.

Thalindra walks a step behind Elowen and Brynja, commanding the center like she was born to it.

Their sheer silks catch the flickering torchlight, their hips swaying to an unspoken rhythm that almost hypnotizes.

I'm half-lost in the sight of them when I see Orion.

A gasp escapes before I can swallow it.

He stands tall above the swirling activity of the corridor, his broad frame radiating strength and command.

His black attire clings to him with sharp precision, a silver sash crossing his chest in stark contrast.

A sword rests on his hip, his cloak pinned to his left shoulder, and his long, silver-streaked hair is pulled back, the sides freshly shaved to reveal the hard angles of his jaw and the deep line of his scar.

The torchlight casts shadows over his face, carving out a vision that is nothing short of hauntingly beautiful.

My chest tightens as my heart stumbles, hammering against my ribs with an erratic beat that I pray he can't hear.

The breath I draw feels shallow, and I force myself to keep my composure with long, deliberate inhales.

Refusing to let anyone see me falter tonight.

But his molten-silver gaze finds me immediately.

My handmaids approach him first, their seductive strides transforming them into something almost otherworldly.

Sirens.

Elowen and Brynja extend their hands, curtsying with a flourish as Orion leans down to kiss each offered hand.

His eyes never leave mine.

Thalindra follows, her silver skirts swishing as she steps forward, her movements a study in poise and presentation.

She turns to me, a playful, knowing smirk on her lips, as if she is unveiling a masterpiece.

"Your Grace," she begins, her tone laced with reverence, "may I present the most delicious of delicacies this Beltane —Her Majesty and future sovereign of Avalon, Lady Tana."

Her words hang in the air as she steps aside, bowing her head along with the others.

Orion crosses the distance between us, his movements deliberate, his intensity palpable.

"Starling," he greets, his voice low and rich as he takes my hand.

His lips brush my knuckles, the touch sending a jolt of heat through me.

"You are but the rarest of jewels, plucked from the very heavens above Avalon."

I smirk, unwilling to let him see how his proximity affects me.

"You clean up quite nicely yourself," I reply, my tone laced with mockery.

Though his raised brow and amused smirk tell me he was expecting no less.

His gaze travels down my form, a slow, unrelenting assessment that makes my skin prickle.

When his eyes land on the holster strapped to my thigh, he slides his large hand firmly around my leg, pulling it upward until I stumble into his chest, bracing myself against him with a surprised gasp.

The scent of leather and cedarwood envelops me, heady and grounding, as my skirt falls away to reveal the empty holster.

His fingers brush the shimmering lotion on my skin, and the contact sends a shockwave straight to my core.

Heat pools low in my stomach, and I grit my teeth, trying desperately to banish the images flashing unbidden in my mind.

Get. It. Together.

His silver eyes lock on mine, the intensity in his gaze grounding me.

"Keep this with you, always," he says, his voice a commanding growl as he pulls a beautiful silver blade from his sash and places it in the holster.

I don't argue, though the sincerity in his tone makes my pulse quicken. There's something almost vulnerable in his expression as he speaks again.

"The glamour will remain, even if you remove it. Only you, and those sworn to your protection, will see it. To others, it will be invisible." His hold on my thigh tightens, pulling me only slightly closer.

A ripple of warmth cascades over my skin as his power surrounds me.

I clutch the fabric of his vest, needing something solid to anchor me as I swallow the moan that begs to leave my throat.

I can imagine that power, already so close to where I

want him, bringing me crashing into pleasure. And God do I want it. But I need to keep focused.

I'm not sure why I feel like a horny teenager, but his closeness is not helping.

A swirl of shadow coalesces behind us, shifting seamlessly into Mor and Hypnos, their arrival silent and seamless.

They fall into step with us immediately, as if they had been part of our entourage the entire way.

Mor gives me a small nod, her crimson eyes sharp against her black tunic and leather pants.

Hypnos, dressed in gleaming cream and gold, offers a brief, reassuring smile before resuming his stoic demeanor.

"There will not be a moment we are not guarding you, starling," Orion says, his voice low as we pass several High Fae lingering in the wide halls.

I scan the crowd, looking for two among them.

The Warden of Thornshire.

And the Glitter Cunt from Shimmertopia.

I can't recall the actual name of her court, so that will have to suffice for now.

The gazes of the spectators follow us, whispers spreading like wildfire. I can't hear their words, but my instincts, and the sharpness of Orion's growl, tell me enough.

The double doors ahead stand closed.

Beyond them lies the vast banquet hall, prepared for days leading up to the celebration.

Just as I ready myself, preparing to take in a deep breath and brace for this shit show, a walking disco ball rounds the corner, jutting out her hip and leaning an elbow against the wall.

Orion halts. His muscles tense beneath my hand. "Liora." His tone is clipped, annoyed.

Ah.

If it isn't Glitter Cunt herself.

CHAPTER 22
Tana

Liona's smile is a masterpiece of venom disguised as charm, her golden skin glowing faintly under the flickering torchlight.

Her breasts are bare, adorned with two gold pieces fixed around each nipple, connected by a chain.

The skirt she wears is merely a gold belt fixed with two long, sheer-gold panels of tulle that cascade down the front and back of her body, each nearly sweeping the floor.

She dips into a shallow bow, her sharp eyes never leaving mine, the smile on her face too perfect to be anything but a mask.

"Your Grace," she begins, her tone a velvet caress, dripping with feigned warmth. "Welcome to Avalon. I am Liona of the Shimmering Court, and I must say, it is such a pleasure to finally meet the realm's chosen queen."

Her gaze lingers on me for a fraction too long before it slides to Orion, softening with an almost intimate familiarity that stabs at me.

"And our steadfast guardian, of course."

"Liona," Orion says tightly. I can't decipher if the word carries irritation or warning. Perhaps both.

I step forward slightly, keeping my hand fixed around his arm. "Lydia, was it?" I offer her the same condescending smile she is giving me.

"It's such a pleasure. I've heard absolutely nothing about you, so I'll be looking forward to getting to know you."

Her lips twitch, but her composure remains intact. "Liona," she corrects. "The mortal has such sharp wit. How charming."

She shifts closer toward Orion, clearly trying to offer one of her nipples for him to suckle if he wants to. The desperation makes me roll my eyes.

"You must know, Your Grace, Avalon's throne is not an easy one to claim—nor an easy one to keep." Her voice drops, sweet as poison.

"After all, some, like myself, are better poised to sit upon thrones than others."

She reaches up, picking a piece of nothing off Orion's silver sash and rolling it between her gold-painted fingers. He bristles and clears his throat but doesn't move away from her touch.

I sense Mor behind us, her shadows cooling the space creep forward—a clear warning that Liona heeds, stepping back.

"I'm certain the realm could always choose another champion." She continues. "Imagine—two queens competing for the crown... and for the hearts of Avalon."

Her eyes run down Orion's tall form with unspoken intent before returning to me. "It would be... unfortunate, wouldn't it? Especially for someone unprepared to face a rival of—superior breeding."

I let her words hang in the air for a moment until the silence grows uncomfortable. She raises her chin and swallows, clearly understanding that she is not intimidating me the way she wants.

I cock an eyebrow, my smile growing sharper. "Oh, you are finished. Wonderful." My incredibly fake smile returns,

"Well, when you find someone of superior breeding, be sure to point them out. I'd love to see what that looks like."

My handmaids try and fail to stifle a quiet laugh, which only bolsters my attitude. Liona's expression falters for the briefest moment, her sharp eyes narrowing just slightly, before Orion cuts in.

"Liona," he says firmly, his voice a blade cutting through the tension. "It's time for the queen to take her place. Please take yours."

Liona hesitates, her bruised gaze darting between Orion and me, but she recovers quickly, dipping into another barely perceptible bow.

"Of course," she says, her voice honeyed once more. "Forgive me, Your Grace, if I've delayed you. I simply couldn't resist introducing myself."

"Consider it done," I say lightly, brushing past her with Orion at my side. "Now run along and take your seat. The chosen queen is ready to enter."

As we stride forward toward the grand doors, I don't look back, though I feel the weight of Liona's gaze lingering —sharp and calculating.

Beside me, Orion's voice drops low, a quiet warning meant only for my ears. "She won't forget this."

Without turning my head, I murmur back, steady and deliberate. "Good."

The festival hall is a kaleidoscope of light, silk, and energy. The air buzzes with music, conversation, and the intoxicating scent of exotic blooms.

Every sound—the tinkling of glasses, faint harp notes—fades the moment we step through the grand archway.

"Her Majesty, Lady Tana, the future queen of Avalon," the herald announces, his voice echoing with authority.

"Accompanied by His Grace, Prince Orion of the Night Court."

The room stills. Hundreds of gazes land on me, dissecting, judging. I force myself to stand tall, chin lifted, as Hypnos drilled into me.

The queen bows to no one. The words steady me as the silence stretches, taut and unyielding.

Then, as if on cue, the Fae bow their heads. The gesture ripples like a wave, silks and jewels glinting under the moonlight spilling through the arched windows.

It feels alien—the reverence as disconcerting as it is surreal.

My instincts itch to crack a joke, but I hold steady,

wearing a calm mask while my pulse thunders beneath the surface. Fake it till you make it.

Beside me, Orion steps forward, commanding the room as effortlessly as the moon commands the tides. He turns, bowing with deliberate precision that makes me itch to roll my eyes.

"Your Majesty," he murmurs, taking my hand and brushing my knuckles with a featherlight kiss.

Heat ripples up my spine—unwelcome and infuriating. Before I can respond, he straightens, his gaze locking with mine for a heartbeat.

"Enjoy the evening."

With that, he vanishes into the crowd, leaving me adrift. The Fae return to their calculated movements, the buzz of conversation swallowing me whole.

I stand there, feeling exposed, like a deer trapped under a predator's gaze.

Thalindra steps forward, her voice soft and steady. "Your Majesty, may I introduce Lady Sylara of Gloamreach, representative of the Twilight Court?"

A tall, crystalline figure with amethyst eyes steps forward, bowing gracefully.

"Your Majesty," she says, her tone unreadable.

Thalindra manages the introductions seamlessly, guiding me through a parade of names, titles, and veiled gazes.

I cling to her steady presence, nodding and smiling politely as required, though the weight of expectation presses heavily on me.

As the dignitaries fade into the throng, I edge toward the

quieter periphery of the hall. My handmaids flit nearby, close enough to intervene but giving me space.

Across the room, I spot Orion returning to the gathering. His silver hair gleaming under the light as he approaches a cluster of Fae.

He's at ease, even charming, his stance open and confident.

He doesn't glance my way, and though I'd never admit it, the lack of acknowledgment stings.

Then I spot Liona, entering only a moment after Orion.

Her golden gown shimmers as she glides into view, catching the attention of everyone nearby. Her eyes find mine across the room, and she smiles—a perfect, calculated weapon.

Turning with effortless grace, she directs her charm at the Fae nearest her, all while ensuring I'm watching.

I turn away, pretending not to care, just as my handmaids leave to fetch drinks.

The reprieve is short-lived. Snippets of conversation drift past me, including one from a male with dark antlers and a gravelly voice.

"The former queen owed me a favor," he says, his tone smug. "I'll collect it from the new one soon enough."

My jaw tightens, but I force myself to keep walking, my expression neutral.

As if tonight wasn't already a minefield, now I have debts I didn't even make hanging over my head.

Before I can stew further, a broad-shouldered figure steps into my path. His chest bears the emblem of the Briar Court, and my heart skips.

A connection to the Warden. Finally.

"Your Majesty," he says smoothly, bowing low. His moss-green eyes gleam with sharp intelligence. "I am Lirian, emissary of Thornspire. King Thorn sends his warm regards and a token of the Briar Court."

He produces an obsidian rose, its intricate petals glinting faintly as though infused with magic.

I hesitate, Hypnos's lessons screaming in my mind. Don't accept gifts.

But before I can decide, shadows coil around the talisman, yanking it from Lirian's hands and flinging it to the ground.

Startled, I look up to find Orion, his silver eyes blazing with cold authority.

"The queen humbly denies King Thorn's marriage proposal," he says, his voice cutting through the hall.

"But do send your thanks when you return to the Briar."

The tension between them crackles, Lirian's polite mask slipping for a fraction of a second before he bows again.

"Of course, I'll extend your sentiments," he says smoothly. "Ruvan has a message to convey of his own. A reminder, really."

He sticks his hands in his trouser pockets and takes a step closer to Orion, lowering his voice so the exchange is just between us.

"Thornspire will not revoke its challenge. He will eagerly meet you in the courtyard at High Shade on the eve of Starfall."

That's in less than a month. Fuck.

I can't wait that long to find a way home. My task

force will begin to notice I'm missing soon, with another week of leave time to exhaust before reporting back to base.

I need to get the fuck out of here.

He vanishes into the crowd, and I whirl on Orion, irritation bubbling to the surface.

"What the hell was that?"

His gaze sharpens as he steps closer, his presence like a shadow wrapping around me.

"You can't afford mistakes, starling. Accepting that would've been disastrous."

"I had it handled," I snap.

"Handled?" His expression darkens, his voice dropping. "You're not just a mortal, Tana. You're the chosen queen of Avalon. That makes you a target for alliances, manipulation, and worse."

I don't need his lecture. What I need is a way to contact the Warden—and Orion's overprotective theatrics just crushed that chance.

My eyes drift to the talisman, now lying innocuously on the floor, its sinister implications lingering.

He steps closer, his voice low and warning.

"Be careful where you tread, Starling. The ground beneath you is thinner than you think."

I glare at him, swallowing my retort. Two can play at this game.

"Noted, Your Grace," I say, my voice icy as I brush past him.

But his presence lingers—a shadow I can't seem to shake.

The hour draws closer to dinner, and I let out a strained breath as my handmaids step back to excuse themselves. Thalindra, ever poised, offers a subtle smile that's both reassuring and teasing.

"You did wonderfully, my queen," she says, her tone warm.

"Thank you," I manage, though my pulse is still racing from the sheer exhaustion of mingling with Fae who seemed just as likely to eat me as bow to me.

My head is thrumming, and while I was able to sneak a few drops of tonic, the thrum between my legs is becoming more of an annoyance.

Elowen gives me a wink before following the others, her silver skirts swaying as the three of them disappear into the crowd.

Without them, I feel exposed again, my fingers brushing the hidden blade strapped to my thigh for comfort.

I watch as one of the castle guards follows their path with a bit too much attention for my liking. He turns his gaze from them to me, his beady black eyes seeming to pierce through me.

I raise an eyebrow in defiance, daring him to continue his stare.

The dinner stretches before us—a decadent feast that could rival the finest banquets on Earth.

The air is thick with tantalizing scents that stir something primal in me: warm spices, sweet fruits, rich meats. Every bite I take is a battle against my own body.

There's something... more in the food. I can feel it, a subtle heat spreading with each taste, coiling low in my belly.

Of course, Mor shows up for the food, sitting several seats down on the opposite side of the table.

I steal a glance at Orion, seated directly across from me. He's perfectly composed, cutting into his meal with all the elegance you'd expect from a prince.

There's no indication that he's affected by whatever aphrodisiac is laced into this food, but his eyes catch mine briefly, and the faintest smirk curls his lips.

Asshole.

I look around me and find Liona seated at the table directly behind me. She has a perfect view of Orion—and he has one of her.

Now I'm not sure if it was me he was looking at or if he was looking past me to the human disco ball.

Around us, the hall has taken on a different atmosphere. Conversations are softer, more intimate. The Fae lean toward each other, their touches lingering, their laughter lower, richer.

The room hums with a tension I can't escape. Even the faintest brush of air against my skin sends a shiver down my spine.

I shift uncomfortably, trying to focus on the customs Hypnos drilled into me.

The queen bows to no one.

Decline gifts.

Don't take an offered drink unless you're ready to bind yourself.

The last one comes to mind as a woman from the Shadow Court approaches with a goblet in hand, her smoke-like hair billowing with every step.

"Your Majesty," she purrs, holding the cup out to me. The liquid inside shimmers faintly, reflecting the dim light like liquid starlight. "A gift from my court. May it signify our humble allegiance to you."

I force a smile, my mind racing. Say no. Say it nicely, but say no.

"I appreciate your kindness," I say, keeping my voice steady, "but I must decline. It would be improper for me to accept such a gesture when I have yet to know your court fully."

The woman's eyes flash with something unreadable, but she dips into a shallow bow before retreating.

Did I offend her? Did I avoid offending her? Who the hell knows with these Fae?

I've managed to keep my composure, and aside from the attempted marriage proposal, it seems to be going well. As long as I can keep myself from having an orgasm at the fucking table.

That would be an embarrassment I'd never live down.

"Hey, the appetizers were so delicious she creamed all over her chair."

At once, the tables are served our first course of the night. Orion acknowledges the lesser Fae with a nod, but I notice no one else.

Recalling how shocking my thanks to Elowen was, I offer a gentle nod of gratitude to the lesser Fae who serves me and watch the appreciation bloom in their eyes at my simple gesture.

I glance down at my bowl of soup. The delicate garnish —a tender flower with petals that reflect the moonlight— floats on top like an artist's flourish.

I select what I think is the correct spoon and dip it gently into the thick, pumpkin-colored soup.

Before I can take a bite, Mor sits up so abruptly that I pause, my spoon hovering between me and the bowl.

Her nostrils flare, and her crimson eyes narrow as she turns her head slowly toward me.

The tension in her body is palpable, her hand gripping the edge of the table like a vice.

Before I can process her shift in demeanor, she's gone in a swirl of shadow, reappearing beside me so suddenly that I jolt back in my seat.

"What the—" My spoon clatters down into the bowl.

Mor leans down, her inhuman eyes flicking from my face to the bowl in front of me. She sniffs the soup, her expression darkening as she straightens and locks eyes with Orion.

"Nightshade blossom," she says, her voice low and clipped.

Orion's reaction is immediate. Shadows ripple around him, his power surging outward in a suffocating wave that makes the air heavy.

The room darkens, the ethereal light dimming as if the very life of the hall has been snuffed out.

The hum of conversation dies, replaced by a hushed, uneasy silence.

The strength of his magic pulses against me, and I want to open my legs and ride the sensation until pleasure washes over me as powerfully as the abilities he controls.

Damn this Beltane Day, I mutter under my breath, my heart pounding as I witness the raw force of his abilities for the first time.

It's terrifying, but there's a part of me—an infuriating part—that feels drawn to it, like a moth to flame, wanting to see more of it.

Orion rises from his chair, his movements slow and deliberate, his silver eyes blazing as they take in my bowl of soup. I look at the bowls next to me.

The others have a garnish, but mine is the only one with this particular flower.

His voice is calm, but there's an edge to it that promises violence as he lifts his eyes, scanning the room.

"Who prepared this?"

Silence is a heavy blanket over the assembly as none dare move, much less breathe an answer.

The shriek of Orion's sword rings across the room as his powerful voice booms.

"Who dares try to poison Avalon's chosen queen?"

My mouth drops as I look at the innocent-looking soup. Slowly, I push the bowl away from me.

Mor remains next to me, her growl so low I think I may be the only one to hear it as she too searches the room for a guilty party.

An older Fae stands, his hands raised in placation.

"Your Grace, it's been ages since we've entertained a mortal. The garnish is harmless to us. I'm sure it was a simple oversight."

"Harmless," Orion repeats, his tone ice-cold. "To you."

The elder Fae falters under Orion's stare, his confidence wavering.

"I do respect you, Eldrin," Orion continues, his voice dropping lower, more menacing. "But make no mistake—I will rip your heart from your chest and let you watch its last beat if harm comes to the queen."

A collective shudder runs through the room as Orion's gaze sweeps over the gathered guests.

"If anyone harms her inside these castle walls," he continues, his voice a blade slicing through the thick silence, "you will answer to me."

Mor, ever watchful, keeps her piercing gaze on the Fae, her crimson eyes sweeping over the crowd like twin daggers.

Slowly, she eases back to her chair, her movements deliberate. The clank of her spoon against her bowl is the first noise to break the heavy silence, signaling an unspoken command to the others.

Tentatively, the rest of the hall resumes their meals, the murmur of conversation gradually rebuilding like a fragile bridge.

But I can't stop watching Orion.

He picks up his bowl and strides the length of the ludicrously long table, his dark cloak trailing behind him like a living shadow. Each step is purposeful, predatory, and my breath hitches despite myself.

I should be pissed. I should hate how he can command attention with a flick of his wrist or a single step.

But instead, my body betrays me—a treacherous heat blooming in my chest as he gets closer.

Several feet away, his molten-silver gaze finally locks with mine. It hits me like a wave, knocking the air from my lungs. I grip the edge of the table to steady myself, my pulse racing so loud I'm sure the entire room can hear it.

When he stops behind me, he sets the bowl down with a quiet finality. His hand brushes my chair as he leans in close, his mouth mere inches from my ear.

His scent wraps around me—leather, cedarwood, and something raw that makes my already frayed nerves snap.

"Apologies, my queen," he murmurs, his voice a low, velvety rumble that vibrates through every inch of me.

I close my eyes.

He grips my chair, scooting me forward toward the table with maddening ease. The movement is subtle, yet the vibrations jolt through me like lightning.

My sensitive core clenches, the relentless teasing of this night pushing me to my limit.

His musky scent consumes me, and his deep voice settles into my bones, igniting something I refuse to name in this crowded hall.

I grip the table with one hand, the other clutching the edge of the chair like it's my only anchor.

My teeth press against my bottom lip, desperate to hold back the treacherous sound threatening to escape.

But it's too much.

A quiet moan slips past my lips, so soft it could have been mistaken for a breath—except Orion hears it.

His eyes blaze with a sudden, scorching intensity, silver burning like molten fire as he looks at me. A flicker of triumph, of knowing, crosses his face, and my traitorous body flushes under his gaze.

What the fuck is happening to me?

CHAPTER 23

A moan.

My queen, who wields her defiance like a blade, moans softly at the simple sensation of a chair moving forward.

Interesting.

I lean closer, my hand brushing against her arm. Her skin pebbles instantly under my touch, delicate goose-bumps spreading like a ripple.

She's trying so hard to keep her composure, but I see through her. I've watched her all night. She's unraveling, thread by delicious thread.

"Fascinating," I murmur, letting my finger trail slowly up the length of her bare arm.

Her sharp intake of breath, the faint quiver in her shoulders—every reaction is etched into my mind. I want to push her further, to see how far this intoxicating dance will go before she breaks completely.

But I won't. Not here. Not with a room full of High Fae watching.

Straightening, I smooth my expression into something

neutral and offer her my hand. "Your Majesty," I say, my voice low enough for her ears alone. "If you'll excuse us."

Tana looks at me, confusion flickering behind her fire-filled eyes, but she takes my hand nonetheless. She's warm, the pulse in her neck beating like the hooves of the fastest shadowmare.

I ignore the whispers and few stares that follow us, but Tana tracks the moans of pleasure from a female Fae who is being pleasured by her mate's hand beneath the neighboring table.

I push open the heavy wooden doors and follow as she exits the suffocating room. The air is thick with the faint scent of jasmine, heady and intoxicating, like the essence of Beltane itself.

I know what my queen needs, and the Solarium will be more than happy to serve her.

"Perhaps Hypnos did not explain our customs well enough," I say, releasing her hand as she falls in step beside me.

The defiant tilt of her chin is already in place. "What customs?"

"Do not blame him. He does not participate. This day marks the start of a new cycle of fertility. It is a celebration of abundance and life."

Her eyes narrow, suspicion glinting in their depths. "An abundance of life, hmm? Is that why everyone out there is acting like they're in a damned orgy?"

I chuckle, the sound low and rumbling. "You are perceptive."

"Oh my God," she groans, realization dawning. "Everyone is horny."

The corner of my mouth lifts. "Not everyone."

Her brow furrows as she studies me, speculation in her gaze before she understands. "Mor wasn't affected. Why is she the only one?"

"She is not Fae, nor is she from this realm," I reply simply, my tone measured.

She crosses her arms, clearly trying to piece it all together. "Well, neither am I."

"Ah," I say, stopping our path and consuming her space until she backs up, hitting the wall behind her. "But there is something about you. Something... undeniable. The land chose you for a reason, my queen."

Her breath catches, and I see it again—that subtle wave of reaction. She stiffens slightly, her skin pebbled where my shadow lingers.

"I, for one, can't wait to find out what that something is."

She clears her throat, but her voice still wavers slightly. "How come you aren't affected, then?"

I lean in, close enough that my breath brushes against her ear. "Who says I'm not?" I whisper, taking in the subtle scent of lavender that lingers on her dark skin.

The sound that escapes her lips—a mix between a sigh and a moan—is like music. Her eyes flutter closed, her defenses slipping for just a moment.

I take a step back, my gaze lingering on her flushed cheeks, her slightly parted lips.

"Come."

With my commanding word, her eyes snap open, that defiance blazing once again. I do not dare hold back the mischief in my grin at the reactions she is feeding me.

They are too delicious to ignore.

The corridor leading to the Solarium is thick with the energy of Beltane, its intoxicating pull heavier with every step.

The faint sounds drifting through the air—soft moans, murmured laughter, the occasional hushed gasp—grow louder as we near the curtain that separates this sacred space from the rest of the castle.

I stop just outside the shimmering fabric, my hand hovering near the edge. I glance at Tana. Her expression is guarded, though her chin is lifted in that defiant way she wears like armor.

This is likely nothing like the mortal world she's accustomed to, and while she hides it well, I sense her curiosity.

"Are you sure you can handle this?" I ask, keeping my voice steady. I am not mocking her.

I genuinely wonder if she understands what lies on the other side of this threshold.

"The Solarium is no mere room; it's a crucible of raw, unfiltered desire. The complete essence of Beltane flows heavily within this space, and none can resist their carnal needs once they enter."

She arches a brow at me, her lips twitching. "It's not my first rodeo."

Rodeo. The word is unfamiliar, but I gather her meaning. A corner of my mouth lifts. "Oh, but it is."

Her eyes flash with challenge, and she smirks. "Well then, giddy up, cowboy."

I blink, thrown off for the briefest moment. "I do not know what that means."

Her smirk widens, and she shakes her head. It's one of the few genuinely entertained looks she has given me since her arrival. "Of course, you don't."

There's a tension in the air between us, sharp and electric, but I let it hang as I pull the curtain aside. The sounds inside swell immediately, the heady atmosphere rushing out like a tide, wrapping around us.

The faintest trace of a smile touches my lips as I follow her inside, watching every careful step she takes.

Tana has no idea what awaits her, yet I see the flicker of curiosity in her eyes, the hunger she doesn't yet understand but can't deny.

A mated pair, clearly overcome with the season's pull, stands near the entrance. Their clothing is already half-shed as they press against each other, mouths locked in unrelenting hunger.

Their hips grind in rhythm, oblivious to the world beyond their connection.

Tana glanced their way, her steps slowing as she takes in the unabashed display of desire.

Further in, a male Fae sprawls on the floor, his head thrown back, his body taut with anticipation.

A female straddles him, riding him with fervent energy, her movements sharp and deliberate as she chases her release. The male clutches her hips, his face etched with both pleasure and restraint as he holds on, determined to let her take the lead.

No one acknowledges our entrance. No bows for the prince. No reverent greetings for the future queen.

The Fae here are consumed by the shifting season, their focus lost in the pleasures of the Solarium. As we move deeper into the space, Tana's gaze flickers over the scene, her eyes wide with wonder and something darker, more primal.

A female lies on a table, her wrists and ankles bound to a spreading bar that keeps her open and exposed. Her body trembles as a male Fae ravishes her with unyielding precision, his tongue and fingers driving her into shuddering cries.

Behind her, another male thrusts into her mouth with calculated power, his gritted teeth belying the control he exerts.

Across from them, a third sits leisurely, stroking himself as he watches the table with a contented smirk.

"He prefers to watch, as his mate is... very well cared for," I murmur, my voice low and deliberate.

Tana startles at the sound, her hand flying to her chest as though I've snapped her from a trance.

She turns to me, lips parted, cheeks flushed. For a moment, it's as if she forgot I was even here.

But her attention doesn't stay on me for long, though I wish it would; her gaze is pulled back to the scene before her, her curiosity unabated.

"Will the other High Fae be coming here—Liona?" Tana

clears her throat, but I don't believe it is because she needs to. "Will Liona be meeting you in here? I can find—"

How curious.

"No, Liona will not be joining the Beltane festivities in the Solarium." I mark this in my memory to explore further.

We continue weaving through the space, and her hand absently rises to her neck. Her fingers rub slow circles along her skin, a movement so subtle it would go unnoticed by anyone else. But I see it.

I see the way her breath quickens, the way her pulse flutters at the base of her throat.

She's fighting it, but the energy of the Solarium is seeping into her, warming her blood and igniting a fire she won't be able to ignore for much longer.

I can't deny the effect it's having on me as well.

My body has been wound tight since I heard the symphony she and her maidens sang this morning, and now... now, I am throbbing, my arousal a persistent ache that presses against the confines of my leather pants.

Every glance at her, every brush of her hand against her skin, sends a jolt straight through me.

We pass a male lounging on a rich velvet chaise, his legs spread wide to accommodate the partner driving into him with unrelenting force.

The male throws his head back, his moans unrestrained, his throat stretched as he devours another Fae's cock.

The sounds, the sights—it's a masterpiece of indulgence, a celebration of connection that leaves nothing to the imagination.

Tana's steps slow, her eyes locked on the scene, and I can see the flush creeping down her neck.

Her hand clutches the fabric of her dress as though it's the only tether she has to keep herself grounded.

I don't say anything, but the corner of my mouth quirks upward as I watch her, waiting for her to acknowledge what this night truly is.

Her gaze darts to me briefly, and I see it in her eyes—the mix of defiance and vulnerability that's become so uniquely her.

She doesn't speak, but the tension between us is electric, an unspoken challenge simmering beneath the surface.

Whatever she thought Beltane would be, she now understands it is far more than just a festival.

It's a living, breathing embodiment of the realm itself, and it is calling to her in ways she never expected.

The moment her gasp breaks the ambient hum of moans and soft cries, I know what's caught her attention.

Tana's eyes widen as she takes in the vast circular bed, its massive size swallowing the center of the Solarium like a decadent sunken oasis.

A dozen or more bodies writhe together, their movements fluid as though tethered by an unspoken rhythm.

The moonlight washes over them, casting a silvery glow on sweat-slicked skin, a river of pleasure ebbing and flowing as they chase their highs.

Her steps falter as her gaze zeroes in on familiar faces among the chaos. On a smaller bed to the left, Elowen is lost to her mate, her cries punctuating the air as he thrusts into her from behind.

Her face is buried between Brynja's thighs, and the sight of Brynja's body arched in a dramatic bow, trembling on the edge of release, makes the air in the room crackle with heat.

"Yes, Wen. I'm coming again," Brynja screams, her voice hoarse and raw as Elowen works her with a hunger that leaves nothing untouched.

My attention shifts as Tana's head tilts, her focus drawn to the frontmost bed where Thalindra kneels like a living statue of lust.

The only adornments on her body are the gleaming silver disks over her nipples. Her legs are spread wide, her fingers circling her clit in languid, deliberate movements that make even me inhale deeply.

Across from her, her mate sits in a plush chair, his gaze ravenous as he devours the spectacle she gifts him.

Tana's breath quickens, her lip caught between her teeth as her chest rises and falls with growing hunger. The pull between them is almost magnetic, and I know she's teetering on the edge of surrender.

My hands move instinctively, sliding around her waist until my palm spreads low across her abdomen.

I pull her flush against me, her soft curves molding to my body.

She leans back, her head finding my chest as her ass presses firmly into me, igniting a fire I've kept banked since we entered the Solarium.

My voice is low and deliberate as I speak into her ear, my breath grazing her skin. "You can do anything you want in here, my queen."

Her soft moan vibrates against my chest, a sound I've become addicted to.

My fingers trace slow, deliberate lines down her thigh, finding the glamoured holster I had crafted for her earlier. With a deft motion, I loosen the clasp and slide the blade free, feeling her pulse quicken beneath my hand.

"You can have anyone you desire," I murmur, my lips skimming the curve of her neck.

The movement catches Thalindra's eye, and she turns, her glossy lips parting in a smile so sinful it could corrupt the stars.

Her gaze locks with Tana's, her hands trailing sensually over her own body as she steps down from the bed with the grace of a predator approaching its prey.

Her hips sway, her steps deliberate as she moves through the writhing figures around her. She pauses, her hands settling on the shoulders of another female.

She leans in, her lips brushing the other woman's ear, her gaze never leaving Tana's.

The second female turns, identical in every way to Thalindra, save for the gleam of darker mischief in her eyes. Together, they approach Tana, their movements like a dance choreographed by desire itself.

"You have a twin sister?" Tana's voice is thick with arousal, her gaze flickering between the pair.

"Serelith," I answer, watching the way the name settles on her lips, watching the way her fingers curl slightly at her sides. I give her a gentle nudge forward.

Her steps are in no way hesitant, her desire growing under the combined intensity of the twins' presence.

The sisters reach her, their hands moving with reverence, removing the sheer fabrics that give the illusion of clothing.

Tana's brown skin gleams under the Beltane moonlight, her curves radiant, her nipples tightening into pebbled peaks as the cool night air kisses her body.

My chest tightens, my restraint slipping with each passing moment. She is perfection incarnate, and the way the twins handle her only adds to the ache building within me.

I step away, moving toward a settee positioned directly across from them. Her eyes track my every movement, her pupils blown wide as her gaze follows me.

She watches intently as I shrug off my cloak, hanging it neatly on the edge of the chair. My vest follows, then my tunic, leaving my chest bare for her to see.

Her eyes trace the lines of my muscles, lingering on the deep scar that slices across my torso.

I sit, leaning back casually as I unbutton my leather pants, my cock straining against the fabric but remaining restrained.

My gaze locks with hers, and I quirk an eyebrow, daring her to let go, to surrender to the night and all it promises.

Tana doesn't move at first.

Not away. Not toward.

She stands there, bare and exposed, though she does not shrink beneath the weight of my stare.

If anything, she rises to it, her chin tilting upward, her spine straightening as if preparing for battle.

Thalindra steps behind her, her hands skimming along Tana's waist, pulling her back into the curve of her body.

Serelith kneels before her, pressing soft, open-mouthed kisses along her thighs, her hands spreading gently across Tana's hips.

Tana's breathing is uneven, her lips parting, but she still holds herself firm.

I grin, slow and knowing. "Fascinating," I murmur, watching her fight herself even now, watching her resist what she so clearly craves.

Serelith's hands travel upward, brushing over the curve of Tana's ass, her nails dragging lightly over the sensitive skin.

Thalindra's lips ghost along the shell of Tana's ear, whispering words I cannot hear, but I see the effect they have. The slight tremble in Tana's thighs.

The way her fingers twitch at her sides as if warring with the urge to reach out and take what she wants.

She wants control. She wants to be the one commanding, dictating the pace, setting the rules.

But here, under the weight of Beltane, of magic, of desire —there are no rules.

I shift slightly, my hand dragging down the length of my thigh, not touching, not yet, but enough to see the flicker of movement in her eyes as she follows the gesture.

She is watching me.

She wants me to watch her.

But she is afraid of what it will mean if she does.

Thalindra's hands move to Tana's shoulders, trailing down her arms before capturing her wrists.

She lifts them, guiding them around Serelith's head, resting them lightly on the twin's scalp, a silent permission.

Tana exhales slowly, her fingers slipping through Serelith's hair, gripping just slightly as the woman's lips move higher along her inner thigh.

I watch as her chest rises and falls with each breath, her body caught between two forces, between the need to hold on and the craving to let go.

Her eyes flick to mine again, something desperate flashing there, something asking. I do not move. I do not tell her what to do.

This is her choice.

She lets out a slow, unsteady breath, her lashes fluttering closed for a moment. Then, her fingers tighten in Serelith's hair, guiding her exactly where she wants her.

A quiet, satisfied hum comes from the woman kneeling before her, and I watch as Tana's lips part, her body tensing before melting between them, surrendering.

A queen surrendering to her own hunger.

To Beltane.

To the night.

And gods, I have never seen anything more beautiful.

CHAPTER 24
Tana

Orion's gaze burns into me like wildfire, and all I want is to feel the heat consume me. He's a force, a magnet drawing me in from only a few paces away, his eyes tracking my every movement with relentless intensity.

I glide my hand up Thalindra's stomach, my fingers brushing against the curve of her chest, and his eyes never leave me.

When I cup her soft, full breast, my thumb grazing her hard nipple, his gaze follows my every shift, every subtle touch.

It's the tremor in Thalindra's body that finally breaks my focus from him. Let him watch.

This hunger has been aching within me all day, and I'm starving.

I take a moment, allowing the warmth and tenderness of her feminine beauty to settle over me before I claim her lips.

The kiss is soft and deliberate, a world apart from a man's caress, which can be claiming and possessive.

This is the kiss of two women, speaking the same

language without words, embracing the unique power we hold in our sensuality. It's sacred—accepting.

Serelith reaches forward, her hands gently caressing me, her lips seeking out bare skin.

My shoulder, my arm, the side of my breast pressed against Thalindra as our bodies merge, molding together.

I break the kiss, and Serelith gently turns my chin, her tongue sweeping across my lips, demanding that I part them.

I give in easily, welcoming her as Thalindra takes my nipple into her mouth. Serelith swallows the sound of my pleasure as her hand slides between my legs, exploring the arousal she finds there.

She pulls her fingers away, tasting the remnants of me.

"Sister, you were not exaggerating," she murmurs, her voice ringing with the same melodic quality as Thalindra's. "Our queen tastes divine."

A male steps forward, his presence commanding. He reaches for Serelith, turning her into his embrace as she wraps her arms around him, and he meets her lips with a fervor that speaks of hunger.

I use the moment to pull Thalindra back toward the bed, settling at the edge as I draw her to me.

My dark gaze shifts to Orion, locking with his, taking in the tightness of his leather pants and the bulge straining against them.

Then my attention returns to Thalindra. I gaze up at her —a silent promise in my eyes—ready to honor her body in ways that will leave her trembling.

I lift her leg, resting it over my shoulder, and Orion's eyes remain fixed on me as I lean in.

The first taste of her is intoxicating—her sweetness flooding my senses as my fingers grip her soft curves.

Orion shifts slightly, lowering the zipper of his pants, giving relief to the pressure building within him.

I claim her, my tongue tasting, devouring as she writhes against me, her body responding to every flick, every pull.

Our eyes remain locked—Orion's gaze never faltering, watching, waiting.

The intensity between us thickens until, at last, I catch sight of his cock, freed and impossibly large.

I nearly whimper against Thalindra's body, my need for Orion intensifying with each passing second.

His large hand wraps around his shaft, moving slowly, deliberately—each stroke drawn out to torment.

His thumb circles the head of his cock before he sucks the precum from his skin, his gaze locked on me like a challenge.

Thalindra shifts beneath me, her body reacting, and I return my focus to her. Her fingers dive into my hair, urging me to stay as she rides my tongue, her release filling my senses as I suck on her clit.

I savor every drop, tasting the sweet culmination of her pleasure. When she's spent, she gently takes my chin, guiding my face to hers.

Though we're the same height when standing, she seems to enjoy looking down at me now, as I sit before her.

"Fuck my mouth, Your Grace?" she asks, a hint of pleading in her voice that I would never deny.

A smirk plays at the corners of my lips, and her expression shifts in response. She positions herself on the bed, perfectly aligned for me to straddle her, ensuring Orion has a clear view of everything.

As I lower myself, I feel the heat of his eyes, watching every move, every shift.

Thalindra begins to lick, and I feel Orion's gaze on my face, watching for any sign, any reaction from me.

His desperation for the details of what unfolds is palpable, and I can feel him—firm and eager—as he strokes himself at the sight of a lover tasting me.

I begin to move, the rush of arousal flooding through me, pooling low in my belly.

Damn, she knows how to eat pussy, and for a moment, I have to close my eyes, surrendering to the pleasure, just feeling the soft flick of her tongue as it teases my clit.

"Eyes on me, my queen." Orion's voice is a deep command, a sharp whip in the air. Without thought, I obey, my gaze returning to his, the pull of his presence undeniable.

The male who captured Serelith releases her, and they look between Orion and me.

"Look at your mate pleasing our queen, lover," Serelith purrs at him, then clicks her tongue, looking at Orion. "Our prince looks quite alone."

She bites his bottom lip, pulling it away as he whimpers for her.

"Crawl. Beg to swallow his cock."

Serelith climbs up beside me, her mouth finding my nipple, her hand gripping my ass as she pulls me closer.

I move my hips, matching the rhythm as Thalindra's mouth works its magic, her tongue flicking against my clit with precision.

The male approaches Orion, crawling to the Prince of Avalon on his knees, eager to serve.

A surge of pleasure makes me tighten, and Thalindra pauses beneath me, her head turning as she glances behind her.

"Our lady likes that," she comments, nodding toward Orion and the male, who is pulling Orion toward the edge of the settee. "She is drenching me in her arousal."

Serelith leans in, her voice a whisper against my ear. "You want to watch the prince get his long cock sucked by our mate, Your Grace?" Her tongue traces the shell of my ear before she bites down gently, her teeth sharp against the sensitive flesh.

"Yes," I breathe out heavily.

As Thalindra sucks harder on my clit, I let out a moan that matches the grunt from Orion.

Their mate wraps his mouth around Orion's cock, teasing the head before plunging down the shaft, taking him deep.

Serelith continues her assault on my senses—her lips on my neck, her fingers on my nipple, her tongue in my ear—as I ride Thalindra's face.

She slides two fingers into me, and I gasp, quickening my movements as my release begins to build, pushing toward the edge.

The tension in the air pulls me higher, to a peak I've yet to fall from.

Orion's eyes are nearly black, his pupils wide with need, as the male before him devours him completely.

Orion's grip tightens on the male's dark hair, his hips thrusting forward as the male descends on his shaft, a primal connection between them.

I can feel it building inside me, the crest of pleasure rising, and I want to fall with him, to collide in that wave together.

We open our mouths, the noises of our pleasure escaping us as the Fae devour us both.

A gut-wrenching scream nearby rips through the air, shattering the moment. The glass ceiling of the solarium around us splinters as darkness rains down.

CHAPTER 25

The sound shatters the air first—a piercing crack that reverberates through the solarium like thunder.

Then, the glass.

Splinters rain down, refracting the Beltane moonlight into a thousand sharp-edged stars. The air is filled with a sudden rush of wind and the collective gasp of the Fae within.

I move without thinking.

Tana is my singular focus, and my shadows coil tightly around us as I push her to the ground, shielding her with my body.

My darkness flings my cape to me, and I cover us, making sure none of the shards can harm her.

A Fae can heal wounds quickly, but not our mortal queen.

Her sharp intake of breath is lost beneath the chaos, but I feel her fists grab at my cloak, her pulse hammering like a war drum beneath her skin.

"Stay down," I command, my voice low and steady despite the rage building within me.

"My knife," she huffs, wriggling beneath me as her hand darts to her thigh—then my hand, recalling that I removed it. She grasps the blade from its sheath before I can stop her.

"You're not getting up," I grit out between my teeth, my shadows pressing more firmly around her, pinning her in place. Of course, she immediately argues, as if she anticipated my refusal and relished the fight.

"You're not my fucking boss."

"Mor!" I summon her without hesitation, my voice cutting through the rising panic in the room.

The room stills for a heartbeat before her arrival. A surge of power ripples through the solarium, and then she is here, shadow-jumping into the space with Hypnos at her side.

But this isn't Mor, who shares meals in the dining hall or banters in sardonic grumbles. No.

This being is darkness incarnate: The Morrigan.

Her transformation is immediate and horrifying. Her skin darkens to a sickly yellow hue, mottled and uneven, as though death itself is crawling across her form.

Her hair, once stark and straight, now drips with viscous black tar that pools in small puddles around her feet. Her eyes—usually deep red—now burn an unholy yellow, glowing like twin suns of malice and power.

The air around her vibrates with a soundless hum of destruction and hunger.

Her voice, when she speaks, is worse than her appearance—a cacophony of whispers and screams, like countless souls speaking through her at once.

"The darkness is here," she proclaims, her many voices cutting through the chaos.

I know she is not speaking of herself but of the blight that is slowly consuming the realm of the Fae—the very darkness that will one day snuff out my own life.

It is an impossible thought. Yet I can't deny it.

Tana looks up, her wide eyes darting in all directions as she scans the scene. Her demeanor shifts against me, her instincts driving her to search for threats, form a plan, and attack.

Admirable but irresponsible.

The obscurity is a swirling cloud of darkness, impossible to catch, even for us Fae, who wield elemental power as easily as we breathe. I fear we may be powerless against it.

"Mor, the wards."

"They are holding," she answers. "Someone opened a door."

My fury combusts into a tempest of rage, and lightning crawls along my skin, aching to be unleashed.

One of our guests is an ally of the disease that swarms our realm, and they have endangered our queen with this act of treason.

I'll have their heads for this. But first, I need to get Tana to safety.

My shadows spread across the castle. This cloud is centralized only here. A shiver rolls down my spine a second before Tana's eyes widen.

It's here for her.

"Oh my god," she breathes, her voice barely audible over the tension crackling in the room.

My head snaps, following her gaze, locking onto

Elowen's mate. His body trembles violently, a deep, guttural sound rumbling from his throat.

His eyes, once vibrant and filled with the glow of Beltane, have turned into hollow black voids, tar-like tears dripping down his cheeks.

The handmaid is desperate to help her mate and is by his side on her knees, tears streaming down her face as she screams her pleas for help.

"Elowen," Tana whispers, her voice breaking with dread as the transformation takes hold.

The male's skin ripples unnaturally, as though something is crawling beneath it, trying to break free.

His hands clutch at his chest, claws sprouting from his fingertips, tearing through his flesh. His mouth opens in a silent scream. His skin rips, elongating his gaping maw in a sickening change.

Jagged fangs emerge from his gums, coated red in his blood.

When the transformation completes, it is as though his body has been turned inside out—veins and sinew exposed, his form grotesque and warped, an abomination of what he once was.

"Help them!" Tana yells, her voice cutting through the bedlam—a mix of anger and desperation that makes my shadows tighten reflexively around us.

She tries to surge forward, to throw herself into the chaos, but I grab her arm, holding her firmly in place.

"We need to get her out of here," I bark, my voice low and sharp as the darkness twists around us, coiling into a protective barrier.

The male Fae, now a grotesque, unrecognizable monster, snarls viciously.

His head snaps toward his mate, and for the briefest moment, something flickers in his soulless eyes.

Then it's gone, replaced by an unrelenting, mindless hunger.

"Elowen!" Tana screams, her panic raw and laced with fury. She struggles against my hold, but I can't let her go.

The male Fae lunges at Elowen, his claws outstretched, his jaw unhinged in an impossible, grotesque arc. It shouldn't be possible.

Every fiber of Fae magic forbids such an act—mates are sacred, their bonds woven into the very essence of our beings.

Yet this darkness seems to twist and corrupt even our most fundamental truths. It has erased all that makes this male Fae and replaced it with something unholy.

"Elowen, run!" Tana's voice is frantic, but Elowen's cries for mercy are met with brutal indifference.

Her mate—no, the creature he's become—slams her to the ground. His claws rake across her flesh as she desperately tries to crawl away.

"Tana, enough!" I snap, yanking her back just as she wrestles against me. "Do you want to die here?"

Her wild eyes burn with defiance, but I don't have time to argue.

I pull my cloak from the shadows, wrapping it tightly around her trembling, naked body. The fabric is enchanted, laced with my magic, but it can't protect her from everything.

I glance at Hypnos, who's already forcing a cornered cluster of beasts to turn on each other with his powers.

"Hypnos, get the queen out of here!" My voice cuts through the air like a blade.

"No!" Tana fights against my hold, her voice shaking with fury. "I'm not running! I'm not leaving them to die!"

"Stupid mortal," I growl under my breath. She doesn't understand the stakes.

This isn't about bravery—it's about survival. And she doesn't realize how fragile her life is here.

Chaos erupts all around us.

More Fae succumb to the darkness, their bodies contorting into grotesque forms.

One male grows additional limbs, each clawed hand lashing out at anything within reach. Another's jaw stretches unnaturally wide, the maw lined with jagged teeth as he lets out a guttural roar.

The sounds of snapping bones and tearing flesh fill the solarium as the once-bright chamber becomes a battlefield.

My shadows coil and lash out, forming barriers to keep the beasts at bay. But the darkness is relentless, seeping through cracks like smoke, twisting reality with every passing moment.

Tana's breathing quickens beside me, her gaze darting to Thalindra, who is trying to fight off her mate as the sickness overtakes him.

The room shifts again, and I feel it—finally recognizing the fractures in the magic around us.

It is the magic of their mate bond snapping.

Thalindra's mate lunges, his teeth sinking into her neck.

The sound of tearing flesh and her strangled scream pierce the air.

"No!" Tana cries out, but the nightmare doesn't end there.

The creature turns, his tar-like eyes locking onto Serelith. With one massive claw, he grabs her face, the sickening crunch of her skull reverberating through the room as her body collapses beside her sister's.

The beast turns its gaze on Tana, letting out an inhuman, guttural cry before lunging at her.

"Not my queen."

My shadows lash out like whips, restraining the beast in an instant.

But a flash of silver arcs through the air as Tana's enchanted blade strikes true, severing the creature's head in a single, precise motion.

The runes etched into the weapon flare brightly before retreating to their dormant state.

Tana stares at the blade in her hand, her chest heaving as she steadies herself.

"Get her out of here, Hypnos!" I bark, my voice carrying over the din.

Tana whirls on me, her fury palpable. "Don't you dare, Orion!"

She sidesteps another beast that charges at her, her movements sharp and instinctive.

But the beasts aren't attacking at random anymore.

They're targeting her.

The darkness is drawn to her, and I won't let it have her.

"Your handmaids are gone!" I snap, my voice laced with the authority she refuses to heed. "If you stay, you'll be next."

The weight of my words doesn't register; she's too blinded by anger and adrenaline.

"I'm not running!" she yells, her voice cracking. "I won't—"

"Now, Hypnos!"

My command booms through the solarium, and Hypnos doesn't hesitate. His magic surges forward, his calm demeanor never faltering as he approaches her.

"Apologies, Your Grace," he says, his voice a soothing balm amid the chaos.

Tana opens her mouth to protest, but her words are cut short as Hypnos' power washes over her. She slumps into unconsciousness, her body falling limp as he catches her.

I weave my shadows into my cloak, wrapping her in an impenetrable shield.

Hypnos vanishes into the shadows with her, his presence gone in an instant.

I know he will take her to safety, but the thought of leaving her unguarded for even a moment gnaws at me.

I turn back to the room, my focus narrowing. The Morrigan's tar-like shadows are consuming the beasts with ruthless precision.

Her voice cuts through the din like a death call, whispering ancient incantations of her long-forgotten realm.

"Target the darkness. I'll get the beasts," I call out, and we unleash absolute night upon the solarium.

The Fae within have either fled or been turned—and none of them will leave alive.

Tonight's battle is far from over, but Tana is safe—for now.

And I'll make damn sure the darkness pays for every drop of blood spilled here.

CHAPTER 26
Tana

Orion is a fucking asshat.

The sharp thud of my boots echoes through the stone corridors of Starfall Castle as I stalk through its halls. Every step feels like an outlet for the simmering anger roiling within me.

My cream-colored tunic clings to me, its soft fabric a poor match for the heat of my temper, and my trousers allow me to move freely, unencumbered.

My hand tightens on the hilt of my knife, ready to jab it into that motherfucker's throat when I find him.

I woke up this morning in my bed, his cloak snuggled around me. It took about five seconds for me to remember the chaos of the night before, and I surged out of bed with vengeance brewing in my stomach.

Turning a sharp corner, I barely notice the startled Fae guard who steps quickly out of my path. His whispers follow me, buzzing at the edges of my hearing, but as I look back, he is gone.

Whatever. Let them talk. Let them wonder why their mortal queen looks ready to spit fire.

"Have you seen Orion?" I demand of a ruby-haired Fae arranging flowers in a large vase.

She startles, giving me a quick curtsy. "The prince regent is in the west wing, Your Majesty."

"Thanks," I mutter before striding away, my fists clenched at my sides as my heart pounds in several erratic beats.

I hear him before I see him—his deep voice carrying through the stone halls. Calm. Controlled. Like nothing happened.

Like last night wasn't a descent into pandemonium, where people I cared about—people I trusted—died.

I step into the doorway of a study, my arms crossed over my chest. He's by the window, moonlight tracing the sharp lines of his profile.

His hair is brushed back, a few stray strands defying the neatness of his appearance.

Shadows coil faintly at his feet, a constant reminder of his power, and they swirl toward me.

"Starling," he says without turning, sipping something steaming and hot.

"Don't 'starling' me," I snap, stepping fully into the room. "What the hell was that last night?"

He turns, his silver eyes meeting mine, and there's a flicker of annoyance there—faint but unmistakable. "That was me keeping you alive."

"Keeping me alive?" I repeat, my voice rising. My eyes flick to the small scratch on his cheek before moving back.

"You knocked me out, Orion. I could've helped! I could've done something!"

"You could've died," he says flatly, stepping toward me, setting his goblet down upon the table. His tone is sharp, cutting through the space between us.

"Do you have any idea what happens if the darkness takes you? If you're consumed?"

My chest tightens, and not just from his words. His presence feels overwhelming in a way I've not felt before. His shadows curl closer as he steps forward.

But I hold my ground, refusing to back down.

"I'm not some fragile doll for you to lock away! I've spent most of my life with soldiers—training them, leading them, fighting with them. I'm not a dainty princess. I'm a fucking weapon."

I throw back, my voice trembling with fury at his underestimation of me.

"And besides—my life was already meant to be cut short! Don't think you're noble for prolonging some nonexistent lifespan for me."

His steps falter, his brows furrowing. "What are you talking about?"

I clench my fists, debating whether to let this part of me see the light. "I'm not going to live a long life, Orion. My heart—"

A knot in my throat makes me force the words. "I have a heart condition. It's only a matter of time before it claims me. So you may as well let me join the fight when I fucking want to.

This will go much easier if you do, *Your Majesty*."

The room suddenly feels colder, his gaze boring into me with an intensity that makes me want to look away.

"You think that settles this?" His voice is low, tight. "You think that justifies throwing yourself into danger?"

I laugh bitterly, throwing my hands up. "It justifies the truth. The realm made a mistake choosing me.

I'm a mortal with a broken heart, Orion.

A queen who might not even live long enough to survive her own trials. How's that for fate? It's a fucking joke—a cruel one."

"The realm makes no mistakes." His expression darkens, shadows flaring briefly at his feet. "You don't understand what's at stake," he says, his voice low and tense.

"This isn't just about you. It's about the realm, the balance of magic, the survival of—"

"Spare me the lecture," I cut him off, stepping closer. "You keep talking about what's at stake, but you won't tell me anything real.

You already put all your faith in me, but you won't even consider that I wasn't supposed to be chosen."

He turns back to me, his eyes flashing with something I can't quite name. For a moment, we're locked in a standoff, the tension between us crackling like a live wire.

"Fine," he says finally, his voice a low growl. "You want answers? Come with me."

Without waiting for a response, Orion strides past me, his shadows trailing behind him like a living, restless cloak.

For a moment, I consider standing my ground, but curiosity and frustration propel me forward.

He moves with purpose, his strides long and unrelenting as I hurry to keep up.

"Where are we going?" I ask, my voice echoing faintly off the narrow stone walls.

"You wanted to know why the realm chose you," he says, his tone clipped. "I'm going to show you."

We descend deeper into the castle, the smooth stone steps turning rough and uneven.

The torchlight grows sparse, casting long, flickering shadows that seem alive. My boots scuff against the stone, the sound stark in the otherwise oppressive silence.

"This feels like the setup to every horror movie ever made," I mutter, more to myself than to him.

He doesn't reply, only stares ahead with a gaze hard as granite.

The tunnel walls widen slightly as we continue, the air shifting from still to alive with faint drafts that tickle my skin.

The stone here is different, etched with carvings I can't make out in the dim light. The place feels ancient—far older than the castle above.

"You're taking me into the forest, aren't you?" I say, my unease growing with each step.

"No," he replies sharply, turning a corner.

Before I can press him further, a sudden rush of wind greets us, cool and bracing. It carries the scent of rain tinged with metal.

The tunnel abruptly opens into a massive stone cavern, the walls stretching high above us and disappearing into shadow.

I stop short, the sheer size of the space stealing my breath.

The ceiling soars overhead, a cathedral of jagged stone glittering faintly with moisture.

In the distance, lightning flashes, illuminating the wide mouth of the cavern that opens out to the night.

This place is as big as an aircraft hangar.

Orion continues on, his long strides carrying him toward the edge of the cavern. I follow with more caution, my boots crunching on loose rock as I take in the massive stone platform.

It juts out like a balcony, overlooking the cliffs of Avalon.

When I step closer, my breath catches.

Far below us, the Misting Lake churns, its waters raging like a tempest. Lightning forks across the dark sky, illuminating the roiling waves.

The mist that always clings to the lake is wild now, swirling and twisting as though alive.

The sight is as beautiful as it is terrifying—a raw display of the realm's untamed power.

"This is definitely not the forest," I say softly, my voice barely audible over the wind.

"No," Orion agrees, his tone heavy. He stands near the edge, his silhouette stark against the storm beyond.

The wind tears at his long cloak, making it ripple as if alive, and I can feel the weight of his presence even with the space between us.

His gaze is fixed on the tempest below, but there's a faraway look in his eyes, like he's seeing something I can't.

Something from the past.

"What is this place?" I ask, stepping closer, my voice lost in the roar of the wind.

"This used to be the heart of Avalon's ancient army," he says, his tone as sharp as the edge of the cliffs. "From here, they defended the realm. They fought... and they fell."

I frown, trying to imagine the space filled with warriors, their battle cries echoing off the stone walls. "What kind of army?"

Orion doesn't answer immediately. Instead, he turns his gaze to me, his silver eyes gleaming in the dim light. "Look behind you."

Confused, I slowly turn, and my breath catches.

The back wall of the cavern is covered in an ancient, massive mural, weathered with time but still achingly vivid.

It spans the entire surface, the artistry breathtaking in its detail.

The center of the mural depicts a line of fierce, winged women, their silver armor catching the faint light that filters into the cavern.

Large, powerful white wings spread behind each of them, their feathers so intricately painted that I swear they might take flight.

On one side of the painting, the warriors charge forward, their weapons raised high, faces set with determination and fire.

But on the other side...

Death and darkness await them.

Shadows rise like a tidal wave, consuming everything in their path. The bodies of fallen warriors litter the battlefield, their wings bloodied and broken.

Young Queen Pandora stands in the center, solemn, her

head cast down as she looks with sorrow at the crown in her hands.

The contrast between the two sides is stark, a grim reminder of the price of war.

I take a step closer, my fingers aching to brush against the cool stone, to trace the edge of one of the wings.

"Valkyrie," I whisper, the word leaving my lips like a memory I don't know I have.

It feels as if that single word could call them to me. Like every set of eyes painted on the stone could turn and look at me.

These are the warriors of Norse mythology—the ones I chose my call sign after.

The ones who walked battlefields, choosing the worthy fallen. And I feel the weight of their judgment still lingering within this cave.

Orion steps closer, his voice low and steady.

"They were Avalon's mightiest warriors—the protectors of this realm. They stood between life and death, wielding power that even the gods respected."

I swallow hard, unable to tear my eyes away from the painting. "What happened to them?"

"They were betrayed," Orion says, his tone laced with a bitterness I've never heard from him before. "One of their own turned against them, opening the gates to the darkness."

I look back at him, my heart sinking. "And now?"

"Now," he says, his jaw tightening, "the darkness has returned. And there are no Valkyrie left to stop it."

The weight of his words presses down on me, but my

eyes are drawn back to the mural, to the fierce determination etched into the warriors' faces.

I can almost hear the echo of their battle cries, feel the energy of their charge.

"And you think I'm supposed to stand in their place?" I ask, my voice barely above a whisper as I tear my eyes from the painting and face Orion. He's a step closer now, so near I can feel his breath against me.

Orion's silver gaze pierces me, his expression unreadable yet heavy with meaning. "It took one Valkyrie to destroy an army," he says evenly.

"To open this realm to a plague that seeks to devour all life. Pandora was the light that fought that darkness, holding it back with every ounce of her being."

The words settle over me like a shroud, the gravity of what he's saying twisting something deep in my chest.

Before I can respond, he steps away from me and gestures for me to follow.

"Come," he says, his voice firm but quieter now, tinged with something I can't quite place. Sadness, perhaps. "There's more you need to see."

I follow Orion back into the tunnel, the oppressive wind outside fading as the stone walls close in around us. The ancient air is damp and heavy, carrying the faint, earthy scent of moss and stone.

The flickering torchlight only adds to the suffocating atmosphere as we descend deeper into the castle.

I don't bother asking where we're going. I know Orion won't answer. His pace is steady, determined. It's like the only part of all this he can control, and he holds onto it as tightly as he can.

The passage narrows, forcing me to walk directly behind him, the rough stone brushing against my shoulders.

The deeper we go, the more the temperature drops, an unnatural chill curling around my skin.

We reach a heavy iron door, its surface pitted and scarred with age. Orion presses his palm to its center, and the metal hums beneath his touch.

A low groan echoes through the tunnel as the door unlocks, swinging inward on rusted hinges.

The air inside is colder, sharper, carrying with it an almost tangible weight.

It's a dungeon.

The narrow hallway stretches ahead, the dim torchlight barely reaching the farthest corners. The cells are empty, their iron bars rusted but still strong.

A cold, oppressive energy lingers in the air, pressing down on my chest like a physical force.

Every step feels heavier, every breath harder to draw.

"What is this place?" I whisper, my voice barely audible over the eerie silence.

Orion doesn't answer immediately. Instead, he leads me to the farthest cell, where the shadows seem darker, deeper.

In the corner, the stone itself looks diseased. Black veins crawl up the walls, their twisted tendrils pulsing faintly as if alive.

The shadows in the corner writhe and shift—an unnatural movement that sends a shiver down my spine.

"What happened here?" My voice cracks despite my efforts to steady it.

"Demeter," Orion says simply, his tone hard as steel. "The darkness within her was a poison. It leeched itself out of her, infecting the castle. This is what remains."

My stomach twists as I recall her tormented form. The weight of it feels unbearable, as though the air itself is alive with malevolence.

"This is how the darkness got into the castle last night?" I ask.

Orion shakes his head, his jaw tightening. "No. Mor and I have been containing this darkness here with wards and our power. What happened last night—"

He pauses, his eyes narrowing. "Someone opened a doorway for it. This was deliberate."

The realization sinks in, cold and cruel.

"Someone let it in," I whisper, more to myself than to him.

Orion nods, his expression dark.

"It took one Valkyrie to bring down an army and invite an unending blight into our realm. That blight is what we fight now. And history is coming back to meet us here in the present."

I stare at him, the weight of his words pulling at something buried deep within me.

"What does this have to do with me?" My voice is sharp with frustration and fear. "I'm not—"

He cuts me off, his gaze unwavering. "Your warriors call you Valkyrie."

The words hit me like a blow, and I reel back, my mind racing to my task force. My friends.

The nickname had always clung to me—it had felt empowering once, respected. My soldiers knew that when I stepped onto the battlefield with them, I had already chosen the outcome of our war.

It was a constant reminder of their commitment to me, their trust in me.

And my commitment to never give up on them.

Now it feels like a curse as it rolls off his tongue.

"How do you know that?" I demand, my voice rising as I push down the feelings of longing that threaten to rise to the surface. A desperation for something familiar. Something that feels like home.

Orion doesn't answer. He only keeps his steely gaze on me.

I swallow hard, the memories of my task force flooding back unbidden.

Our last mission. Their teasing. The comfort of being in their presence. The switch from family to a band of warriors, ready to die for each other.

In that rainforest, I had felt the oppressive weight of the air behind us, the sense that something unseen was watching me.

My stomach twists as I recall looking back into the darkness of the trees—only to see rich shadows looking back at me.

"Mor," I whisper, the realization cutting through me like a blade. "Mor told you."

Orion nods, his expression grim. "She watched you, starling. Watched your warriors.

Their dedication to you and your dedication to them. It was a Valkyrie who started this with an unspeakable betrayal.

Perhaps it will only take one more Valkyrie to restore it —to bring balance back to the realm."

I shake my head, irritation pushing past the distraction of what he's been showing me.

"But you had already decided I was going to be taken by then, right?" My voice is sharp again, accusatory. "Don't act like that was a factor in your bringing me here. Why are you so set on this?"

Orion takes another step forward, his silver eyes burning with conviction.

"Because perhaps the realm sees something you don't. It doesn't make mistakes, starling. You were chosen—not by accident, but because you are what Avalon needs."

He pauses, his gaze unwavering as he seems to memorize every speck of brown in my eyes.

"You are to be the brightest star that burns in Avalon's sky—the light that will chase away the darkness."

He raises his hand as if he will move my hair out of my face, but then drops it. "

I just need you to believe it."

CHAPTER 27
Tana

The castle is a maze, its halls stretching endlessly in every direction, each turn revealing something new and unexpected. Orion and I emerge from the castle's lower levels, with Hypnos waiting for us at the door.

"Lady Liona requests a word, Your Grace." Hypnos tries to keep his tone low, but that name rings out, and I force myself to remain relaxed.

Orion looks at the ground first, then at me for only a second before nodding to his friend.

"Excuse me."

Liona clearly has history with Orion, and while it's not my business, that history could still be present. In the solarium last night, things got—confusing.

I close my eyes as memories of Elowyn and Thalindra's deaths flash in my mind.

Before the attack, a moment passed between Orion and me. Something that felt real and natural.

It's clear the Fae are very open when it comes to their sexual dynamics, but something about Liona grates on me, and I don't want any involvement with her if I can avoid it.

I need to make it clear to Orion that last night won't repeat itself, nor will it go further.

Seeing the warrior's mural and the darkness contaminating the dungeon leaves me with more questions than answers. I can't sit still.

The walls of my room feel too imposing without the comforting presence of my handmaids, who would tell me about Fae customs and what to expect.

The weight of everything is just too crushing. I need to move, to explore, to escape—if only for a little while.

I wanted to explore the gazebo I found yesterday, inspect the stones, and examine the surrounding space for etchings or carvings that might tell me more about it.

But when I looked out across the parapet, I saw Orion and Liona enjoying a stroll across the lawn.

I'll pass on the sword in the stone for now.

My boots echo softly against the stone floors as I wander, passing doorways that lead to libraries, storage rooms, and balconies overlooking the mist-shrouded expanse of Avalon.

Every corner of Starfall Castle seems steeped in history, the very stones humming with ancient power.

The occasional whisper makes me feel like someone is walking behind me more than once.

I was warned—many of the Fae who arrived at Beltane may likely stay until the end of the moon cycle. But these whispers feel ominous, like a warning.

Shivers rush down my back, and I turn, but no one is there. It's like the walls are alive, watching me, waiting for something.

I don't have a destination in mind. I'm only wandering the halls, turning down paths that don't make my head thrum.

Until I can talk with Hestia, I'm testing a theory to see if it's the magic of the realm causing my headaches and dizziness.

As I turn down a narrower hallway, my fingers brush absentmindedly against the cool stone walls.

The corridor is dimly lit, the torches fewer and farther between. It feels forgotten—this part of the castle—untouched by the bustle of Fae life.

It may be a nice hiding spot if I need to run away from another tutoring lesson with Hypnos, but at the very least, the pulsing in my head is nothing more than a soft thrum.

That itself is approval enough that I should check this out.

Stopping at a doorway, I look at the carved stone. Etched over the curve of the header is a word that means nothing to me, but curiosity tugs at me, and I push it open.

Cool air greets me, carrying the faint sound of trickling water, calling to me like a siren.

A narrow spiral staircase winds downward, the steps carved into the stone and worn smooth by centuries of use.

The walls and ceiling are covered in a stunning mosaic, the tiny tiles forming a depiction of Avalon's eternal sky.

Constellations sparkle faintly in the dim torchlight, the artistry so detailed it feels as if the night sky has been captured and brought indoors.

Gripping the handrail, I begin my descent. The air grows

warmer with each step, the faint scent of minerals and damp earth wrapping around me.

The staircase is tight—the kind of space where two people would have to turn sideways to pass each other—but it feels comforting rather than claustrophobic.

If someone were to come down here to attack, they could only come single file.

My mind goes directly into captain mode, assessing my exit points.

The final step deposits me into a chamber that feels otherworldly. A natural hot spring rests at the center, its surface steaming faintly in the warm air.

The pool is surrounded by smooth stone, its edges shaped into natural seats.

Bottles of oils and vials of powders line a stone shelf nearby, their delicate labels marked with swirling Fae script.

The room itself is bathed in a soft glow from the torches mounted on the walls, their light reflecting off the water and casting shimmering patterns across the ceiling.

I let out a long breath, tension easing from my shoulders as I take in the sight.

This place feels untouched by the weight of the realm—a quiet sanctuary hidden deep within the castle. And it's exactly what I need.

Rushing back to my room, I quickly undress and don a silky, short robe that ends above my knee.

I nearly forget my knife and sheath, so I dart back into the room to grab them.

"Always keep it close." I mock Orion with a sneer, as if I need help from a prince with my weaponry.

Back in the grotto, my robe discarded, my knife resting on top of it, the warmth is a shock—but a welcome one.

It seeps into my muscles, loosening the knots tied tight from the chaos of the past day.

I sink deeper, the water lapping at my shoulders, and let out a sigh as the tension slowly drains from my body.

The oils I pour in mix with the water, their sweet, earthy scent rising with the steam.

I lean my head back against the smooth edge of the pool, staring up at the shimmering mosaic above as my headache evaporates with the vapor.

This moment—this tiny, stolen moment—is the first peace I've felt since I was dragged into this world. But even as the water soothes my body, my mind refuses to quiet.

The memory of Beltane, the dungeon, the Valkyrie mural, and the darkness infecting the castle—all of it churns in my thoughts.

I glance toward my knife. The blade gleams faintly in the torchlight. I can almost feel it in my hand, slicing through an alpha shifter or using it to drain a vampire.

It feels like a companion from the life I left behind.

A life that feels impossibly far away now.

With a sigh, I close my eyes, the heat and the scent of the oils wrapping around me like a cocoon.

The storm of my thoughts rages on, but for now, I let myself drift in the warmth of the water.

My eyes pop open to the dim glow of the torches, the steam still curling lazily around me.

For a moment, I feel disoriented, the soft ripple of water the only sound in the grotto.

The warmth of the water must have lulled me to sleep, but something spurred me awake.

A faint scuff against stone—soft, deliberate.

My body stiffens, the peaceful haze of the hot spring replaced by a sharp jolt of adrenaline.

I strain my ears, trying to catch the sound again. My hand moves slowly through the water, careful not to disturb it, reaching for the edge of the pool where my knife lies with my folded clothes.

Every movement is measured, deliberate, my breaths shallow to keep from making a sound.

Nothing. Only silence greets me now.

Silence so heavy it grips the back of my neck, sending a shiver down my spine.

I let out a small breath, trying to reassure myself. Maybe it was nothing—a trick of my mind, still half-caught in the haze of sleep.

Or the castle shifting in its ancient bones, its stones settling. My fingers relax their grip on the hilt of the knife.

Then I hear it again.

A boot on stone. The faintest scuff, deliberate and slow, as if whoever is on the stairs is trying not to be heard.

My pulse quickens, hammering against my ribs as I instinctively crouch lower in the water, making myself smaller.

My eyes dart around the grotto, searching for an escape or somewhere to conceal myself. The stairs leading down to the pool are narrow, curving just enough that the bottom portion is partially hidden by the stone.

If I can get there, I'll at least have a vantage point to see who's coming before they see me.

The water ripples softly as I move, gripping my knife in one hand while steadying myself against the slick stone edge with the other.

Every muscle in my body is coiled tight, the weight of the blade grounding me as I inch toward the pool's steps.

The room feels like it's holding its breath with me, the tension pressing against my skin like a second layer.

I pause at the base of the steps, closing my eyes for a moment and willing the room to remain silent. Each drop of water echoes in the grotto, each soft sound amplified in the quiet.

If I make a single splash, I'll give myself away.

Please, I plead silently, as if the room itself could hear me. *Don't betray me.*

And then, impossibly, the water answers. The first step I take out of the shallow pool is silent—no ripples, no sound, just the smooth, noiseless shift of liquid around my foot.

My eyes snap open, and I glance at my knife. The faint,

intricate runes etched along the blade shimmer with a soft silver glow, a light that wasn't there before.

A warm pulse passes between my hand and the blade. *Magic.* Something imbued in the runes must be responding to my need.

I don't have time to question it. Carefully, silently, I climb the steps, my breath shallow, the glowing blade steady in my hand.

The thought of magic working in my favor steadies me, sharpening my focus. My feet touch the cool stone floor of the grotto, and I slip into the shadowy alcove beneath the curve of the stairs.

Crouched low, the edge of the stairs obscuring most of my view, I strain to hear anything beyond the blood rushing in my ears.

My grip on the knife tightens, the runes still faintly glowing. This hiding spot feels secure, but doubt worms its way in.

What if it's just Orion, skulking in after me to talk? Or perhaps *Glitter Cunt* is coming to nag me to death with her superiority complex and insecurities.

I roll my eyes at the thought of that and wonder if I would cause a war by stabbing her.

Maybe this spot isn't as secret as I thought. Maybe it's a favorite haunt among the Fae who live here, and I've only made this a dramatic misunderstanding.

But then I see a shadow stretching long across the dim light spilling into the grotto. My stomach clenches, my pulse hammering in my chest.

The figure descends the last few steps, their movements deliberate, calculated. They carry no torch, no visible light, only the gleam of moonlight filtering in through the mosaic ceiling above.

The faint shimmer of something metallic catches my eye.

My breath catches as I make out the silhouette of a knife clutched tightly in their hand. It's raised high, poised for a strike.

My mind goes blank for a moment before the weight of the truth crashes into me like a wave.

This isn't Orion. This isn't some friendly castle Fae checking on their queen.

Someone is coming to kill me.

The moment I see the glint of the raised blade, my training kicks in. Every ounce of fear, doubt, or hesitation vanishes, burned away by years of instinct and discipline.

My body moves on autopilot, every muscle remembering its purpose. This isn't the first time someone has come for me, and it won't be the last.

I think of the Fae in front of me as nothing more than a vampire back on Earth. I've slain hundreds of those. He's just another mark, another tally on my kill score.

I am an assassin of the gods, and whoever thought they could take me out will learn that lesson in their last moments.

The figure steps off the staircase, his boots touching the stone floor of the grotto. My eyes sweep over him, taking in the details. *Male.*

Unknown to me. Not surprising—I barely recognize

anyone here. He's of average height for a Fae, which is to say taller than most humans, but not enough to intimidate me.

His grip on his blade is solid but untrained, giving him away as someone who has never truly faced death before.

He will now.

CHAPTER 28
Tana

As soon as his weight shifts onto the floor, I strike.

I step out from behind the stairs, silent as the grave thanks to the blade's enchantment. The runes glow faintly, as if feeding off my resolve, and I bring the knife up in a single, fluid motion.

My free hand grips his head, holding it steady as I drag the blade clean across his throat.

The motion is quick, precise, efficient. It's the kind of kill that makes no room for error.

The blade bites deep—so sharp that his breath catches in his throat before the blood even starts to flow.

His eyes widen in shock, his mouth opening to scream or beg or curse, but nothing comes out. The gurgle that follows is wet and final.

I step back as his body crumples to the floor, lifeless. His knife clatters against the stone, the sound loud in the silence.

Blood spills freely now, pooling beneath him and staining the pale stone a dark, gleaming crimson.

I take a slow breath, lowering the knife but keeping my grip steady. My heart is pounding, but not with fear. It's the rush of battle, the calm clarity that always follows a clean kill.

The glow of the blade's runes fades slightly, as though the magic is satisfied with its work.

I crouch to inspect the fallen Fae, my knife still ready just in case. The stillness of his body confirms his death, but I can't ignore the tension that keeps my senses on high alert.

I quickly fix the silk robe around me, thinking of who I should report this to first. Rushing out of here in a panic, confessing to killing a Fae, could mean my own death sentence.

The shadows in the room sway, and I turn around, preparing for someone else to descend the stairs.

The only thought in my mind is: *this is twice now I've been attacked while naked.*

Maybe I should keep my clothes on from here on out.

A swirl of darkness flourishes across the grotto, the room's temperature seeming to plummet.

My grip tightens on the blade as I rise, readying myself for another attack.

Instead of another assassin, Mor and Orion materialize from the shadows, their forms solidifying like specters called from the void.

Orion's expression is starkly different from his usual composure—panic flickers in his eyes before it's quickly replaced by a fierce, almost feral anger.

Mor, on the other hand, looks entirely amused, her crimson eyes sweeping over the scene and settling approvingly on the dead Fae at my feet.

"What in the name of Avalon happened here?" Orion

demands, his voice sharp and cutting as he eats up the distance between us. His silver eyes lock onto mine, a storm brewing within them.

I straighten, holding my chin high despite the fact that I'm dripping wet, wearing nothing but a silk robe, and standing in the aftermath of an assassination attempt. "Exactly what it looks like," I say, my voice steady.

"He tried to kill me. Now he's dead."

Orion's jaw tightens as he glances at the body. His hands clench at his sides, and shadows whip at his feet, betraying the rage simmering beneath his controlled exterior.

"This is exactly why you need to take my warnings seriously," he growls, grabbing my upper arm in a firm grip. "One of the courts just tried to assassinate you."

"I don't need you to babysit me or clean up my messes," I snap back, yanking my arm away. "But if I'm to be the queen... then that makes me the boss of you. So, you can take care of this mess for me."

I turn on my heel without sparing him another glance. Walking away—barefoot and unapologetic—my wet hair dripping, I ascend the narrow stone steps.

"Where are you going?" Orion calls after me, his tone sharp and commanding. "Stop being reckless."

I keep going and hear him following after me.

"This is foolish, and you fucking know it."

Ooh, finally, the put-together prince shows he's not entirely made of polished marble.

"Do you even know what it feels like to be the only mortal here? I'm here because of you. *Suffocating,* because of you!" I bite back as he walks next to me, meeting my brisk pace easily.

His shadows ripple as he follows me, his presence looming larger with every step.

"I'm trying to protect you," he says, his voice measured but firm. "To serve you as my queen."

The Fae we pass quickly move aside, their quiet conversations pausing completely to watch us bicker down the halls.

"I wouldn't need you to protect me if I weren't here!" I whisper-yell, the words cutting through the air as I reach my room. The thick door is heavy in my hand as I slam it behind me.

Of course, Orion is here—my own shadow that I can't shake no matter how hard I push. His hand thumps against the door, keeping it from closing on him.

"You're going to need all the allies and protection you can find if you are going to survive the Fae." His anger is palpable now as he presses into my room.

My chest heaves with the force of my emotions, and before I can stop myself, I spin around, snapping at him.

"I hate you. I hate you for fucking bringing me here. So run to your annoying glitter princess and leave me alone."

The declaration hangs between us, thick and charged as we stand in silence. But it's the second part of my statement that I wish I had held back.

It makes me look like a jealous, pathetic little girl, and he knows it.

I can practically see him rolling my last words over in his mind.

Dissecting them. Preparing himself to use them against me.

The walls feel closer than before, the air heavier. My heart pounds, and my skin flushes when I realize he is standing far too close.

My nipples pebble against the slick robe, and I take in a sharp inhale of air.

Orion notices in an instant, and I watch as his anger shifts into something darker, more consuming. His pupils dilate, his breathing deepens, and his tone softens to a low, seductive drawl.

"It doesn't seem like you hate me," he says, stepping closer, his gaze burning into mine.

I swallow hard, my body betraying me as his nearness and scent—a heady mix of leather and cedar, so uniquely him—intoxicate me.

"There are other ways I'm happy to serve my queen," he murmurs, his voice like a caress.

His hand moves to the silk belt at my waist, his fingers brushing against it as though testing my resolve.

"All you have to do is ask," he whispers.

His fingers toy with the silk, his touch featherlight, waiting—*waiting* for me to be the one to break first.

I can't. I *won't*.

Heat rises in my cheeks, and I fight to remain defiant, though I know he can see through the thin veneer of my resistance.

Especially after what happened at Beltane.

The beginning of something was laid bare between us,

and we both know we're attracted to each other as much as we annoy each other.

My pulse quickens as his fingers toy with the belt, as though daring me to give in.

"I can take care of myself in that area as well," I answer, just as smooth and quiet as him, gripping the belt and sliding it from his grasp.

I step back, sitting on the edge of my bed, the robe short enough to reveal most of my bare legs. I lean back slightly, letting him drink in the sight of me, knowing full well the game we're playing.

His lips curve into a faint, knowing smirk. "I bet you won't," he challenges, his voice low and velvety. "My new queen is all talk."

The air between us is electric, a charged current neither of us is willing to break first.

I know exactly what he wants—he wants me to give in, to let him have the control he craves, to yield myself to him like I had *almost* done in the solarium, when our gazes locked and everything else disappeared.

But I won't give him that satisfaction. Not yet.

Not until I know what Liona is to him.

Not until I *make* him burn for it first.

Meeting his heated stare with a boldness that sends a thrill through me,

I slide my hand to the belt of my robe. Slowly, deliberately, I loosen it, letting the silk fall open to reveal my bare body.

The cool air brushes against my peaked nipples, sending

a shiver across my skin as I spread my legs, fully exposing myself to him.

His eyes darken—molten silver with a hunger that could consume me whole.

"Trying to get some pointers for your lovers, *Your Grace*?" I croon, my voice low and taunting as I slide my hand down my stomach, my fingers moving with purpose toward my wet, throbbing heat.

"Or are you not sure you could pleasure a mortal?"

I see the way his jaw tightens, the faint tick in his brow as he fights for control.

His erection is straining against the tight leather of his pants, and the sight of it sends another rush of arousal coursing through me.

But he doesn't move. Doesn't break.

His restraint only fuels the fire building inside me.

"Why don't you enlighten me, *starling*?" His voice is calm—dangerously so—but the tension in his body betrays him. "What would you command your willing servant to do?"

The words send a spark through me, igniting something reckless and wild.

Slowly, deliberately, I drag my touch up the slit of my cunt, gathering my arousal on the tip of my finger. I hold his gaze as I circle my clit in lazy, teasing strokes, the fire in my belly growing hotter with each pass.

His breath catches, just for a moment, and his hands flex at his sides. The shadows that always linger around him seem to writhe and twist, responding to the unspoken desire simmering between us.

But he doesn't move.

Doesn't give in.

It's a battle of wills now, and I'm determined to win.

"Is this what you wanted to see?" I ask, my voice dripping with mockery and defiance as I arch my back slightly, angling myself to give him the perfect view.

My body is trembling, not from fear but from the sheer intensity of the moment, from the raw, primal connection between us.

His gaze never wavers, but I can see the cracks forming in his composure—the way his pupils dilate, the tension in his shoulders as he fights the urge to close the space between us.

The air feels heavy, charged with the weight of everything unspoken.

"Keep going," he commands, his voice dropping to a rough, husky whisper that makes my core clench. "Show me, *starling*. Show me what you'd have me do."

I want him to break. To *lose* control.

But as my fingers circle faster, the pleasure building to an unbearable peak, I realize—*I* might be the one who shatters first.

The air between us is molten, and every word I speak feels like a match striking against a blaze.

"I would have you on your knees, crawling to me. *Begging* for a taste of my sweet pussy."

The rush of tingles rippling across my skin is matched by the flicker of tension in his jaw, the way his composure falters for just a moment.

"I would have you licking me, sucking me until I can't stand it anymore."

My fingers quicken their pace, and my breath catches in my throat.

The fantasy plays out vividly in my mind—his strong hands gripping my thighs, his mouth worshiping me. It's almost too much, but there's no stopping now.

"And after?"

His voice is deep, rich, and it wraps around me like a velvet shroud.

The sound alone sends a fresh wave of heat pooling between my legs.

My hips start to roll in slow, deliberate movements, countering the rhythm of my fingers, and I close my eyes briefly, surrendering to the sensation.

When I open them again, he's moving.

Slow, measured steps bring him closer, like a predator closing in on its prey.

"If you did a good job," I say breathlessly, the heat in my words unrelenting, "I would let you fuck me with those long fingers, thrusting them into me while I come around them."

He stops at the foot of the bed, his boots planted firmly between my legs.

He's so close now—close enough to touch if he wanted.

His hands could reach out and glide up my thighs, claim me entirely.

But he doesn't.

He just stands there, towering, his presence suffocating in the most intoxicating way.

"Show me," he murmurs, his voice low and commanding.

He leans forward slightly, his gaze heavy on me, and it feels as though his words alone are a touch against my skin.

I shift back, resting my feet on the bed's edge, letting my knees fall open as I recline fully.

The vulnerability of the position only fuels the fire burning inside me, and the heat in his eyes matches it perfectly.

"Let me see my queen's glistening cunt," he says, and the way he growls the words makes my body tremble.

My fingers pause their movements, anticipation coiling in my belly, and he takes another step forward.

Slowly, deliberately, he leans over, collecting saliva in his mouth.

The moment his spit lands on my pussy, my body jolts, and a whimper escapes my throat.

The simple act feels so intimate, so possessive, that I almost come from it alone.

I drag my fingers through the added moisture, mixing it with my arousal, and the smirk that tugs at his lips is equal parts wicked and knowing.

The mirth in his dark eyes tells me what I've only just realized: I'm not the one in control here.

I've been playing into his game all along.

But I'm not about to let him win without a fight.

I push two fingers inside myself, my palm pressing against my clit to create the friction I need.

A gasp leaves my lips, my back arching as the pleasure builds, and all the while, his eyes never leave me.

"Keep going, starling," his voice drips with molten temptation, low and devastating.

Damn him.

I want that voice closer. I want to feel it murmuring into my ear as his lips, his tongue, blaze a path down my neck.

I want him to pull my nipple into his mouth, to devour me entirely.

Instead, I do it for him.

My hand moves to my breast, my fingers rolling and pulling at the peak. My hips grind against my hand as I follow the lead I accidentally handed over to him, my movements desperate and aching.

"What else, my queen?" His words send a shiver through me.

The shadows at his feet darken, growing richer, deeper.

Tendrils of his power unfurl, creeping toward me like they have a mind of their own. Two ribbons of darkness snake around my ankles, and I gasp as a sharp jolt of pleasure shoots through me.

"Would you have me show you how much my shadows desire you?" His voice is a dark melody, every syllable wrapping around me like silk.

"How desperately my darkness longs to *taste* you?"

I actually fucking whimper at the offer.

"Does my starling like the idea of my shadows flicking your little clit, making your legs twitch?"

My starling.

The way he says it, low and possessive, sends me spiraling.

"Yes," I pant, the heat of my impending release coiling tighter.

The shadows glide up my legs, their touch cool and electric against my heated skin.

It feels like two strong hands kneading my thighs, coaxing every ounce of tension out of me.

I'm teetering on the edge, desperate for more, desperate for him.

I need that power to thrust into me, to shatter me, to catch me as I fall.

The tendrils trail higher, their cool caress brushing closer to my core. My breathing hitches, anticipation building with every second.

Just as they're about to reach me, I pull my hand away, ready to surrender to his power completely.

My fingers move to my nipples, twisting them hard, bracing myself for the shadows' touch.

And then... *nothing.*

The tendrils retreat, dissolving into nothingness as Orion steps back.

The grin that spreads across his face is one of smug, calculated satisfaction.

My body screams in frustration, the absence of his touch a cruel betrayal.

"What the fuck," I growl, sitting up abruptly, my head spinning with unmet desire and raw fury.

"Well," he drawls, pausing at the door and resting his hand on the handle. His silver eyes gleam with unrepentant mischief. "It's a shame you don't want any help."

And just like that, he opens the door and disappears into

the hall, his long strides echoing in the distance. I stare after him, my jaw slack in disbelief.

A growl of pure rage erupts from my throat.

I grab the nearest pillow and hurl it with everything I've got. The thud against the closed door does nothing to satisfy my irritation.

I wish it were a rock against his head.

"I hate you!" I yell, my voice carrying down the hallway.

The only response is his deep, wicked laugh, echoing back to me.

CHAPTER 29

The painting looms over me, a testament to the past and a cruel reminder of what lies ahead.

My grandmother, Queen Pandora, is depicted mid-trial, her silver hair flowing like a storm's wind.

The brushstrokes capture the unyielding resolve in her gaze, the gleam of her blade, and the shadows of her enemy—the darkness she held at bay—depicted as a swirling cloud of obscurity.

It seems only a black stain on the canvas now. The artist immortalized her triumph, but in the end, the cost of her crown was great.

It cost the realm the Valkyrie, handed over by an unfaithful sister of the blade. It cost my grandmother her immortal life—betrayal at the hands of her own daughter.

It is as if this darkness searches for a single point of entry, exploits it, then rushes in like a relentless tide to drown everything it touches.

"Staring at ghosts won't solve this, Orion."

Mor's voice cuts through my thoughts. It's blunt, as always, and carries the faintest edge of amusement.

Her shadows slither behind her as she steps into the room, carrying the scent of night and damp earth.

The darkness that rests in the corners flocks to her like sheep to a herder.

"It reminds me of the stakes," I reply, keeping my tone even. "Tana doesn't see what's at risk yet."

"Neither does she care," Mor retorts, grabbing an apple from the platter set on a nearby table. She sits in one of the table's wide chairs, placing her feet on the table, one boot crossed over the other.

"And why would she? The realm dropped her here like a lamb among wolves."

"She's not a lamb," I say eventually, my voice tight. "She's more capable than you give her credit for."

"Every lion thinks he is the largest and strongest of his pride until he faces a pack of lions, bigger and stronger. Then he sees the true measure of himself," Mor replies, biting into the apple with a loud crunch.

Her crimson eyes gleam with weariness at the increased patrols. "She's mortal. She has her own battles, her own life back on Earth. You brought her here; don't pretend that doesn't matter."

Hypnos clears his throat, a small sound that cuts through Mor's barbs as he joins us.

"She took Demeter's execution harder than she lets on," he interjects smoothly.

"Her defiance is a shield. She's grieving—questioning everything, Your Grace. She only needs space to do that."

"The realm made it complicated," I say, my jaw tightening. "Revealing her mortality to the Fae only added fuel to the fire."

Mor scoffs. "It's not just complicated, Orion. It's dangerous. The courts are already circling like vultures. Beltane wasn't a random attack of the darkness—it was calculated.

At least one of the courts aims to overthrow the realm's choice and is willing to hand over Starfall to do it."

"And now," I add, my voice hardening, "after the attack in the grotto, we can assume it's more than one. No single court would risk such an overt move unless they believed they had allies."

"The first plan failed, so there was a second plan ready." I mutter the words more to myself than to my companions. The weight of that truth settles over us, each of us lost in our own thoughts for a moment.

Hypnos breaks the silence. "We need to know where the ten courts stand. Who will be loyal, who remains undecided, and who is our enemy. Without that knowledge, we're flying blind."

"We can't leave Starfall vulnerable." I shake my head. "What of the wards, Mor?"

"I've strengthened them, weaving extra measures into the dark shield around the castle. It's holding for now, but the darkness is persistent. It's probing, testing for weaknesses."

"And the patrols?" I press further, knowing myself that the walls around Starfall are attacked nightly by creatures of obscurity hunting us.

She shrugs one shoulder, her expression unreadable.

"The creatures are bolder. More of them, and they're hungrier. They've been corrupted, like the Cŵn Annwn.

I killed three near the outer wall last night—none of them went down easy. Each looked more twisted than the one before it."

My shadows curl tighter around me as I feel the tension of the realm pulse with anticipation.

"We'll start with the obvious courts." With a deep sigh, I turn to Hypnos. "Were you able to determine who or what invited the darkness into the castle during Beltane?"

Hypnos adjusts the high collar of his cloak, his pale eyes reflective in the dim light.

"I was able to sift through the residue of emotions left behind," he answers, his tone steady, though his words carry the weight of what he has uncovered, and I know I'm not going to like what he has to say.

"There was a talisman, discarded in the ballroom. It was steeped in malice, deceit, and dark energy."

A talisman.

I close my eyes, fearing I know what is to come.

By the sacred moon of Avalon, give me patience.

Hypnos's ability to sense and manipulate emotions is powerful, but even more powerful is his gift of reading lingering imprints tied to specific events or objects—the empathic echoes left behind that only those with sight like his can see and interpret.

He raises his hand. The ripple of his opaque power reveals a ball of protective energy, the dark omen held protectively inside.

My jaw tightens seeing the object again. It was the same

talisman offered by the emissary from Thornspire—the supposed token of King Thorne's "welcome" for our new queen.

The very one I flicked away from Tana before she could touch it.

I gave her my rage when really I was angry at King Thorne.

I do not like the attention the Briar is putting on our mortal queen.

The Warden, challenging her life. The king, making an offer of marriage.

It smells like a brewing war.

If I were honest with myself, I would admit my jealousy seeing Thorne's offer to Tana—one he deemed so insignificant he didn't even declare his intentions in person.

I should have paid closer attention, but I let Tana distract me. I took her contemplation over the object as consideration of the Briar King's offer.

"This was the doorway," Hypnos declares with finality, pulling me from the swirl of anger rising within me.

"Perhaps it was a ruse?" Mor suggests, taking two more apples from the platter, biting into one first and then the other.

Hypnos considers Mor's implication, nodding thoughtfully.

"It is possible there was never any intention of proposal after all. It was merely a means to get the doorway inside Starfall without raising suspicion."

"What else did you find?" I fight to keep my tone even against the guilt and frustration straining within me.

"The stone the talisman is carved from," Hypnos explains, his voice taking on the patient tone of someone explaining something to a particularly stubborn child.

"It's from Evershade. Specifically, from the mines in Lord Umbriel's domain. It's a powerful conductor for dark magic, and Umbriel hoards it like a dragon hoards treasure."

"Evershade," I mutter, the name heavy with history and mistrust. The realm of Eternal Night is infamous for its ruler and the secrets its shadows conceal. "Umbriel wouldn't part with such a stone unless he had something to gain."

"Exactly," Hypnos says, his gaze sharp. "Which means Thornspire is likely not acting alone."

The realization settles over me like a weight.

If Thornspire enlisted Evershade's resources, then this wasn't just a matter of one court conspiring against Tana.

It was a conspiracy that could unravel Avalon itself.

Rest assured, where two gather in darkness to gossip and plot, more will not be far behind.

I must stop the spread of dissent across the courts before it spirals out of control.

"Has Hephaestus learned anything about the blade used in the assassination attempt?" I ask, my voice tight with urgency.

Hypnos shakes his head. "Hephaestus says he's never seen anything like it. The runes carved into the blade aren't in any known language.

He's searching the archives of Avalon's forgotten tongues, but it's slow work. The blade's craftsmanship is exceptional—almost too perfect. It wasn't made by any common hand. It may even predate the courts as we know them."

Predate the courts.

My mind churns, trying to piece together how this fits with Umbriel and Thornspire.

A talisman from one court, a blade of unknown origin, and a conspiracy that seems to reach further than we thought.

Mor finally pushes off her chair, her eyes narrowing. "So, what's the plan? March into Evershade and the Briar with swords raised, or will there be talking to death?"

I glare at her, the heat of my frustration boiling to the surface. "We start with Umbriel. He knows something, and I intend to find out what."

"And if he doesn't feel like sharing?" Mor asks, her voice laced with challenge.

"Then we make him," I say, my shadows flaring briefly at my feet.

Hypnos watches me closely, his pearly eyes steady. "Evershade first, then Thornspire. But you need to tread carefully, Orion. Umbriel plays a long game, and we're stepping onto his board."

"I know the risks," I say, my voice cold. "But we don't have time for caution. Every moment we wait, the darkness gains ground, and Tana nears her first challenge of the realm. She has already found the sword."

Hypnos's interest piques at that mention.

"Let's bolster the wards and double the patrols—again. If more corrupted creatures approach the castle, I want to know about it immediately. No matter where we are in Avalon, I want to know."

Mor tosses her half-eaten apple onto the table and stretches lazily, but there's nothing idle in the sharp gleam of her crimson eyes.

"Then we'd best be on our way."

As they leave, I turn back to the painting of my grandmother. The light in her eyes, the determination in her stance.

Tana has the same fire, whether she realizes it or not.

But fire can burn as easily as it can illuminate.

And if I push her too far, *I* might be the one to snuff it out.

CHAPTER 30
Tana

The courtyard is quiet tonight, the stillness broken only by the soft rustle of leaves in the cool breeze. I lean back on the stone bench, staring up at Avalon's sky.

It's vast and endless—the kind of sky you could lose yourself in if you weren't careful.

The stars here seem sharper, brighter than those back on Earth, as if this realm polishes its night to perfection.

I sigh, my thoughts circling back to the chaos of the past few days, and it's all just *so much*. Like I'm being dragged down into something I might never escape.

A reflection within the night sky grabs my attention, and I strain my eyes, trying to focus on it.

At first, it's subtle—a faint shimmer just at the edges of my vision. I blink, thinking it's a trick of the light, but it's there, unmistakable.

A soft, rippling glow, like moonlight caught in water. It drapes over the castle, a dome of shimmering energy that feels alive, pulsing faintly as if it's breathing.

I stand, captivated. *Has this always been here? How have I never noticed this before?*

The way it shifts and bends, catching the faintest hues of silver and blue—it's... beautiful. Strange, but beautiful.

As I watch the phenomenon, I feel a familiar pull—that undeniable sense of being watched by a familiar stare. Slowly, I lower my gaze to the ground below.

Orion is there.

Of course, he is.

Standing at the edge of the courtyard, his figure is outlined by the faint glow of the shimmering veil. His gaze is fixed on me—piercing and unwavering.

There's something about the way he looks at me, like he's seeing too much. Like he *knows* too much. It makes my skin prickle, and not entirely in a bad way.

He nods once—a silent acknowledgment.

I roll my eyes, crossing my arms. If he thinks a little nod is going to smooth things over after earlier, he's out of his mind.

Mor and Hypnos stand beside him, their presence unmistakable even in the dim light. Mor's crimson eyes glint faintly as she shifts, the shadows around her moving like living creatures.

Hypnos, as always, is unnervingly still, his calm an almost physical thing.

I watch them more closely now. The shimmering veil around the castle isn't just some natural spectacle—it's *coming* from them.

Their power intertwines in the air, weaving together to form the protective shield.

Mor's darkness flows in sinuous tendrils, blending with Hypnos's translucent energy, while Orion's shadows anchor the entire structure like the foundation of a fortress.

It's impressive.

Terrifying, but impressive.

My gaze flicks back to Orion. His face is calm, unreadable, but I can sense the strain in the way his jaw tightens—the faint edge of tension in his stance.

They're giving their energy, their power, to maintain this shield—to protect the castle.

To protect *me*.

The thought twists something in my chest—an uncomfortable mix of gratitude and guilt.

A hulking figure joins them, and I'm pulled from my thoughts.

Hephaestus strides across the clearing toward the group, his gait uneven on the rough terrain.

The wooden prosthetic he crafted himself thuds softly against the stone, but he walks with purpose, his broad shoulders and easy confidence defying the limp.

Hephaestus glances up and spots me. His face lights up with a grin, and he raises a hand in greeting.

I can't help but smile back, the tension in my chest easing a little. Hephaestus has a way of making things feel less... *heavy*. Less *impossible*.

The shimmer of the veil fades, the glow of power withdrawing into its sources.

Mor's shadows slink back into her, Hypnos's aura dims, and Orion's own darkness retreats, though I still feel the residual hum of it on my skin—a faint, protective current that won't quite let go.

It's calming.

And unnerving.

All at once.

The group turns, heading toward the front of the castle, Hephaestus falling into step with them.

Orion pauses only briefly, tilting his head in the same direction. A clear signal. *Come.*

For a moment, I toy with the idea of staying right where I am, giving him the finger, and refusing to be dragged into whatever plans he has.

But curiosity—and that infuriating need to *prove* myself—wins out.

I take a deep breath and follow, heading toward the front of the castle.

When I reach the drawbridge, I stop short, my breath catching.

Three massive horses stand before them, tethered but restless, their dark pelts seeming to *absorb* the very darkness around them.

And I find I can't look away.

They're unlike any horses I've ever seen—bigger, taller, more muscular, with proud, arched necks and intelligent eyes glowing faintly like embers in deep ash.

Their manes ripple like flowing ink, the ends disappearing into nothing like fog.

Their hooves—nearly the size of my head—are ironlike, polished steel-gray. They strike the ground as I approach with the sound of distant thunder.

Amazing.

I wonder what they sound like running at full speed.

One of the beasts turns its head toward me, snorting softly, and I find myself stepping closer.

Its massive frame should be intimidating, but there's a curious softness in its gaze as it watches me approach.

"Hey there," I murmur, holding my hand out instinctively.

The horse sniffs at my fingers, its warm breath washing over my skin before it nudges its head against me.

I laugh softly as it presses its face against my shoulder, its massive head heavy but oddly gentle.

My hands instinctively move to scratch behind its ears, and it seems to *melt* under my touch, its eyes half-closing in contentment.

"You're not so scary, are you?" I say, scratching along its jawline.

That's when I notice the massive fangs, like those of a lion, hidden within its powerful jaws.

Maybe a little scary.

Another horse takes a step closer, sniffing me with curiosity, while the first reaches to the ground, munching on a soft tuft of grass.

My brief moment of awe is interrupted as I notice something that immediately sours my mood.

There are only *three* horses.

I pull back from the curious beasts, crossing my arms over my chest as I turn my glare toward Orion.

His expression doesn't change, but I see a faint flicker of amusement in Mor's crimson eyes.

She nudges Hypnos with her elbow, and he tilts his head slightly toward her, his lips curving into the faintest smirk.

"Don't tell me you were betting on this," I snap, narrowing my eyes at Mor.

"We were," she replies bluntly, taking a bite of the apple she's still holding. "And we won."

My glare shifts to Orion, but not before I shake my head at the way Mor refers to herself in a plural sense.

"Where's my horse?"

"You do not have a horse. The Duskbane chooses its rider, not the other way around." Orion's voice is even, clipped. "And simply put, you're not coming."

I scoff, stepping closer. "Excuse me?"

"It's too dangerous," he continues, his tone unyielding. "This isn't up for debate, *starling*."

That fucking nickname grates along my skin. I press my lips into a thin line.

"Don't call me that, and I don't recall asking for your permission." I plant my hands on my hips, my irritation spiking. "Where are you going?"

"To ensure the attack on the castle—and on you—does not go unanswered." Orion's voice is cold, formal. "Fae do not tolerate such offenses. Justice must be served."

"And I'm supposed to just stay here and wait for you to *handle* it?" I snap. "Newsflash, Orion: *I'm* the one they attacked, and *I* took down my would-be assassin, thank you. I have a right to be part of this."

"You have a right to stay alive," he counters, his voice hardening. "And you can't do that if you're charging head-first into danger without thinking."

"Without *thinking*?" My voice rises, my anger spilling

over. "I'm not some reckless child, you asshole. I've fought battles and made decisions that saved lives—"

"This is not Earth, *starling*." Orion steps closer, his silver eyes flashing. "This is not *your* world. You do not understand what you're walking into."

"Do. Not. Call me that." I punch out each word, my fury a live wire beneath my skin.

"And I understand *enough*," I snap back, meeting his gaze without flinching.

"You keep talking about *protecting* me, but all you're really doing is keeping me in the dark—locked away like some damsel in the highest tower. How am I supposed to lead if you don't let me *see* what I'm up against?"

I don't give a shit about being queen. But I *do* want to speak with the Warden.

If the talisman their representative offered me—and the assassin in the grotto—have anything to do with them, Orion will be going straight to the very court I need to question.

Playing along is my best chance to get out from under Orion's suffocating watch.

The tension between us is palpable, crackling like a live wire.

Behind him, Mor looks entirely unbothered, idly tossing the core of her apple to one of the horses.

Hypnos remains stoic, though there's a faint crease in his brow, and I wonder if he can *see* through my lies—to the truth of my plan.

Orion swings himself onto his horse with practiced ease,

his broad frame fitting seamlessly into the saddle. Hypnos follows, helping Mor onto her horse.

She can't be more than five feet tall—she would need a *damn* ladder to mount this beast on her own.

"It's too dangerous," Orion says, his voice cutting through the quiet tension. His silver eyes meet mine, hard and unyielding.

"We don't know who our allies are. We don't know who our enemies are. Until we do, it's better that you remain here—within the castle walls, within the wards."

I open my mouth to argue, but he cuts me off, his tone sharp, brooking no argument.

"And it's not just your safety. If someone retaliates, it won't just be *you* they target. The castle could be attacked again. The village below Starfall could be attacked. The Lesser Fae depend on the protection of the High Fae—our strength, our power. You need to understand the innocence at stake.

That is where our fight is. *Not* here, arguing over your wounded pride."

His words hit me like a slap—sharp, undeniable.

The image of the village flashes in my mind: children playing in the streets, shopkeepers tending to their wares, lives so fragile compared to the dangers lurking around every corner of this realm.

I clench my fists, frustration boiling in my chest.

But I can't deny the truth in his words.

"I'm not *happy* about this," I say tightly, glaring up at him. "But *fine.* I'll stay."

He nods, though his expression doesn't soften. "We'll be

gone several nocturns. Stay close to Hephaestus. He and his wife, Hestia, will look after you."

I cross my arms, huffing. "And what am I supposed to do while you're off playing John Wick?"

Orion flicks the reins, urging his horse forward with a click of his tongue. "Stay out of trouble," he says, his tone clipped.

Then, as if to twist the knife, he adds, "Try making a friend. I hear Liona is *quite* entertaining."

I freeze.

That bastard.

"Fuck you," I seethe, not even caring how loud I am—or if that glittered-up bitch can hear me.

Hypnos turns his horse, readying to follow after his prince.

Before he does, Hephaestus steps forward, a warm smile softening the tension in the air. "My wife's been cookin' up somethin' special in honor of hostin' the queen," he says, his voice gruff but warm.

"She's been chatterin' on about it for *days*, aye."

I glance at him, my irritation wavering slightly at his genuine warmth. "*Special*, huh?"

"Oh, aye." Hephaestus nods, his face lighting up with pride. "Hestia's honey-roasted boar, done up with her wild truffle glaze. Rare as hen's teeth and *twice* as delicious."

At the mention of food, Mor straightens in her saddle, her crimson eyes glinting with sudden interest.

"We *love* wild truffle," she says, her tone uncharacteristically eager. "May we stay for dinner, too?"

Orion groans, clearly unimpressed. He flicks the reins,

urging his horse forward with a click of his tongue. "We don't *have* time for this, Mor."

But she's undeterred, her horse stepping forward at a leisurely pace. "Is that a *no*?" she calls after him, the faintest trace of mischief in her voice as she prods her horse into a trot to catch up.

Orion doesn't answer, his broad shoulders stiff with exasperation as he leads the way.

Hypnos follows silently, his expression inscrutable—though I catch the faintest twitch of his lips, as if he's holding back a smile.

Mor glances back at me, her crimson eyes gleaming.

"Save me some, *Your Majesty*."

I roll my eyes—but I can't help the small laugh that escapes me as she spurs her horse onward, her shadows trailing behind her like a restless storm.

CHAPTER 31
Tana

The warmth of Hephaestus and Hestia's home is the first thing I notice as I step inside.

It smells like roasting meat and freshly baked bread, the kind of comforting aroma that makes me momentarily forget I'm in an unfamiliar realm where danger lurks around every corner.

Their home is cozy, filled with worn wooden furniture and soft cushions, the walls lined with shelves of books and knickknacks that seem to hold years of stories.

It feels lived in, loved, and I'm glad to get out of the stark castle.

Hestia greets me with a wide smile, her deep-crimson hair tied back into a neat braid.

She bustles around the kitchen, her energy boundless as she sets plates and utensils on a sturdy oak table.

"Come in, my queen," she says warmly, waving me toward a chair. "Sit, sit. Dinner is nearly ready."

Hephaestus follows behind. I can't help but smile as I sit. "Thank you for having me."

"Nonsense," Hestia says, waving off my gratitude as she

places a steaming platter of honey-roasted boar in the center of the table. "It's an honor to host you."

The room fills with chatter as their children dart around, excited and curious, stealing glances at me before scurrying away.

It reminds me of home—of the weekends and holidays I used to spend with one of my soldiers and his family.

Five kids under one roof, chaos and laughter in equal measure. I was their honorary aunt, always there for cookouts and celebrations.

The memory brings a bittersweet ache to my chest, a longing for home softened by the genuine warmth of this moment with new friends.

Dinner is a feast. The boar is tender and flavorful, the glaze rich with the earthy sweetness of truffle. Hestia piles my plate high, and I don't have the heart to refuse.

Between bites, Hephaestus shares stories of his time as a blacksmith, his booming laughter filling the room as he recounts mishaps with molten iron and stubborn apprentices.

He tells a fantastic story of losing his leg to a dragon. I'm fascinated until several of his children pipe up, all of them discounting the tale, arguing that he has told them different stories.

Fighting the giants of Mont Michel. Slaying the wyrm of Lambton. It seems he spins a fresh tale for each newcomer, so no one knows the true story.

After the meal, the children gather around the hearth, their eyes wide with anticipation as Hephaestus leans back in his chair, a glint of mischief in his gaze.

"Shall we tell a tale tonight?" he asks, his deep voice rumbling like distant thunder, drawing eager nods and wide-eyed murmurs from the children.

Hephaestus lifts a hand, and the flames in the hearth leap higher, swirling and shifting as if alive.

The children gasp as shapes begin to form in the fire—figures of light and shadow, flickering with the movement of the flames.

"This here," he begins, his words rolling with the weight of tradition, "is the tale of Queen Pandora's trials. A tale of bravery, sacrifice, and the kind o' strength that lights up the darkest of nights."

I lean forward, captivated as the fiery figures dance, depicting a long-haired woman standing tall amidst swirling darkness.

Hephaestus's words weave a vivid picture of Pandora's strength, her unyielding resolve as she faces impossible challenges to prove herself worthy of the crown.

Each trial is a test of will, of sacrifice, of her ability to endure and overcome.

The visions begin as Pandora pulls a sword from the ground, and my heart lurches into my throat. I try to take in every detail, hoping to see clues that may help me.

With sword in hand, she charges forward through a confusing labyrinth of darkness.

The Trial of the Heart and the Trial of Shadow.

These first two trials are the ones I have studied most, with Hypnos acting as my tutor.

Pandora then battles a raging storm in the Trial of the

Elements. She faces the tall-standing stone that I recall seeing in the vision from the Lady of the Lake.

Then Pandora decides between two paths in the Trial of Sword and Chalice.

This is where the accounts of the trials become confusing, with too many variations recorded. One thing is agreed upon: the final trial is the Trial of Fate.

Something within me assures me that one will be the most difficult of them all.

I hope to be spared having to complete all the trials. If I'm lucky, I'll either bargain for a way back home, or the realm will realize its mistake and release me from this burden.

As the children head to their beds and we tidy the kitchen from dinner, curiosity pulls my thoughts downward.

How long had Pandora known she was to be queen before her first trial, and how did she recognize it had begun?

It gnaws at me, building the dread within me as I watch the moon darken when the rolling black cloud of obscurity dances across the sky.

"When will my trials come?" I wonder aloud, the question slipping out before I can stop it.

Hephaestus pauses, his gaze turning thoughtful as he regards me. "When the realm deems ye ready," he says finally, his tone softening, though his words hold steady as iron.

"It'll call on ya, Queen Tana, when the time is right. And

mark my words—I'll wager every bit of my forge and hammer on ye being up to the task."

I nod, though his answer doesn't bring me comfort.

The flames in the hearth have settled back into a steady glow, but their warmth doesn't reach the unease settling deep in my bones as I look back to the sky, tracking the looming cloud of darkness overhead.

A sharp pang in my skull makes me wince, and I pinch the bridge of my nose, squeezing my eyes shut.

"Lady Tana, are you okay?" Hestia's tone carries her worry. "Here, I have more drops for you."

She squeezes some of the bitter potion, and the pounding eases to a dull pulse, but one that still thrums with an annoying beat inside me. "I was hoping to talk to you about these headaches," I begin, pocketing the vial.

"I've noticed times when the headaches are an annoyance but not bothersome. But when they are most intense, it seems to be around areas where magic or something about the realm is very potent—like the lake or the caves down there."

My hosts gasp, and Hephaestus looks off in the direction of the caves, though we can't see them from here.

"You have visited the Sanctum of Echoes?" Hestia asks, as if I just confessed I'm wearing a bomb that will detonate in thirty seconds.

"If that is what the creepy cave below the village is called, then yes."

Hephaestus nods once in disbelief but otherwise just folds his hands over his broad chest.

"It is possible the magic of the realm is battling you, Lady Tana. Or rather, you are battling the realm."

Her smile is warm but carries the weight of truth. "I believe it is a sign you are not yet accepting your place here. Yet."

I'm not sure who she is trying to convince, adding that final word—*yet.*

As if knowing my fate is sealed and it's only a matter of time before I stop fighting it.

I figured out pretty quickly that Hestia has been visiting the castle more to keep an eye on me while Orion and the others are away.

Yesterday, she introduced me to two new handmaids. Part of me wanted to dismiss them—the loss of Brynja, Elowen, and Thalindra still fresh on my heart.

But I know that would be offensive, and it helps to have others who know the castle and the Fae well.

Aeris and Theren are a mated pair. Aeris seems delicate, like the petals of a flower.

Her skin is a lovely shade of pale purple, her hair a dark amethyst, and her eyes a rich blue. She is patient and serene, and I can tell she is the voice of reason for her mate.

Theren is tall with a strong build. His skin and hair seem to have an almost golden tone when candlelight or torch-light strikes him just so.

His green eyes have an almost feline quality to them, and they gleam with mischief.

When I suggested we go rummage through Orion's room, Theren agreed it was a splendid idea. Aeris crossed her arms, a look of annoyance on her face, and stood between us and Orion's door.

"The prince may very well have wards on his door. Have you thought of that?" She literally grabs Theren by his ear and pulls him back down the hall.

"You may open that door, and one of His Majesty's lightning bolts will strike you in the ass."

I burst out laughing, appreciating that they aren't a stuck-up pair of Fae assigned to spy on me and report my every infraction to Orion.

In fact, aside from the company, I have a feeling Theren was chosen specifically for protective duty should we encounter another unexpected attack.

I put our time to good use, using the extra hands to help me clear the dead vines and overgrowth from the gazebo. Something about freeing this sword from the stone is the start of these fucking trials—I just know it.

I'm hoping that by clearing away the vegetation, we'll find something to help me figure out how to jump-start all of this.

Of course, I'm not making much progress because of this particularly stubborn vine that refuses to be pulled up.

I glare at the stubborn little bastard clinging to the soil like it has some divine right to exist.

"You're just a plant," I mutter under my breath. "Why are you making this so personal?"

Elyra hums nearby, her voice light and melodic as she pulls small clumps of invasive plants growing around the large boulder. "You're doing quite well, Your Grace."

Theren snorts from where he's leaned against a pillar, arms crossed, his smirk firmly in place. "Define *well*. She's losing a battle to a particularly aggressive patch of dirt."

I shoot him a look over my shoulder. "Who exactly told you it was break time?"

Before Theren can come up with a smart-ass reply, a voice interrupts—smooth, saccharine, and instantly grating.

"Well, well, what do we have here? The chosen queen of Avalon, reduced to a gardener."

I don't even need to look up. There's only one person who could turn up her nose in that specific, insufferable way.

"Linda," I say, yanking the weed free and tossing it into Elyra's basket with a little too much force. "What a pleasant surprise."

"It's Liora," she corrects, her tone as sweet as poisoned honey.

"Right," I reply, standing and dusting my hands off on my skirts. "That's what I said."

It's my own personal pain in the ass in gilded form. She's bathed in gold, as I've come to expect—her gown shimmering like liquid sunlight despite the moonlit darkness around us.

She walks around the stone, and I squint at her when she runs a gold-painted finger across the hilt, barely touching it as if it's contaminated.

"What can I do for you?" I huff out, sitting back on my heels, resting my hands on my thighs.

Her every movement is carefully executed, as if all of Avalon is watching her and admiring her beauty.

She doesn't simply stand—she poses, making sure her figure is perfect and her radiance is on full display. That must be fucking exhausting.

"I'm simply missing Prince Orion," she says smoothly, stepping closer. "When we are apart, I always feel incredibly... lonely.

I thought perhaps you would enjoy getting to know me better since you have no other purpose at this moment."

I let out a soft laugh, shaking my head. "Oh, that is very thoughtful of you, Lilith." I stand, patting the dirt from my hands and making sure to fling some in her perfectly poised direction.

Elyra busies herself with the basket, but I catch the faintest twitch at the corner of her mouth. Theren, on the other hand, lets out a quiet cough that sounds suspiciously like laughter.

Liora's smile tightens for a fraction of a second before she recovers. "It's just that I've known Orion for centuries. We're very close, you see.

I can't imagine how hard it must be for him to act as your chaperone during this trying time, especially when there's so much history between us."

I clench my jaw but force myself to keep my tone light. "Funny, I don't recall him mentioning you—ever."

She carries on like she never heard me, her hand going

back to the hilt of the sword, and for some reason, I want to chop her hand off for touching it.

"We've shared... many moments together. He's always been protective of me, always looking out for what's best for Avalon." She steps closer, her voice dropping to a conspiratorial whisper.

"He's always been willing to do whatever it takes to save the realm. Even if it means... sacrifices." She looks me up and down as if I'm covered in horse shit.

The insinuation in her tone is clear, and I contemplate just headbutting her, one good time. But she is clearly here to goad me, and I refuse to give her the satisfaction.

"Sacrifices," I echo, arching a brow. "Like putting up with your company? That would explain his patience."

Elyra's head ducks slightly, and Theren doesn't even try to hide his smile this time.

Liora's smile sharpens again, her golden glow seeming to intensify as she closes the distance between us.

"You know, Tana," she says, her tone almost pitying, "Orion and I have been betrothed for quite some time." She smiles, and I know I've let my mask slip at her words.

I have to admit they hurt.

"Once he no longer needs you to secure Avalon's future, he and I will marry. It's what's best for the realm."

My chest tightens, but I keep my expression neutral.

"Betrothed, huh? How quaint. Tell me, Lyra, do you rehearse these little monologues, or do they just come to you naturally?"

Her eyes flash with irritation, but she presses on.

I straighten, waving her off like an afterthought. "Good

chat, Leanne. Now, if you'll excuse me, I have far more interesting weeds to pull."

Liora hesitates, her jaw tightening, before she strides away, her golden gown shimmering with every pissed-off step.

Once she's out of sight, I exhale sharply, turning back to the overgrowth. Elyra is standing nearby, her arms crossed, while Theren leans against the gazebo, his smirk practically carved into his face.

"What?" I ask, raising a brow.

Theren shrugs, the smirk remaining. "Just thinking it's a shame we're in perpetual night. That burn deserved some sunlight."

I roll my eyes. "That was the lamest thing I've ever heard in my life."

With my head down, I go back to clearing the gazebo, thoughts of what Liora said stewing in my mind.

Orion has been very persistent about me staying here and righting this wrong about the darkness.

What if what Liora claims is true? What if he only plans to use me as a means to that end and then dispose of me?

It's those thoughts that make my anger simmer as I keep working.

Not the images of Orion and Liora together.

Not the thought of what they could have been doing when they were both missing from the Beltane celebration at the same time.

Conspiring?

Fucking?

I swallow down my anger at that one.

Like I've said before, it's none of my business.

CHAPTER 32

The border of Evershade looms before us, a stark line where the lush darkness of Avalon deepens into an abyssal black—the kind that swallows all light.

The air is heavier here, charged with the unmistakable hum of power. I rein in my horse, feeling its unease beneath me as Mor comes to a stop by my side.

We rode our Duskanes through the Evenfall until first shade begins creeping over the horizon.

These horses are made for the job. Running at full speed, their hooves leave faint scorch marks that vanish moments later, as if the ground forgets their touch.

The thunderous sound of their stampede warns of our arrival, and now that we rest, they take in the darkness and shadows around them, their stamina recovering.

As soon as we finish here, they will be ready to carry us to the next court with just as much speed.

The path ahead is shrouded, Evershade's entrance marked by obsidian pillars adorned with glowing runes. Beyond, the landscape seems alive, shadows twisting and pulsing like a living organism.

The realm of Lord Umbriel is as much a prison for light as it is a fortress of power.

Mor's crimson eyes narrow as we sit in silence. The oppressive stillness stretches on, broken only by the occasional rustle of unseen creatures lurking in the trees.

"They know we're here," she says, her voice a quiet snarl. "And they're making us wait."

I grip the reins tighter, frustration simmering just beneath the surface.

Umbriel. Always playing games.

He isn't rejecting us outright—that would be a slight too blatant even for him. But he's stalling, making it clear that we're at his mercy before he grants us passage.

"They've been expecting us," I say, my voice calm but clipped. "This is deliberate."

Mor doesn't respond immediately, her gaze fixed on the darkened path ahead. Then, with a slow, deliberate motion, she raises her hand.

Shadows coil around her fingers, writhing like living smoke. The air thickens, and from her palm, a crow takes shape, its body formed of pure darkness, its glowing yellow eyes piercing through the gloom.

The creature caws once, a sound that echoes unnaturally in the stillness. Mor nods at it, her expression cold and unyielding.

"Go," she commands, her voice low and resonant.

The crow launches into the air, its wings silent as it cuts through the oppressive shadows. The spectral bird disappears into the void, its yellow eyes the last thing to fade.

"Do you think he'll ignore that?" I ask, keeping my tone neutral.

"We are no Fae." Mor leans back in her saddle, her expression inscrutable. "Umbriel won't ignore a message from us," she says, her words laced with a quiet threat.

"He may toy with you, Orion, and your court politics, but he knows better than to play games with The Morrigan."

Her bluntness earns her a glance, but I don't bother challenging her. She's right.

Umbriel's games are calculated, designed to test patience and resolve. But Mor's presence here changes the stakes. The Morrigan is a force even Umbriel hesitates to provoke.

We wait in silence, the tension between us palpable.

My thoughts drift to Tana—her stubborn defiance, the way she looked at me in the courtyard.

Scenarios of what rebellions she may be causing in her never-ending quest to annoy me run through my mind.

I wonder if I will find Liora alive when I return.

I have to admit, even I am becoming frustrated at the realm's timing to begin Tana's trials.

If I could protest to our guardian moon and urge Tana's ascension to immortality, to the crown, I would do it.

But all I can do is sit here at the border of shadows and darkness, waiting on a pompous court ruler to remove the stick from his ass and let us in.

So, I push out the thoughts of Tana and instead allow my irritation to stew on Umbriel.

The crow will deliver its message, and then we'll see if he has the spine to keep us waiting.

If he does, my patience won't last, and neither will Mor's.

And when that happens, even Evershade will tremble.

I will happily split this eternal darkness with the bolts of my lightning and watch as The Morrigan consumes all that Evershade hides in its shadows.

CHAPTER 33
Tana

The castle is unnervingly quiet—the kind of silence that makes you double-check shadows for things that aren't there.

A draft of cool air slips past me, brushing against the back of my neck like a ghost with a secret. Every creak of the ancient floors feels amplified, but I keep moving, staying close to the walls, my bare feet silent against the cold stone.

If anyone catches me, I'll definitely be in for a lecture about royal propriety or some other Fae nonsense.

But this has to be done tonight.

Twelve. The number has been gnawing at me all night since I looked through one of the archive's old books. Twelve beasts, twelve beams of moonlight, twelve symbols in the carvings around the castle.

It's everywhere, as if the whole realm is screaming at me to pay attention.

And I think I've finally figured it out—the sword isn't about strength or worthiness. It's about timing.

If I'm right, the moonlight is the key.

As I looked through the ancient books, something about

Liona's presence here didn't sit right, and I think there may be more truth to her taunts than I'm supposed to believe.

Her absence during the Beltane celebration, then her return just before the dark attack happened in the Solarium.

I had asked Orion if she would be coming in there, and he said she wouldn't. Was that because she already knew what would happen?

And was Orion supposed to lure me there?

I've been thinking about it. Playing on the heightened moods and senses caused by the Beltane moon was the perfect distraction.

No one was looking at anything else—not even me. My guard was completely down, and the attack happened.

When Orion saw I wouldn't go down so easily, he had Hypnos get me out of there, and they tried again.

Liona summoned Orion, and he went to her. I roamed the castle and was attacked in the grotto when I had no way out—when I would be in the pool and vulnerable.

But the knife Hephaestus gave me was an advantage. Maybe one Orion didn't count on.

He'll be sure to correct his mistake next time.

Well, I'm not going to wait around for a next time.

If I'm right, the moonlight should unlock the stone's grasp on the sword. Then I'll use it as my bargaining chip with the Briar Court and purchase a one-way ticket home.

I need to do this tonight—leave before the castle staff rises for their morning chores.

The sword and I need to be on our way to the Briar Court before they realize I'm gone and alert Orion.

I'm betting everything on his response.

I think he would rush back to the castle first to see for himself. I'll stage my room to look like someone attacked me. He'll be looking for clues about who it could have been.

By that time, I should be walking into the Briar Court, haggling over the sword for an audience with their king and a way home.

First things first—I need to get this sword out of the stone.

The air grows colder as I make my way through the outer halls, sharp enough to make me shiver despite the adrenaline humming in my veins.

The stone walls seem to close in as I pass through the last corridor, heading toward the side doors that lead to the gardens.

This part of the castle always feels alive at night—every groan of timber and shift of shadows putting me on edge.

I crack open the heavy side door, wincing at the low groan of the hinges. For a second, I freeze, my pulse pounding in my ears.

No shouts, no footsteps.

Just the wind whispering through the trees beyond the garden.

I slip outside, letting the door ease shut behind me, and take a deep breath. The crisp air bites at my skin, but it clears my head.

The gardens stretch out ahead of me, the moonlight making everything look sharper—like the world's been etched in silver.

The gazebo looms in the distance, its pale stone glowing faintly, almost like it's waiting.

I move quickly but carefully, avoiding the paths and sticking to the grass to keep quiet. My gaze darts around, scanning the shadows for any sign of movement.

I don't know if there are guards patrolling, but I'm not taking any chances.

Reaching the gazebo, I stop at the edge, catching my breath. The vines that once choked the structure have been stripped away, leaving it bare and gleaming.

The sword stands in the center, and I smile when I see its hilt catching a beam of moonlight.

There's a faint silver glow around it, pulsing softly—almost like it's alive.

"I knew it."

My heart pounds as I step inside, the cool stone underfoot grounding me. Wrapping both hands around the hilt, I grip it tight.

The metal feels warmer than I expected, as if it's been waiting for this moment too.

"Okay," I mutter, bracing my feet. "Let's see if I'm right."

I pull.

Nothing happens.

My jaw clenches, and I shift my stance, throwing more weight into it.

The sword doesn't budge.

A flicker of doubt tries to worm its way in, but I shove it aside.

I'm not giving up. Not after everything I've been through.

This time, I grip the hilt harder, planting both feet firmly on the stone. I take a deep breath, feel the cool air fill my lungs, and pull with everything I've got.

The sword doesn't just move—it sings.

A low hum vibrates through the air as the blade slides free from the stone, smoother than I ever thought possible.

The sound reverberates in my bones, almost drowning out my gasp of triumph.

My chest heaves as I hold the sword up, its silver glow brighter now, casting pale light across the gazebo.

"Got it," I mutter, a fierce grin spreading across my face.

But the moment is short-lived.

The temperature plummets—sharp and sudden—and a whisper brushes past my ear.

Not a voice.

A thousand voices, overlapping and incomprehensible, hissing with venomous intent.

My breath catches, and I whip around, the sword trembling slightly in my hands.

The darkness outside the gazebo churns, thick and alive, pouring toward me like smoke with a mind of its own.

"What the hell—"

My words are cut off as the cloud of shadows slams into me, a solid, ice-cold force that knocks me backward into one of the stone pillars.

Pain explodes across my back, and the sword flies from my hands, skittering across the stone floor of the gazebo.

My lungs seize, air refusing to come, and I crumple to my knees, gasping—unable to take a breath.

The whispers swell, circling me, taunting me.

I clutch my ribs, willing myself to move, to grab the sword, to do something.

But before I can even crawl toward it, a figure steps into the gazebo, cutting through the oppressive shadows like a gold beacon.

Liona.

She's radiant, bathed in an otherworldly glow that glints off the silver sword lying at her feet.

Her golden gown ripples unnaturally, as if the fabric itself is alive, moving in response to the dark energy swirling around us.

Her eyes gleam with conquest as she crouches and picks up the sword, holding it like it was always meant to be hers.

"Well, isn't this just perfect?" she purrs, her voice smooth as honey and twice as sticky. "I was wondering how long it would take you to figure it out, little mortal. I should thank you, really."

I force myself to sit up, every movement sending sharp stabs of pain through my ribs. "Don't mention it, Lenox. Happy to help."

Her smile sharpens, the edges of her teeth catching the silver light.

"It's Liona, darling," she says, her tone dripping with mockery. "But I don't expect you to remember things like that. After all, you are a simple-minded mortal who doesn't belong here. You're not one of us, and you never will be."

I grit my teeth, willing my voice to stay steady. "Funny. I'm the simple-minded one," I wince against the pain in my ribs, "yet you couldn't pull the sword."

"Don't mistake usefulness for intelligence." She steps

closer, the sword glinting in her hand. "You were a means to an end. But now? You're just in the way."

Liona stands to her full height, her grin turning seductive.

"Isn't that right?" she calls over her shoulder.

Before I can reply, another figure steps into the gazebo, his presence as cold and deliberate as the shadows around us.

My stomach twists.

Orion.

His silver hair catches the faint glow of the moonlight, but there's nothing warm about the way he looks at me now.

He stops just behind Liona, his hand sliding around her hip, low on her stomach, as he pulls her into him.

The gesture is intimate, possessive, and it sends a spike of anger through me.

"You performed perfectly, starling," he says, his voice low and smooth. His lips trail up Liona's neck, and she visibly shivers. "But you, my love, you've done well."

Liona tilts her head, giving him better access, her smile widening. "Was there ever any doubt?"

I can't move.

The pain in my chest is nothing compared to the icy realization settling over me.

"You," I say, the word barely more than a whisper. "You've been using me this whole time."

Orion's gaze shifts to me, his expression unreadable.

"Of course I have," he says simply. "You should've known better."

The casual cruelty in his tone makes my breath hitch. Every warning, every doubt I'd ignored crashes over me in a wave, and I feel like an idiot for not seeing it sooner.

But anger flares to life alongside the pain, and I force myself to my feet, swaying slightly but standing tall.

"Well," I say, my voice biting. "You got what you wanted. So, what now? You two going to run off into the moonlight and take the throne?"

Orion smirks, his fingers moving Liona's golden hair off her shoulder.

"Something like that."

Liona raises the sword, her golden glow intensifying.

"Do it," Orion says softly, his voice coaxing and cruel in her ear. "End her."

For a moment, I think she'll hesitate.

But her eyes meet mine, and there's no doubt, no mercy in them.

The blade comes down in a swift arc.

I twist to the side, hoping to avoid the worst of it.

Pain explodes in my side as the sword pierces flesh.

I gasp, my lungs seizing as my knees hit the dirt.

My hand flies to my side, the sharp sting grounding me in the now as reality surges forward.

Where the fuck am I?

My head swims, and for a moment, the realm is spinning too fast.

Moonlight filters through the dense canopy above, its silver glow casting fragmented patterns across the forest floor.

The forest.

I'm outside.

I'm in the forest.

Panic claws at me as I take in my surroundings. The castle walls loom behind me, the gate wide open—something it's never been. I'd tested that myself. More than once.

The cold realization washes over me: I'm beyond the wards. Beyond the safety of the castle.

My abdomen burns, and I glance down. Blood glistens on my fingers where they're wrapped around the hilt of my dagger.

The blade is buried shallowly in my side, its edge biting into my palm as if I'd been gripping it in desperation. But my other hand is wrapped firmly around the handle.

Did I stab myself?

My breath comes in sharp bursts as I pull the dagger free, hissing through clenched teeth at the fresh wave of pain.

Blood seeps from the wound, dark against the pale moonlight.

I press my hand against the gash, my thoughts racing.

How the fuck did I get here?

That dream—that fucking dream—or was it real?

Liona. The sword. Orion.

It had felt so vivid. So cruelly tangible.

My legs are shaky as I stand, the cool forest air brushing against my sweat-damp skin.

I need to get back within the castle's protective walls.

Within the shield that keeps the darkness out.

A soft crunch on the forest floor makes me freeze.

The sound of footsteps.

The rustle of leaves and twigs sends adrenaline spiking through my veins.

Any number of beasts roam these woods.

I've heard Mor talking about them nearly every day for a week.

I narrow my gaze, searching between the trunks for movement. Assessing how much time I have to run to the castle gate.

Movement.

A dark figure steps from behind a thick tree trunk.

A familiar stare locks onto me.

A Lesser Fae.

One I recognize.

The guard from Beltane.

The one who stared at me too long in the archives.

The one whose eyes crawled over my handmaids like they were a feast he couldn't wait to devour.

Now, his predatory smile cuts through the shadows as he steps into the clearing, his boots crunching softly against the earth.

I shift my grip on the dagger's handle, my hand slick with my own blood.

"Orion said you can't hurt me within the castle walls," I say, keeping my voice steady despite the hammering of my heart.

His grin widens, teeth flashing in the faint light.

"You're not inside the castle walls, though. Are you?"

The words hit me like a blow.

The specifics of the command that left me vulnerable. Exposed.

"Within the castle walls."

That's what Orion had said.

And that's exactly where I am not.

I keep my eyes firmly on him, calculating my options.

More rustling in the leaves makes my stomach tighten, and I grimace against the pain.

Figures emerge from the trees, their silhouettes tall and imposing.

Three—no, four.

Four male Fae step into view, each one wearing dark tunics and trousers—some clad in the same dark armor as the first guard.

Their faces are shadowed, but the way they carry themselves tells me enough.

They mean to capture me.

Their knees are slightly bent, their hands stretched out before them, moving at a snail's pace—slow, deliberate.

They don't want me to run.

The whispers return, faint and insidious, rustling through the air. I can't tell if they're real or a trick of the realm, but they set every nerve in my body on edge.

"Stay back," I warn, gripping my dagger with blood-slick hands. My voice is sharp, slicing through the thick tension.

The guard chuckles—low, dark, and menacing—as he takes another step closer.

"You think that little knife will save you?"

"I think it'll hurt like hell when I slice your balls off."

I snap the words back, shifting my stance.

My legs are unsteady, but I refuse to let him see it. I take one slow step back toward the gate behind me.

The dagger feels heavier than it should, but I tighten my grip.

Ready to strike. Ready to kill if I have to.

The tension stretches, a taut string ready to snap.

I move back half a pace.

They match it, closing in.

The guard lunges.

I react on instinct, sidestepping and swinging the blade in a quick arc.

The tip catches his cheek, slicing cleanly through skin.

He jerks back with a grunt, his hand flying to the fresh wound. Blood seeps between his fingers, dark and glistening.

His eyes meet mine, blazing with fury.

I don't have time to revel in it.

Another Fae lunges.

I drive my elbow into his nose.

A sickening crunch—bone shattering beneath the force.

He stumbles back, hissing a curse.

But before I can move, another set of hands—strong, unyielding—wraps around me from behind.

I thrash, twisting in his grip, but his arms are like iron.

Squeezing. Constricting.

The first guard wipes the blood from his cheek, his mouth curling into a sneer.

"You're going to pay for that," he snarls, his voice a venomous growl.

The whispers grow louder, wrapping around me like a noose as I ram the back of my head into the Fae crushing me.

CHAPTER 34

orion

The horses' hooves clatter against the damp stone path as Mor and I leave Umbriel's court behind.

The thick, oppressive air of Evershade hangs heavy around us, a lingering reminder of how utterly unhelpful the visit has been.

Umbriel's refusal to cooperate is frustratingly expected, but his smug aloofness grates at me like jagged glass.

"The Lord of Shadows," I mutter, my grip tightening on the reins. "More like the Lord of Circles. He says plenty and yet nothing."

Mor's crimson eyes flick toward me, amusement curling faintly at the corner of her mouth.

"You expected something different? Umbriel thrives on riddles and ambiguity. It keeps his enemies guessing. And his allies," she adds pointedly.

"Allies?" I snort. "He's a liability, not an ally."

Mor shrugs, the movement causing her shadows to ripple and shift. "Perhaps. But his games serve a purpose, even if we don't like it. Still, his indifference to the stone is suspicious."

"That stone," I growl, my jaw clenching. "We're no

closer to answers. He didn't deny it came from Evershade, but he didn't confirm it either."

"Because denial would be a lie, and confirmation would be an admission of guilt," Mor replies coolly, her tone tinged with disdain.

"Umbriel's not stupid enough to implicate himself outright. He knows you would have grounds to execute him on the spot."

The path curves ahead, and our horses meander along, their pace unhurried despite my mounting frustration.

I glance at Mor, who is preoccupied with peeling another piece of fruit she must have tucked away in her cloak.

She seems utterly unaffected, as usual, her nonchalance only feeding my irritation.

As the border nears, Hypnos comes into view. He stands beside his horse, the creature as still as a statue beneath his hand.

His pale, colorless eyes are distant, his expression impassive—unreadable to anyone unfamiliar with him. But I know him too well.

The slight tension in his shoulders, the subtle weight in his stance—it's enough to tell me his efforts have been as fruitless as my own.

When we are close enough, I ask the question already burdened with the answer. "Thornspire?"

Hypnos inclines his head, his voice calm yet tinged with quiet disappointment. "Denied entry. King Thorne's emissary claims he is indisposed."

"Indisposed?" Mor echoes, her scoff cutting through the damp air. "Cowardly bastard."

"Indeed," Hypnos replies, his tone clinical and detached as always. "The timing is . . . suspicious."

I grit my teeth, irritation bristling under my skin. The courts are playing games while the darkness claws at Avalon's heart. Before I can respond, Hypnos suddenly freezes.

His head snaps westward, and the glow of his eyes intensifies—a stark, unnatural brightness illuminating his face.

The horses shift uneasily, their hooves scuffing against the ground as though they, too, feel the shift in energy.

A cold knot tightens in my chest, a leaden weight dragging down every instinct as I follow Hypnos's gaze.

Mor and I remain within Evershade's boundary, still wrapped in Umbriel's oppressive wards.

Hypnos, however, stands in the lands between courts, unbound by their influence, untethered by their enchantments.

His gaze locks beyond the horizon to the west. To Starfall.

"Orion," Hypnos says, his voice soft—quieter than a whisper yet deafening in its gravity. "Something's wrong."

The knot in my chest twists tighter. Dread rushes through me like glacial water as I look westward, the wordless warning filling the space between us.

"Go!" The shout tears from my throat as I slam my heels into my horse's flanks. It lunges forward into a gallop, its powerful strides devouring the distance.

Beside me, Mor spurs her mount with the same feral urgency, her beast moving like an extension of her will.

The thunder of hooves echoes in the air as the border of Evershade looms closer.

The moment we cross, the weight of Umbriel's wards falls away, and Starfall's sirens crash into my awareness like a breaking dam.

The alerts slam into me—a torrent of fragmented warnings and desperate pleas from the magic tethered to my will.

The din pounds in my head, a cacophony of chaos that I shove aside to focus.

The darkness around us shifts, pressing at the edges of my mind. The wards at Starfall are fraying, their edges strained against a force I can't yet see. Shadows flicker at the corners of my vision, their desperate whispers begging for aid.

Mor growls low beside me, her darkness curling around her like living things. "The wards are barely holding," she says, her voice tight with tension.

"Starfall will hold." The words are as much a command to the castle as a reassurance to myself.

My horse pounds forward, hooves striking the ground like thunder, but it feels like I am moving too slowly. The distance to Starfall feels infinite. It has to hold.

"Mor." My breath comes in hard pants as I push my horse even faster. "Let me speak to Badb."

I always feel the shift take place—the moment when one soul steps back and another takes control.

Mor's posture shifts, almost lengthening, her spine

straightening. She moves the reins in her hands. Mor is left-handed. Her older sister is not.

If I were looking at her eyes, the crimson hue would have given way to gold.

"The Battle Crow is always here, Prince Regent," comes Mor's voice, but it is no longer just hers. It is layered, deeper, resonating with an eerie certainty. Badb has taken possession of Mor's body.

I don't waste time with pleasantries. "Send your Cacophony ahead. I need to know what's happening at Starfall."

Badb nods, her tone edged with a subtle amusement that seems out of place amidst the chaos. "And we will locate your queen."

Before I can respond, the shift in power rolls off her like a tidal wave.

Shadows pour from her body—an oily, rippling darkness that catches the wind and fractures into hundreds of crows.

Their cries fill the air, harsh and piercing, as they surge upward in a living tempest.

Their wings blot out the massive moon, the sky darkening with their violent flight.

The flock races forward, a murderous blur of feathers and claws bound for Starfall. Badb watches them, spurring her horse into a gallop, her gilded gaze fixed on the horizon.

The trees blur past in a chaotic streak of shadow and moonlight, the horizon seeming to shift and stretch as Badb's murder of crows surges ahead.

"It is a false attack," Badb finally says, her voice cool and certain. Relief wars with confusion as my heart stumbles, then picks up its frantic pace.

"A test?" I grit out, the words feeling foreign on my tongue.

Badb nods, her gaze distant. "The dark Obscura tests the boundary. The wards are anxious, Prince Regent. Starfall screams into the night. The castle sends you a message."

My jaw tightens. "Where is Tana?"

"The castle weeps for the Queen," Badb murmurs, her gaze snapping to me. Her voice is devoid of its usual sharpness, tinged instead with something raw. "Orion, she is in danger."

The world feels like it tilts on its axis, but I don't falter. "Summon my Shadowmare," I bark, the command more instinct than thought.

Badb doesn't respond with words. Instead, her shadows writhe and coil, manifesting the creature from the void. My Shadowmare materializes, its obsidian form shimmering with an unnatural sheen. Its glowing silver eyes meet mine, and I waste no time.

With a single leap, I'm on its back, spurring it forward even before my boots are fully settled in the shadowed stirrups.

The creature obeys without hesitation, its massive hooves finding an impossible speed as it breaks ahead of Mor and Hypnos.

With a mighty flap of the beast's great obsidian wings, the mare reaches for the dark sky.

"Find her, Badb."

My anger claps with the growing thunder as lightning flashes in the West.

I don't slow.

Not for the return of the Cacophony, not for the chaos waiting ahead.

The castle is mine to protect.

Tana is mine to protect.

And I tear through anyone who dares threaten what belongs to me.

CHAPTER 35

Tana

The world seeps into focus like a slow drip of poison, every drop accompanied by pain. My head throbs in relentless rhythm with my heartbeat, the ache crawling down my neck and into my shoulders.

The sharp sting on my cheek pulls me further into awareness.

Someone slapped me. Hard.

My eyes flutter open, but the effort feels monumental. Everything is dim, hazy. One eye refuses to cooperate, swollen shut and pulsing with cruel insistence.

The other strains against the low light, taking in the outline of a dingy cabin.

This place smells like shit.

My arms ache, stretched high above my head. Rope bites into my wrists, coarse and unforgiving.

My feet barely brush the dirt floor, leaving me swaying unsteadily in the stagnant air.

Stretching, I can touch with one toe, and the reprieve on my arms is minuscule—but at least it's something.

The castle guard I have affectionately dubbed Sewer

Breath and four other Fae were waiting for me, somehow knowing I would emerge from the protection of the castle.

Every one of these bastards was bleeding by the time the largest finally knocked me out.

I don't know how long we've been at this cabin, but it's likely been nearly a day. The denim-hued morning of Avalon greeted me when I first woke up in this godforsaken place.

They've been at this for hours, and I feel like I've been out just as long.

A flash of lightning illuminates the room for a split second, followed by thunder that rolls endlessly across the darkened sky.

The sound rattles through the cabin, blending with the pounding in my head.

I blink against the pain, trying to focus. It's a mistake. The world tilts dangerously, and I fight the urge to retch.

My den of torment is nothing more than a cabin that stinks of sweat and piss. It's small, cramped, with soot-streaked walls from the old fireplace.

The haze in my mind recedes slowly, and the pain in my body sharpens as I try to catalog each wound that was there before I lost consciousness again.

The stab wound in my side—from my own dagger. The one I dropped onto the forest floor, the one that only those sworn to protect me will be able to see.

Hopefully, they'll find it, see the blood, and know something is wrong.

The beating they gave me when I first got to the cabin left me with a swollen eye, a busted lip, and at least one broken rib. I'll count the bruises later—when these mother-fuckers are dead.

The dozens of shallow cuts on my legs, arms, and stomach have stopped bleeding, but I'm expecting Stabby Fae to slice me more at some point and bring out a fresh wave of blood loss.

He's the big Fae who locked me in an unbreakable hold.

He will likely be my biggest obstacle in getting out of here.

They took a break to cook themselves some kind of roasted hare.

Swamp Breath used the time to cut my nightgown open and grope me while he jacked himself off, his cronies laughing like it was a fucking game.

A shiver courses down my spine, unbidden, as the memory claws its way back. The sickening heat of his breath on my neck. The rasping whispers of all the vile things he planned to do once they were finished with me.

The way his hands roamed—intrusive and slimy—while he pumped himself like the pathetic, disgusting creature he is.

He was about to bring himself to orgasm and wanted to shoot his load on my stomach.

He moved from the side to my front, looking down at his tiny pecker for a second and then at me.

"You're going to smell like me for days, Que—"

That's when I broke his nose, slamming my head into his pockmarked face, reveling in the sickening crunch and his howls of pain.

It was worth the punch that knocked me out.

So now I'm waking up for a second time with these assholes. My eyes strain to focus as Swampy comes back into view.

He's so close I can smell the rot of his breath, his face split into a wide, menacing grin—covered in his own blood. His eyes shine with malicious glee as he tilts his head, studying me like a predator sizing up its prey.

This bitch does not know the meaning of personal space.

"There she is," he says, his voice low and mocking. "Thought I lost you for a moment there, Queenie."

He smacks my cheek three times, pissing me off with each strike.

Jerking my head away, I spit blood in his face, the metallic tang still thick in my mouth.

"—the Briar Court." The whispers of Stabby Fae and another wander over to me across the hut. "You know Ruvan wants her," he says.

"Yeah. And we saw their emissary approach the mortal during Beltane. Prince Orion did not like that."

He sings the last several words with a grin, amusement dripping from his tone.

"Right, then, we'll send an offer to Thornspire first and see what they are willing to pay for the realm's chosen queen." I catch the malice dripping off the imposed disgrace.

The irony of this is not lost on me.

A bit of karma, you could say. My own ruse backfiring and manifesting into reality.

I was going to stage a queen-napping, steal the sword, and head to the Briar Court for my bargain home.

It seems I'll be making it there after all—just without a sword and with my ass beat.

Well, if they're looking for a payout, they'll have to hand me over in one piece . . . hopefully. Plus, I assume they will need to transport me somehow for the exchange.

I'll likely have a multitude of opportunities for escape, seeing how these guys are fucking idiots.

"Oy, boys." Swamp Breath calls out. "Our toy is awake again."

Thunder rolls outside again, and my body screams in protest. I force myself to lift my head, even as the room tilts precariously.

I need to focus, to push through the pain, and keep these assholes on edge.

"You guys ready to get your asses kicked again?" I mutter, every word fighting through my dry throat.

The castle guard steps back, his cruel grin still plastered across his filthy face. My one good eye follows his movement, then flicks to his small pack of tormentors.

They're just as grimy as he is, their clothes tattered, their faces smudged with dirt.

But it's the way they look at me that sends a chill through my veins—a gleam of cruelty and hunger in their eyes that makes my skin crawl.

"I think you've got this situation twisted around, Queenie."

Big Stabby licks his lips, his gaze trailing over me, admiring his work—and probably envisioning more.

Another Fae cracks his knuckles, a slow, deliberate motion that echoes in the small, oppressive space.

They're silent, but their intent is clear.

So let's piss them off.

"I think you hit like a little bitch." I let out a weak, rasping laugh, though it burns in my throat. "Is this going to be it? Six of you?"

My voice is hoarse, barely above a whisper, but I make sure it carries enough disdain to prick their fragile egos.

"Is that how many you need to gang up on a mortal?"

The guard's grin falters for a split second, but he recovers quickly, stepping closer again. "You've got quite the mouth for someone hanging by a thread," he sneers, looking up at my bound hands.

I let my head drop forward, feigning exhaustion, then glance up at him from beneath my lashes.

"You're not very bright, are you?" I rasp, licking the blood from my lips. "Let me make this simple for you. You've got five more minutes to walk out of here alive."

That makes them laugh, the sound rough and grating, like broken glass. More lightning strikes—seemingly closer. A storm howls in the distance, raging toward our rotting shack.

The guard leans in again, his face inches from mine. "You don't look like you're in any position to be making threats, Queenie."

I force another weak chuckle, coughing as I do. "Not a threat," I whisper, my lips curving into the faintest smirk. "Just a fact. Let me go, and maybe—just maybe—you'll live to see another night."

A sharp crack of lightning punctuates my words.

Their laughter dies down, replaced by a tense silence.

One of the Fae in the back shifts uncomfortably, but the guard doesn't budge. He grabs my chin roughly, forcing me to look at him.

"You think you're scary?" he growls. "You're nothing but a mortal playing pretend in a world that'll eat you alive."

I glare at him, my vision swimming. "Maybe," I whisper, my voice trembling but steady enough to drive the point home.

"But you have no idea what kind of nightmare you just brought into your pathetic little lives."

The storm outside roars, lightning flashing through the cracks in the hut, illuminating the unease flickering in some of their eyes.

They don't know me—not really—but that's what I'm counting on. Let them wonder what I'm capable of. Let them doubt.

"She's bluffing," Stabby's gravelly voice barks from the back of the hut. He stands, a much more imposing figure than Swamp Breath.

Laughter swims eerily in his dark eyes as he walks slowly across the small cabin. Each step makes the space seem smaller and smaller.

Reaching the crackling fire just a few feet away, he lifts a metal poker that had been sitting within the hot embers.

Oh, fuck me.

It's not a poker.

It's a branding iron.

They must have put it in the embers while I was out. Now I'm almost thankful Swampy woke me up with a slap rather than searing that into my skin.

I swallow carefully, making sure to keep my gaze hard on him as he grips the branding iron in his large hand. The tip glows orange-red, hungry to sear into the closest hide—and unfortunately, that might be me.

Lightning cracks again, and it feels like it's right outside.

Three intense snaps of raw power rain down from the sky.

Crack.

Crack.

Crack.

The shadows of a horde of birds fly overhead, lit up by the white bursts of lightning. Their calls echo ahead of them as they race the approaching tempest.

The heat from the brand grows dangerously close, the glowing tip nearly kissing my skin. My breath catches—shallow and erratic—as I brace for the searing agony.

I'm shaking—not from fear, but from the rage boiling just beneath my skin.

This bastard doesn't know it yet, but he's just sealed his own fate.

The storm outside rages, the wind howling like a pack of wolves, shaking the fragile walls of the hut. The lightning is relentless, each strike illuminating the filth-streaked faces of my captors.

The air feels alive, charged with something electric and primal, and I swear I can feel it vibrating in my bones.

The Fae with the branding iron leans closer, his grin wide and cruel, his foul breath mixing with the acrid smell of burning metal.

"Let's see how loud you can scream, Queenie."

The castle guard steps behind me. His grin is twisted, his eyes alight with perverse anticipation.

He grabs my cheeks roughly, puckering my lips and forcing my stare ahead. His other arm wraps around my waist, keeping me from swinging.

The others are watching, their cruel laughter echoing faintly over the storm, as if feeding off my impending pain.

I focus on Stabby's dark eyes as he lifts the iron closer to my side, the heat making me sweat.

I bite down hard on the inside of my cheek, tasting blood, using the sharp pain to keep me grounded.

I won't give them the satisfaction of seeing me break.

Thunder rumbles like a god's wrath, shaking the earth beneath us. The sound grows louder, more insistent, as if it's building toward something catastrophic.

A blinding flash of light explodes through the hut, the door shattering into splinters that scatter like deadly rain.

The world around me is a chaos of sound and light, but all I can register is the piercing white static that's taken over my vision.

My ears scream with a high-pitched ringing, drowning out any other noise.

The air feels thick, oppressive, as if the explosion has sucked all the life out of the room and left me floating in its void.

I blink rapidly, trying to focus, to ground myself, but my sight is a blur of dark shadows and ghostly streaks.

A shape moves nearby—large and undefined—and I squint against the disorientation.

My heartbeat pounds in my chest, frantic and uneven, the only tether I have to reality.

A muffled voice filters through the fog, distant and distorted, like a sound trapped beneath the surface of an ocean.

I can't make out the words, but the tone is sharp, commanding, and it sends a shiver down my spine.

Blinking again, the shapes around me begin to solidify. Shadows give way to faint outlines, colors bleeding back into the world in a slow, agonizing crawl.

My breaths are shallow and ragged, but I force myself to steady them, to push through the pain and confusion.

The hut comes into focus in fragments—bits of shattered wood, the flickering light of the fire.

To my right, the Fae who held the branding iron is staring back at me. His eyes are wide and lifeless, frozen in a mask of shock.

The branding iron is no longer in his hand. Instead, it's embedded in his forehead, pinning him to the wall like some grotesque trophy.

Blood trickles down his face in thin rivulets, glinting in the firelight as if mocking the life that once coursed through him.

A figure steps into my line of sight—tall and imposing.

My vision is still blurred, the edges of him wavering like a mirage. The movement seems both too fast and too slow, surreal in the chaos.

White hair catches the dim firelight, glowing like a beacon, and the familiar scent of leather and smoke washes over me.

Orion.

I blink rapidly, trying to sharpen the world around me. His quicksilver eyes lock onto mine, their usual intensity softened by something that feels foreign—sorrow.

There's an apology in his gaze, as if my battered state is a burden he can't bear but doesn't know how to carry.

The dream I had is the first recollection that swarms in my mind. The hurt of his betrayal.

But it was just a dream.

Perhaps a premonition.

His lips are moving. I can see the shapes they form, the urgency in his expression, but my ears are still ringing, drowning out whatever he's trying to say.

He snaps his fingers near my face, and the sharp motion finally breaks through the fog.

The muffled ocean of sound begins to fade, replaced by a pop in my ears, the painful pressure finally easing.

"Tana," he says my name like a prayer, and the word reaches me.

I blink at him, my mind sluggish and still catching up.

My name.

He said my name.

He's never called me by it before—not once.

The way it falls from his lips—it's different. Not a barked order. Not a teasing nickname.

But something softer. It wraps around me, familiar yet foreign, weaving itself into the air and grounding me.

"Y-you said my name," I manage to whisper, my voice hoarse and rasping, barely audible over the crackle of the fire and the distant storm outside.

I don't know why it's important to point that out, but it's the only thought my mind can process.

His brows knit together, his eyes scanning my face as if searching for what I'm holding onto, what part of me is still fighting to stay present.

"Yes," he says, his tone quieter now but no less urgent. "I'm here, Tana."

The way he says it again, with that same careful reverence, sends a ripple through me.

It's grounding and disarming all at once, as if the chaos around me dims just enough for me to breathe again.

My fingers twitch against the bindings at my wrists, the first flicker of life returning to limbs that feel heavy and foreign.

I swallow hard, forcing my focus back to the here and now.

The man before me is real.

His voice is real.

And he said my name.

Orion bends down, his movements deliberate yet impossibly gentle as he begins untying the rope binding my ankles. His fingers work quickly, the rope falling away with little resistance.

I can't tear my gaze away from him, from the quiet fury simmering just beneath the surface of his composed exterior.

Beyond him, the remnants of the hut come into sharp focus.

The entire wall and door are gone—blown away with the force of the lightning strike. The storm rages outside, flashes of silver light illuminating the destruction like a surreal painting.

Broken beams jut out at odd angles, and the acrid scent of burnt wood mixes with the damp, electrified air.

My captors are still alive—for now.

They dangle in the ruined space, their feet kicking uselessly against the air.

Their faces are twisted in agony, contorted into expressions that would almost be pitiful—if they weren't the monsters who did this to me.

Shades of red creep into their skin, deepening to an ominous purple as the life is choked from them.

The source of their torment is clear.

A river of shadows streams from Orion like a living entity, each tendril coiling tightly around their necks. The tendrils undulate like serpents, cruel and purposeful, holding the Fae aloft as if they weigh nothing.

Orion doesn't even glance their way.

His focus is entirely on me as he straightens, turning his attention to the ropes binding my wrists.

The tenderness in his movements is a sharp contrast to the deadly grip of his shadows. His eyes meet mine briefly—soft yet burning with an intensity that makes it hard to breathe.

"Which one of them did this to you, Starling?" His voice is low, almost tender, but it carries the weight of a storm.

I swallow hard, my gaze darting to the suspended Fae.

All of them.

They all did something. Their twisted laughter, the sting

of their blows, the branding iron poised to scar me—it's all still fresh, a cacophony of pain and humiliation.

My swollen face and bruised body are proof of their collective cruelty.

My voice catches in my throat, but I don't need to answer.

Orion reads my silence for what it is.

His jaw tightens, and a flicker of something dark flashes through his silver eyes. His shadows pulse, tiny sparks of lightning traveling their lengths.

I suddenly realize—he is the storm outside.

It's his anger.

"Please understand me," Orion says, his tone calm but deadly, the weight of his promise hanging in the air. "Each of them will die tonight."

The rope around my wrists loosens.

Before I can react, he scoops me into his arms with careful precision, cradling me as if I'm made of glass.

My head rests against his chest, the racing rhythm of his heartbeat grounding me even as chaos swirls around us.

A single tendril of shadow winds up to my wrists, effortlessly untying the rope and letting it drop to the ground.

"I only need to know who was responsible," he continues, his voice soft yet sharp, cutting through the storm outside. "So I can ensure they are tortured appropriately for this offense."

The world feels unsteady beneath me as Orion sets me down, his hands lingering just long enough to make sure I won't collapse.

My legs are shaky, my body weak, but I manage to stay upright.

His cloak wraps around my shoulders, warm and heavy, the faint scent of him—a mixture of clean woodsmoke and something spiced—filling my senses.

It's comforting, grounding, even though everything else feels like it's spiraling out of control.

My eyes go to the Fae who watched me in the castle. The one who stepped out first from behind the tree.

Marking the guilty offender, Orion's shadows hunt.

First, it is the guard's who acted together.

Their heads tipped back, their mouths forced open by the stream of darkness that flows into them.

My stomach curdles as their intestines are pulled from their bodies, out through their gaping mouths.

Stretched around their necks and pulled tight at once, bones crack as they fall. Joining the debris of the shattered hut.

The guard who dragged me into this nightmare hangs suspended in midair, his face twisted in terror as Orion's power works him like a predator toying with its prey.

The tendrils of shadow slither into his chest, splitting it open with a sickening, wet sound. His ribs crack, parting like the covers of a book.

Blood splatters everywhere, painting the dirt floor and walls in dark streaks.

"He did this?" Orion's gaze flicks to my slashed night-dress, cut from neck to hem, exposing me.

I nod, my fingers tightening around the edges of the cloak, and I keep my eyes on the unfolding scene.

The guard's screams don't reach me.

I can see his mouth open wide, his face contorted in agony, but all I hear is the sound of my own ragged breathing.

The shadows strip him of his trousers next, exposing him fully before surging back to finish their work.

My stomach turns as they rip his genitals away, the brutal motion so fast it feels surreal. Then they shove the severed flesh into his mouth, the force of it silencing him forever.

He gags on his own cock, his body convulsing, but there's no mercy in the relentless tendrils that hold him.

I keep my eyes open, firmly watching so the image is burned into my mind.

The shadows pull his hands together, binding them tight in front of him.

They surge deeper into his chest cavity, and with a violent yank, they extract his heart and drop it into his cupped hands.

The severed organ beats once.

Twice.

Then stills.

He pales rapidly, the blood leaving his body in a torrent, pooling beneath him in a growing crimson lake. His lifeless body sags, the shadows discarding him like rubbish.

I don't realize I'm trembling until Orion steps in front of me again, his worried eyes meeting mine.

There's something soft in his gaze now, something almost tender, and it shouldn't feel as reassuring as it does.

"Let's find you some clothes, Your Grace," he says, his voice quiet and steady.

CHAPTER 36
orion

The stench of the hut is suffocating, a mix of sweat and rot clinging to every surface. It's everywhere—on the walls, in the air, and worst of all, on her.

The faint scent of her tormentor lingers on Tana's skin, and it fills me with a fresh wave of fury that simmers just below the surface. I shove it down, focusing on the immediate task.

Clothing. She needs clothing.

I move through the cramped, filthy space, my jaw clenched so tightly it aches.

The floor is uneven beneath my boots, littered with broken furniture, scraps of fabric, and things I don't care to identify.

My shadows ripple around me, feeding off my anger, and I don't even bother reining them in—nor the storm outside.

A pile of discarded garments catches my eye near a corner. The fabric is rough and worn, but it'll have to do. I sift through the pile, finding a tunic and trousers that look close to her size. Not perfect, but practical.

Next, I spot a pair of boots shoved haphazardly beneath a small table. I pull them out, examining them quickly before adding them to the bundle in my arms.

I don't let my gaze linger on Tana, though I can feel her shivering behind me.

She's wrapped in my cloak, clutching it tightly around her shoulders, but it's not enough to shield her from the chill of what just happened.

The sound of her uneven breathing grates against my composure, her pain a constant reminder of how close I— the realm—came to losing her.

She was reckless. Stupid. She could have died.

The thought alone makes my blood boil.

Turning back toward her, I hold out the clothes and boots, keeping my expression carefully neutral. My voice is tight, clipped, as I speak. "Here. Get dressed."

She looks up at me, her one good eye dull with exhaustion and pain, but I don't meet her gaze. I can't. Not right now.

"I'll wait outside," I add, my tone betraying none of the rage burning in my chest.

Without waiting for a response, I turn on my heel and step out of what's left of the hut, letting the cold night air hit me like a slap.

It's a relief after the oppressive stink inside, but it does little to cool the fire raging within me.

I keep my back to the dwelling, clenching and unclenching my fists as my shadows writhe around me like restless animals.

I release the storm, the air heavy with the scent of rain and earth. Though the distant growl of thunder in the sky warns that my temper is precarious at best.

She doesn't realize how close she came to the edge.

And what pisses me off more is that I nearly didn't arrive in time to pull her back from it.

My shadowmare pants softly, her starlit mane shimmering even in the dim light. She's restless, her wings twitching, needing rest after the hard flight that delivered us here.

I press my forehead against her snout, grounding myself in the steadiness of her presence.

"You did good, girl," I murmur, my voice low, the words meant for her ears alone. My hand lingers on her sleek neck as I send a silent command.

She is too exhausted to carry two riders back.

Without hesitation, the mare spreads her wings, their dark expanse cutting through the night as she leaps into the air.

She soars upward with grace, a creature of shadow and starlight, and vanishes into the night, her path aimed toward Starfall.

When I turn back, Tana is standing a few paces behind me, silhouetted by the dim moonlight, watching the vacant sky where the flying steed just vanished. She holds my cloak in her arms, her face drawn.

Even in the dark, I can see the faint gleam of blood on her, a reminder of how close I came to losing her.

"Do I need to carry you?" I snap, the edge in my voice sharper than I intend.

I regret it immediately, but I can't take it back. The words are out, cutting through the night.

Her head whips toward me, her good eye narrowing in disbelief. She uncrosses her arms, standing taller despite the tremble in her frame.

"You've got something to say? Then say it, Your Highness," she shoots back, her tone biting and loaded with sarcasm.

The title rolls off her tongue like a curse, and it sparks a fire in my chest I can't extinguish.

"Don't push me, Tana," I warn, my voice low and cold. "Not right now."

"Oh, forgive me," she says, stepping closer, her movements as jagged as her words. "Did my near-death experience inconvenience you? By all means, let me apologize for the trouble."

My fists clench, the scent of her blood and that godsforsaken dagger wound driving my rage to the surface.

"You shouldn't have been out of the castle to begin with! What the hells were you thinking, leaving the wards like that?"

She stops dead in her tracks, her lips parting in disbelief before curling into a bitter smile. "You think this is my fault?"

"Isn't it?" I counter. "You've been looking for a way to run since the day you got here. Don't tell me you didn't see my absence as your opportunity."

Her laugh is sharp and humorless as she takes a step closer, her good eye blazing.

"You arrogant, self-righteous ass. You really think I'd run

without a plan?" she says, her voice laced with venom. "For the record, if I wanted to leave, I wouldn't be careless enough to run barefoot, in my fucking nightdress, in the middle of the night, without a damn plan."

The words hit harder than they should. I tell myself it's the insult, not the implication.

"Then why were you outside the wards?" I press, my voice like steel.

"Oh gee, I just thought, 'You know what? I want to take a nice stroll in the death-forest and then stab myself with my own fucking blade while I'm sleeping.'"

She lifts the hem of her tunic, showing me the deep gash in her side that begs to be mended. "Then, to top things off, I called dipshit and his band of merry morons to snatch me up, beat the fuck out of me, and rape me."

The weight of her words slams into me like a blow.

My chest tightens as I process what she just said.

"Did they . . ." I grit the words between my teeth as red rage fills my vision.

"No, they didn't," she snaps, her anger relentless. "Because I broke that motherfucker's nose."

Her words hit harder than I expect, shaking the foundation of my assumptions.

"Why didn't you tell me this sooner?" I ask, softer now.

She lets out a humorless laugh. "Tell you? When, Orion? While I was dodging their branding iron, or maybe when you were busy glaring at me like I'd betrayed you?"

I step back, my throat tightening as her words hammer into me.

She doesn't give me a chance to respond, plowing forward with the force of a storm.

"I didn't run away from the castle," she says, her voice lower now but no less firm.

"Something . . . something brought me outside the wards. Made me try to kill myself, but—I think even in my sleep I fought back. The blade stabbed into my side, not my abdomen. I don't know what it was. But the guard—he was there."

Her good eye holds mine, unwavering, and I see the truth there, raw and unvarnished.

"I fought back," she continues, strength creeping into her voice. "Against every one of those pricks. I left my dagger for you to find. I wasn't planning on giving up, and I damn sure wasn't planning on giving in."

I stare at her, the weight of her words pressing against the anger and fear that have been my constant companions since I found her.

She fought.

Even against impossible odds, she fought.

She puts her hand lightly on my forearm, pulling my attention back to her. "Put some faith in me," she says, her tone soft but firm. "The realm has. Now you need to."

My rage ebbs, replaced by something heavier—something that feels like shame.

My eyes drift over her, really seeing her injuries for the first time. Small cuts crisscross her exposed skin, bruises blooming on her arms and legs, her throat.

She's battered, but not broken.

The evidence of her fight is written all over her, and it

was there in the bloodied faces of the Fae I'd torn apart in that hut.

"Tana," I murmur, the edge in my voice gone. "I . . ." The apology sticks in my throat, but I push it out. "I'm sorry. I shouldn't have—"

Her lips twitch into the faintest hint of a smile. "You're damn right you shouldn't have."

Her faint smile fades as I take a breath, steadying myself. I owe her more than just an apology; I owe her an explanation.

"This is important," I begin, my voice softer now but still carrying the weight of my words. "Not just to the realm. To me."

She tilts her head slightly, her expression curious but guarded. I press on, my gaze steady on hers.

"I'm the grandson of the realm's first chosen queen. Pandora," I say, the name heavy on my tongue. "Her legacy is all that's left of my family. I'm the only survivor."

Her brows knit slightly, but she doesn't interrupt. I keep going, the words spilling out like they've been waiting to be said.

"Every day, I've fought to protect what she built. To keep the throne safe from those who would take it, challenge it, destroy it."

I pause, my eyes flicking to the distant horizon as the memories press in. "I've kept it safe . . . for the queen. For you."

She exhales softly, her gaze flickering with something I can't quite place. I look back at her, my expression softening despite the gravity of what I've just said.

"And I'll give my life to keep it safe," I add, a lighter tone creeping into my voice as I attempt to diffuse the weight of my confession. A smirk tugs at the corner of my mouth. "Not to give you any more ideas to try and kill me again."

That earns me a small, genuine laugh from her, though it's cut short by a wince of pain. She presses a hand lightly to her side, her good eye narrowing at me.

Despite her obvious discomfort, there's a spark of warmth in her expression now.

She holds out her hand, palm up, a gesture of peace. "We'll call it even," she says, her voice steady despite the strain in it. "But on one condition—you stop treating me like an infant. No more pushing me to the side."

I glance at her hand, the slight tremor in her fingers, then back to her face. There's determination in her gaze, but also an unspoken vulnerability.

I reach out, clasping her hand gently, and nod. "Deal."

Her grip is steady but brief as she pulls her hand back.

"Good," she says, brushing off the moment with a slight roll of her shoulders.

I clear my throat, my tone turning practical. "Can you walk, or should I carry you?"

Her displeased look is immediate and sharp, making me grin for the first time in what feels like days. It's a rare, genuine humor that surprises even me.

"Don't push it, Your Grace," she mutters, the mocking emphasis on the title making me chuckle.

Without waiting for a reply, she turns and begins walking, her pace slower but steady now. And surprisingly, she's headed in the right direction.

I fall into step beside her, matching her slower stride.

For the first time since this whole ordeal began, it feels like we're walking the same path.

The battlefield between us has found peace—for now, it would seem.

We'll see how long it lasts.

CHAPTER 37
Tana

The soft drizzle taps against the leaves above as we make our way through these sparse woods.

The rain is light, barely more than a mist, but it's enough to seep into my skin and add to the chill creeping through me.

I cross my arms over my chest, suppressing a shiver, but before I can say anything, Orion wraps his cloak around me.

I've told him I don't need it twice already, even though he clearly knows I do.

He reaches into his belt and holds something out to me.

My knife and sheath.

"Thought you might want this back," he says, his voice calm but laced with the faintest hint of regret.

I take it, the weight of it familiar and grounding in my hand. "Thank you," I murmur, strapping it to my thigh. The leather feels like a lifeline, and I feel a rush of relief having it with me again. "I feel better already."

He nods, his expression unreadable, but I catch a flicker of approval in his silver eyes before he looks away.

We walk in silence for a moment before I notice something odd. The direction.

"Wait," I say, narrowing my gaze as I glance around. "We're not heading toward the castle anymore."

Orion gives me a sidelong look, clearly impressed. "You've got a good sense of direction."

"I'm a captain in the special forces," I remind him, a slight edge in my voice. "On Earth—Gaea, as you like to call it—that means something.

I'm not just some lost mortal wandering in your woods. I'm a fierce warrior where I come from."

He raises an eyebrow, the corner of his mouth twitching as if he's fighting a smile. "Noted."

I roll my eyes but let it go, focusing on the path ahead. "So, why aren't we heading back to the castle?"

"The walk would take several days," he admits, his tone practical.

"Our horses need rest, and the magic in this part of the realm has been damaged. We're on our own for now. I'm looking for a shortcut."

His words settle over me, and I find myself strangely at ease despite the circumstances. The silence between us feels comfortable, not forced. It's a stark contrast to how we usually are—barbed words and tension.

With this newfound truce between us, curiosity stirs in me, eating me alive.

"So, fess up." I nod at him. "What's the deal with Glitter Cunt?"

Orion throws his head back, and his laugh fills the forest. I don't think I've ever heard him actually laugh before, and I'm mesmerized by it.

"I believe you are referring to your closest friend, Liona?"

I raise an eyebrow at him, unimpressed. "You did just give me my knife back. I can stab you."

God, his fucking smile is beautiful. His silver eyes seem darker and have an actual goddamn glimmer to them.

"When we were younglings, Liona's father petitioned my grandmother for a marriage match between her and me."

So, he is fucking engaged to her. I swallow down the immediate irritation that answer raises within me.

"My grandparents were matched and married for duty. For the realm. However, when my grandfather passed—young, in battle—Pandora married again, but for love. Her true mate."

"Like fated mates? Is that a real thing?" My voice rises an octave higher.

"It is indeed. A fated pair is an unbreakable bond, and my grandmother wanted to give me that chance."

He looks at the ground and sticks his hands in his pockets. I watch the way his forearm muscles move before I look ahead.

"During our Dawning years, we were forced to be friends, to get to know each other. I had hoped Liona would find her mate or perhaps die in a tragic accident; however, I was not so blessed."

He holds back his grin and cuts his eyes at me. I admit it: I like hearing this.

"By the terms of the agreement, I was required to wait until we both reached the prime of our immortal lives to decide whether to marry her or not.

I have decided I would rather saw my own head off and let the wild boars feast on it than tie my life to hers."

I snort a laugh, wincing and covering my split lip. "Jesus."

Orion stops, turning to me and retrieving a handkerchief from his pocket. He holds it up to my lip, his other hand gently holding my chin.

He looks at my mouth only a second before he looks into my eyes.

I swear I can feel the weight of his gaze drop to the pit of my stomach.

"Any other reason you didn't want to marry her?" I try to act like I'm not holding my breath waiting for the answer.

"No reason I'm willing to admit." His thumb strokes my chin once, and he pulls away, leaving behind a chill where his warmth just was.

He falls back into silence, walking again, looking around the woods at the swaying trees as if they're fascinating.

I catch up to him, chewing on my cheek, enjoying hearing him tell me about his younger self.

"Your grandmother," I begin, testing the waters of a new conversation. "Pandora. What was she like?"

He glances at me briefly, a faint smile softening his usual stern expression.

"She was... remarkable," he says after a moment. His voice carries a mix of reverence and warmth. "You would have loved her. She also had a sharp tongue she could wield as easily as a sword."

"I like her already," I tease, intrigued.

But my boots sink deep into the saturated mud with a wet squelch. The earth is slick from the rain, and I struggle to pull my foot free without toppling over.

"Here," Orion says, stepping closer and offering his hand.

I take it. His grip is strong, steady, and he pulls me out of the mud with surprising ease.

I murmur a quick thanks and stomp the mud from my boots as best I can, feeling his eyes on me.

He seems lost in thought for a moment, his gaze distant as he smiles faintly. "Pandora was…"

Before he can finish, the ground beneath us shifts with a sudden, ominous groan. My breath catches, and we both stare at each other for a beat before the earth gives way beneath our feet.

Mud and debris slide around us as we tumble down a collapsing mudbank, the world spinning in a chaotic blur of dirt and roots.

There is a moment of freefall, disorienting in total darkness until I hit the ground. The impact knocking the wind out of me as we come to a stop at the bottom of a steep incline.

The damp earth clings to my clothes, the chill biting deeper into my skin as I struggle to catch my breath and fight against Orion's heavy ass cloak.

"Orion?" I call out, my voice shaky as I push myself onto my knees, scanning the darkness for him.

"I'm here," his voice comes from a few feet away, steady but tinged with irritation. He sits up, brushing mud from his hands. "Well, that wasn't the shortcut I had in mind."

The air in the cavern feels heavy, the damp earth pressing down on me as I try to regain my bearings.

But my pulse spikes when I catch the sudden shift in Orion's posture. His body is tense, coiled like a spring, every line of him brimming with alertness.

"What is it?" I ask, keeping my voice low, though the weight of the question thrums in my chest like a drumbeat.

Orion doesn't immediately answer. His sharp silver eyes sweep the space around us, lingering on the dark tunnels that branch off from the cavern where we've fallen.

There are several of them, each gaping like the maw of some ancient predator. They're enormous, easily large enough to fit a subway car through.

But it's the way the walls are carved—rough and uneven, as if gouged by something immense and unrelenting—that sends a shiver down my spine.

Something alive made these tunnels... something huge.

Orion crouches low, pressing his back against the dirt wall, and motions for me to join him. The urgency in his gesture leaves no room for argument.

I move quickly, my knife already in my hand as I take a position beside him.

In a low, steady tone, he begins to speak as he removes the clasp of his cloak from my shoulders and places it on the ground.

"This is a burrow. And if I'm right, it belongs to the Questing Beast."

"The Questing Beast?" I repeat, my whisper barely audible. The name sends a ripple of unease through me, and I glance at the cavernous tunnels again.

"What the fuck is that?"

His jaw tightens, and for a moment, I think he won't answer. But then he exhales quietly, his gaze still fixed on the nearest tunnel.

"A creature of legend. The head of a serpent, the body of a leopard, the haunches of a lion, and the feet of a hart. It makes a strange sound—like barking, or questing—that's how it got its name."

I swallow hard, the image forming in my mind far worse than I'd imagined. "And it's down here?"

Orion's expression hardens. "Most likely. The tunnels are unmistakable." He glances at me, his tone dropping further. "It's fast, lethal, and relentless. If it finds us, it won't stop until we're dead."

My grip on my knife tightens, the metal digging into my palm. The stillness of the air suddenly feels oppressive, as if the darkness itself is waiting for something.

"So, what do we do?"

"We need to find a way out without disturbing it," Orion says, his voice calm but purposeful. He gestures toward the tunnels with a slight tilt of his head.

"One of these might lead to the surface. But if we choose the wrong one..." His words trail off, but the implication is clear.

The beast is down here somewhere, and every choice we make could bring it straight to us.

The air ripples as Orion's shadows unfurl, stretching out from him like a living net of darkness.

They slither silently across the cavern floor, disappearing into the gaping tunnels and sweeping along the rough dirt walls.

The way they move is almost hypnotic—graceful and deliberate, as if they're searching for something unseen.

A few of the shadows curl around my ankles, their touch cool and featherlight as I run my fingers through them.

For a moment, the tension in my chest eases, the sensation oddly comforting, like a reassuring hand on my shoulder.

I glance down at them, then up at Orion, curiosity getting the better of me.

"Are these... yours?" I ask quietly, watching the shadows shift and writhe. "Or do they have a mind of their own?"

He doesn't immediately answer, his gaze fixed on the tunnels as his shadows continue their silent exploration. But then, he glances at me, a flicker of amusement in his quicksilver eyes.

His lips curve ever so slightly, a hint of a smirk that sends a ripple of heat through me.

"A little of both," he replies, his voice low and smooth, like a secret meant just for me.

The gleam in his eye lingers for only a heartbeat before he turns his attention back to the task at hand. But it's enough to leave my heart racing—a distraction I don't need in a place like this.

Orion's focus sharpens, his shadows pooling back to him, their paths seemingly decided.

He gestures toward one of the tunnels, the largest of the group, its entrance sloping upward ever so slightly.

"This way," he says, his tone clipped but calm.

I follow him, gripping my knife tighter as we step into the yawning darkness. His shadows move ahead of us, lighting the way with faint, shimmering traces of starlight woven into the black.

The air grows colder, heavier, the quiet punctuated only by the soft crunch of our boots on the dirt floor.

Every step feels like a gamble, but I trust him—and his shadows.

Orion moves through the tunnel with an uncanny grace, every step deliberate and soundless, like a predator on the prowl.

It's as though he's hunting the Questing Beast, rather than the other way around.

The way his shadows curl and stretch ahead of him only adds to the predatory aura surrounding him, a reminder of just how dangerous he truly is.

I keep close, my knife in hand, though I'm certain I wouldn't stand a chance if that monster appeared.

My eyes flick to him, watching the sharp precision in his movements.

There's no hesitation, no wasted effort. He exudes control, and it's both reassuring and unnerving.

He glances over his shoulder, his voice barely above a whisper. "Did the guard say why they wanted you?"

The question catches me off guard, though I suppose I shouldn't be surprised he's thinking strategically even now. I let out a soft breath, my voice low as I answer.

"They planned to sell me to Thornspire. Said it was because of the marriage offer and how you reacted to it."

His jaw tightens almost imperceptibly, and for a brief

moment, there's a flicker of something—unease? Regret?—in his expression.

It's gone just as quickly, replaced by the stoic mask he wears so well.

"I reacted as any ruler would," he says defensively, his tone firm but not unkind.

I hadn't meant it as an accusation, but his sudden need to justify himself raises an eyebrow.

Before I can push further, he adds, "I would've reacted the same way to any unapproved overture. Their attempt to manipulate you was unacceptable."

His shadows shift subtly, as if responding to his mood, but he steadies himself, his focus returning to the tunnel ahead.

I let the silence stretch for a moment before changing the subject. "Did your visits to the courts turn up anything?"

"No," he admits, his voice clipped. "And we had to cut the visit short. The wards around the castle were assaulted by the darkness."

I stop mid-step, alarm racing through me. "The village?" I ask sharply. "Were the lesser Fae harmed?"

He shakes his head, glancing back at me briefly. "No. The darkness didn't breach the wards. It was only testing the perimeter, searching for weaknesses."

His calm tone does little to ease the knot in my chest. "Is that... normal?" I ask, gripping the knife tighter.

"No." He hesitates, his stride faltering for the first time. His next words are measured, heavy with meaning. "The darkness does not typically attack the castle."

I wait for him to elaborate, but he doesn't. The silence

that follows is more unsettling than anything he's said so far. My voice drops, barely a whisper.

"Then why attack it now?"

His silver eyes meet mine, a shadow passing over his face as he finally answers, his voice low and steady.

"Because it's here for you."

CHAPTER 38
orion

A low, guttural bark echoes down the tunnel, vibrating through the ground beneath my boots.

My head snaps toward the sound, my senses sharpening as the air grows heavy with the unmistakable tension of a predator stirring.

"Did Fluffy wake up?" Tana's voice is breathless, her attempt at humor failing to mask the unease creeping into her tone.

I smirk despite the situation. "Seems so," I reply, though my attention remains fixed on the darkness behind us. "We need to move."

We quicken our pace, our boots crunching softly against the packed dirt of the tunnel floor. My shadows coil tighter, stretching behind us to monitor the space we've just passed.

They ripple with unease, their agitation matching my own.

A deep snarl reaches us—low and resonant—followed by a rush of warm air. The Questing Beast is closer than I thought. Too close.

Tana glances over her shoulder, her steps faltering

slightly. "How fast is this thing?" she asks, her voice tight with tension.

"Fast," I reply, my tone clipped. "It strikes with the speed of a viper."

I can feel her glare even as she keeps moving. Her tone sharpens as she hisses, "Of course it does."

"Also, it can turn invisible," I add, as if it were an afterthought.

"For fuck's sake." She stumbles slightly, shooting me an incredulous look. "You're telling me this now?"

I don't respond, only gesture for her to keep moving. There's no time for debate or sarcasm. The beast is awake, and it's hunting us.

We break into a light jog, the sound of our steps blending with the faint snarls and growls echoing through the cavern.

My shadows pulse, brushing against the walls and the air ahead of us, searching for a path that will give us an edge —or at least buy us some time.

Behind us, the snarls grow louder, more distinct. The Questing Beast is nearing, its presence pressing against the edge of my awareness like a vice.

Tana glances at me, her breaths coming in quick, shallow bursts. "Let me guess. We're running straight into its lair, aren't we?"

"If we don't keep moving, it won't matter where we're running."

The tunnels twist and turn as I lead the way, my shadows reaching ahead, feeling for paths, for safety—or for danger. Tana follows close behind, her breaths shallow but steady. She's keeping up, though I can sense her weariness.

It radiates off her in waves, but she masks it well. She's a fighter, through and through.

A curse slips from my lips as my shadows pull back abruptly, their whispers warning me of what lies ahead.

Before I can stop us, the tunnel widens, opening into a vast chamber. I freeze, my arm shooting across her, my hand gripping her hip as I pull us into the shadows of the nearest wall.

Her sharp intake of breath tells me she's seen it too.

Crouched in a shadowed alcove ahead, illuminated faintly by the phosphorescent glow of fungi clinging to the walls, is the beast. Or rather, a juvenile one.

Its form is both alien and majestic—a strange, mismatched creature that shouldn't exist. The head of a serpent sways slightly as it rests, its body sleek and spotted like a leopard, with powerful haunches that resemble a lion's.

Its deer-like legs twitch, muscles coiling and uncoiling even in sleep.

"Shh," I whisper, my voice barely audible, my lips brushing her ear as her soft hair tickles my nose.

For a fleeting moment, I allow myself to notice her scent —warm and heady, despite the grime and blood that contaminate her sweet aura.

The thought lingers for less than a second before I force it away.

"It's only a juvenile," I murmur, my breath warm against her skin.

"It hasn't seen us yet. Their eyesight isn't sharp at this age, but their hearing and sense of smell are. Stay close to the wall and move with me. Slowly. Quietly. Understand?"

She nods beneath my hand, her pupils blown wide. I let my hand fall from her mouth, taking her hand in mine.

I keep my shadows pressed firmly at our backs, deepening them into a silent, impenetrable wall of darkness.

Tana's gaze flicks back to the beast, her brow furrowing. She leans closer, whispering softly, "That's a juvenile? It's the size of a damn truck."

My heart thrums faster when she covers my hand with her other.

"Be grateful its parents aren't here," I reply, my tone low but firm.

She exhales shakily. "Thank God for small mercies, I guess."

"That's not a mercy," I tell her, glancing at the creature as it shifts slightly, its serpent head lifting lazily to sniff the air.

My jaw tightens, and I lean in closer to Tana, our proximity a necessity in this moment. "If the parents aren't here, it means they're hunting."

Her body stiffens beside me, and I see the realization dawn in her expression. She whispers, her voice barely audible, "Hunting us."

I nod grimly. "If this one alerts them, we're dead."

The weight of my words hangs between us, as heavy as the air in this cavern. I tilt my head toward the far end of the chamber, where another tunnel beckons—a possible escape.

"Follow me," I whisper, my shadows swirling protectively around us. "And don't make a sound."

We creep along the perimeter of the cavern, every step calculated and measured. The air is stifling, thick with the earthy musk of the creature, and my shadows pulse around us, wrapping Tana and me in their protective embrace.

My eyes remain locked on the sleeping beast, its massive body rising and falling with each slow breath.

Tana follows just behind me, her movements surprisingly quiet for someone without Fae-stealth training.

I glance back at her briefly, her face set in concentration as she mirrors my cautious pace.

We're nearly there, the tunnel across the cavern calling to us like salvation.

Then, the beast stirs.

My heart hammers as its serpent-like head lifts, its glowing eyes scanning the air rather than the cavern. It's not looking at us, but its movements are deliberate—searching.

A forked tongue flicks out, tasting the air, and I know immediately—it's aware of something different. Us.

It rises on its mismatched limbs, its leopard body moving with eerie grace as it stalks toward the tunnel we came from. Relief flickers in me for a moment—it's heading in the opposite direction.

If we move faster, we can slip into the next tunnel unnoticed.

I glance back at Tana, silently urging her forward with a sharp gesture. She quickens her pace, her boots stepping carefully over loose stones and debris.

Then her boot catches on a rock.

It's not much—a small stumble, her balance recovering almost instantly. She doesn't make a sound, but the faint scuff of leather against stone echoes in the quiet cavern like a shout.

The beast stops.

Its head snaps up, the forked tongue darting out again. A low, guttural bark erupts from its throat, reverberating through the chamber like a warning bell.

My blood runs cold as it tilts its head back, barking louder, the sound a desperate cry for help.

Then the ground beneath us trembles.

A rumble rolls through the cavern, growing louder with each passing second.

My shadows ripple and tighten instinctively around us as the answering calls of the beast's parents boom through the tunnels like thunder.

"Tana, run!" I bark, my voice sharp and commanding as I pull her forward.

We break into a sprint, the rumbling calls behind us growing deafening.

The cavern is alive with sound now—the snarls and growls of the parents, the frantic barks of the juvenile, and the pounding of our boots as we race for the tunnel.

"Faster!" I snap, glancing over my shoulder to see the shadows of the parents spilling into the cavern like a living nightmare.

The juvenile turns, its glowing eyes locking onto us as it hisses, its sleek body coiling like a spring.

"We need to move!" I shout, pulling Tana beside me as the juvenile lunges.

We bolt into the tunnel, the narrow passage swallowing us in shadow. The tight space amplifies the pounding of our feet and the roar of the beasts behind us. Subtlety is no longer an option; the only thing that matters now is speed.

Tana moves with surprising agility beside me, her stride strong and purposeful despite her injuries. There's power in her movements—the kind of raw, unrelenting determination I've only seen in seasoned warriors.

For a mortal, she is remarkably fast, her breath steady and controlled as she pushes forward.

I keep pace, my shadows spreading ahead and behind us like an extended sense. Then a sharp pang of awareness barrels into my powers. One of the beasts is too close. Too fast.

"Tana, keep running!" I bark, skidding to a halt and spinning to face the threat.

I pull my bow of shadows in one fluid motion, the string taut before the thought fully registers.

The beast is invisible, but I don't need to see it. I can feel the vibrations of its heavy footsteps, sense the ripple of displaced air as it barrels toward me.

I fire.

The arrow soars through the darkness, guided by years of honed precision and the keen instincts that have kept me alive.

The satisfying sound of impact echoes back to me, and the beast howls in pain, its form flickering into visibility as the arrow of my power pierces its flank.

Its serpentine head thrashes, golden eyes blazing with fury.

I don't wait to admire my work.

Turning on my heel, I sprint after Tana, the shadows wrapping around me like armor.

I catch up to her quickly, her pace unbroken as she surges forward, glancing back briefly when she hears me approach.

"Was that—" she starts, breathless but steady.

"The male," I cut in, my tone clipped. "The female is still out there."

Her eyes widen slightly, but she doesn't falter. "And she's worse?" she asks, her voice tight with effort.

"Much worse," I confirm grimly. "Larger. More vicious."

Tana doesn't respond, but her jaw tightens, and she picks up her pace. Good. She understands the gravity of the situation, and for now, that's all that matters.

We press on, the tunnel winding and narrowing as we run.

Behind us, the guttural snarls of the injured male echo faintly, and I know it's only a matter of time before the female catches our trail.

The tunnel spills out abruptly onto the edge of a jagged cliff, and Tana's momentum nearly takes her over the ledge.

She flings her arms out for balance, her boots skidding on the loose rock, and I act without thinking.

My shadows snap forward, coiling around her waist like living ropes, yanking her back just as her toes flirt with the empty void.

She stumbles into me, and I steady her with my arm wrapped securely around her waist.

Her hand covers mine instinctively, her fingers curling into my knuckles.

"Thanks," she breathes, her voice tight with adrenaline but steady.

I nod, releasing her reluctantly. "Stay close."

The ravine stretches before us, its sheer walls plunging into a churning, tumultuous river far below.

Whitecaps crash against jagged rocks, the sound deafening even from this height.

Ahead, a strange column of water rises, defying gravity as it spirals upward toward an unseen destination. It's exactly what I was hoping for.

Tana is already scanning the space, her sharp gaze taking in every detail. She squints at the rising column, her voice rising over the roar of the river. "Is the water flowing upward?"

"It is," I confirm, a flicker of satisfaction in my tone. "It's our shortcut."

She shoots me a dubious look, but there's no time for debate.

"You're just going to have to trust me," I add as we take off.

Before she can respond, the air behind us erupts with a deafening roar.

The tunnel wall explodes outward in a shower of dirt and stone as the female beast barrels through, her massive form a blur of lethal intent.

Her golden eyes lock onto us, and her claws swipe forward, aiming directly for Tana.

Tana's reflexes are faster than I expect. She ducks and rolls, narrowly evading the razor-sharp talons, and doesn't stop moving.

Her blade is in her hand in an instant, and without hesitation, she flings it with perfect precision.

The knife lodges deep into the beast's foot, pinning it to the rocky ground with a sharp, metallic hum.

The beast lets out an enraged bark, thrashing against the binding.

Tana doesn't waste a second. She sprints forward, leaving her blade buried in the beast's paw.

Her instincts are good—every second counts.

I catch the faint glow of the rune on the knife as the beast struggles to free itself. The blade doesn't budge.

No matter how hard it yanks, it stays firm, and realization dawns.

The magic.

Tana's will is holding the blade in place, whether she realizes it or not. The runes respond to her intent.

It's either a lucky coincidence or a sign that she's beginning to grasp their power and how she can wield it.

"Keep moving!" I shout, gesturing toward the rising column of water ahead.

Behind us, the beast's bellow of fury echoes through the ravine, shaking the very ground beneath our feet.

The roar of the water drowns out almost everything as I hold my hand out to Tana.

"Take my hand!" I yell, my voice barely cutting through the cacophony.

Her fingers grip mine firmly, her strength surprising even now.

"We're jumping?" she shouts back, her voice tinged with both defiance and uncertainty.

"Yes," I answer, my eyes locking with hers. "Take a deep breath."

Just as we step to the edge, I fling a ribbon of shadow behind me. It streaks toward the beast, wraps around the hilt of Tana's blade still buried in its foot, and yanks it free.

My own will merging with hers.

The creature lets out an enraged bellow, but the knife sails through the air, clean and true.

I catch it mid-flight, just as we leap into the water column.

We plunge into the rushing torrent.

The force of the water grabs us instantly, pulling us upward with relentless speed.

The world darkens as we are propelled through the column of water, the rushing current turning everything into a deafening blur.

Tana gasps against my chest, her hands clutching my tunic with a death grip.

I tighten my hold around her, my shadows wrapping around her body, insulating her against the crushing force of the ascent.

But doubt creeps in.

How long can a mortal hold her breath?

I can feel her pulse hammering against my arm, her body tensing as she fights against the instinct to breathe in.

I don't know how much longer she can last, and panic claws at my gut.

The water feels endless, and the pressure builds with each passing second.

Then, suddenly, we are spat out into the Misting Lake.

The chill of the lake's depths bites into my skin as we crash into the still, dark water. We're deep—far deeper than I anticipated—and the surface is an agonizing distance above.

Tana is still in my arms, her face strained, her lungs clearly burning for air. I don't let go, nor do I take time to think.

I kick hard.

I propel us upward, summoning my shadows to grip at the pockets of darkness within the water, pulling us toward the surface as fast as possible. Every ounce of my strength goes into reaching the light above.

Tana's movements turn frantic, her body thrashing.

Hold on, Starling.

With one final surge, we break through the surface.

Tana gasps, sucking in a desperate breath before coughing violently. I keep her head above the water, my grip unwavering as I tread us closer to the shore.

Our breathing is labored, the exertion and relief mingling in every heave of our chests.

Castle Starfall looms above the mist-shrouded lake, its dark towers rising through the haze like a sentinel. I glance at it briefly, but my focus remains on Tana.

She is my priority.

She crawls onto the emerald sands of the lakeshore, her body shaking as she coughs up water and gulps in air. I follow close behind, my own breath steadying as I watch her.

Then she freezes.

A pair of boots planted firmly in her path.

Her head tilts upward, and her gaze meets Mor's crimson eyes.

"You look like shit," Mor says flatly, her tone as bland as ever.

Tana lets out a breathy laugh, a mixture of exhaustion and disbelief, then collapses onto her back on the damp sand.

CHAPTER 39
Tana

Mor strides up the beach with her usual calm confidence, a leather satchel swinging at her side.

She hands it to Orion without a word, her crimson eyes flicking toward me briefly before she turns to inspect the shoreline with that sharp, unbothered demeanor she always carries.

"What's that?" I ask, still seated on the soft, emerald sand, my muscles aching despite the relief of solid ground.

"Something from Merlin," Orion replies, his concentration unwavering as he inspects the contents of the bag.

He crouches beside me, opening the satchel and pulling out a series of small vials and jars. "An old friend of my grandmother and an exceptional alchemist."

"Oh my God. There are fucking wizards," I mutter with a huff, still catching my breath.

He selects two vials filled with a shimmering, golden liquid and holds them out to me. "Drink these. They'll help with the pain and speed up the healing process."

I hesitate for a moment, eyeing the vials warily. "Are

they poison? What if they taste like... I don't know, swamp ass?"

Orion raises a brow, his expression almost amused. "You survived a Questing Beast and a group of murderous Fae. Surely you can stomach a little potion."

Point taken. I take the vials and unstopper one, sniffing cautiously. To my surprise, it smells faintly of honey and herbs. Shrugging, I down it quickly, followed by the second.

The effect is almost immediate.

Warmth spreads through my body, radiating outward from my chest.

The aches in my muscles fade, disappearing as if they were never there, and the persistent throbbing in my eye begins to subside.

I touch my side gingerly, astonished to feel that the wound is no longer painful.

"That's..." I trail off, genuinely at a loss for words. I collapse back on the sand with a relieved sigh. "Thank you."

"I need to check the wards," Orion nods, standing and glancing toward the castle's looming silhouette in the distance before looking back at me. "You'll..."

I wave him off. "I'll be fine."

He hesitates only a second before handing me my knife again. I hadn't even realized he retrieved it, and I smile at the offering. He turns to Mor and gestures for her to follow.

She gives me one last glance, and I think I catch the faintest twitch of approval in her expression before she vanishes into the mist with him.

The knock at my bedroom door startles me as I fasten the sash of my robe.

On my way up to my room, I had to command my new, panicked chambermaid back to her quarters for the evening with her mate.

I took a scalding bath, rubbing the lotions and salves into my wounds, fascinated as I watched them heal right before my eyes.

Even my self-inflicted stab wound is little more than a faint pink line. It may not even leave a scar.

I step lightly across the room, opening the door to find Orion standing there.

He's clean too, and he looks much more refreshed from our trip through his shortcut.

His stark-white hair glistens as though it's just been dried, and his scent wraps around me—a subtle mix of pine and something warm and musky.

It's grounding and unnervingly inviting.

"I came to check on the salves," he says, his voice low, steady. "To check on you."

The honesty in his tone throws me slightly off guard, and I hesitate for just a moment before stepping back to let him in.

He moves into the room, his presence as commanding as ever, though his posture is more relaxed now.

"I'm impressed," I tell him, lifting one arm to show him the smooth, unblemished skin where only an hour ago bruises and cuts had marred it.

"This stuff works wonders. I've got a few spots on my back I couldn't reach, but if that's all I walk away with, I'll count myself lucky."

Orion's sharp eyes scan me briefly before he retrieves one of the salves from the bathroom.

"Nothing less than exceptional will do for the queen of the Fae," he remarks, his tone lighter than usual, but there's a sincerity beneath it that makes my chest tighten slightly.

"Turn."

I shake my head, a soft laugh escaping me. "Are you really going to keep calling me queen? I may prefer Starling."

He chuckles. "It's true," he says simply, motioning for me to turn around. "Even if you have not yet faced your trials."

Or remain in denial. Those are the words left unspoken.

I slip the robe from my shoulders, and it drapes low at my back.

"Hold still," he murmurs, his voice closer now. Orion gently moves my hair aside, his touch careful and respectful.

His fingers brush against the bare skin of my back as he applies the cool salve, and a shiver runs down my spine— not from the temperature, but from the sensation of his touch.

"You really don't have to do this," I manage, my voice softer than I intended.

"I do," he replies, his tone firm but kind. "Your strength

isn't in question, Starling. But even the strongest deserve care."

His large hand work the salve into my back attentively. His other hand grips my hip, holding me steady, and it's far too intimate for my sanity.

The room feels charged, the tension thickening with each slow stroke of his hand over my skin.

His fingers press into the muscles along my spine, working out knots I didn't realize I had, and my breath hitches despite my best efforts. Heat pools low in my belly, igniting a fire I can barely control.

I clench my fists against the urge to lean into his touch, to let the sensations take over, but it's futile.

My body betrays me, arching ever so slightly into his hold.

A low, rumbling sound escapes him—almost like a growl—and it vibrates through me, pooling straight where I don't want it to.

My eyes flutter shut as both of his hands slide up to my shoulders, kneading with expert precision.

A moan slips past my lips before I can stop it, soft but unmistakable.

The air between us becomes stifling, heavy with something unspoken.

His breath brushes against my ear, and I shiver as his voice, low and rich, breaks the silence.

"You didn't need my help before," he murmurs, the memory of that night weaving through his tone. His lips are so close I can feel the heat of them.

"Has that changed?"

My throat tightens, my breath catching in my chest. I force myself to steady my voice, but when I finally speak, the words come out softer than I intend.

"I don't... I don't need your help."

It's not a lie. I don't need him. I don't need anyone.

But wanting him?

That's an entirely different matter.

His hands pause for a fraction of a second—just long enough for me to feel the loss when he lets go.

My body protests the distance, but Orion carefully pulls the robe back over my shoulders, the silk sliding softly against my skin.

Then, with deliberate gentleness, he turns me by the arm until I'm facing him. His silver eyes search mine, and the weight of his gaze is almost unbearable.

He takes my hand in his, fingers brushing over my knuckles as he lifts them to his lips.

"If you change your mind..." His lips graze my skin, impossibly soft. "...all you have to do is ask."

Before I can find my voice, he releases my hand, steps back, and strides toward the door.

The lingering warmth of his touch stays with me, even as I watch him leave.

A moment later, I hear the soft click of his door across the hall shutting.

The room suddenly feels too quiet. Too empty.

I let out a shaky breath, running a hand through my damp hair.

Damn him.

Damn me.

Damn this.

My mind churns with a thousand thoughts, each one more chaotic than the last.

I can't let him distract me, not if I'm going to figure out how to survive this realm—how to get back to Earth.

I need to set boundaries. Clear ones.

Orion's presence is like a storm, and I can't let myself get swept away.

I march across the hall, my bare feet silent against the cold stone floor.

I reach his door and knock harder than I intend, my resolve steeled for a confrontation.

But when the door swings open, and I see him, everything—every carefully constructed wall, every ounce of stubborn determination—melts away.

His expression isn't the cocky mask I expected.

It's raw.

Vulnerable in a way that takes my breath away.

The silver in his eyes gleams like molten metal, charged with an emotion he's trying—and failing—to hide.

He looks broken, like he's spent years fighting a battle he doesn't know how to win.

My breath catches, and I falter, just staring at him.

Every logical thought vanishes, leaving only the pounding of my heart and the ache I feel deep in my chest.

"I'm asking."

The words escape me before I can think them through.

I can't tell if it's him or the tendrils of his shadows that reach me first.

One moment I'm standing in the hall, and the next, I'm

surrounded—by him, by his power, by the heat of his body and the intoxicating scent of him.

His lips crash against mine, and the world explodes.

The kiss is everything—hungry, desperate, overwhelming.

It's a clash of wills, a battle for control, as frustration and irritation turn to searing passion.

His hands are in my hair, his shadows curling around my waist, pulling me flush against him as my hands tangle in his tunic, fisting the fabric like it's the only thing keeping me grounded.

Every nerve in my body ignites, the tension between us building until it feels like it might shatter us both.

His tongue sweeps against mine, and I taste him—wild and untamed, like the storm raging outside.

I can feel his restraint slipping, the barriers he's so carefully built crumbling with every touch, every gasp, every broken moan that escapes my lips.

And I don't care.

I don't care about the realm, the throne, or the endless questions that haunt me.

In this moment, there's only him—his lips on mine, his hands on my body, his shadows wrapping us in a cocoon of darkness and desire.

It's too much, but it's not enough.

I want more.

I need more.

And from the way he growls against my mouth, I know he does too.

In one fluid motion, my robe is gone, floating to the floor like a whisper of silk, leaving me bare to the heat of his gaze.

His large hand wraps around my throat, his lips still locked on mine as he kicks the door shut and walks me back to the wall.

The stone is cold against my ass, but I shiver from the chill of his power slinking around my wrists, pulling my arms over my head.

"Just like the first time I saw you." His deep voice breaks as he trails fire down my neck, his fingers kneading my breast with a possessiveness that makes me moan. "Are you ready to feel me, Starling?"

I nod, unable to make the words leave my throat as his shadows caress my legs, moving upward.

"The darkness in me craves you as much as I do." He runs his tongue up the length of my neck. "Will you let us both taste you?"

My eyes are half-lidded as he holds my stare. His grip around my wrists replaces the shadows.

"It was torture," He sucks on my neck. His grip on my wrists tightening. "Beltane—absolute fucking torture. Not tasting you myself."

He licks long and slow up my neck, my chin, before taking my mouth against in another harsh kiss.

He pinches my chin between his thumb and forefinger. "Answer."

The cool tendril of obscurity winds around my thighs, the sweet caress making me arch my back, my nipples brushing against Orion's tunic.

"Can the darkness within me have a lick of that sweet cunt?"

Oh, my God.

"Yes." My eyes roll closed as one of those dark ribbons of his power strokes through my wet arousal.

"Oh," I whisper.

"Fuck." Orion grunts, leaning his head against mine. "Delicious."

I open my eyes to see him wet his lips. I lean forward, capturing his bottom lip between my teeth as his power swirls around my clit.

"Mmph." It brings me to the tips of my toes as his darkness strokes me.

"Orion." My head falls to the side when he rakes his teeth over my nipple, the tender bite making me cry out as his powers set a rhythm that will quickly have me coming against the wall.

I move my hips, chasing the pleasure while he brings it rushing forward.

"Look at me, Tana." He grabs my chin again, and the rumble in his tone pulls my eyes open. "Let me watch you come."

Orion places a peck on my partially open mouth. "I've not even touched you yet, Starling, and your soaked pussy is throbbing for me."

"Orion, I'm—"

"—going to give me every drop of your pleasure." He takes over my sentence as his powers flick across my clit, making me cry out with each thrum.

"I know, my queen. Give me what I want and come for me."

As if my orgasm obeys him, the climax surges forward. He keeps his hold on my wrists as my body writhes against the wall.

The effort to keep my eyes open—to not close them and fall into the sensations of this moment—is monumental.

The tendrils of his power stroke and suck, wringing every gasp and moan possible as I ride the waves of my climax.

As my breaths settle, my cunt still throbbing, Orion's hand slides under my thigh, lifting me like I weigh nothing, his strength as effortless as it is intoxicating.

My legs wrap instinctively around his waist, and I capture his mouth with mine, grasping each side of his face with my hands.

He growls his approval, the sound vibrating through my chest as he sucks on my neck.

Before I can process the shift, he's crawled onto his bed and drops me in the center.

It's the same bed—the massive expanse of black-satin sheets—that surrounded me when I first woke up to this nightmare. But now, they feel like something entirely different.

The cool fabric caresses my skin like a dream, contrasting the heat radiating from Orion as he towers above me.

His silver eyes burn as they rake over my body, and I can't look away, pinned by the weight of his stare.

My legs are spread, and his hands run up the inside of my thighs, his hungry stare fixed on my wet pussy.

In one swift motion, he pulls his tunic over his head, revealing the hard planes of his chest, the tattoos that snake down his neck to his shoulder and arm, and the scars that speak of battles fought and won.

He is magnificent. He's a storm—the chaos and the calm all at once—and I feel like I'm drowning in him.

"You're perfect," he murmurs, his voice rough and full of reverence.

A darkness closes over his face as he slides his belt from his leather trousers, dragging it down my nipple, then the other. But it's not a leather belt.

It's a belt of his shadows, and I shudder at the cold against my hot skin.

"One day, I'll see how beautiful you are with my knots binding you."

He lowers himself over me, his lips finding my breast. The kiss is no softer this time than before. The hunger still simmers beneath the surface, waiting to consume us both.

"Spreading you open for me," he continues, his path moving down my body.

"Choking you while my cock splits you in two."

He whispers the last words against my pussy before he inhales the scent of my arousal like it's a drug.

My groan is a plea wrapped around my pleasure.

His tongue flicks against my center, and a sharp gasp escapes me. Every nerve in my body ignites, fire racing through my veins.

He doesn't rush—no, that would be too kind. Orion

takes his time, tasting me, exploring me, devouring me like I'm the only thing in the world that exists.

He sucks my clit into his mouth, his tongue swirling in slow, deliberate circles. My breath catches, the intensity building with every pass of his tongue.

"Orion," I pant, his name spilling from my lips like a prayer.

I arch into him, my hand grasping his hair as I grind my hips. He moves one of my legs, letting me wrap it around his neck, pulling his mouth into me so I can fuck his face.

My hand grazes his pointed ear, and his pleasured moan surprises me.

I lift my head, watching him work my pussy, and I stroke his ear again.

"You like this, baby?" I coo at him, both hands tenderly massaging his ears.

He breaks away from my cunt, his mouth dropped open as he moans against the movement of my hands.

It's intoxicating, watching him.

Opening his eyes, he fixes them on me with a predatory stare and crawls up my body.

He rubs his erection, still captured in his leather trousers, along my pussy, grinding into me as I stroke him.

"Fae ears are very sensitive, Starling." He licks and then sucks my bottom lip. "You want to make me come in my pants before I've fucked you with my thick cock?"

Holy fucking shit. Potty-mouth Orion is a sight to behold.

"Maybe I do." I whisper next to his ear and watch his skin pebble.

I run my tongue up his ear.

He wraps his arm around my hips, pushing my pussy into his cock, pulsing against me. He's barely holding it together, and both of us will come undone in a matter of seconds.

This isn't how I want him to come. I want him spilling his orgasm deep into me.

"But I'll save that for another time."

I sweep my tongue into his mouth, then open my eyes, staring into his.

"Right now, I want your mouth back on my cunt."

He growls into my neck, marking me with his teeth.

"As you wish, my lady."

His arms wrap around my legs, holding my pelvis while he works me.

Watching me writhe at every touch, I cry out when a tendril of darkness curls up my leg, gliding over my stomach and caressing my breasts, teasing my nipples into hard peaks.

I bow off the bed, the sensation overwhelming as his long fingers join his tongue's exploration. Two slide into me —slow and deliberate—curling in a way that makes stars burst behind my eyelids.

Then another, his movements syncing with his tongue —stroking, teasing, coaxing me higher and higher.

The shadows hold me and begin to move, their silky tendrils brushing over my skin—stroking, caressing—adding to the unbearable pleasure.

One slides between my thighs, joining Orion, a cool contrast to the heat of his tongue and fingers.

I cry out, the sound raw and guttural, as the darkness fills me alongside him—stretching me, claiming me.

I'm teetering on the edge, every nerve in my body screaming for release.

"Yes, Orion, make me come again."

Orion groans against me as a new wave of pleasure courses through me. His shadows tighten their grip, the tendrils around my breasts twisting just enough to send a sharp spike of pleasure-pain that tips me over the edge.

"Oh, fuck, yes." My body convulses, my cries echoing in the room as wave after wave crashes over me.

Orion doesn't stop—his tongue and fingers working me through the aftershocks, his shadows holding me steady as I come undone beneath him.

When I finally collapse, boneless and trembling, he pulls back, his lips glistening with my arousal, his silver eyes molten as they lock onto mine.

His shadows release me, sliding away like a retreating tide, and I can finally move again. My chest heaves as I try to catch my breath, but all I can do is stare at him—utterly wrecked.

Orion only stops long enough to remove the rest of his clothes. His massive cock—hard and hanging low.

And fuck if I don't want him to slam his dick into me with everything he has.

He grips his base, sliding his hand up, rubbing his head with his thumb.

I sit up, sliding to the edge of the bed, mouth open. I watch him as I lick the precum from his tip, then suck the head of his cock into my warm mouth.

"Fuck me," I tell him, gripping his dick, squeezing his hard shaft, and stroking, sucking.

"Is my queen starving for my cock?" he growls, his voice low and commanding as he holds the back of my head, his fingers threading into the tight curls of my hair.

He lets me work his long length into my mouth until I'm gagging on the size of him.

"Mmm." I moan against him, taking him further, again and again, spit leaking down my hand.

"Beg for it, Starling." He lets his head drop back, his voice traveling across the ceiling. "Beg me to fuck you like you've never been fucked before, my queen."

"Oh God, Orion," I choke out, my voice hoarse. "Yes."

"Tell me, Starling."

He slides himself out of my mouth and crowds me until I crawl my way back toward the headboard.

"How much dick do you think you can take before you cry out for me to stop?"

He fists himself, rubbing the head of his cock against my clit.

I'm getting wetter each time he talks, my legs twitching with each touch on my cunt, and I need more. I need to be full of him.

"Please, I need you. I need you inside me. All of you."

I bite his lip as he lines up with me. "Give me everything."

"If my queen commands it."

He grips my thighs, opening me wide, fixated on my dripping cunt.

Positioning himself at my entrance, and in one swift

motion, he thrusts into me—my arousal helping him glide in without effort.

The stretch is overwhelming, his cock filling me completely, reaching places no one ever has before. My scream is soundless, my head thrown back as I adjust to the sheer size of him.

"Fuck," he groans, his voice rough with restraint. "This little mortal pussy is so tight—my cock is suffocating in you."

His hands grip my hips, holding me steady as he buries himself to the hilt.

His ravenous eyes are locked on the point of his entry, obsessively watching himself thrust into me again and again.

"You were made for this, Starling."

His words unravel me—dirty, raunchy, reverent—all at once.

"So fucking beautiful," he murmurs, his pace slow and deliberate, each thrust designed to drive me mad.

"You feel incredible."

His thrusts send me into another universe of pleasure.

"Look at your perfect pussy. The queen of Avalon, taking her prince's cock so well."

The praise, the filthy words, the way he looks at me like I'm the only thing in this realm—it's too much.

When a tendril of his power snaps against my clit like a whip, my body combusts again, my walls clenching around him as another climax rips through me.

I cry out his name, lost in the overwhelming ecstasy, and

he follows me, his movements becoming more frantic, more desperate as he chases his own release.

Orion and I lose track of time as we lose ourselves in each other. His stamina is unlike anything I've ever encountered—relentless, insatiable.

Every time I think we're done, that we've wrung each other dry, he proves me wrong. He doesn't even seem to need a break between his climaxes.

It's as if he can't breathe unless he's buried deep inside me, and I know for certain—fucking a mortal man will never compare to this.

One night of pleasure with Orion—of him bending me over his bed, pounding into me from behind, grasping my hips when I ride his cock or fuck his face—he's ruined me for anyone else.

By the time we're truly spent, our bodies are tangled together, melted into the luxurious satin sheets of his massive bed.

The muscles in my legs feel like jelly, my chest rising and falling as I take a deep, contented breath.

I lean up to him, my breasts pressing against his chest as I kiss him deeply. His lips are soft but firm, his tongue claiming mine with the same possessiveness he's shown all night.

His arm around me rubs affectionately along my back as I rest my chin on his chest.

"I want you to promise me something." I rub a finger down the thin scar on his cheek.

"I have a feeling this promise will not be in my favor, Starling." He smirks. "What is your request of me?"

The words are stuck in my throat, holding us in limbo as the moment stretches out.

"If there is a way for me to go back to Earth, to go home, will you promise to let me know?"

One thing I have learned here: Fae bargains are no fucking joke.

If I'm going to give this a shot—to try, really try—I need to know it's my choice.

Orion's expression shifts—from curious to disappointed. He recovers quickly, pushing back the emotion and nods. "I promise."

I take in a deep breath, releasing it slowly as I lean forward and kiss him.

Just as his hands begin to roam my body again, I feel the telltale hardness against my thigh.

I grin against his lips, pulling away just enough to look him in the eyes. "You're unbelievable," I murmur, a chuckle in my tone.

His silver eyes gleam, his hands sliding down to grip my hips as if daring me to leave.

"I am merely serving my queen, Starling."

The way he always says "my queen" instead of "the queen" does something to me—and I admit, I like it.

Sitting up, I press a kiss to the tip of his cock, earning a deep groan. That thing deserves a fucking trophy. But not today.

The cool air brushes over my skin as I slide off the bed and pick up my silk robe from the floor.

"Well, thanks for this," I say casually, throwing a glance and a wink over my shoulder as I saunter toward the door.

"It's just what I needed."

Orion props himself up on his elbows, watching the sway of my hips.

"What, no cuddles?" he teases.

Without looking back, I chuckle and lift my middle finger in response.

His laughter follows me as I open the door, leaving him behind.

The heat of his gaze lingers on my skin long after the door shuts.

CHAPTER 40

The shift in Orion is there, subtle but there. He's more watchful, more deliberate in his movements when I'm near. His touches linger a little longer, his words softer.

Not that he's any less commanding or frustrating, but there's an unmistakable shift. It's like he's decided something about me, something he hasn't shared yet.

He's been honest about their failures with the courts.

He explained in detail how Evershade's ruling Fae, Umbriel, was as unhelpful as one might expect from someone with that much power and that little interest in anything outside his own borders.

Hypnos fared no better at the Briar Court, where his entry was flatly denied. Orion's frustration simmered below the surface as he spoke, but he never let it boil over.

I've decided the Briar Court is a bad idea, likely filled with selfish pricks that wouldn't bargain with me to go home.

They would just fucking kill me. So, I've abandoned that plan since Orion gave me his word.

My time now will be better spent working to find out

how the one-way door opened, so I can open it again. And preparing to kill the Warden of the Briar when he returns to call in his challenge.

"Why don't we all go to the Briar as a royal convoy or something? Those dickheads thoughts Thornspire would want to *buy* me from them."

Orion releases a possessive growl as I remind him of this. "If I'm there they may let us in, and you guys can snoop around while I—entertain their king or something."

A.K.A.: Convince him to collar his Warden.

"There will be no *entertaining* of anyone until we know their role in planting the doorway on Beltane. Let's not forget Ruvan has placed a threat on your life."

That seemed to settle the matter.

For now.

Orion took me to the top of Starfall's walls and showed me the creatures that lurk in the darkness just beyond the castle's protective wards.

I wasn't ready for them.

They're monstrous things—oversized canines with bodies that look as if they've been flayed alive, their skin dark and leathery, stretched tight over unnaturally muscular frames.

Their fangs glint in the moonlight, and two enormous tusks curve forward from their lower jaws, each the size of my forearm.

I couldn't stop staring.

One prowled close to the wards, its movements sharp and predatory. It snarled, revealing rows of jagged teeth that seemed designed to tear through anything unlucky enough to cross its path.

"They're called Cŵn Annwn," Orion explained, his voice low in my ear as he stood behind me.

"Creatures born of the darkness, corrupted beyond reason. They won't stop until they've consumed everything in their path."

"Charming," I muttered, swallowing hard as I watched the beast. I didn't even realize I was pushing my ass into Orion until he grabbed my hip.

I can't help but feel intoxicated when I'm around him now. Since I've had a taste of him, I want more. We both knew what we wanted in an instant without saying a word.

I turned around with lust in my eyes and unbuttoned his trousers. He met me with a ravenous glare of his own.

Orion spun me back around and lowered my pants quickly pushing into me from behind, the snarls and low growls of the dark beasts below us filling the air.

"Wear a fucking dress next time."

He growled against my ear as he started thrusting into me, his hand reaching around for my clit.

My heart raced—not just from the beasts below but from the way he spread my legs, knelt before me, and worshipped me as if I were the most sacred thing in existence.

He lapped at my pussy, making me come again, cleaning his own cum as it dripped out of me.

His tongue may be my favorite thing about this realm. That and the way his formalities turns filthy when my cunt is involved.

Tonight, an electric hum runs through me for an entirely different reason. Tonight, I'm joining Mor on patrol.

I've been waiting for this since she suggested it. The anticipation thrums in my veins—a chance to do something familiar, something that reminds me of the missions I ran with my team.

Only this time, I'm stepping into the unknown with a dark enchantress who could outmatch any soldier I've fought beside.

As I secure my knife to my thigh and pull on my boots, a grin tugs at my lips.

Finally.

Action. Purpose.

A chance to prove I'm not just some mortal queen playing at being Fae.

Maybe tonight, the realm will finally hand me one of its trials.

Mor walks ahead, her crimson eyes scanning the shadows like a predator assessing its territory.

She's quieter than usual, her sharp tongue dulled, the ever-present swish of her shadows subdued. A strange disappointment clings to her.

"You seem extra pissy today," I say, keeping my tone light.

She doesn't slow, doesn't even glance back, but her voice drifts toward me like smoke. "We were hoping for something more... eventful on your first patrol."

"You wanted trouble?"

"We wanted to see what you're capable of." Her shadows coil slightly, like a snake tightening around prey.

A slow smile tugs at my lips. "Well, that's almost touching. Don't worry, Mor. Trouble usually finds me first."

Her eyes finally flick to me, a faint smirk gracing her otherwise stoic face. "We hope so."

As we continue our patrol, the silence stretches, broken only by rustling leaves and the distant cry of a beast in the woods.

Mor moves like a shadow, her presence as closed off as her emotions.

It's part of her charm—if you can call it that. But she's a puzzle, one I can't help but want to solve.

"I've been meaning to ask," I say, breaking the silence again. "How did you know the garnish on that soup was poisonous? Back in the dining hall?"

Mor slows slightly, crimson eyes narrowing as if debating whether to answer. "We were mortal once. Long ago."

The words hit like a stone in my chest. Mor—with her shadows, her strange way of referring to herself as *we*, and her power that feels both ancient and otherworldly—was once *like me*?

"You were mortal?" The question slips out before I can stop it. "What happened?"

She doesn't falter, eyes fixed ahead as if my question is nothing more than a passing breeze. "That is a story for another time." Her shadows ripple, a silent warning not to push.

I chew on her response, treading carefully. "What about your powers? The transformation—when your skin changes, your voice… when it sounds like more than just you."

She pauses for a fraction of a second before continuing. "We walk with the dark realm at all times. The realm of Elysium."

"Elysium," I repeat, testing the word on my tongue. It sounds hauntingly beautiful. "That's not a place I've heard of."

"No, you wouldn't have." Her tone is measured. "Elysium is not like Avalon or your Gaea. Those are realms teeming with life, brimming with light. Vibrant, growing worlds."

She stops walking, turning to face me. Her shadows dance at her feet, responding to the shift in her attention. "Elysium," she continues, "is a shadowed thread in the tapestry of creation.

Like the dark veins that run through marble, it weaves into every realm, seeping into their cracks and crevices."

A chill prickles my skin. "You make it sound… alive."

"It is," she says simply. "Alive and endless. It is not evil, as mortals might imagine, but pure, unyielding shadow—the counterbalance to light. And it is always there, watching, waiting."

I glance at the shadows clinging to her like a second skin. "And you… you're connected to it?"

"We are." Her crimson eyes gleam faintly. "It's raw, untamed power courses through us. When you see our transformation, when our form shifts, it is Elysium *begging* to be unleashed. We must never allow it without restraint."

The thought sends a shiver through me. "That doesn't scare you?"

Her lips twitch into what *might* be a smile, though it's hard to tell. "This is our penance. We made peace with it long ago, Your Grace. Fear would do us no good."

I nod slowly, trying to process it all—Elysium, the idea of its darkness threading through everything. "And Avalon? Does it—?"

"Elysium touches Avalon as it touches every realm," she interrupts. "Even here, in a place of life and power, the shadow runs deep. You've felt it already, haven't you?"

I think of the darkness pressing in on my dreams, a living thing. *Yeah, I've felt it.*

"Then you understand," she says, her voice softer, almost kind. "The moon and starlight cannot exist without the darkness."

Mor resumes walking, shadows whispering at her heels. I follow, my mind racing. *If Elysium's influence is growing, if the balance is shifting...*

Watching her, it strikes me how seamlessly she wields its raw power. It's not just magic—it's as if she *is* Elysium's anchor in this world.

I hesitate before speaking again, the weight of her presence making my question feel almost intrusive.

"The realm you came from... your mortal realm," I begin carefully. "What's it called? Does it... teem with life, like Avalon?"

She stops completely. Her shadows tighten around her, curling in close like a protective barrier. "That is enough questions."

So, I shut the fuck up.

As we continue the patrol, the silence stretches between us, but my curiosity finally gets the better of me.

I glance at Mor, her crimson eyes scanning the shadows like a predator searching for prey.

"Why do you refer to yourself in the plural sense?" I ask, my tone light but genuinely curious. "You keep saying 'we' like you're a crowd."

Mor doesn't look at me, but this time I catch the unmistakable curve of her mouth into a faint, sardonic smile.

"Three is a crowd," she answers cryptically, the words as much a riddle as a response.

I blink at her, completely thrown. "Wait—what does that even mean?"

Before she can answer—or deliberately *not* answer—a guttural growl echoes through the trees.

My attention snaps forward as a pack of monstrous creatures emerges from the darkness, their skinned, inside-out appearance making my stomach churn.

Their leathery hides glisten in the moonlight, and their exposed teeth drip with saliva that steams in the cool night air.

"Shit," I mutter, gripping the hilt of my knife. "Cujo's cousins, I presume?"

Mor's lips curl in something resembling a grin, her crimson eyes gleaming with excitement.

"Excellent," she murmurs, anticipation lacing the single word.

"Are you ready, Your Grace?"

I smirk, adrenaline surging through me. "Please. They're just baby wolf-shifters."

Mor doesn't respond, already stepping forward, her shadows unfurling like a living storm.

I move alongside her, my knife steady in my grip, the familiar weight grounding me.

The first beast lunges. I sidestep with ease, driving my blade into the base of its neck in one swift motion. It lets out a strangled cry before collapsing, and I spin to meet the next one.

Fast, but predictable.

I drop into a crouch as another leaps, slashing its belly open midair. Its dark blood splatters across the ground as it tumbles, lifeless.

Mor is a blur beside me, her shadows slicing through the pack with brutal precision. But I hold my own. My blade finds its mark again and again, my movements fluid, rhythmic.

One of the beasts gets too close, claws swiping at my leg, but I'm faster.

I twist, grabbing its head and slamming it into the ground before driving my blade into its throat.

It twitches once, then stills.

Mor watches me from the corner of her eye, her grin widening slightly as she dispatches two more with a single wave of her hand.

"You're holding up better than I expected," she muses, almost approving.

The snarls thin out, the remaining beasts falling one by one. As the last creature collapses under Mor's shadows, she crouches over its body, movements deliberate as she extends her hand toward me. "Your blade."

I hand it over, watching as she extracts two massive fangs, their blackened tips glinting in the moonlight.

"What are those for?" I ask, wiping the blood from my blade onto my pants.

"Hypnos wants to study them." She slips the fangs into a pouch at her side. "See what's turning these creatures into such atrocities."

I glance at the mangled bodies as they dissolve into ash, their twisted forms fading into the darkness seeping into every inch of Avalon.

"Think he'll find anything useful?"

Mor straightens, her shadows coiling around her like a cloak. "If there's an answer, Hypnos will find it. That is his nature. Let's go."

Her darkness surges over me—cold, suffocating, overwhelming. It's nothing like Orion's shadows, which wrap around me like an embrace.

Mor's power is raw, consuming, dragging me into a void where time and space cease to exist.

When I blink again, we're back in the castle, standing in the hall with the round table. The sudden shift is jarring—the cool forest replaced by the dimly lit room and its crackling fire.

I stagger slightly, still reeling.

"Warn me next time," I grumble, glaring at Mor.

"We did." She smirks, dropping a bloodied tooth into a small pouch before tossing it to me. "Consider it a lesson in adaptation."

I catch the pouch, peeking inside to inspect the teeth when my stomach growls.

"I'm hungry enough to eat a horse. Hell, I'd kill for a cheeseburger from Mike's right now."

Mor halts mid-step. Her entire frame freezes, shoulders tensing as though I've uttered something profane—or incomprehensible. Slowly, she turns toward me, crimson eyes wide and… shocked?

I pause, wondering if I've accidentally blasphemed some sacred Fae law against eating beef.

Or horses. Or both.

"What?" I ask cautiously. "Did I say something wrong?"

Mor tilts her head, her expression uncharacteristically open—almost vulnerable in its astonishment.

"You like cheeseburgers?" Her voice carries a strange mix of disbelief and reverence, like I've just revealed an ancient, forbidden truth.

I blink. Of all the things to unsettle the formidable Mor, I never would've guessed cheeseburgers. "Uh… yeah? Of course. Who doesn't?"

She steps closer, studying me as though searching my soul for deceit. "They are our favorite," she declares, her tone nearly solemn.

"We made a friend before we captured you. He made us cheeseburgers."

I bristle slightly at captured, but I'm too thrown to argue. Mor—sharp-tongued, terrifying, shadow-wielding Mor—is practically revering the concept of a cheeseburger.

It's bizarre. And honestly, kind of endearing.

"They're not hard to make," I say slowly, wary of where this is going.

Mor's jaw drops. "You can make them?" Her voice is barely above a whisper.

I choke back a laugh. "Yeah... they're not exactly complicated."

Her reaction is instant. Mor straightens, her shadows swirling with what can only be described as excitement.

"We must make haste for the kitchens," she declares, utterly serious. "You must show us how to make these cheeseburgers at once."

I stare at her. "Right now?"

"Yes." Her expression is unwavering. "We cannot delay."

I glance at the bloodied fangs in my hand, my damp boots, and the exhaustion weighing on my limbs.

But the look on Mor's face—somewhere between grim determination and barely restrained joy—makes me sigh.

"Fine," I say, shaking my head with a grin. "Let's go make some cheeseburgers."

Mor's expression remains impassive, but the slight curl of her lips and the way her shadows swirl just a little faster tell me she's genuinely pleased.

For the first time, I wonder if beneath all the darkness and danger, Mor has far more humanity than she lets on.

And, apparently, a profound love for cheeseburgers.

CHAPTER 41

The unmistakable hum of a dream presses against my awareness, the surreal clarity of it tipping me off.

Tana hasn't argued with me once, hasn't met my words with sharp retorts or stubborn defiance. She's too... compliant, too focused on me. That alone tells me this is not reality.

But I don't care. I have no intention of waking from this.

Her dark eyes, like pools of molten onyx, pin me in place as she rides me.

Her hands grip my chest for balance, her nails digging into my skin just enough to sting—to remind me that even in dreams, she is power and passion incarnate.

Her full breasts sway with her movements, the dark peaks of her nipples begging to be taken into my mouth.

And I oblige, leaning up to capture one between my lips, sucking and nipping as a low, guttural moan escapes me.

"Mate," she whispers, her voice husky and full of command.

Pain lashes through my chest—sharp and undeniable—

a bitter reminder that this cannot be real. That word—mate —is a word I cannot afford.

"Mate me, Orion," she demands, her tone taking on a sultry edge as her fingers fist in my hair, pulling me closer.

My teeth graze her nipple, and her hips roll in perfect, torturous circles that drag every nerve in my body closer to the edge.

I want her. Gods, I want to mark her, to claim her, to make her mine in every sense of the word. The primal urge is undeniable, roaring through me like a beast caged too long.

"I cannot," I shudder, my voice breaking even as my hands grip her hips, pulling her down harder against me.

My heart clenches—not from passion but from guilt.

I cannot do something so cruel to her. My heart will fail one day, and if I tie a mate to myself, their life will end with mine.

Tana has a future. The realm needs her. She is vital in a way I can never be. I am a tool for the throne, a fleeting moment in its legacy. She must live.

The realm needs her. It does not need me.

"Mate me," she breathes again, arching her back as her hands slide over her breasts.

Her words and movements are a siren's call, impossible to ignore as her hips undulate, pulling me deeper.

Outside, lightning cracks, flashing like the heavens themselves are protesting the torment of this dream. The sound echoes through the space, amplifying the raw need building between us.

I'm losing my grip, feeling my control splinter as her body tightens around me.

She leans back, exposing the elegant curve of her neck, the roll of her hips keeping me fully sheathed within her.

Another crack of lightning illuminates her, bathing her sweat-slicked skin in an ethereal glow as the orgasm washes over her.

Her cry of pleasure is all it takes to shove me over the precipice.

I feel my hand now, the slickness of my palm as it slides along my cock.

The dream shatters like glass, and the sensation of release slams into me—a guttural groan tearing from my throat as I come, hot and hard, spilling across my stomach.

Reality sets in as I open my eyes, the dim light of my chamber a stark contrast to the vivid fantasy that lingers.

My chest heaves, the remnants of pleasure tangled with the heavy weight of guilt as I stare at the mess I've made.

"Tana," I whisper hoarsely into the silence, her name a curse and a prayer all at once.

Another sharp crack reverberates through the night, but it's no lightning strike.

The sound has a precision to it, a controlled force that lightning lacks.

A weapon. An attack.

My blood ignites, molten fury surging through my veins as realization strikes.

Someone has dared to harm Starfall. My Starfall.

In an instant, I'm out of bed, dragging on my pants, my sword a comforting weight in my grip.

I hastily grab yesterday's tunic from the floor and wipe off the last evidence of my dream.

Flinging my door open, my shadows pulse around me, responding to my rage and unease.

I'm a storm through the halls, my bare feet slapping against the cold stone as I sprint toward the source of the disturbance.

Each crackle of that foreign sound pushes me harder, my grip on my sword tightening until my knuckles ache.

I burst through the door, a war cry on my tongue, my blade raised and ready to strike down whoever has the audacity to—

I stop instantly.

The scene before me is... bizarre, to say the least.

The blade in my hand feels heavier than it should as I lower it, the tension in my body still coiled from the imagined threat.

I scan the scene before me—no ambush, no dark beasts.

Just Mor and Tana sitting at a table, surrounded by an absurdly mundane platter of food.

It takes a moment for my eyes to focus on it properly.

Cheeseburgers.

Mor had called them that when she first returned from Gaea with a greasy sack of the realm's delicacy. I'd nearly forgotten the name.

Yet there they are, stacked high on a wooden tray between them as if the castle's safety isn't perpetually at risk.

My confusion must be written across my face because both of them are staring at me as though I've just grown another head.

Nearby, Hephaestus, oblivious to my arrival, is tinkering

with the odd weapon Tana first used when she arrived in Avalon.

He closes one eye, aiming at a target set far beyond the castle gates, then squeezes the trigger.

The weapon booms, and the parcel screams through the air, striking dead center on the mark.

"You okay there?" Tana asks, amusement lacing her voice as she takes a bite of her cheeseburger. The unapologetic grin on her face only makes the situation more surreal.

I exhale slowly, swallowing down my embarrassment.

"I thought there was danger," I explain, stepping closer to the table. My voice is calm, collected, even though my nerves are still frayed from the lingering tension of the dream I woke from.

I don't miss how her gaze slides over me, lingering on the lines of my stomach, the faint sheen of sweat still clinging to my skin from the rush to get here.

Her attention sharpens, almost predatory, when her eyes dip lower, tracing the deep V at my pelvis.

Heat surges in her gaze, and it takes everything in me to keep my own composure.

"Let me have one," I say, gesturing toward the platter of cheeseburgers, eager for something to redirect the tension.

Mor's hand lashes out, smacking mine away with surprising force.

"There are not enough," she declares, her voice curt and utterly serious.

I arch a brow, gesturing at the clearly overfilled platter.

"There are dozens. You can spare one."

"We cannot," Mor snaps, her tone brooking no argument.

Before I can challenge her further, Tana lifts her own patty of meat, surrounded by bread, her lips curling into a sly grin.

"Here," she says, her voice dripping with mischief. "Have a bite of mine."

The world narrows for a moment, my focus entirely on her as she holds the food offering out to me.

The gesture is deliberate, her eyes dancing with a playful challenge.

I lean forward, keeping my gaze locked on hers, and take a slow, deliberate bite.

Her fingers brush my lips as I do, and the intimacy of the moment hangs heavy in the air.

Mor lets out an exaggerated scoff, breaking the spell.

She slides off the table and snatches the platter of cheeseburgers, marching toward the castle.

"We will lose our appetite watching the prince attempt to woo the queen," she mutters darkly. "And we will not have the taste of our cheeseburgers sullied."

Tana laughs, warm and genuine, and Hephaestus joins her, his deep chuckle echoing through the courtyard.

I shake my head, following Mor's retreat with my eyes.

As she passes Hypnos, she thrusts a cheeseburger into his hands without breaking stride.

Hypnos inspects it briefly, then takes a bite as if this is entirely normal before following her into the castle.

"Of course, Hypnos can have one," I mutter under my breath.

Tana smirks and her voice pulls my attention back to her. "What's up with those two?" she asks, taking another bite of her burger.

I hesitate, considering the complexities of Mor and Hypnos's relationship, before settling on the simplest answer. "They are... complicated."

She hums in acknowledgment, clearly not expecting more, and my eyes linger on her as she sticks the tip of her thumb into her mouth, sucking the juices from the cheeseburger off it.

Her devilish grin meets my gaze, and a surge of heat flares in my chest, making my composure slip for just a moment.

Releasing a heavy sigh, I straighten. "I need to speak with Hypnos," I say, my tone a little too firm as I turn on my heel and walk back toward the castle.

I don't look back, but her amused chuckle follows me, embedding itself in my mind like a brand I can't shake.

I need to dunk myself in an arctic pool.

The dim light of the lower castle levels casts elongated shadows, dancing along the ancient stone walls as I descend the spiraling staircase.

This part of Starfall is rarely visited—a labyrinth of forgotten halls and storerooms that hold the weight of Avalon's history.

I find Hypnos in the archives, his pale, unseeing eyes scanning the air before him, as though he can see more than the countless scrolls and tomes stacked precariously on towering shelves.

He doesn't acknowledge me immediately, though I know he senses my presence.

His fingers hover over an ancient text splayed open on the table before him.

The faint glow of his magic shimmers around the edges of the tooth Mor delivered to him earlier, suspended midair as if caught in an invisible web.

"You've been down here a while," I say, stepping closer, my voice breaking the silence. "What have you found?"

Hypnos tilts his head slightly, his blank eyes turning in my direction.

"Strange things," he says, his tone clinical but edged with unease. "This tooth carries an energy signature unlike anything I've encountered before."

I frown, my gaze narrowing on the object in question. "Strange how?"

"The darkness is threaded into it, yes," Hypnos continues, his voice measured as he turns back to the tooth.

"But its origin is peculiar. It does not resonate with the magic of any of the ten courts."

The weight of his words pushes into my gut like a physical blow.

"What?"

Hypnos lowers his hands, letting the tooth drift down to the table. His brow furrows slightly, and he exhales.

"I've checked and rechecked. The magic within does not come from the ten known courts of Avalon.

Its energy is entirely foreign to them."

I step closer, the implications swirling in my mind.

"That's impossible. Everything in Avalon—every beast, every Fae, every shadow—can be traced back to the court of its origin. If it's not from one of them..." My voice trails off, my thoughts racing.

A memory surfaces, unbidden: Tana standing in the round council chamber, her sharp eyes lingering on the marred spot in the stonework surrounding the great table.

Her voice rings in my ears, matter-of-fact and insightful.

"There are spaces for twelve," she had said, tracing her finger along the table's edge. *"The symbology here is clear— twelve courts were intended, even though there are only ten now. What happened to the other two?"*

I inhale sharply, my heart pounding as the realization takes shape.

"Missing courts," I murmur, more to myself than to Hypnos. "Could it be...?"

Hypnos doesn't answer immediately. Instead, he rests his hand on the table, his head tilting as though listening to something far away.

"If there were once twelve courts," he says slowly, "and two have vanished, their magic would not have simply disappeared.

It would have lingered, dormant, waiting for something —or someone—to awaken it."

The pieces begin to fall into place, but the picture they form is grim.

I meet Hypnos's pale gaze, his calm demeanor doing nothing to quell the storm in my mind.

"Are you saying one of the missing courts could be the source of the darkness?"

"It's a possibility," Hypnos replies, his voice measured but grave. "A dangerous one."

The implications send a shiver down my spine.

The darkness that has plagued Avalon—that seeks to consume it—it could be tied to the remnants of a forgotten court.

A court that once held power equal to any of the ten but was erased from memory for reasons unknown.

My mind races with questions.

If this is true, what happened to the missing courts?

Were they destroyed, exiled, or did they choose to vanish?

And most importantly—if one of them is the source of the darkness, what could they possibly want with Tana?

And with Avalon?

I grip the edge of the table, my knuckles whitening.

"This changes everything," I say, my voice low.

Hypnos nods solemnly.

"Indeed, it does."

I linger.

A million thoughts racing through my mind. All of them leading back to a dark skinned woman with lush hair the strongest storm couldn't dare tame.

"Hypnos?" I keep my eyes on the parchment and ancient text. "While in Gaea with Mor, you witnessed many of the mortal's modern customs?"

"I did, my friend."

"Tana–"

The words stall in my throat, suddenly feeling ridiculous for my curiosity.

"Tana performs a sort of hand gesture, quite often." I think back to the many occasions when her middle finger is shoved toward me.

A look of irritation or defiance in her eyes when she does it.

I mimic the gesture to my old friend.

"What could it mean?"

Hypnos grins. "Ah, my prince." He struggles with the explanation.

Not because he does not know its meaning. But because he does and he's making a decision of how to inform me.

"It can be interpreted in two ways." He explains it to me as if I'm a youngling, receiving my first lesson of the stars.

"In one instance, it means *'leave me alone'*, or *'go away'*."

"Mmm," I hum. Raising one eyebrow to the ceiling in thoughtful contemplation. "And the other?"

"I may have this incorrect, but a gesture to indicate ones interest in another." He pauses. "Sexually."

Interesting.

"A way to say–*'fuck you'*. If I may be so crude, your grace."

I nod my head in agreement. The grin I'm trying to stifle fighting me. "We will interpret it as the second, then."

I pat my friends, shoulder, satisfied to have learned the mystery.

Turning, I begin to walk away and then think better of it. "Only to me, of course." I must clarify this oversight.

"For everyone else, it shall be the first." I declare it as if I will make it law.

"Indeed." Hypnos tries and fails to hide his humor. "A wise conclusion, your highness. As always."

CHAPTER 42

Tana

This pounding headache is proof I'm not compatible with Avalon.

Hestia insists it's just the realm's magic trying to *fuse* with me.

But I'm not Fae. Not immortal. The magic has nowhere to go.

I asked Hypnos if mortals who once visited Avalon experienced this—headaches, dizziness, this *constant* pressure. They didn't.

Lucky me.

Drinking water from the misting lake helps, as do the relief drops Hestia keeps forcing on me, but the dull, relentless throb behind my eyes is wearing me down.

Taking a swig from my hip flask, I follow Mor and Hypnos into the heart of the forest surrounding the castle.

The trees here are ancient, their massive trunks twisted with time, branches clawing at the sky like skeletal fingers.

Moonlight barely cuts through the dense canopy, casting the ground in an eerie, perpetual twilight.

The air is charged, heavy with an unseen energy that prickles against my skin.

Avalon's magic is thick here. Suffocating.

Hypnos leads the way, moving with the unhurried grace of someone who knows exactly where he's going.

His Sensor abilities guide him effortlessly through the labyrinth of trees, his presence unnervingly calm.

Mor walks beside me, her shadows slithering around her ankles like restless pets. She's quiet, but her crimson eyes scan the forest with sharp, surgical focus.

If *she's* on high alert, that can't be good.

"Are you going to tell me why this meeting is so important?" I ask, breaking the silence.

"The Woodland Fae are... unique," Hypnos replies, his tone detached. "Their magic is ancient, rooted in Avalon's earliest days. If anyone can trace the origin of this darkness, it's them."

"And they're just going to *help* us?" I press, barely suppressing my skepticism. "Out of the kindness of their hearts?"

Mor chuckles, low and amused. "Kindness? No. Curiosity, maybe. Or the chance to remind us of their superiority."

Great. Arrogant Fae with ancient magic. What else is new?

The path narrows, trees pressing in, their twisted roots threading through the damp earth.

The air is thick, heavy with the scent of moss and decay.

I duck beneath a low-hanging branch, my fingers instinctively brushing the knife strapped to my thigh.

Small comfort, but a comfort nonetheless.

"We're close," Hypnos murmurs, his voice softer now, as if the forest itself demands silence.

I glance at Mor. Her expression remains unreadable, but her shadows—normally shifting and restless—have stilled, clinging to her like a second skin.

They're *listening*.

To *what*, I'm not sure I want to know.

We step into a clearing. I expect to find our new companions waiting, but the space is empty.

Mor drops onto the forest floor, leaning back against a gnarled tree trunk.

Without ceremony, she pulls a flank of roasted boar from her satchel and starts eating, as if everyone casually carries *haunches of meat* around.

I sigh and sit beside her, picking up a dried twig and breaking it into small pieces before tossing them aside. Around us, withered ivy clings to the trees—once wild, now brittle and dead.

Something about it makes my skin crawl.

The forest here is dying.

Veins of decay weave through the land, siphoning Avalon's life like an open wound.

Beside me, a sapling struggles to exist—a frail thing, barely half a foot tall.

Once, it might have become one of these towering trees, but now its blackened stem and brittle leaves whisper of defeat.

Not yet.

I pour water from Avalon's Misting Lake over its shriveled roots, rubbing a dried leaf between my fingers.

"One more shot, little guy," I murmur before turning my attention back to Hypnos and the woods.

A shift in the air makes my shoulders tense. Hypnos feels it too, his already straight posture lengthening.

Magic thickens around us—something old, something watching. The Woodland Fae are near.

Mor remains unbothered, still seated, still eating. My gaze flicks back to the sapling just in time to see green spreading across its branches, soft evergreen leaves unfurling where rot once clung.

A small smile tugs at my lips. I unscrew my flask, take a swig. This stuff is magic.

The Woodland Fae emerge, so seamlessly blended with the forest that I almost miss them.

They are unlike any Fae I've encountered. Their bark-textured skin bears the knots and swirls of ancient trees, moss and ivy weaving through their vine-like hair.

Their eyes are pure black—depthless voids, unreadable and unsettling.

One steps forward, antlers crowning his head like twisted roots.

He tilts his head, studying us with an intensity that makes my spine itch, but I refuse to look away.

"Hypnos," he says, his voice deep, like old wood creaking in a storm. "You bring outsiders into our domain."

Hypnos inclines his head. "I seek your wisdom, Elder Oryn. We have encountered something beyond the knowledge of the courts."

Oryn's gaze flicks to Mor, then to me, lingering longer than I like.

"This mortal?" he muses. "Why do you bring her here?"

I cross my arms, cocking my hip. "This mortal is involved just as much as you."

"Lady Tana is the Queen chosen by the realm," Hypnos replies evenly. "And she is correct. This concerns us all."

Oryn's brow lifts, his expression unreadable. "The realm's chosen," he murmurs. "How... unexpected."

He moves closer, slow and deliberate, like a tree bending in the wind. Every instinct screams at me to step back, to run, but I hold my ground.

The pressure hits me—his magic, dense and suffocating, slamming into me like an oncoming storm.

It's overwhelming.

I push back, biting down on the strain, letting a small smile curve my lips.

"Hm," he hums, his dark eyes trailing over me, measuring. "What is it you wish to show us?"

Hypnos withdraws the collection of teeth Mor and I gathered on patrol.

These dark creatures stalking the woods all bear the same taint, a corruption he believes is spreading.

Oryn lifts one of the largest fangs, turning it between his fingers. The clearing stills, tension thick as mist.

Then, his expression darkens.

"This knowledge does not come freely," he says, his tone weighted with expectation. "If you wish to understand the origin of this... anomaly, there will be a price."

Hypnos, ever composed, tilts his head slightly. "And what is it you seek in return?"

Oryn's black eyes narrow. "We desire—"

A chime interrupts him.

Not a normal sound, but something *other*. A delicate, ethereal tinkling that grows louder with every breath.

The Woodland Fae stiffen, their bark-like faces contorting into snarls as flurries of tiny lights burst into the clearing.

Sprites.

The Sprites blur through the air in flashes of color, their bell-like voices ringing with laughter. Their high-pitched chimes scatter like wind through the trees.

The Woodland Fae react instantly—with malice.

"Pests," one of them growls, extending a hand. Vines snake up from the ground, twisting into a living net that ensnares the tiny creatures mid-flight.

A collective chime of alarm ripples through them as they push and pull against their prison.

Anger flares through me before my mind catches up. My knife is in my hand in an instant, its weight grounding me as I surge forward.

My palm slams against the Fae's chest, my foot hooking behind his leg. He topples, stunned, as I press my glowing blade to his throat.

The rest of the Woodland Fae whirl toward me, their expressions twisting with fury.

A cold blast of air at my side warns me that Mor has shifted, her power unfurling.

The growl that leaves her throat—layered, voices melding together—is a warning, a threat.

Oryn steps forward, his void-black eyes locking onto mine. "You dare—"

"Yes, I dare," I snap, my voice sharp as steel. "They're tiny. Harmless. And you think they warrant an attack?"

"They disrupt the balance," another Fae hisses, bark-like skin creaking as he shifts closer. Hypnos rests a hand on the hilt of his sword.

I bark out a laugh, gesturing to the net of vines still constraining the Sprites. My grip tightens on my dagger, its runes pulsing brighter.

The Fae beneath me swallows hard. "You mean *your* balance. Your fragile egos. Didn't realize 'balance' meant bullying creatures a tenth of your size."

I press the blade closer. "Let. Them. Go."

The Fae mutter curses under their breath but don't move. Oryn's gaze flickers to my knife, unease tightening his jaw. Perhaps the runes glowing along its steel remind him I am not entirely powerless.

His composure cracks, frustration lining his features. "For what reason?" he finally grits out. "What do you want, mortal?"

I hold my stance, tilting my chin just enough to make it clear I *won't* back down.

"Information," I state evenly.

"Tell us about the tooth and release the Sprites. We part ways, and your friend here walks away intact."

Silence stretches through the clearing, tension coiling thick in the air. The Woodland Fae exchange murmurs, their bark-like skin creaking as they shift uneasily.

Oryn's jaw flexes. Then, begrudgingly, he nods. "Very well. We will not harm them."

At his silent command, the vines loosen, falling away.

The Sprites vanish in a flurry of chimes and light, slipping into the night like they were never here.

I release the Fae beneath me and slide my blade back into its holster. The magic fades from the steel, leaving only the echo of chimes behind.

"Okay, then," I say, stepping back toward Mor and Hypnos. "Talk."

Oryn straightens, his movements stiff with irritation, but when he speaks, his voice is measured.

"The tooth carries the mark of an ancient blood-magic. A kind that binds itself *not only* to living beings—but to the realm itself."

My frown deepens. "What kind of blood magic?"

His gaze darkens. "Woodland Fae would never taint our perfection with such a blight. We do not practice such magic. But as part of the land, we *feel* its mark. It is woven into the roots and rivers, into the very air we breathe."

He's being vague—just helpful enough to seem cooperative, but keeping real answers just out of reach.

"Bound by *who*?" I press. "And for *what purpose*?"

Oryn's lips curve slightly, the faintest hint of condescension. "How am I to know, mortal?"

I step closer, voice hardening. "Oh, I think you *do* know. You just don't want to say."

Something flickers in his expression. A nerve hit. He knows more than he's letting on.

"Do you require further information, mortal?" His tone is careful now, measured.

My mind races, trying to connect the dots. The tooth. The blood-magic.

The darkness creeping through Avalon. It all feels like pieces of a puzzle—one that's still missing too much.

I make a calculated gamble. "Are there courts missing from the realm?" My voice sharpens. "Are they tied to this darkness?"

Oryn's face shifts. A subtle, practiced neutrality, but *too* neutral.

"That," he says coolly, "was not part of our bargain."

His voice is final. A door slammed shut.

"You asked about the tooth. I have given you what I can." His unreadable black eyes hold mine. "Our conversation is concluded."

"Wait—"

But he steps back, his form blending into the shadows of the trees as if he were never truly there.

The other Woodland Fae follow suit, their retreat as swift and silent as a falling leaf.

Within moments, the clearing feels emptier, as though their presence had been nothing more than a passing breeze.

Frustrated, I let out a breath and Mor steps closer, her power retreating within her, returning her appearance to her usual state.

"That went better than expected," she says dryly, though there's a hint of approval in her tone. "For what it's worth, they've never spoken that much to me."

"Yeah, well, it wasn't enough," I mutter, glancing at Hypnos, who looks as pensive as ever. "What do you make of all that?"

His colorless eyes flick toward me, his voice calm but weighted.

"It's clear there is more they're not saying. But they're right about one thing: this blood-magic is ancient. Older than Avalon itself perhaps."

"And the courts?" I press.

Hypnos hesitates, then shakes his head. "If there are missing courts, their absence is woven deeply into this mystery. It's something we'll have to uncover ourselves."

"Fuck," I whisper, my frustration simmering beneath the surface. I should have been vaguer when I struck that bargain. Fucking literal assholes.

I follow behind Mor and Hypnos, my thoughts tangled in the frustration of our fruitless encounter with the Woodland Fae.

The forest around me shifts—its vibrant greens and dappled moonlight swallowed by a creeping stillness. The air turns heavier, colder.

My boots crunch against brittle leaves, but the sound feels distant, as if muffled by an unseen barrier.

Then my foot catches on an exposed root, and I stop.

The path is gone.

So are Mor and Hypnos.

The forest around me is blackened, stripped of life. Trees

that once stood proud are skeletal, their bark twisted and charred as if scorched by an ancient fire.

A suffocating weight presses down, thick with despair and something far more insidious.

A prickle of unease creeps along my skin. I'm being watched.

I stay still, scanning the treeline, searching for what I know is there.

The movement is so subtle I almost miss it—a woman, or something shaped like one, standing at the grove's edge. A spectral.

She's carved from shadow, so dark she nearly vanishes into the void between the trees.

She doesn't move, yet her long, dark hair stirs unnaturally, caught in a breeze I can't feel. Her form ripples, neither solid nor entirely incorporeal.

I can't see her eyes, but I feel them locked on me.

She reminds me of the Lady of the Lake, as if she carries magic so powerful it bends the world around her.

A hand grips my arm.

I jolt, sucking in a sharp breath as I spin to find Hypnos beside me. His pale eyes hold an unusual intensity, his expression uncharacteristically severe.

"Remain on the path, Your Highness," he says, voice firm. "Do not let the darkness lead you astray."

I glance back toward the figure, my pulse hammering. "What happened here?" My voice is quieter than I intend. "Do you see her?"

Hypnos doesn't look, doesn't acknowledge her presence at all.

His focus stays locked on me, as if forcing himself not to turn. "The darkness has consumed this part of the forest.

To disturb the darkened grove is to court its wrath."

His voice is steady, but something in it—something just beneath the surface—tells me he knows something is there. He just won't admit it.

The figure remains still, her presence both unsettling and compelling.

My instincts scream at me to look away, but curiosity roots me in place. A part of me itches to march over and demand to know what the fuck she wants.

But I don't. I'm not an idiot.

"We should go," Hypnos urges, his grip loosening, though his touch is still firm. "This is not a place to linger."

I force myself to nod, my legs heavy as I step back. But before I turn away, I steal one last glance. She hasn't moved, hasn't made a sound, yet something in her posture feels expectant—as though she's waiting.

The oppressive air clings to me as I follow Hypnos back to the path. The weight of the grove lingers, pressing against my spine like unseen fingers.

Whatever darkness has taken root here, it isn't just lingering.

It's alive.

And it's watching me.

CHAPTER 43
orion

The castle breathes differently on the eve of Bloomrise.

The stones seem to hum beneath my boots, pulsing with restless anticipation.

Excitement lingers in the air, a tangible thing, as the Fae gather to witness the only sunrise that graces our eternal darkness.

This Bloomrise is unique.

Not only will Avalon disperse the first seeds of life, heralding the season of fertility and birth, but it will also occur just after Starfall—the end of a moon cycle when the stars rain down from the dark sky.

It is rare for the two events to collide. A coincidence I believe has everything to do with the arrival of our new queen.

The stars will fall, and life will rise.

A prophecy of what Tana will bring to the realm of the Fae.

I finish giving orders to a lesser Fae, my voice clipped and final as they depart, leaving me seated at the head of my table, dozens of tasks still to oversee.

Preparations must be flawless.

Bloomrise isn't just Avalon's singular sunrise—it's a mirror, reflecting the fractures beneath the polished veneer of Fae courts.

A weakness exposed for those keen enough to see it.

Behind me, the distinct ripple of an unwelcome presence slithers into the edges of my awareness, like cold fingertips brushing the nape of my neck.

A scent—sweet as rotting fruit beneath polished perfume.

Liona.

Her aura brushes against mine before her shadow does, as if she revels in announcing herself without words.

I stand, as duty dictates, but I don't turn. I don't need to.

She circles like a predator without prey, only the pleasure of pacing.

"You're such a dutiful regent, Orion." Her voice is velvet laced with thorns, each word dipped in seduction, but I hear the bitterness threaded beneath.

She steps closer, the faint shimmer of her signature gold dust catching in the low light, casting fragments of false stars against the dark stone walls.

A finger traces along my shoulder—light as a whisper. The touch is a calculated intrusion rather than affection.

I let her.

To flinch would be to give her something to savor.

She thrives on the reaction she doesn't deserve.

Positioning herself between me and the table holding the scatterings of my First Shade's orders, I glance down, giving her the faintest nod her station earns.

Liona is unapologetically bare, as she always is—adorned only with glimmering powder dusted across her collarbones and the curve of her hips, jewels draped like afterthoughts meant to distract from the hollowness beneath her beauty.

Fae vanity incarnate—wrapped in gold and self-importance.

Her eyes gleam, sharp and calculating, as she raises herself to sit on the table's edge. The smile on her lips is nothing more than a weapon disguised as charm.

Her posture is meant to entice, to tempt me into sampling what she continues to offer.

Her hopes of swaying my marriage decision back in her favor remain her constant ambition.

I arch a brow, keeping my voice cool, detached.

"Liona. Shouldn't you be somewhere more... relevant?"

She laughs softly, the sound like silk sliding over steel.

"Oh, darling Orion. Relevance is subjective. I find myself exactly where I need to be."

She props one foot upon the arm of the chair behind me, the scent of her arousal offending my senses.

"Imagine the strength we would wield together," she purrs, leaning back slightly, her fingers lazily tracing patterns along the exposed skin of her thigh.

"The bond of our houses restored, the realm united under us as chosen mates. Your rejection of the alliance forged by my father and your grandmother was premature, perhaps... emotional."

I don't dignify her words with a response, giving my attention to the ancient tapestries hanging along the walls.

Irritation creeps beneath my skin—a slow burn simmering in my chest.

Liona, undeterred, shifts closer, her fingers now trailing from her throat down the curve of her breast—her body an offering wrapped in nothing but gold dust and misplaced pride.

"You could have this, Orion. Power. Beauty. A union that would make the courts tremble."

Her hand lingers, her movements deliberate, ignoring the sharp edge of my growing frustration.

She leans in, her lips a breath away from my ear, her words a venomous caress.

"Think of what we could be. The strength we could wield. You, the shadow of Avalon. Me, its golden light."

I finally meet her gaze, my voice low, threaded with warning.

"Your desperation is showing, Liona."

She freezes—just for a breath—then forces a sharp, brittle smile.

But the glitter in her eyes flickers—not with desire, but with something darker.

Something territorial.

Because this isn't about me.

It's about Tana.

Liona places her other foot upon the rest of my chair, bracketing me between her legs—akin to a venomous spider weaving its deadly web.

"She's a distraction," she hisses, her tone sharper now, layered with hatred beneath the velvet.

"A mortal whore passing through shadows that will be gone in a blink."

Red rage blots out my vision.

My hand wraps around her throat, slamming her back onto the table.

The wood cracks beneath her skull, and I relish the sound.

"And yet," I sneer, my grip tightening, "she haunts you more than I ever could."

But her response renders me frozen in disgust.

She clasps my wrist firmly—then her breast with the other.

Her legs slither around me, and with a dramatic arch in her back, she writhes and moans, eyes closed, mouth parted.

"Yes, my prince."

In a blink, I understand the manipulation.

Disappointment is fleeting—blasted away by the hushed gasp I hear from the doorway.

Then the sound of Tana's boots treading away from the scene.

Liona's true smile can never be mistaken for beauty.

She is a grim taunt of evil, like a lake maiden rising from the swamps of Mirevalis, hungry to consume the flesh of the living.

I tighten my hold around her throat, watching the panic flood her eyes as the fine bones in her neck snap.

Lowering to her ear, I deliver my promise.

"Touch me or speak of Lady Tana again, and I will rip

your arms from your body—alleviate you of the flesh that offends my queen."

My shadows unsheathe my blade.

The darkness I command pries open her vile lips, and I pinch her poisonous tongue between my fingers.

"I will cut the tongue from your mouth."

My power urges the blade upward, digging its sharp point into the underside of her tongue.

She whimpers—a tear rolling down her face.

"I will bury you far beneath the soil of Avalon, where no one will hear your screams."

The blade moves farther.

"You will remain there, until your pitiful limbs regenerate, and you can dig yourself out of your own grave."

The gleam of my blade shines at me, having pierced her foul tongue fully.

I release my hand from her throat, tugging the knife toward me—forcing her to sit up, or lose her tongue.

"How long do you think it would take you to fully regrow your arms?"

She cries, trying to hold still.

Her blood runs down my hand, absorbing into the cuff of my ivory tunic.

"Unless you wish to find out," I murmur, yanking my knife from her mouth, slicing her tongue like the forked serpent she is, "do not push the limits of my patience. Or my hospitality in entertaining you within my castle walls."

Flicking her blood from my blade, I leave her weeping on the table.

To find Tana.

"**S**tupid motherfucker," the chosen queen of Avalon curses through her teeth as she yanks at a vine.

On her hands and knees, she rips at the twisting tendrils that spiral from the ground, coiling around the impaled blade fused with the rock that holds it.

"Do you mean the vine?" I smirk, crossing my arms over my chest and leaning against the gazebo's stone pillar.

"No."

She doesn't look at me. Sitting back on her heels, she rubs her forehead with her arm.

"Starling, what you saw was not—"

"Was not what it looked like?" She impales me with her eyes, and I can't deny it—I almost wish she'd look away. Anger mixes with something else she's trying desperately to hide. Pain.

Her gaze flicks downward, first to the blood on my hand and sleeve, then lower—to my trousers. Liona's annoying gilded sheen lingers on the fabric, and I sigh, closing my eyes against my continued stupidity.

"You literally have Glitter Cunt's... cunt glitter... on your crotch."

Tana stands and brushes her hands across her thighs, ridding her palms of dirt as she walks out of the gazebo surrounding the sword.

"Save it. We fucked, you two fucked. It's no big deal."

"It is." I push off from my post and follow her with slow, deliberate strides. "Liona is as calculating as a cobra.

She goaded my wrath, and I stepped into her deception. It was aimed at you, and I failed to realize it soon enough. I apologize."

Tana stops, crossing her arms over her chest, and I praise the stars for the strength they give me to refrain from casting my eyes downward. "And the blood?"

Now is when I give up my fight. I let myself drink in the beautiful, lethal woman before me, my smirk settling easily into place as I come to a stop in front of her.

She cranes her neck, looking up at me.

The anger is cooling. But the pain remains.

"I sliced her tongue in two for speaking offenses against my queen."

I pinch Tana's chin between my thumb and forefinger, dragging my tongue along my bottom lip as I devour the sight of her.

"Well," she exhales, releasing some of the emotion that had flooded her upon witnessing my indecency with Liona. "Your queen approves of this."

She feigns indifference, but the bitter sting of what she witnessed lingers in the set of her mouth.

Leaning down, my lips skim hers—not quite a kiss but still a caress.

"I'm sorry," I whisper.

Then I claim her mouth.

My hand wraps around her waist, slides down the perfect curve of her ass, and pulls her into me.

One touch of her skin against mine, and my cock is as hard as the stone keeping the ancient sword a prisoner.

She moans, and I drink it in, taste it on my tongue, as her arms wrap around my neck.

My hand roams up her back, beneath the coiled curls of her wild hair.

Fisting the tangles, I tug gently, forcing her head back, offering her throat to me.

I flick the button of her pants open, sliding my hand between her legs as my tongue runs the length of her neck.

"Fuck, Starling."

My fingers sink into her.

She's dripping.

"My queen is always so wet for me."

She shudders against me as I rub slow, teasing circles around her clit.

Tana rises onto the tips of her boots, clutching my neck for balance.

"Will you let me fuck you, my lady," I murmur against her lips, "with the hand that bears the blood of your enemy?"

She gasps when I flick her clit with fast, precise strokes.

"Yes." She grabs my wrist, holding me to her.

Sliding two fingers inside her, I groan as her tight, perfect cunt clenches around me.

I want it to be my cock her pussy is strangling.

But I can be patient.

Her hips rock against my hand, her moans unraveling me as she climbs toward her peak.

And then she comes undone, her pleasure crashing over

her as I thrust my fingers deeper, curling them against the soft, throbbing walls of her pussy.

"That's it, Starling."

She soaks my hand, her body trembling as my thumb works her sensitive bud until she quivers with every touch.

"Oh, fuck, Orion—"

I swallow her cries with my mouth, taking her lips with the same desperation that lives in my blood.

Her pants are a fucking problem.

I tear my hand away, growling as I drop to my knees.

"I said wear a fucking dress."

Fisting the leather, I rip it down the seam, and now, nothing is hidden from me.

"Did you seriously just—holy shit." She clinches my hair.

And then she's gone. Her voice, her thoughts, her disbelief. Lost in my pleasure my tongue gives her, and I taste her like I've been starving.

I groan against her slick, swollen cunt, my lips closing over her clit as I suck, savoring every delicious drop of her release.

With one hand, I free my cock from the confines of my pants. Fisting my length, I worship my queen with my tongue.

"Now," I rasp, my voice heavy with need. "Get the fuck down here and ride me."

Her desperation matches my own, and she doesn't hesitate. She straddles me, grabbing my cock in her small, sinful hand.

She isn't gentle when she squeezes—

And fuck, the stars above Avalon have never burned so bright.

She drags her wet pussy along my hard shaft, coating me in her arousal.

Tana toys with me, rolling her hips, teasing the head of my cock, until I'm trembling with restraint.

And then—finally—she takes me.

She impales herself on my length, stretching, consuming me, squeezing the soul from my fucking body.

"Gods, you feel so fucking good inside me." Her hands grip my face, her lips crashing against mine as she devours me.

I hold her tight, kissing her back with the same wild desperation.

She fucks me like she owns me—like I belong to her—like I am nothing and everything in her hands.

Tana tips her head back, and the moonlight kisses her beautiful, dark skin.

"Come on, Starling." I grip her hips, thrusting up into her with deep, punishing strokes. "Soak your throne so every Fae knows who owns the prince's cock."

She smirks, her lips curling into something wicked. "My throne?"

She changes the rhythm, grinding down on me so deep I see fucking eternity.

I fist her hair, pressing my forehead against hers, aching to spill inside her.

"Yes, Starling." I kiss her, gasping against her lips. "Anywhere the queen sits is her throne."

Her pussy squeezes me like a vice. I lose myself.

I drown.

"And when we go back inside, it will be my face."

"Orion." She's nearing her crest.

"I'm going to eat this delicious pussy until you can't scream anymore."

"Fuck, yes."

"The entire castle will hear you drown me with your sweet cunt."

She calls my name, her tight, desperate pussy squeezing me as her orgasm begins.

I hook my arms around her, grasping her shoulders, pulling her hard against me with each thrust as we come together.

She never looks away from me, and something within me cracks open.

A faint tether of some kind, peeking out of my heart—almost reaching for her.

So... curious.

Tana slows her movements and licks her lips.

I track the motion, hungry to feel her mouth on me.

She leaves my lap, but I grab her chin, not letting her retreat.

"Clean up your fucking mess first, Starling."

The dark desire that slides over her face is breathtaking, a beautiful veil that sharpens every feature.

On her knees, she spreads them, lowering her chest to the ground as her warm tongue licks my length.

She bathes me, worships me, consumes me.

And I am still so fucking hard for her.

Suddenly, I need more.

I need to feel her throat tighten around me as she swallows every drop of my release.

And she's ravenous for it.

She fists my cock, sucking me hard, hollowing her cheeks as she takes me deep—deeper still.

I'm long—too long for her. Her lips stretch around my girth, and Gods help me, I want to fuck her mouth.

I want to hold her still and slide into her until there is nothing left of me. Until there is nothing left of her.

Ruined.

Ruined for any other cock that dares come after me.

"I'm going to come for you, Starling."

I grunt, my words driving her down on my cock harder.

And fuck, I want it.

"You'll swallow every drop, won't you?"

I fist her hair, anchoring myself, my other hand braced behind me so I can watch my beautiful queen gag on my dick.

I am so deep she can't breathe, but she doesn't let up.

"Oh, fuck me, Tana."

I moan when I hit the back of her throat, and she keeps going.

"Fuck me so good."

She pushes beyond her gag, tears streaking down her face.

Her nails dig into my thighs—

And I am undone.

She chokes on me as I groan, my cock throbbing, spilling into her waiting throat.

She moans, licking up every drop before turning her drunk, dazed gaze on me.

Her fingers still wrap around my shaft when I pull her toward me.

I press my lips to hers, tasting the remnants of my release.

"Give me these lips, Starling," I whisper against her mouth.

Because I'm just getting started with you.

"You know, the legend of the sword in the stone is famous in my realm too?" I lie on Orion's chest, tracing the long lines of the scars that mar his pearly skin.

"Really?" He raises an eyebrow, interest flickering in his silver eyes, and I rest my chin on my hand.

"Mhm."

"Tell me the legend."

Orion turns onto his side, resting his head against his hand. I turn as well, mirroring his posture. The thin black satin sheet rests low on my hip.

"Well, there was a sword called Excalibur—"

"Already wrong." Orion runs his thumb over my exposed nipple. "My cousin wields the sword of truth."

I smack his hand away. "Pay attention."

He smirks, reaching for my breast again. "I'm paying very close attention to the very perfect breasts of my sovereign."

Scooting closer, he wraps his arms around me, burying his face in my cleavage.

I laugh as he pepper-bites his way around my breasts.

"Please, continue." He exhales against my skin, his breath warm.

"There was an old kingdom that lost its king, and this crazy old wizard named Merlin—"

"Merlin!" He laughs. "He is crazy. This part is very true."

"So, crazy wizard man said only the true ruler could remove the sword from the stone." I finish the story, then tilt his face toward mine and kiss him. "So, tell me the real story."

"I'm afraid the truth is less heroic." The playfulness in his eyes dims, replaced by something darker.

He rolls onto his back, one hand behind his head, gazing up at the ceiling.

"It is the site of the Valkyrie's betrayal."

Well, damn. I didn't expect that.

"The sword is named Veilcleaver and belonged to the strongest of the Valkyrie. The darkness twisted her loyalty, and she drove it into the ground, breaking open the veil that held back the Obscura—unleashing it upon Avalon."

"Shit." I roll onto my back as well, staring up at the ceiling, Orion's words replaying in my mind.

"It started the Great War that ended the Valkyrie, and the darkness remains."

Orion faces me again, propping himself up on one elbow. His fingers trace the dark edge of my nipple, making it peak at his touch.

"Does the sword call to you?" His rich tone turns husky as he leans down, rolling his skilled tongue over my breast before sucking my nipple into his mouth.

My fingers tangle in his hair, and he hums approvingly.

"Yes." I whisper the admission, a secret I'm not supposed to share.

"I think it called to my grandmother as well." His voice is low, pensive.

"I would often find her in the gazebo, looking at it with great sadness. Sometimes touching the hilt, as if it were speaking to her."

"Hm." I contemplate his words as he gives my other breast the same reverence. "Hopefully, it was just as much of a confusing asshole for her as it is for me."

Orion chuckles, running his hand down my stomach and between my legs.

Surprising me, he hooks his arm around my knee and pulls me on top of him, straddling his chest.

"It will come, Starling." He kisses the inside of my thigh. "But at this moment, it is your turn to come."

He kisses my other thigh, and my pussy is soaked, already aching for his mouth again.

"So, sit." His voice is reverent. Commanding.

"Your throne awaits."

Three sharp bangs on the door jolt me awake.

I sit up abruptly, clutching the sheet to my chest as Elyra and Theren rush in, their faces etched with urgency.

"We must make haste, my lady." Elyra's voice is tight as she strides to the tall windows.

She yanks the heavy dark curtains apart, letting in the muted, silvery light of Avalon's early morning.

The usual dark denim haze has softened today—brighter in a way that feels unnatural. A signal. The coming sunrise in a realm built on shadow.

I open my mouth to ask what's happening—

But it slams into me like a blow to the chest.

Ruvan Kael.

Fucking Warden of the Briar.

"Ruvan," I breathe, swinging my legs over the edge of the bed.

"Yes, Lady Tana. We must ready you." Elyra rushes us across the hall to my room, already moving with practiced efficiency.

I grit my teeth, irritation prickling beneath my skin. Not just at Ruvan, but at myself.

How did I let this sneak up on me?

Oh, I know. Orion.

The infuriating Fae Prince that must had sneaked out of his bed without waking me.

My mind betrays me with flashes—Orion's mouth, his hands, his endless talents that are far too distracting.

In the bedroom.

The dining hall.

The hallway.

Gods, even the fucking courtyard.

I scowl at the memory, pushing it aside. *Focus, Tana. You're about to be challenged to the death.*

Elyra pulls me to my feet, her hands untangling my sleep-mussed hair. "Theren," I snap, shaking off the lingering haze of desire and sleep, "go to Hephaestus. Tell him I need a blade."

Theren nods sharply, already halfway to the door. "What kind?"

"He'll know which one to send."

He vanishes down the hall in a sprint.

Elyra braids my hair back from my face with a tightness that mirrors the knot in my chest. She dresses me in fighting leathers—supple, snug, built for movement.

Light armor follows—shoulder guards, forearm bracers, a chest plate. Not a full suit, which I'm glad for.

The armor I'm used to is tech—Gaea's best.

I exhale slowly. *Home.*

The thought slips in so easily now. I shake it away.

The sword in the stone would come in handy today. A pang of regret flickers through me. I should have claimed it. But Hephaestus will choose well.

He made my enchanted knife—the one that bends to my will in ways I don't understand.

And he cares about me. He'll send something that will help me today.

CHAPTER 45

orion

The sky stretches wide and restless above Avalon, shades of dark steel bleeding into the faint bruising light of the impending Bloomrise.

I ride the winds astride Omen, my Shadowmare's wings slicing through the thin veil between Evenfall and First Shade.

Each powerful beat sends ripples of shadow trailing in our wake, echoes of a realm that refuses to be forgotten, even as the sky brightens.

Skyfall Castle looms in the distance, etched in stone and secrets, its wards pulsing faintly against the tide of Fae gathering for the celebration.

I weave through the currents of magic, senses stretched thin as I reinforce the barriers, threading shadow into the seams where cracks threaten to form.

With so many Fae arriving, alliances brittle as glass, I take no chances. I won't make the same mistakes I did during Beltane.

A sharp pull tugs at the edge of my awareness—something that refuses to be ignored.

My pulse spikes, a visceral instinct screaming beneath the calm veneer I wear like armor.

I narrow my gaze, invoking my Fae sight, the world sharpening into harsh, unforgiving clarity.

In the castle courtyard, Tana stands armed, poised like a warrior carved from flame and fury, facing Ruvan Kael.

A snarl curls my lip, rage flaring hot and immediate. That bastard. I know his kind—all pride and poison, masked beneath thorns and honeyed words.

He will cheat. He will twist the rules, do whatever it takes to kill her.

Because that's what cowards do when faced with someone who threatens their fragile power.

His quarrel is with me—it always has been. He denied the loyalty of his court simply to spite me, and Thorne is all too happy to let this play out, waiting to call off his Warden at the last moment.

But Ruvan will pay the price for his treachery today.

I yank Omen's reins hard, my grip fierce. She answers without hesitation, a dark blur against the paling sky, her wings stretching wide, catching the wind with brutal grace.

We rush forward, cutting through the thin veil of clouds like a blade.

Still too far away, the clash begins.

Tana shifts into a defensive stance, her body coiled with intent. Ruvan charges, his movements precise, calculated. But so is she.

I lean forward, urging Omen faster. The sky betrays us, its growing light thinning the shadows, making it harder for her to Shadow Jump.

My power feels distant, stretched thin against the dawn that will taunt us tonight.

Their swords meet, the clash of steel sharp even against the wind roaring past my ears. Ruvan drives her down, forcing her to the ground—but my anger falters, replaced by something sharper, more visceral.

She's in control.

I see it in the angle of her hips, the calculated twist of her wrist.

She wants him close.

And when he overcommits, leaning in with the arrogance of a man who thinks he's already won, she strikes.

Tana drives her feet up, slamming them into his groin with brutal precision. Ruvan grunts, his body recoiling, but she doesn't stop.

She uses his momentum, kicking him over her head with fluid grace, a predator disguised in mortal skin.

He crashes onto his back behind her, breath stolen by the impact.

Tana doesn't hesitate. She surges to her feet, her sword an extension of her will, and brings it down on him with a force that feels like destiny forged in steel.

I push Omen faster, but in that moment, I know—

She doesn't need me to save her.

She never did.

But I will damn myself to the darkness of Elysium before I let him touch her.

I rise from the saddle, balancing with ease born from ages of battle. My legs steady against the shifting currents, Omen's wings a dark blur beneath me.

I wait, timing the arc perfectly as she sweeps over the castle, the courtyard below opening like a wound carved into stone.

Thunder growls, distant but rising, fueled by my rage.

Lightning surges through me, pooling in my palms until it forms twin staffs of crackling, blinding power.

My pulse beats in tandem with the storm brewing in my chest.

Ruvan staggers to his feet, shaking off the dust, his sword raised to strike Tana again.

But I will not afford him this opportunity.

I step off Omen's back, falling with purpose, a comet trailing darkness and fury.

The wind screams past me, but I hear nothing but the roar of my own blood, the sharp snap of my magic coiling like a beast unleashed.

I land hard, the ground cracking beneath the force, dust and stone exploding outward in a ring of raw energy.

I rise from the crouch, lightning snapping out like a whip, precise and unforgiving.

It coils around Ruvan's sword, searing metal and bone alike.

With a sharp tug, I rip the weapon from his grasp, sending it clattering across the courtyard.

My gaze locks with his, a warning etched in every shadow around me.

Ruvan straightens slowly, a sneer twisting his features.

"Afraid she can't fight her own battles, Regent?"

I step forward, lightning flickering like restless serpents

along my arms, my voice a low growl dripping with loathing.

"No," I say, dark and final. "I'm here to make sure you die screaming."

Ruvan's sneer deepens, but I see the glint of unease beneath it. He's realizing—too late—that this fight isn't one he'll walk away from.

He lunges, quick, his magic snapping out in jagged crimson vines, thorned and writhing, desperate to sink into my skin.

I meet him with shadow and lightning, my power surging in a violent collision that sends shockwaves through the courtyard.

The gathered Fae press back, wide-eyed, whispers slithering through the air as we fight.

He is strong, fast, but I am faster.

I twist, dodging his strike, shadows sliding over my skin like armor.

My lightning cracks against his vines, searing through them, but he adapts, using them to pull me forward, forcing me close.

His fist slams into my ribs, pain flaring sharp and immediate, but I don't falter. I use the momentum, ducking low, twisting behind him. My shadows coil around his legs, locking him in place.

Tana gasps from somewhere behind me, her voice caught in her throat, but I can't afford to look at her.

I can't let her see the strain, the way my vision blurs at the edges, my heart hammering harder than it should.

The price of my power gnaws at me, but I shove it down, forcing my body to obey.

Ruvan snarls, his vines writhing wildly, trying to break free, but I don't give him the chance.

I move, swift and merciless, lightning crackling in my hands as I slam my fist into his face. The impact sends him staggering, blood spraying across the cracked stone.

He barely catches himself before I'm on him again, driving my knee into his gut, wrenching his arm behind his back until I hear the sharp pop of bone dislocating.

He howls, dropping to one knee, but I don't let go.

"I should carve the rot from your body," I snarl, voice low, venomous, my grip tightening. "You're a parasite, clinging to a throne that does not belong to you."

His laughter is wet with blood, but the arrogance hasn't left him. He spits at my feet, grinning through crimson-stained teeth. "Kill me, and Thorne will make sure your queen suffers."

The storm inside me surges, howling for blood. I tighten my grip, shadows rising like a black tide, my lightning crackling, ready to end him, to make sure he never touches her, never breathes another threat against her.

I lean in close, letting him feel the weight of my rage.

"You won't live long enough to see it."

I drive my sword through his chest.

The blade sinks deep, piercing flesh, bone, and stone beneath him.

His body seizes, his mouth falling open in a silent scream as my magic floods through him, searing every nerve, every vein, consuming him from the inside out.

Lightning bursts through the wound, a violent surge of raw power that shatters the ground beneath us. His breath stutters, his eyes wide, disbelieving, before the light in them vanishes.

I rip the sword free, letting his body crumple to the earth.

Silence swallows the courtyard.

The gathered Fae stare, stunned, some in horror, others in awe. The scent of scorched flesh lingers in the air, but I don't acknowledge it. I don't look at them. My gaze finds only one person.

Tana.

She stands at the edge of the courtyard, her expression unreadable, her fists clenched at her sides.

Her dark eyes flick to my shaking hand, the way my fingers tighten around the hilt of my blade, the slight tremor I can't hide. I know what she sees.

The toll this battle has taken. The exhaustion creeping in, the weight pressing down on my chest, the darkness I can't keep at bay.

Her lips part, but before she can speak, Mor steps forward, her voice cool, unimpressed. "Well, that was dramatic."

The tension shatters. The spell breaks. The moment of death and violence fades just enough for the world to tilt back into place.

I exhale, forcing my body to move, to turn away from the ruin of Ruvan Kael.

I dip my head toward Tana in a shallow bow, my voice steady despite the tremor beneath it. "It has been my honor to serve as your champion, my lady. Rejoice in your victory."

Her gaze sharpens with concern, flicking to Mor.

"Take us to the caves at the base of the cliffs," she orders, her voice steady despite the spectacle she just witnessed.

Mor's shadows rise, dark tendrils wrapping around us, swallowing us whole.

The courtyard vanishes, replaced by the damp, suffocating darkness of a cave I know too well—the place where I watched the prophecy of my death, and later, the vision of Tana's arrival.

The walls seem to pulse with memory, shadows lingering like echoes, and I stumble, bracing my hand against the rocky wall.

Tana wastes no time wrapping her arms around me, hoping to help steady me.

She turns to Mor, her voice sharp, her eyes never leaving me. "Get back up there. Make sure they don't kill each other."

Mor smirks, her presence a dark comfort. "And if they do?"

Tana doesn't flinch. "Then you kill them."

Mor's grin widens with sinister delight. "You will make an excellent Fae Queen."

And then she vanishes, swallowed by shadows once more, leaving me with the woman who sees everything I try to hide.

CHAPTER 46
Tana

Orion is hiding something. I don't know what, or how I know, but I'm certain there's something he isn't telling me.

The power he released... I've never seen anything like it. In all my years fighting immortals, battling vampires, slaying werewolves—nothing compares.

And it took a toll on him.

He is not invincible. His well of power is not endless. Or maybe it's supposed to be, but something is wrong.

Like the darkness siphoning the life from the realm, maybe there's something draining him too.

All I know is, he was paler than usual. A light sheen of sweat gathered along his hairline, and he was trying to hold back the tremor in his hand. Something told me the Fae can't see him like that.

As soon as Mor leaves us, the endless thrumming in my head increases. The atmosphere in the cave thickens, pressing against me, saturated with magic. Fae power.

It's trying to rip through my skull, banging against me with each heartbeat.

If the magic is this strong, it has to help restore him.

He seems to follow my unspoken thought, moving toward the rear of the cave—toward the shallow pool where I first encountered the Lady of the Lake.

Each step is harder to take, and Orion doesn't resist when I wrap an arm around him to help.

His fingers brush against the wall, unsteady. I unclasp his belt, letting the weight of his sword's scabbard drop to the ground with a heavy thump.

"You just—can't keep your hands off, huh, Starling?" His words slur slightly, and I swear to God, if his big ass collapses before making it to the dark pool, I'm going to be pissed.

I tell him as much.

He snorts, a half-hearted sound.

He stands long enough for me to remove his boots and tunic. I only manage to unbuckle his trousers before he all but tumbles into the water.

He lowers himself in, releasing a deep, satisfied sigh.

His arms stretch along the pool's ledge, head tilting back, silver eyes closed as he breathes deeply.

The pool is massive, but it must be shallow. Near the rear of the cave, the still surface churns. I feel the shift in energy a second before the Lady rises from the water.

Only the top of her head and eyes emerge, watching us. It's unnerving.

She stares, silent, unmoving. It reminds me of a crocodile lurking beneath the surface, waiting to snap its jaws shut.

I blink.

And suddenly, she's at the pool's edge, right beneath me.

"Fuck me." I gasp, stumbling back a half step.

Orion grins, but his eyes remain closed.

The Lady reaches out, her cold, webbed fingers wrapping around my wrist. A pulse of energy rushes through me—not words, not images, just pure will.

I understand her meaning immediately.

I need to get in there with him.

This is fucking weird.

The water remains still as the Lady drifts backward, her pale form slowly sinking beneath its murky depths.

Releasing a sharp exhale, I begin unlacing my boots. "This place is fucked up, you know that?"

Orion's voice is rough. "That is one way to describe it." He dips his chin, taking a mouthful of water before spitting it out.

I shed my light armor, then remove my tunic and leathers. Orion cracks an eye open, watching as I step into the pool naked.

I only meant to sit beside him.

But he reaches for me, wrapping his arms around my waist and pulling me into his lap.

He exhales, pressing his forehead to mine. I wrap my arms around his neck, our bare chests flush, his heartbeat a steady, grounding rhythm.

I try to match mine to his. The erratic pulse makes it impossible, but the attempt calms me.

It clears my mind of everything—the battle, the blood, the torment that just took place.

"Thank you for fighting for me," I whisper, my lips brushing against his.

He opens his eyes, color slowly returning to his skin. One hand grips my hip; the other cups my face.

"I will fight for you until the stars reclaim me."

He doesn't give me time to respond before his lips claim mine.

The kiss is slow, languid, easy.

His cock swells between us, thick and ready. The water sloshes as I sink down on his length, taking him fully.

Our moans echo through the cavern.

I close my eyes, losing myself in sensation.

The movement of the water, the stretch of him inside me, the way every vein along his shaft drags against me with perfect friction.

The cave begins to glow.

I blink, startled. Around us, the pool glows silver, pulsing with light. The magic seeps into him, the water flowing into his skin, rejuvenating him as I ride him.

His arms tighten around my waist. His mouth finds my collarbone, my shoulders, then my lips. A deep warmth spreads through my chest, like fire burning from within.

Orion's tongue sweeps into my mouth.

And suddenly—I hear him.

"Starling."

I gasp, body tensing. What the fuck?

I jerk back, stopping mid-movement. "What was that?"

Orion's wide stare matches my own, but the shock doesn't last.

His grip tightens, spinning me so my back meets the pool's ledge as he drives back into me.

The surprise giving way to a feral possessiveness.

I cry out, the sound reverberating through the cave.

"Tell me you can hear me, Starling."

His voice is in my fucking head.

And it feels... good. Warm. Safe. Like being cocooned in absolute comfort and security.

"Yes," I breathe as he thrusts harder, my walls clenching around him. "Oh, God... yes. I can hear you."

"Then tell me."

He pauses, waiting.

"Tell you what?" My voice is a broken whisper.

His fingers slide between us, pinching my clit.

I arch, gasping. "Oh, God."

Orion's voice is low, amused. *"Who is this god you call to make me jealous?"*

He shifts, lifting my legs over his arms, holding me wide open.

"Where is he so I may slaughter him, too—" he bites my neck, marking me *"—and bring you his head as my offering?"*

Holy fucking shit.

Every word is spoken directly into my mind.

Orion is merciless. His thrusts are deep, brutal. My back scrapes against the ledge, the burn only adding to the pleasure.

"Rub your clit for me, my queen."

My hand moves without thought. My fingers circle my swollen bud as he pounds into me.

"I am the god of lightning."

Electricity crackles, zipping along my skin, biting at my nipples.

"Of shadows."

He grunts, slamming into me, his pace unrelenting.

"And I am the god that makes your pretty pussy weep."

My moan shatters. *Yes, fuck, yes, you are.*

"Orion," I cry, body clenching, the orgasm tearing through me like a supernova. "Oh, fuck—I'm coming—"

"Pray to me, Starling, for the pleasure I give you."

His grip tightens around my throat, cutting off my scream as I shatter around him.

Lightning flashes. The water pulses silver.

Orion grunts. His hand circling my throat, his thumb on my pulse.

His cock throbs, spilling into me with pure, electrified release.

For a moment, there is nothing.

Then the glow fades.

I press a hand to his chest, my other brushing against his cheek. He turns into my touch, lips pressing against my palm.

"Do you feel better?" I whisper.

Orion exhales, voice rough, satisfied. "Anytime your sweet cunt is wrapped around me, I feel amazing."

CHAPTER 47

The air is thick with the scent of lavender oil and rosewater as Theren and Elyra bustle around me. They're quiet and efficient, their relaxed chatter a faint hum in the background.

Their presence is a solemn reminder of what happened before the last Fae celebration I was getting ready for—the hours leading up to Beltane, when Brynja, Thelindra, and Elowen had attended to me with care, their laughter filling the room.

Their quick camaraderie put me at ease in this strange world.

A lump forms in my throat at the memory, the sharp contrast between their gentle smiles and the bloodbath that followed.

I flinch as Elyra adjusts the intricate belt at my waist, her hands brushing against my skin. The moment is fleeting, and she doesn't notice, but the memory lingers, clawing at the edges of my mind.

I force myself to focus on the present—on the woman reflected in the mirror before me.

The dress is unlike anything I've ever worn. The fabric is

nearly sheer, a shimmering silver-blue that catches the light and gives the illusion of starlight cascading over my skin.

The panels barely cover my breasts, the thin material whispering over my nipples with every breath I take.

A belt of silver, encrusted with sapphires, cinches at my waist, drawing the panels together to drape elegantly down the front.

Behind me, layers of ethereal tulle cascade from my hips, covering my ass and flowing into a train that trails behind me like a cloud.

My blade, glamoured away, rests securely around my thigh.

It's revealing—scandalous, even—but undeniably regal.

My hair flows freely down my back, a cascade of dark curls meticulously styled to frame my face and tumble over my shoulders.

When they place the crown on my head—a delicate circlet of silver and sapphire—it feels heavier than I expected.

As it settles into place, the mates step back, their work complete, leaving me alone with the reflection in the mirror.

For the first time, I don't just see myself.

I see a queen.

The realization sends a shiver down my spine. I'm not sure if it's fear or pride—or something far more complicated.

My hands brush the edges of the dress, smoothing the fabric as I stare at the woman looking back at me.

Strong.

Confident.

Powerful. Not yet a queen fit for Avalon—yet so far from who I used to be.

"You're ready, my queen," Theren says, clearing his throat.

I take a deep breath, straightening my shoulders. For tonight, I'll play the part.

I only need to be careful that the woman who arrived in Avalon is the same one who leaves it.

I can't allow myself to get swept away by the glamour of what is around me—or who is around me.

I expected Orion to escort me, as he had on Beltane, but it's Mor who strides down the hall with me. She's not adorned in finery or playing the part of a regal attendant.

No, she's dressed like a sentinel of darkness itself, her black cloak shifting like liquid shadows as she approaches. Her crimson eyes survey me with that calculating gaze I've come to expect.

"The sooner we arrive, the sooner we can get this over with," she says, her tone lacking its usual sharp edge.

I scoff, adjusting the weight of the crown on my head. "Oh, don't be a party pooper."

Mor narrows her eyes at me. "We do not understand that reference, so we will contemplate whether we are offended or not." With a nod, she steps aside, leaving me in front of the hall's massive double doors.

The low murmur of voices beyond grows louder, a crescendo of expectation until someone inside announces, "Presenting Queen Tana, the Chosen of Avalon, Lady of Starfall."

Jesus, the titles are getting longer by the day.

The doors swing open with a dramatic flourish, revealing the grandeur of the hall beyond. The noise grows deafening as hundreds of high Fae, dignitaries, and rulers from the ten courts turn their attention to me.

The sheer variety is overwhelming—skin in every hue from golden to ice-blue, hair shimmering like molten silver or braided in midnight strands.

Some glow softly, like walking constellations, while others seem to draw in the light around them, shadowy figures wrapped in mystery.

I stand at the top of a grand staircase, my heart thudding painfully against my ribs as the sea of faces tilts upward.

For a moment, I'm frozen, unsure of how to step into the world they've thrust me into.

And then my eyes find Orion.

He stands at the base of the stairs, clad in the same colors of Starfall that I wear—silver and deep, rich blue. The cape draped over one broad shoulder sways as he takes a deliberate step forward, his silver eyes fixed on me.

There's no mistaking the expression on his face. It's reverence—a raw, unguarded admiration that sends a flutter through my chest.

He looks at me like I've cast every star in the sky just for tonight's celebration.

The storm that brews in his gaze is fierce, commanding, but it's the calm I find within that chaos that steadies me.

Ironically, it's his tempest that grounds me, giving me the courage to take the first step down the stairs.

The room seems to fall silent as I descend, each step measured and deliberate. The train of my dress whispers against the marble, the faint sound drowned by the roaring of my heartbeat in my ears.

I can feel their eyes—their judgment, their curiosity—but it all fades into the background as Orion extends his hand to me.

I take it, his touch warm and solid, and suddenly, the daunting crowd feels insignificant.

"You are breathtaking," he murmurs, his voice low enough for only me to hear.

I meet his gaze, and for once, the words that usually tumble out of me so easily are lost. Instead, I allow myself a small smile—one that conveys everything I can't seem to say.

Tonight, I have a game to play. And if I falter, I know the storm at my side will hold me steady.

We face the crowd, and the sea of Fae before us bends as one—a synchronized wave of reverence. Heads bow low, knees bend in submission, a display of unity—or perhaps fear—for Avalon's chosen queen.

But not all follow suit.

One figure remains upright amidst the sea of deference, golden and gleaming like the sun itself. Liona.

Her head is high, her gilded hair catching the ambient light, and her lips curl into the faintest hint of a smirk.

The defiance is subtle, but it's there, and it halts the moment like a knife slicing through silk.

Orion stiffens beside me, his hand tightening into a fist at his side. His voice comes low, barely audible across my mind, but it rumbles with quiet authority—the kind that leaves no room for argument.

"Do not look away from her until she bends her knee."

How the fuck am I supposed to answer a goddamned mind reader?

I keep my gaze locked on Liona, my pulse quickening with the need to fling my blade into her throat. That would shut her the fuck up.

Orion snickers—as if he perhaps heard me. Liona meets my stare with a smugness that ignites a challenge I'm all too ready to answer. I would cut this bitch from her cunt to her cocky smile.

Finally, with a mocking smile, Liona lowers herself into the shallowest of bows.

"Good girl," I murmur under my breath, enough that Orion hears me. I catch the slight twitch of his lips before he straightens, releasing the room from its suffocating stillness.

As we descend the remaining stairs, I lean closer to Orion, my irritation getting the better of me. "I may kill that bitch before sunrise," I murmur.

Orion turns his head to meet my gaze, his expression unreadable, his tone calm and even. But the weight of his words lands like a thunderclap.

"I'm not sure you could best Liona, Starling. But I would enjoy watching the attempt."

CHAPTER 48
orion

The instant my words reached her ears, I saw the shift in Tana—the way her breath caught, the momentary flicker of something raw in her eyes before it was extinguished.

I felt the chill when her hand slipped from mine, the warmth replaced with a void that I hated more than I should.

But most telling, most important of all, was the way she threw up her walls. Her defenses rose like iron gates, her spine straightened, and her gaze hardened.

She was no longer just a mortal woman in an immortal court; she was a soldier stepping onto a battlefield, her weapons sharpened and ready.

Good. That's exactly how she needs to be tonight— sharp, steady, and fierce.

As we continue forward, I allow myself a brief glance at her. Tana's face is composed, her expression a mask of calm indifference.

But I can feel the fury burning just beneath the surface, a furnace ignited by Liona's little display.

It's there in the set of her jaw, the fire in her gaze. Liona believes there is still a game to play, but she's underestimated my Starling.

She doesn't realize she's just handed Tana the perfect excuse to show these courts exactly what she's made of.

I almost pity the lords and ladies of Avalon. *Almost.*

I've endured enough of Liona's calculated flirtations, her attempts to ensnare me with her body, the traps she set for weaker Fae to stumble into.

All of it designed to provoke Tana, to unbalance her.

She isn't here to win me over; she's here to play her games, to make Tana falter in front of the entire court.

But I know what burns in Tana. Lighting that furnace of anger doesn't weaken her or make her irrational; it tempers her. Hones her into the weapon she's been crafted to be.

And tonight, I have unleashed her on the courts of Avalon.

As we step further into the grand hall, the murmurs of the gathered Fae rise and fall like a tide. Their eyes flicker between Tana and me—gauging, measuring.

But I see them linger on her, the mortal queen, their curiosity tinged with doubt. They don't know what to make of her yet.

Good. Let them wonder.

Tana pauses just a step ahead of me, her chin lifting as her gaze sweeps the room.

I know the look in her eyes—the assessment, the cataloging of every exit, every threat. It's the same look she gave me the first time she realized I was more than a spoiled prince.

The same look she'll give anyone who dares underestimate her tonight.

I lean closer to her, my voice low enough for only her to hear. "Let the games begin, Starling."

CHAPTER 49
Tana

The sound of laughter and the clink of crystal goblets fills the ballroom, a cacophony of wealth and power parading as civility.

I keep my chin high, and my steps measured, a picture of poise and control, though my insides feel like a raging storm.

Orion's words linger like a bitter aftertaste, but I shove them aside.

I'll handle the courts tonight. On my own.

The gazes of the High Fae follow me as I move through the throng, curious and piercing. Whispers trail in my wake, each syllable carrying the weight of scrutiny and doubt.

I take a breath and square my shoulders. They can watch all they want. I'm not here to be their spectacle.

"Queen Tana," a smooth voice greets me, pulling me to a stop. I turn to find myself face-to-face with the Lord of the Celestial Court.

He is tall and lean, with pale skin that seems to shimmer faintly under the ballroom's golden light.

His eyes, an eerie silver-blue, seem to hold galaxies within them.

"Lord Caelith," I reply, inclining my head just enough to show respect without yielding an ounce of authority. His lips curl into a faint smile, one that doesn't quite reach his eyes.

"It is an honor to finally meet the mortal chosen by the realm itself," he says, his tone dripping with something between curiosity and condescension.

"A rare occurrence indeed."

"I hope your sentiment of rare does not imply unworthy, Lord Caelith," I respond smoothly, letting a hint of steel edge my words. "Surely the realm's choice should be cause for celebration, not suspicion."

His smile widens, but it's a cold thing, like moonlight on ice. "Of course, Your Majesty. Forgive me if my intrigue seems misplaced.

It's simply... fascinating to consider what—qualities the realm might have found so compelling in a mortal."

I step closer, meeting his gaze head-on. "Perhaps it saw the same qualities in me that it once saw in Pandora.

I have come to learn she exuded impressive strength, resilience, a refusal to be underestimated."

My voice lowers, taking on an edge that cuts through the thin veil of politeness.

"But perhaps it saw something else—someone willing to do what must be done to protect this realm. It does not seem the Fae are dedicated to their own survival. The realm has looked elsewhere for it."

Caelith's expression falters for the briefest moment, a flicker of surprise breaking through his practiced facade.

It's gone as quickly as it appeared, replaced by a shallow bow.

"Indeed," he murmurs, his tone quieter now. "Perhaps the realm chose wisely after all."

"Perhaps," I echo, my gaze steady as I hold his for a beat longer than necessary. Then, with a small nod, I step past him and continue through the crowd. "Please, excuse me."

The tension in my shoulders eases slightly as I put distance between us, but I know this is just the beginning.

The other courts will be watching after that exchange, taking note of how I carry myself, how I respond.

If I falter even once, they'll pounce.

Good luck with that, I think grimly, my lips curving into a faint smile.

I weave my way toward another group of dignitaries, each step a deliberate choice.

The sound of laughter and the hum of conversation dulls as Liora steps into my path, drawing every eye in her wake.

Once again she is entirely nude, her golden skin shimmering like molten sunlight, her body adorned only with elaborate jewels that sparkle under the soft glow of the room's chandeliers.

Her presence is arresting, her beauty undeniable, but there's a sharpness beneath the glamour—a weapon wrapped in gilded silk.

"Hmm," Her gilded eyes look up amusingly at the crown in my hair. "Cute crown."

"Well, look at you. Saying big words and everything." I answer back in a sing-song voice. "And not even a lisp."

I snag a small plate with cheeses and cured meats. Taking my hidden dagger, I flip it between my fingers and spear a piece of cheese. Keeping my eyes on her as I take it from the knife with my teeth.

"Tell me, *Lady* Tana." Liona crosses her arms and runs a few fingers delicately across her collarbone. "Did our prince still smell like me when he ran after you?"

She makes a point to look at Orion with her large doe eyes, literally batting her eyelashes and the impulse to roll my eyes as hard as possible is nearly painful to resist.

What makes this ever better is Orion is paying no attention to our conversation.

He appears wholly engaged in conversation with the Lord of Evershade. But I know better. The flicker of shadows around me is subtle but unmistakable.

He's aware of every move I make, of every word spoken around me, even when he pretends not to be.

"Oh, you mean when he made me come while he still had your blood on his hands?" I take another piece of cheese while she tenses her jaw. "Yea, but I thought the stink was just from the Swamp Court."

"The realm can choose whatever trash it wants." She steps to me but truthfully, her being nude takes any element of intimidation she's trying to convey.

I just cannot take her seriously. "You should know, the Fae can also choose a champion."

I make a point to look just behind her; my brows pinched in confusion.

She is taken aback and hesitates, before turning to look

as well. "Sorry, I was just looking for the fuck I'm supposed to give."

A Lesser Fae walks by and I nod to get their attention. Handing them my plate, I give a small smile. "Thank you." I offer quietly.

The Fae clears their throat and walks away quickly as my politeness causes a few High Fae to turn their heads. *Pompous assholes.*

"Look, Lenora," I slide my dagger back into its home where no one can see it again. "I know you think your sparkle pussy is super special and I'm sure you give fantastic head."

She gasps at my crude response.

"But that doesn't mean they want to see you sit that smelly cunt on Avalon's throne, baby. Or else they would have put you there by now."

I reach up and pat her cheek lightly twice. "But hey, tits up, girl. It's supposed to be a fun night. You look like you sucked on the asshole of a Questing Beast."

Mor half chokes, half coughs. Unlike Orion is who doing a good job of blending in and feigning disinterest, Mor is making sure every Fae in the room knows she is serving as my guard this evening.

Her dark gaze shifts quickly from Fae to Fae as they move around me. Her shadows are deep and rich, roiling off her like smoke.

"Smile, have a good time." I hand her a flute of bubbling Fae wine. "You can go back to your frigid bitch ways tomorrow."

I lock eyes with Orion over her shoulder. He's looking at

me. A smirk on his lips as he raises a cup a mead to his mouth, looking back at his companion.

Hypnos walks in front of my view, two large, gold coins between his fingers that Orion plucks.

That fucking son of a bitch.

He set me up, intentionally to piss me off. And they placed bets on the evening.

I glare at him, and I know he feels it. I know he can sense the shift in my demeanor and the smug-ass grin sliding across his face makes me want to slap him.

Yes, let the games begin, Orion.

Without another word, I glide away, spotting Hephaestus and Hestia. Lesser Fae who shouldn't be here mingling with high brow, but who would question Orion inviting them.

I know they are here to serve as more eyes on my safety. Liona's golden figure disappears into the crowd with a huff as she realizes I ended her conversation to speak with someone of a station she considers below her.

"What a bitch." I mutter into Hestia's ear as she places a kiss on my left cheek and then the right.

"See, my love." Hestia's eyes shine bright with amused approval. "I told you, not to worry." She speaks to Hephaestus who looks about as comfortable here as he would diving into a briar patch.

"Our Queen is fairing just fine on her own tonight."

CHAPTER 50
orion

The grand hall pulses with life—candlelight flickering against jeweled gowns, the sharp clink of glasses raised in toast, the low hum of conversations threading through the air.

Bloomrise Night is everything Avalon prides itself on: a dazzling spectacle meant to unite its courts. But all I see are the fractures.

My eyes follow Tana as they have since the moment she entered. A vision of strength, draped in silver and blue, every inch the queen Avalon has chosen.

Antagonizing her earlier had been a gamble, but one that paid off. She's been magnificent, holding her own against the sharp tongues and sharper gazes of the Fae.

Every challenge thrown her way, she dismantles with effortless precision. *She's proving herself.*

Not just to them, but to herself.

Yet, I see it—the flickers of hesitation in her gaze, the subtle tension in her shoulders when she thinks no one is looking. *She still plans to leave.*

The mortal realm calls to her like a siren song of familiarity and comfort, and I have nothing to compete with that. *But I want her to choose this.*

To choose Avalon.

When Liona approached her earlier, I fought the urge to intervene. Watching the Shimmering Court's viper circle her, taunting with veiled barbs, was like witnessing a predator toying with its prey.

But Tana *wasn't* prey. She held her ground, meeting Liona's words with the cutting precision of her own. The flicker of anger in Liona's gilded eyes had been *delicious.*

Still, I hadn't anticipated *this.*

Tana's gaze flicks toward me, her lips curling in a teasing smile as she brushes her fingers along the arm of some lesser lord, tilting her head in laughter at whatever insipid thing he's saying.

She *knows* I'm watching.

She's doing this on purpose.

I can feel the storm rising within me, jealousy simmering beneath my skin, but I let her play her game.

She thinks this will shake me. That I'll break first. But Tana doesn't understand *me.*

The Fae are not selfish in pleasure. I had no problem watching her take her handmaids to bed on *Beltane*—in fact, I enjoyed it.

But watching *this* insipid fool ogle her breasts as she squeezes his forearm?

That makes me want to tear down the castle walls and beat him to death with Starfall's stones.

My shadows ripple at my feet, betraying my rising agitation, but my expression remains neutral. The others may not see it, but *she* does. *She always does.*

When our eyes meet again, she raises a single brow, smirk widening as she touches the hand of a Frosthaven prince.

Calculated. Deliberate.

My jaw tightens, and I turn away, forcing my attention to the Evershade lord beside me. But even as we exchange pleasantries, I'm *acutely* aware of her every move.

I hate how much she's gotten under my skin.

No. That's a lie.

I hate how much I *enjoy* it.

The night drags on, a whirl of politics and pretense, but the space between us feels more like a battlefield than a ballroom. Every glance, every lingering touch she bestows upon another Fae, is a challenge.

And every step I take closer to her is an answer.

She's daring me to make a move.

And gods help me, I just might.

The shift in the room is subtle at first. Conversations dim, replaced by an almost reverent hush. I find Tana midthought, her head tilting slightly as she lifts her gaze to the high windows above the ballroom.

Following her line of sight, I see it—the moon's light dims, veiled by a shroud of dark clouds, casting the *Night Court* in a deeper shade of shadow.

It's time.

She sensed it before anyone else.

A silent announcement ripples through the gathering, Fae drifting toward the balconies and courtyards with measured purpose. I follow at a deliberate pace, keeping Tana in my periphery as she steps outside.

When I reach the stone railing of the largest balcony, the sight before me steals my breath.

The field stretches endlessly, its surface pulsing with bioluminescence.

Flowers bloom in waves of shimmering light, petals unfurling in a slow, hypnotic dance. Soon, they will release their spores—tiny stars of blue, green, and pale gold, carried upward on the wind, spreading across Avalon.

A promise of new life.

But tonight is different. *Bloomrise* is occurring on the night of *Skyfall*.

Tana tilts her head to the heavens as the stars brighten, then begin to fall. Colors more beautiful than jewels flare as the stars shoot through the night.

A cry rings through the sky as meteors streak across the horizon, plummeting like falling embers.

I am privileged to watch the parade the cosmos gives us at the close of every mooncycle and yet, I never tire of it.

The falling stars vanish behind the dark mist of the lake, swallowed by Avalon's endless night.

And then, as the final star completes its descent, the field *responds*.

The glowing petals intensify, lifting from their stems, drifting upward like fireflies in the dark.

The sky, moments ago streaked with dying light, is reborn—filled with floating blooms that chase the fallen stars, reclaiming the night.

I've only seen this once before. Long ago.

It was magnificent then.

But now?

Now it feels transcendent.

Perhaps it isn't the event itself.

Perhaps it's her.

Tana stands slightly apart from the others, her dark skin illuminated by the soft glow of the spores.

The shifting colors dance across her features, accentuating the sharp cut of her cheekbones, the fullness of her lips, the quiet wonder in her expression.

She looks as if she belongs to this moment—woven into the splendor rather than an observer of it.

It's almost too fitting.

Bloomrise marks the propagation of life, the renewal of Avalon's cycle. And yet, this—*her*—is the truest renewal the realm has seen in an age.

How could it be mere coincidence that she arrived in this season, when even the land itself seems to respond to her presence?

The thought settles in my chest, heavy, both awe-inspiring and terrifying.

Then she moves. A subtle shift, as though sensing the weight of my attention. Slowly, her gaze sweeps the crowd, searching—until it lands on mine.

I don't look away. *I can't.*

While the other Fae marvel at the luminous display, I remain rooted, *captivated by her.* She catches my gaze, her brows knitting together for a fleeting moment before her expression softens.

Something passes between us—an understanding, unspoken but undeniable.

The air between us crackles, a tension neither of us will name. All night, we've played a dangerous game—not one of physical peril, but something far riskier.

The kind that threatens to unravel defenses we both pretend to hold firm.

I've been careful. Too careful. Shielding *her* not from my heart, but from her own.

My fate is sealed—the numbered beats of my heart are unchanging. But hers? She believes it to be fragile, broken beyond repair. I see it differently.

Her heart is strong.

Resilient.

Destined to beat for Avalon—once she accepts it.

Without breaking our shared gaze, we both move—not toward each other, but toward *Starfall.*

Step by step, our paths weave together like threads in a tapestry, yet never quite touching.

She reaches a door first. Pauses. Her hand lingers on the handle, her eyes still locked on mine.

Then she disappears inside.

Moments later, I take another passage, only to find myself somewhere else entirely. Not near her. Not where I *want* to be.

The castle hums around me, its ancient corridors shifting. I breathe deeply, shadows stirring in response, brushing against me like loyal hounds seeking direction.

They move at my will, fanning outward, searching.

And then—they *find her.*

My feet move without hesitation.

She's waiting for me.

Tana stands in an alcove beneath the grand staircase, turning slow circles as if deciding where I'll come from. Her frustration is evident in the sharp set of her jaw, the way her arms fold across her chest, her hip jutting in irritation.

She's still punishing me for *Liona.*

Her defiance is as sharp as ever, and I should brace for the verbal lashing to come.

But the *true* punishment is standing there, bathed in the soft spill of moonlight, her sheer dress clinging to every lush curve.

The delicate fabric teases at what it fails to fully conceal —*full breasts, a narrow waist, the soft flare of her hips.*

A torment I wouldn't wish away for anything.

She's a storm wrapped in beauty, her very presence a challenge.

And I am a man who *cannot resist answering one.*

I step into the alcove, my gaze locked on hers. Hands in my pockets, I aim for the illusion of casual nonchalance, though my heart pounds a thunderous beat.

I'm not sorry for what I did—*she needed that push.* Yet, if she demanded I grovel at her feet, I *would.*

A contradiction in flesh and shadow.

"Liar," she accuses, her voice low and sharp. One word, sliding between us like a blade.

A pulse of anger and desire surges through me, and before I consciously will it, my shadows react.

They rush forward, coiling around her wrists, pinning

her against the stone wall with a force both gentle and unyielding.

A sharp inhale.

Her breasts rise with the motion, straining against the sheer fabric, her body bound in the most maddening way.

I step closer, slowly. Deliberately.

"Motivator," I counter, voice low, the syllables rumbling deep in my chest. *I refuse to let her label stick.*

Everything I did—every move I made—was to *spur* her onward, to make her *brilliant,* to make her strong enough to stand against anyone.

Even me.

Her eyes narrow, dark fire sparking behind them. She tugs at her bonds, but the shadows hold, anticipating her every movement. Her lips press into a thin line, her breath shallow, controlled.

The air between us thickens.

She does not flinch.

Neither do I.

Her chin tilts upward in defiance, and my shadows shift slightly—not to hurt, merely to *remind.* A challenge she refuses to back down from.

She swallows, and I watch her throat work, the lamplight casting highlights along her collarbone. Her scent— warm, feminine, *infuriatingly* tempting—taunts my senses.

Another step.

She *lets* me get close.

My lips graze the column of her throat.

Her skin is warm, softer than I like to admit. I flick my

tongue out, tasting her. A whisper of salt, of something *sweet*, uniquely *hers*.

My shadows dissipate, releasing her wrists, but she does not move. Not to fight. *Not to run.*

Instead, my fingers encircle her throat in a possessive grip, firm but not harsh, a declaration of control she could challenge if she chose.

She *doesn't*.

My other hand slides down, capturing her leg behind the knee. With little effort, I lift it to my hip.

The shift brings her body flush against mine, my arousal pressing into the softness of her, drawing a sharp gasp from her lips.

Her head tilts, baring the smooth curve of her throat. *An invitation.*

Her hands rise to my shoulders, steadying herself—*or pulling me in.*

I tighten my grip just enough to feel her pulse hammer against my palm.

"What," I murmur, voice rough, lips brushing the shell of her ear, "can a Prince do to earn his Queen's forgiveness?"

Her breath ghosts over my skin, warm, teasing. Then, her lips part, her voice laced with fire and command.

"Get to your knees."

Her words punch through me—unexpected, undeniable. A slow, knowing smile curves my lips, and without hesitation, I drop to one knee. Then, the other.

At her feet.

My hands rest on my thighs, my posture expectant, waiting for her next decree.

She watches me, dark eyes gleaming with something predatory—something that stokes the inferno inside me.

Then, with deliberate grace, she lifts her heeled foot, resting it against my thigh. The shimmer of the delicate shoe catches the light, but it pales in comparison to *her*.

Her brow arches. A silent command.

I obey.

Reaching out, I remove her shoe with careful precision, cradling her foot in my palm as my thumb brushes over the soft arch.

I lift her leg slightly, pressing a slow, deliberate kiss to the inside of her knee.

Then lower—to the curve of her calf, the delicate bone of her ankle—until my lips find the top of her foot, reverent, worshipful.

My breath hitches. My chest tightens.

When I glance up, her gaze locks onto mine, her lips slightly parted, her chest rising in a steady, controlled rhythm. *Power* glows in her eyes, making my blood sing.

And I wait. *Eager. Willing.*

For her next command.

For *her*, I would kneel a thousand times over—if the beats of my heart would last that long. *If that were the case, I might even tell her of my devotion.*

But my heart is finite. And some truths are too cruel to lay bare.

She shifts, lifting her other foot onto my leg, granting me the same privilege. Without hesitation, I repeat the gesture, removing the second shoe with the same care.

My mouth follows, trailing lower—kissing the length of

her calf, the dip of her ankle, the delicate arch of her foot. Each kiss is deliberate. A silent vow.

Her hands find my shoulders, her grip featherlight, but the weight of her intent is undeniable. Using the leverage of my thighs, she lifts herself onto the narrow stone ledge behind her.

The space is barely enough, yet she perches with effortless grace, turning the balance of power in her favor.

Her toes rest on my legs, pointed, poised.

Then, with the languid elegance of a queen claiming her throne, she spreads her legs.

The shimmering panels of her dress part like a veil, falling aside.

And she is bare to me.

My breath catches. *Gone is my composure.*

She glistens in the low light, slick and waiting, a silent invitation that steals the last thread of restraint from my grasp.

I ache to touch her.

My hands twitch against my thighs, straining against my own discipline.

But I stay where I am—*kneeling at her altar, captivated and powerless in the presence of her beauty.*

"Tana," I murmur, her name slipping from my lips like a prayer.

Behind me, my shadows coil and shift, restless, eager, their hunger a mirror of my own. But I hold them back.

This moment belongs to *her.*

I lift my gaze, waiting. *Seeking.*

Her permission.

Her command.

Her lips curve into a knowing smile, her dark eyes gleaming with the fire of a queen who knows exactly the power she wields.

"Well?" she taunts, her voice a sultry whisper, each syllable curling around me like a spell. "Are you just going to sit there, or are you going to *serve your Queen*?"

The words ignite something feral inside me. *Something primal.*

I lean forward, my hands sliding up the soft skin of her thighs—only for her to *tsk*, amusement flashing in her gaze.

"Uh-uh," she murmurs, tilting her head in mock reprimand. "You're a naughty prince."

Then, slow and deliberate, she presses her foot against the ache straining beneath my pants.

I bite back a groan, my jaw locking as pleasure and frustration coil in my gut, tightening like a vice.

Fuck.

She knows *exactly* what she's doing.

"No touching," she purrs.

I still, my muscles taut with restraint, my breath coming harder now. *She is testing me.* And I will *gladly* let her.

My voice is low, rough, scraping over the syllables like gravel. "What would you have me do, my Queen?"

She leans in, her lips a breath away, her words a command wrapped in velvet.

"Tie your hands behind your back," she whispers. *"Use your shadows."*

A wave of heat courses through me as I obey, summoning my power with nothing more than a flicker of thought. My shadows wind around my wrists, pulling my arms behind me, securing them in inky bonds of my own making.

I could break free in an instant.

But I won't.

Because this is where I belong—bound to her will, *offering myself in service.*

Tana spreads her legs wider, the sheer panels of her gown falling aside like veils parting for a goddess. She leans back against the cool stone, her posture regal, commanding.

And the sight of her—*open*, waiting—makes my pulse hammer in my throat.

Her arousal glistens in the dim light, her scent washing over me in waves, *rich, intoxicating, absolute.* A queen's offering, but more than that—her claim.

I breathe her in. *Let her consume me.*

My head lowers, my lips brushing over the soft skin of her inner thigh—a silent vow, a whispered prayer.

Then, with deliberate slowness, I part her with my tongue, and the sound she makes—the sharp inhale, the soft, shuddering sigh—sends a fresh bolt of hunger through me.

She tastes like *ambrosia*, a maddening mixture of heat and honey that I would gladly drown in.

My tongue strokes her in slow, reverent circles, drawing her pleasure out inch by inch, savoring every gasping breath, every quiver of her body.

Tana's hips begin to move, rolling in slow, languid circles, guiding me, *owning me.* Her fingers tangle in my hair, gripping tight as she holds me *exactly* where she wants me.

Her moans—soft at first—grow louder, rising like a hymn to the gods as I tease, lap, *devour* her.

A wicked smirk ghosts my lips as I deepen my strokes, flicking my tongue just so—

And then she presses the arch of her foot against the *aching*, straining length beneath my pants.

A growl rumbles through my chest, the vibrations sending a shudder through her.

She does it again, grinding her heel against me, *knowing* how it affects me, *knowing* I can't do a damn thing about it with my hands bound.

"Closer," she pants, breathless and *commanding*.

I obey instantly, shifting closer on my knees, pressing into her as she hooks her leg over my shoulder, drawing me deeper into her heat. My tongue works her harder, my hunger insatiable.

Then—

Footsteps. Voices.

They echo down the corridor, growing closer.

Tana stiffens slightly—but not with fear. No, she grips my hair *tighter*, her fingers fisting with *purpose*.

A sickly sweet voice slithers through the space.

"I'm sure Lord Orion cannot resist the temptation of two High Fae ladies such as ourselves." Liora's words are poisoned honey, meant to wound. "He will forget his little mortal in an instant."

The giggle of another woman follows, their presence drawing nearer.

Tana's head tilts back, her breaths quickening. Then, she meets my gaze—dark, defiant, *daring*.

"Don't stop."

I wouldn't *dream* of it.

Her body trembles as I roll my tongue over her swollen clit, my groan sending another jolt of pleasure through her. Her muscles tense, her thighs clenching around me.

Then—

A *gasp*.

A sharp inhale.

The footsteps *halt*.

They see us.

Tana doesn't falter. If anything, she grinds harder against my mouth, chasing the climax building within her.

"Orion is—" Her voice catches as I suck her clit between my lips, teasing with my teeth, and she *surges* forward, riding the pleasure I give her.

I hum against her, pressing deeper, pushing her over the edge.

"Orion is *very busy right now*," she breathes, and her voice is drenched in satisfaction, edged with a moan.

Let them watch. Let them *see*.

See what it means for her to have the *devotion* of Avalon's prince.

Liora's huff of frustration cuts through the alcove, sharp and brittle. I can *feel* her rage simmering beneath her gilded mask, can *hear* the barely concealed humiliation in her breath.

She turns to leave—

But Tana stops her.

"You have not been *dismissed*, Fae."

Her words rise like smoke, soft and teasing, but laced with steel.

Silence.

The weight of her command settles over the space.

Fae honor *demands* respect in the presence of the realm's chosen queen. Liora *cannot* leave until Tana *releases* her—not without irreparable disgrace. And Tana *knows* it.

A slow, knowing grin spreads across my lips.

She's going to make Liora *watch*.

Watch as I *worship* her.

Watch as I *ruin* her.

And so, I *do as my Queen commands*.

My tongue works her with relentless precision, stroking, teasing, drinking her in. She bucks against me, thighs trembling, her moans now shameless, unrestrained.

Her nails rake against my scalp, the sharp sting making my cock throb painfully.

My shadows tighten around my wrists, the restraint a delicious torment I endure for *her*.

Her climax *slams* into her, hard and unyielding.

Her body arches, her release soaking my tongue, her cries ringing through the alcove like *victory bells*.

I *devour* every drop of her.

Only when the last tremors subside does she release me, her grip on my hair loosening. I look up, drinking in the sight of her—flushed, breathless, *triumphant*.

Then, she speaks.

"That will be all."

Her tone is *cool command*, the words cutting like glass.

"You may leave."

Footsteps retreat—sharp, hurried, *furious.*

Only once the Fae are gone does Tana reach down, fisting the lapels of my shirt in both hands as I breaking my shadows binding me.

She yanks me to my feet.

"Orion," she whispers, my name a plea, a demand, a promise.

And that's all I need.

I *surge* forward, my lips crashing into hers, bruising, devouring. My hand knots in her thick, curling hair, tilting her head back to bare her throat to me.

My free hand drops to my pants, unlacing them in a single fluid motion, freeing my aching cock.

It's heavy, throbbing, *starved* for her.

I pull her legs around my waist, pinning her to the stone wall, my length pressing against the slick heat I've just worshiped.

Then, my voice, raw and guttural, a command of my own:

"Now, give your naughty prince this tight *pussy.*"

And in one sharp thrust, I claim *her* as she has *claimed me.*

CHAPTER 51
Tana

The morning air is cool against my skin as I step onto the balcony, the thin silk of my nightgown fluttering in the soft breeze, and I'm drawn to the open air beyond.

The sight that greets me makes my breath hitch.

Orion lounges on the roof adjacent to his balcony, his body a study in effortless masculinity.

Reclining with one arm behind his head, his long white hair spills like silk against the dark stone tiles.

His other hand holds something that looks suspiciously like a rolled joint.

He's shirtless, his torso bare to the fading moonlight, the silver glow casting shadows across the ridges of his chest and abdomen.

His pants sit low on his hips, partially undone, teasing the deep V of his pelvis and the thin trail of hair leading below his waistband.

As if sensing my presence, he turns his head, his silver eyes locking onto mine. A smirk plays on his lips—the kind that makes my heart race and my blood simmer.

"The sun is nearly here. It's dreadful."

Without a word, I climb onto the roof and straddle his hips, my silk nightgown riding up my thighs as I settle against him.

"It won't be so bad."

His cock hardens beneath me, straining against his pants as I roll my pelvis over him, slow and deliberate.

He groans softly, the sound reverberating through his chest as his free hand finds my hip.

He takes a lazy drag from the joint, his eyes never leaving mine. Sitting up, he leans in, the scent of him—smoke and spice—washing over me.

He holds the smoke in his mouth, his lips inches from mine.

"Open," he murmurs, his voice low and commanding.

I obey, parting my lips, and he exhales the smoke into my mouth, the intimate gesture making my pulse quicken.

I inhale deeply, savoring the heat of it before tilting my head back to release it into the night sky.

The silvery tendrils rise and disappear into the darkness, but I feel his gaze on me, heavy and unyielding.

"You're trouble, you know that?" he murmurs, his voice rough as his hand slides along my thigh, his fingers skimming the bare skin beneath my nightgown.

"And you like it," I reply, my lips curving into a teasing smile as I roll my hips again, grinding against him in a way that makes his breath hitch.

I slide off his lap, my nightgown brushing against his bare skin as I settle beside him.

The cool stone roof presses against my back, but I barely feel it when his arm curls around me, pulling me close.

I rest my head on his chest, the steady rise and fall of his breath a comforting rhythm beneath my cheek.

The stars above us are endless, scattered like shattered diamonds across a velvet canvas.

For a moment, the world is quiet—nothing but the sound of the breeze and the distant hum of Avalon's nocturnal life.

Pink and orange take over the deep navy and violet sky. I can already tell the small sun will be no match for the one on Earth.

This "sunrise" will merely be like the last light of day when the sun snuffs itself out, resting until morning.

I grow quiet, too, my thoughts swirling.

And you like it.

Orion didn't agree with me. He didn't admit it. I know it's ridiculous to even want him to, but a part of me wishes he had. Because then it wouldn't just be me feeling like this.

But it's foolish. I can't afford to get attached here.

Except . . . I'm afraid it's already too late.

I glance up at him, his face turned toward the sky, his expression unreadable. He's guarding himself just like I am.

I can feel it.

There's a distance in his gaze, a wall that I recognize because I've built the same one around myself.

It's a skill I've mastered over the years—keeping people at arm's length. It started when I was young, a military brat hopping from base to base, never staying long enough to form real connections.

My father's promotions came like clockwork, each one uprooting our lives before I could plant any roots.

Now it's different, but the result is the same. I push people away because I know what's coming. My body reminds me every day.

The faint pang in my chest, the occasional dizziness, the moments I feel like my heart might stop entirely.

I'm going to die.

And I've made peace with that.

Or at least, I thought I had.

But the idea of leaving someone behind, someone who might mourn me, who might grieve over the void I leave—that's what terrifies me. That would be selfish, wouldn't it?

Yet, lying here, his warmth anchoring me to the present, I wonder if maybe, for the first time, I want to be selfish. If only for a little while.

Orion takes another drag from the joint, the faint floral and earthy scent drifting between us, then offers it to me.

I take it, the soft glow of its embers lighting the space between our faces.

As I inhale, the smoke carries a pleasant lightness to my mind, relaxing the tightness that has pounded behind my eyes since I arrived here.

I exhale slowly, letting my head sink further into his chest, my leg instinctively hiking over his.

His hand moves to my thigh without hesitation, his thumb brushing softly along my skin in soothing strokes.

There's comfort in the way he touches me—an unspoken connection that makes my breath hitch even in this haze of calm.

"What is this?" I ask, taking another hit, the blend filling me with a warmth that's almost as intoxicating as his presence.

He chuckles low in his chest.

"It's Lunabloom," he says, naming the Avalonian herb with a hint of amusement in his voice. "Calms the mind. Eases tension. I keep some for when . . . I get chest pains."

His tone shifts slightly, the weight of his admission subtle but unmistakable.

The words settle in my mind like heavy stones, and I roll them over, my thoughts clouding the lightness in my body.

Chest pains.

That could mean so many things, but knowing him, it's something he hasn't fully shared—perhaps with anyone.

Orion notices, of course. He always does. Placing a soft kiss on my temple, he shifts, propping himself up on one elbow to look at me.

"What thoughts trouble the queen?" he asks softly, his movements never faltering, but his eyes remain fixed on mine, piercing through the fog in my mind.

I hesitate, my thoughts tangled in a mess I can't seem to unravel. I open my mouth to speak, but the words catch in my throat—too raw, too revealing.

Instead, I close it again, the weight of silence pressing between us like a stone.

"You still doubt your place here?" Orion's voice cuts through the quiet, low and almost . . . vulnerable.

It's not what I expect, and it throws me off balance. His usual sharp confidence is softened, and for a moment, I glimpse something beneath the surface—something he never shows.

His silver eyes meet mine, steady and searching, as though he's trying to uncover my secrets without forcing me to say them aloud.

I exhale, finally pushing the words out, though they feel jagged and rough in my throat.

"I do," I admit, my voice barely above a whisper.

He studies me, his gaze intense but unreadable. Then, with a quick flick of his fingers, he tosses the smoldering ember into the night. Rising smoothly to his feet, he extends his hand toward me.

"Come on," he says, his voice low but firm. "I want to show you something."

I blink, caught off guard.

"Where are we going?"

"You'll see." A faint smirk tugs at his lips.

CHAPTER 52
orion

The woods hum softly around me, their quiet stillness a comforting contrast to the chaos of Starfall.

This place feels like Avalon's heartbeat—ancient and steady.

My steps are instinctual here, a rhythm I've known since boyhood. The soft crunch of leaves beneath my boots and the occasional rustle of branches overhead blend into a melody of familiarity.

The forest has always been mine—a haven where the prince's crown weighs nothing.

Omen's reins are in my hands as my dark-winged horse walks beside me.

I glance over my shoulder at Tana. Her leathers fit snugly, and I notice she left her dagger at the castle.

She walks with purpose, her steps deliberate but not hesitant. It suits her, this untamed backdrop.

The tension she carries within Starfall's walls has lessened out here, and I can see the military precision in her movements—the captain she was on Gaea.

Here, she's not pretending to belong; she just does.

I slow my pace, letting her catch up as I spot a low bush heavy with berries.

"These," I say, crouching to pluck a handful of the deep-red fruit, "are starfruit berries. Sweet, but they pack a kick."

I hold one out to her, suppressing a smirk. "Try one."

She hesitates, her dark eyes narrowing at the small fruit before rolling it between her fingers and popping it into her mouth.

Her expression shifts as the flavor hits her—a burst of tart sweetness—and she blinks up at me in surprise.

"You weren't kidding."

The corner of my mouth lifts as I toss one into my own. "I wouldn't lie about the forest."

Ripping several berries from the bush, I offer them to Omen, who already knows the snack is for her and takes them greedily.

Tana chuckles, stroking the mare's soft mane.

The woods grow denser as we move further in, the ancient trees towering above us, their canopies forming a woven tapestry that dims the light.

The moss beneath my boots glows faintly in patches, soft and vibrant against the muted browns and greens of the forest floor.

I speak softly as we walk, my words flowing easily—descriptions of the vines coiling around trunks and the properties of the bioluminescent moss that glimmers faintly in the dark.

Tana listens intently, her dark eyes flicking to each thing I point out, absorbing my words like she's anchoring herself to this place.

There's a rare, quiet reverence in her expression that tugs at something inside me—a part of me I thought I'd locked away.

She doesn't just listen; she understands, even if she doesn't realize it yet.

This realm isn't just my home. It's hers too.

The silence deepens, the forest wrapping around us like an ancient cocoon. My senses sharpen as we tread deeper, and just as I start to think the stillness might stretch too long, a flicker of movement catches my eye.

I halt, holding out an arm to stop Tana.

A faint scratching dances through the underbrush. My breath stills as the creature steps into view.

"An Aetherlynx. A cub."

Its sleek, dark fur does not yet have its swirling obsidian patterns that help it blend with the forest.

Its elongated ears turn and perk as the curious little babe sniffs the air at our arrival.

Tana smiles, kneeling down and holding out her hand.

My breath catches at the massive paw of the mother as she steps out from the dark brush.

She blinks, her eyes flashing between deep violet and molten gold, shifting with the light.

They are breathtaking.

"They're rare," I murmur, keeping my voice low so as not to startle them. "They are rarely seen and never let anyone get close."

But as if defying my words, the little creature steps toward Tana. It studies her for a moment before moving closer, the glow of its young eyes casting soft hues across her face.

I hold my breath as the pup sniffs at her palm, the mother joining its babe.

Tana is breathing heavily as the adult nudges her hand, allowing her to stroke its fur. The faint shimmer of its coat reflects in her eyes, and for a moment, the forest itself seems to hold its breath.

My chest tightens at the sight.

This is Avalon's magic at work—choosing her, acknowledging her.

The lynx recognizes something in Tana, something I've seen from the moment she stepped into this realm, even if she's too stubborn to see it herself.

Omen snorts, stomping a hoof on the dirt ground. The mother lynx growls softly and takes a step back, her long ears flicking once before she disappears into the trees.

Tana rises slowly, her gaze fixed on the spot where the creature vanished.

"That was . . ."

"Incredible," I finish, my voice tinged with awe.

I step closer, my eyes lingering on where the massive lynx and her babe had stood.

"They don't trust easily. I am certain it saw in you what the realm also sees."

What I see.

She glances at me, her expression unreadable for a moment. But I see the flicker of doubt—the hesitation that still lingers in her.

She doesn't believe it yet, but she will.

Avalon doesn't make mistakes.

And neither do I.

Tana glances at me, her expression a mix of surprise and something deeper, but I'm already moving, leading Omen further into the woods.

The path changes beneath our feet, the soft crunch of earth giving way to the springy cushion of moss.

Above us, the trees weave a canopy of shadow and moonlight, the silver beams spilling through like a blessing from the heavens.

The sound of water reaches my ears first—a steady, rhythmic roar that grows louder with every step.

Then, the forest opens, and the sight before us steals the breath from my lungs, just as it always does.

A waterfall cascades down a rugged cliff face, its frothy waters spilling into a lagoon that glows faintly with reflected moonlight.

Moss and bioluminescent flowers surround the pool, their ethereal light painting the scene in hues of blue and silver.

The air is crisp and cool, carrying the faint, intoxicating scent of wild blossoms.

It's a sanctuary—a glimpse of Avalon's untouched beauty.

I step to the edge of the lagoon, letting the serenity seep into me.

Omen lowers her snout to the water, drinking before turning away to forage around the ground for moonshrooms.

The tension that often coils tight within my chest eases

here, in this place where the land still thrives unspoiled. I unfasten my leathers without a word, the motions fluid and practiced.

My tunic is the first to go, and I hear Tana's sharp intake of breath behind me.

"You couldn't warn me we'd be swimming?" she says, her tone teasing.

I glance over my shoulder, a smirk curling my lips.

"Would you have said no?"

She rolls her eyes but doesn't argue, her hands moving to the buckles of her own gear. I turn back, letting my pants drop and stepping out of them.

The cool air brushes against my bare skin, invigorating and grounding me in this moment.

I don't rush her—I want her to take in this place, this moment.

And perhaps, a little selfishly, I want her to see me here, in the heart of the woods where I feel most myself.

Tana hesitates for only a moment before stripping down. The moonlight caresses her skin, turning her into a vision that even the gods of Avalon would envy.

My gaze drags over her slowly, unabashed in my appreciation.

I step toward her, my hands finding her waist and pulling her against me.

Her breath catches, her body pressing flush to mine, her warmth chasing away the night's chill.

Her dark eyes search mine for a moment before I lower my lips to hers. The kiss is slow, deliberate—a melding of passion and reverence.

Her skin is soft beneath my hands, and I let them roam, memorizing every curve, every dip. I trail kisses down her neck, savoring the shivers that ripple through her.

When my lips find her breast, I take her nipple between them, my tongue teasing before I release her with a grin.

"The fragrances of Avalon taste delicious on you," I murmur, my voice low and filled with heat.

She swats my arm playfully, her eyes narrowing in mock annoyance, but her lips curve into a smile that tells me she's just as captivated by this moment as I am.

Without waiting, I turn and dive into the lagoon, the cool water enveloping me in its embrace.

When I surface, I glance back to see her standing at the edge, hesitating for only a second before she follows.

The water parts around her as she glides toward me, the moonlight reflecting in her dark eyes.

She looks otherworldly, a goddess carved from the night itself.

I swim to the base of the falls, disappearing behind the rushing water into a hidden cave.

The curtain of falling water glows faintly, casting the space in a shifting, ethereal light.

The walls and ceiling shimmer with vibrant rose-colored algae, their glow illuminating the otherwise dark cavern. It's alive again—like Avalon itself, breathing with new life.

The cave shines around us, its walls alive with light, but my focus is entirely on her. The soft pink glow of the algae paints her skin in warm hues, each curve and dip illuminated like an artist's masterpiece.

Her arms wrap around my neck as if they belong there,

her touch soft but certain. My hands rest on her waist, instinctively sliding lower to cup the firm, inviting curves of her bottom.

I can feel her warmth even through the cool water.

"This place suits you," I say, my voice low and almost reverent. My fingers knead her gently, the action unbidden but impossible to stop. "Untouched, wild, breathtaking."

She lets out a soft laugh, the sound echoing softly in the enclosed space.

"I think you're describing the cave, not me."

I shake my head, a small smirk tugging at the corner of my lips. "Am I?"

Her cheeks flush, the pink glow deepening across her skin, and I find myself leaning closer, the urge to taste her again overwhelming.

"I haven't been here in centuries," I admit, my lips grazing the shell of her ear. "The glow of the algae died long ago. This place was just darkness."

Her head tilts slightly, her eyes searching mine. "Then why bring me here?"

"Because it came back," I answer, my voice steady but laden with meaning. "The light returned."

She blinks, her expression softening as my words sink in.

I trace my thumb gently along her cheekbone, then let my hand glide lower, skimming the curve of her jaw and resting at the base of her neck.

Her pulse thrums beneath my fingertips, steady but quick, and it matches the rhythm of my own heart.

The air between us thickens, charged with an unspoken tension that neither of us seems willing to break.

Her gaze drops to my lips, and I take it as permission, closing the distance until my mouth captures hers.

My other hand slides further down, pulling her body against mine as the world narrows to the feel of her, the sound of her soft sighs, and the warmth of her touch.

My lips leave hers reluctantly, the taste of her still lingering as I trail slow, deliberate kisses along the line of her jaw.

Her skin is warm beneath my mouth, soft and impossibly addictive.

I move lower, pressing my lips to the curve of her neck, then lingering at her collarbone, where her pulse flutters like a trapped bird.

Her legs wrap around my waist as I lift her, her thighs pressing against my hips with an urgency that matches my own.

Her arms encircle my neck, and I catch her mouth in a searing kiss, losing myself in the warmth and taste of her.

When I push into her, we both groan, the sound muffled by our shared kiss.

The tight heat of her envelops me, and for a moment, nothing exists but the feel of her—soft, yielding, and perfect.

Our movements sync naturally, her hips meeting mine with every thrust as the water laps softly around us.

I can't get enough of her—the way her body responds to mine, the way she gasps my name between our kisses, the way her nails rake gently down my back.

It's all too much, too consuming. And I want more. I always want more of her.

But deep in the corner of my mind, there's a truth I can't ignore, no matter how much I want to: this is wrong.

As much as I wish it weren't, I know it is.

I shouldn't be doing this—not because I don't want her, but because I do. Because I want her too much, in ways I can't allow myself to.

My heart isn't mine to give, not when its time is borrowed.

To let her fall for me would be the ultimate cruelty.

I force the thought aside, focusing instead on the way she feels in my arms, the way her kisses ignite every nerve in my body.

If this is to be the last time, then I'll memorize everything—the way her breath hitches when I thrust deeper, the way her skin glows in the pink light of the algae, the way she whispers my name like a prayer.

This moment isn't mine to keep, but I'll savor it as if it were.

Because after tonight, I know I have to let her go—not only from my bed but from the part of my heart that's already claimed her.

CHAPTER 53
Tana

The vibrant energy from the lagoon still hums through me, my skin warm and tingling as Orion and I finish dressing.

He adjusts his quiver and bow, his fingers lingering over his belt for a moment before glancing at me.

His silver eyes drop to my hand, and for a second, his expression is unreadable, as though he's weighing a decision he hasn't yet voiced.

Apparently, he makes his choice.

With a quiet exhale, he takes my hand in his, the simple contact grounding me in a way I don't fully understand.

He says nothing as he leads me away from the lagoon, and I don't press him.

The quiet between us feels too sacred to shatter.

His obsidian horse follows as we walk in silence. Eventually, the path feels familiar, though it takes me a moment to place it.

Then the forest thins, and the memory clicks just before my stomach sinks.

This is where I saw that dark ghost between the trees.

The blight looms ahead.

The forest gives way to a barren expanse, its once-towering forms reduced to brittle, blackened husks.

The ground beneath our feet fades from the lush green of Avalon's thriving woods to an ashen gray, as though the very life has been burned from the soil.

It's not just death that clings to this place—it's something darker. Heavier. Malevolent.

I stop in my tracks, my breath catching as I take it in. The air is different here—thinner and colder, laced with an acrid bitterness that makes my skin crawl.

The horizon stretches ahead, a wasteland of shadows and ruin that seems to go on forever.

"What is this?" I ask, my voice barely above a whisper.

"These are the Wastelands," Orion replies, his voice low and measured.

He doesn't look at me, his gaze fixed on the charred expanse ahead. "The edge of Avalon's reach. There's nothing beyond this but death."

The weight of his words settles in my chest, heavy and unrelenting. "What happened here?"

"The darkness consumed everything here. A long time ago, this land was vibrant, alive. But it was devoured—dark Obscura, unlike anything Avalon had seen before.

It spread like a disease, consuming everything in its path. Now, it's nothing but ash and shadows."

I look out over the desolation again, unable to reconcile how a place as breathtaking as Avalon could be marred by something so terrible.

"What kind of evil exists that could do something like this?" I ask, my voice tight.

Orion's jaw flexes, his gaze hard as he surveys the wasteland. Omen grows more tense by the second, stomping her hooves and shaking her head.

"My grandmother fought to keep the darkness at bay for centuries. She poured everything she had into holding it back. But with her death . . ."

He trails off, his voice growing quieter. "It's spread."

The weight of his words settles heavily between us, and for the first time, I see something in him I haven't seen before—vulnerability.

Orion kneels, his movement deliberate, and gestures for me to join him.

I hesitate for only a second before lowering myself to the ground, the cool ash biting through the leather of my leggings.

"Place your hand on the earth," he instructs, his voice a calm undercurrent in the still air.

I mirror him, pressing my palm to the ashen ground. It's cool, lifeless, and unyielding beneath my skin.

I glance at Orion, who closes his eyes, his features softening as if he's listening to something far away.

"Close your eyes," he says, his tone steady. "And listen. Feel. The realm speaks to you, Tana."

I do as he says, squeezing my eyes shut and straining to hear whatever it is he's talking about. At first, there's nothing but silence—oppressive and cold.

I open my mouth to tell him as much, but then I feel it.

Faint, so faint I might have missed it if I weren't so focused—a pulse.

It's steady, rhythmic, and impossibly familiar.

My breath catches as I realize it's beating in perfect time with my own heart.

I snap my eyes open, staring at Orion in disbelief.

"I felt it," I whisper. "It's . . . alive."

His lips curve into the faintest smile, his silver eyes opening to meet mine.

"The realm is alive, Tana. Even here, in the shadow of death, its heart beats. And now, it beats in you."

I don't know what to say.

The pulse I felt was real, yet it was so much more than that. It was an echo of something ancient, something powerful. A connection I didn't think I could feel, and now I can't ignore.

Orion reaches for my hand, his touch warm and grounding against the chill of the blighted ground. Slowly, he lifts it and presses my palm flat against his chest.

His heart beats beneath my fingers—steady but faint, as if it's speaking a language I can't quite decipher.

"Close your eyes," he whispers, his voice a low murmur that curls around me like a protective cloak.

I hesitate for a moment, then obey, shutting out the world around us.

My focus narrows to the feel of his heart beneath my hand, its rhythm echoing faintly through my fingertips.

Then I feel it—a skip.

The rhythm falters, just for a fraction of a second, uneven and unsettling. Orion's body tenses under my touch.

My eyes fly open as I gasp, staring up at him in stunned realization.

"You . . . your heart . . ." The words catch in my throat.

His silver eyes hold mine, unflinching. There's no pity there, no fear—just quiet acceptance.

"The hearts of the Fae beat with the realm," he says softly, his tone calm but heavy with meaning. "Its pulse is ours, its rhythm our own. And for some of us . . ."

He trails off, his gaze distant as if he's searching for words that might soften the truth.

"For some of us, we can feel the end coming long before it arrives. We sense the finality, the moment when the path stops, and there's nothing more."

The depth of his confession hits me like a tidal wave.

He's dying.

My hand stays where he placed it, the irregular beat beneath my palm a cruel reminder of his mortality. My throat tightens, but I manage to whisper,

"You've known this . . . all along?"

Orion nods slowly, his expression somber yet resolute.

"One day, my heart will stop. But that's not what matters. What matters is that when the darkness comes for me, Avalon's heart will still beat.

And now, with you here . . . it will."

His hand covers mine, his gaze unwavering.

"You carry that pulse within you, Tana. You feel it, don't you? The connection. The realm chose you because you are its hope. You only have to believe you can make that destiny real."

The sincerity in his voice washes over me, tangling with the disbelief and the ache building in my chest.

Then—movement.

Beyond his shoulder, the spectral woman stands under the shadow of a dead tree.

She watches us.

Her long, dark hair billows as though caught in a phantom breeze, her presence heavy and hollow, like an echo left behind in a room long abandoned.

I freeze.

Omen whinnies sharply, bucking. Orion grabs her tether, struggling to steady her.

The shadows move again—faster this time.

Not shadows.

Living things.

My breath catches as my vision sharpens, locking onto the sleek, twisting figures circling behind the ghost.

Cŵn Annwn.

A lot of them.

A sudden, brutal scream rips through the air.

High-pitched. Desperate.

The sound of someone begging for their life.

Then another.

And another.

The cries rise, blending into a chorus of the damned.

My stomach twists violently as the truth sinks in.

"They're attacking a village."

CHAPTER 54

Tana

"They'll never stand a chance," Orion says, his voice grim as he climbs onto Omen's back. The dark horse seems to sense the danger as soon as we do and is already prepared.

"That village is full of lesser Fae—they don't have the power to fight off the Cŵn Annwn on their own."

"We need to help them."

"We need weapons first." Orion holds out his hand, and I grasp his forearm, swinging onto Omen's back behind him.

I barely have time to grip his waist before the shadow-mare takes off, wings flaring wide as a dark void swallows us whole.

The portal rips open, and it feels the same as Mor's shadow portal—thick and cold, like a slimy, viscous cloud of nothing.

The darkness absorbs all light, leaving nothing for the eye to see.

In the blink of an eye, we're back in the castle courtyard. I'm off Omen's back before Orion is shouting orders. "Get your dagger and handmaids."

Darkness spews from him like a rolling fog, fast and low

to the ground. He's searching for who is present, summoning the castle guards—perhaps even Hephaestus for weapons.

I sprint through the halls, my boots striking fast and sure against the stone. The castle blurs around me as I push forward, instinct taking over.

Move.

Get ready.

Get to the village.

I pass Theren and Elyra on the way, catching their attention instantly. Their eyes sharpen as they fall in step beside me, no words needed.

They see my expression, they sense the urgency, and they move.

We reach my room, and I barely have time to inhale before I'm speaking. "Cŵn Annwn. In the forest. I need my armor."

Theren is already moving to my closet, Elyra securing her hair back, readying to help me. We need a plan. We need weapons—

My fist closes around the handle of my blade, securing it quickly around my leg when the door to my room releases a slow squeal.

What the fuck?

I look up quickly, locking eyes with Orion. He says nothing, standing in the doorway. He doesn't need to say anything—I know in an instant what he's going to do.

Dropping my dagger, I rush to the door.

The sharp click of the lock is like a gunshot to my senses.

"No." The word is out before I even think—pure instinct

and rage. My fists bang on the door as I try the handle. It's fucking locked.

"Orion!" I snarl, slamming my palm against the wood, twisting the handle again. It doesn't budge.

I spin to the windows, ready to climb down the damn castle walls if I have to, but before I even reach them, they slam shut.

Not just shut—sealed.

A cold wave rolls through the room, his darkness coiling through every crack, sinking into the walls, locking every exit, making it impossible to open.

My breath hitches, rage flashing hot in my chest as I turn in a circle.

"You did not just lock me in here," I yell at no one, knowing he'll hear me. This fucking asshole knows he's making an enemy out of me by keeping me from the fight.

This is what I'm trained for—what I've been honed for.

"Dammit!" I bang my fist against the glass pane, and it rattles.

Theren stands with my thin armor in his arms, eyes wide with shock. Elyra moves into action. "This way, my lady."

She picks up my blade from the floor, rushing to the closed bathroom door. "The prince may have overlooked the servants' passages. We hid them as Queen Pandora lost her mind."

The three of us rush into the room.

"Just before her death, she was not herself." Elyra takes the armor from Theren and begins helping me with it. "She would often get lost in the servants passages so we covered them."

Theren's large hands grip each side of a heavy armoire, carefully sliding it aside.

The outline of a door slowly reveals itself as he moves the giant piece of furniture.

Finished with my armor, Elyra secures my thigh holster as I pull a wide elastic band around my head, sweeping my thick hair back.

Elyra wastes no time pushing against the hidden door—it pops open.

"Yes!" I hiss, following Elyra inside with Theren close behind. Our feet rush through back halls and down narrow stone steps.

The passage opens up as we near the ground level, the ceiling slightly higher.

"This way, my lady." Elyra opens a door, depositing us just outside the kitchens.

"I need a sword," I pant as we keep moving.

"Hephaestus!" My voice rings out as we burst through the castle's side door, the wide steps leading down to the lakefront village just ahead.

I push ahead of my aides, taking the steps two at a time. "I'll need a horse," I call back over my shoulder. "Or find Mor."

"Mor and Hypnos are escorting Ruvan's body back to the Briar," Theren's voice bounces between the cliffs as I rush down.

As soon as my feet hit the base, I push off toward Hephaestus's blacksmith shop—but he's not there.

Several Flame Sprites take turns jumping on a blower, stoking Hephaestus's forge fire. They pause, looking at me as my eyes scan the building.

"Where is he?"

They point in the same direction—to my right.

Hestia's bakery.

I rush next door and burst inside, the scent of fresh bread and sweet rolls hitting me.

"Hephaestus!" I call out, moving quickly toward the rear of the bakery. "I need a sword."

"Ah, lass," Hephaestus crams the rest of an icy sweet roll into his mouth, crumbs dusting his long auburn beard.

"Ye'll no' be convincin' me tae get me hands lopped off by a pissed-off prince. Go fetch yer own bloody sword."

"If only you knew where to find one, Your Majesty." Hestia teases with a knowing smirk.

The sword-in-the-fucking-stone.

"Oh, kiss my ass. That sword is stuck forever inside that stubborn-ass stone."

Hephaestus leans forward, a chilling seriousness darkening his gaze.

"Then be more stubborn than the stone." He speaks each word slowly, the weight of them sinking into my resolve.

My eyes narrow as I hold his stare. Then I turn on my heel and leave the bakery.

I run through the castle grounds, my breath sharp in my chest, my heart racing just as fast as my feet. The night air is thick, the scent of damp earth clinging to my skin as I push forward.

The gazebo looms ahead, half-buried in shadow and ivy

—a forgotten relic hidden at the edge of the castle's grounds.

Nearly every day I've come here, peeling back the vines, tracing my fingers over the ancient carvings in the stone.

I've thought of everything I can to pull this godforsaken blade from its prison.

I've scoured every book, searched every image, even dreamt of the sword clutched in my hands. But it's still here.

My eyes lock on the sword, buried in the heart of the stone.

It shouldn't be possible—nothing should be able to remain untouched in Avalon's endless night.

And yet, the blade gleams as if it were forged yesterday, the intricate hilt catching the faint silver glow of the full moon overhead.

My pulse pounds in my ears as I step closer, the ancient power humming beneath my feet.

I reach out, wrapping both hands around the hilt. The metal is cool, pulsing with something I don't understand—something deep and old.

I brace myself and pull.

Nothing.

My grip tightens, fingers straining, arms shaking as I yank with everything I have. My feet dig into the stone, my breath comes in sharp gasps, but the sword does not move.

I grit my teeth, adjusting my stance. I try again. And again. And again.

Nothing.

A growl rips from my throat. My hands tremble with frustration as I release the hilt and stagger back. My heart is pounding. My muscles burn. I glare at the sword like it's mocking me.

I need this. I have to take it.

I spin on my heel, pacing the length of the gazebo as my fury builds, my blood boiling hotter with every second.

"You have got to be fucking kidding me," I snap, throwing my hands in the air. "Is this some kind of joke? Do you think this is funny?"

The realm does not answer.

I clench my jaw, my nails digging into my palms.

"I don't have time for this! There's a village under attack. People are dying, and I'm standing here playing your twisted little game."

The air around me is still, heavy, as if the land itself is listening. I don't care. Let it listen.

"I don't know what you want from me!" I shout. "Some grand revelation? Some lesson I'm supposed to learn?

Because I don't have time for that. I don't care if I'm not worthy or chosen or whatever other bullshit this sword is waiting for. I don't care. I need it."

My voice cracks, the weight of everything pressing down on me. My hands tremble at my sides, fury and desperation warring in my chest.

"I..." My hands run down my pants before I wrap them back around the hilt. "Am not leaving."

At the corner of my vision, I see movement. The Fae have come out to see. They have come to watch if I will be able to free the sword.

I chuckle to myself.

Fucking watch me, then.

"I am not leaving without this fucking sword," I swear, my voice low and sharp as a blade. I pull.

"Whatever magic binds it," I grit out, my hands slipping. My arms shake. But I'm locked in. I'll pull my fucking arms out of their sockets before I let go of this handle.

"Whatever test this is—drop it. Right. Now."

My palms tear as the metal bites into my flesh. I bite down, channeling every ounce of myself into my hands locked around the hilt and my feet, pushing off the stone.

My blood runs down the silver, warm and red.

Above me, the clouds shift. A gentle wind stirs, peeling them back from the full moon, bathing the blade in radiant light.

My legs shake, but the rumbling beneath me is not coming from me.

Pebbles on the ground tremble and dance as the quaking earth grows stronger.

A vibration travels up the sword, rattling my bones.

I squeeze my eyes shut, releasing a guttural growl into the Avalonia night. The earth is quaking, and it feels like I'm at its epicenter.

Like the realm is trying to hold on to its last grip on the sword.

Well, I don't fucking think so.

"Give me my fucking sword!" I cry out, as if the realm will hear me. "It's my right!"

I grit out the last words as the final cloud slips away from the moon. A beam of silver light catches on the blade, illuminating the rivulets of blood trailing down its sharpened edge.

As if my blood were the key, the sword releases.

Just like in my dreams, it screams as I rip it from the stone that has confined it.

The rumbling ground stills as a shockwave of moonlight rushes outward in all directions—a pulse of energy that races across the realm, carried by the wind.

I stand upright, chest heaving, the sword heavy in my grasp.

I move my gaze to the Fae gathered around.

Theren and Elyra are near the front, and they are the first to bend their knees—bowing to the queen who pulled the sword from the stone.

Tears glisten in Elyra's eyes as she covers her mouth to hold back a gasp.

Hestia, a wide, beaming smile on her beautiful face, looks to Hephaestus, who does nothing to hide the tears running down his cherry-red cheeks.

A scabbard rests in his big hands.

Movement at the back pulls my attention as the rest of the Fae bow in reverence.

Fucking. Liona.

She backs away, horror widening her eyes as she retreats toward the castle.

Yeah, run, you little bitch.

I step toward the castle, and Hephaestus meets me in the center, holding the scabbard out to me.

"I knew you had it in you," he whispers as I sheath the sword.

The corner of my mouth lifts in a small grin. "Thanks for the push, big guy."

I fix the scabbard over my shoulder, the weight of the blade resting between my shoulder blades.

Now.

Lifting two fingers to my mouth, I blow.

A shrill whistle cuts through the night.

It's time to call a ride.

CHAPTER 55
Tana

"You do not have a horse. The Duskbane chooses its rider, not the other way around."

Oh yeah, asshole? I don't have a horse, huh? I don't... I have three.

Thunder rolls in the distance as storm clouds flash on the horizon. It's in the direction of the village.

Orion is already locked in the battle he tried to keep me from. Tried and fucking failed.

Above anything else, I'm a fighter. A warrior. If there is anywhere I belong, it's in the middle of a fight I know I shouldn't be able to win. But I'll be damned sure it's going to be me walking away as the victor.

Rolling thunder grows closer, and I realize it's not just the storm—it's the horses. I knew they would come, and the sight of the three massive steeds galloping toward my call lights a fire within me.

The lead horse—the one I petted before—reaches me first and rears on his hind legs. The ground quakes when the horse lands, a deep snort echoing into the darkness.

This horse knows there is a fight somewhere and is just as eager as I am to be there.

Swinging my leg, I hoist myself up, grabbing the horses onyx mane. "Let's go raise some fucking havoc," I say quietly, menace dripping from my tone.

With a kick of my boots and a click of my tongue, I urge the steed on, and he takes off like a bolt of lightning.

My thighs squeeze against the horses sides, keeping my chest and head low. It's like riding my motorcycle.

Ash and embers explode into the air as each hoof strikes the ground, leaving a scorched trail that fades with each step.

I'm not sure if these horses can use a shadow portal like Omen can, but at the rate they're running, we'll be at the village in a matter of moments.

They somehow know exactly where I want to go.

My eyes widen at the wide columns of smoke rising into the sky.

I only hope I'm not too late.

Smoke stings my eyes as I race through the trees, the scent of burning wood and scorched flesh thick in the air.

The night is alive with chaos—screams echo through the valley, shrill and panicked, drowning beneath the snarl of beasts and the crackling roar of flames.

My horse's hooves pound against the earth—faster, faster—shadows and fire blurring past me as we descend on the ruined village below.

The first thing I see is death.

Bodies litter the ground, twisted and torn, their blood soaking into the scorched dirt.

Lesser Fae—many of them too small, too fragile to have stood a chance—are crumpled in the streets, their wings bent at unnatural angles, their delicate bodies left broken in the glow of the burning homes around them.

The fire paints everything in violent shades of gold and red, flickering against the onyx fur of the Cŵn Annwn, the monstrous shadow hounds that stalk through the ruins.

I tighten my grip on the reins, my heart a hammer against my ribs.

This shouldn't have happened.

A blast of black lightning rips through the battlefield.

A hound lurches back from its lifeless victim with an earsplitting snarl, its body convulsing before it's flung into a burning building.

Orion stands in the wreckage, wreathed in shadow and crackling darkness, his power curling around him.

The flames seem dimmer where he stands, swallowed by the raw, unfathomable void that churns at his fingertips.

His power is dark, consuming, terrifying—and yet he wields it with devastating precision.

A second hound lunges at him, jaws snapping. Orion moves like a storm, fast and merciless, his magic searing through its form before it can even touch him. The beast collapses in a heap of blackened smoke and smoldering embers.

Castle guards fight at his back, their blades flashing through the night, but they are outmatched.

The Cŵn Annwn do not tire.

They do not bleed like mortal creatures. They persist.

And I should have been here.

A fresh surge of rage claws up my throat, hot and bitter, nearly choking me. Instead of bringing me here—instead of letting me fight—Orion wasted time locking me away, as if I were some fragile, breakable thing.

As if my hands weren't made for this.

A shriek pierces the air, yanking my attention toward the chaos ahead.

A Fae child, no older than five, scrambles backward on their hands and feet, their wings fluttering in panicked, jerky movements.

A hound looms over them, massive and nightmarish, its blackened maw dripping with something thick and tar-like.

My vision blurs with fury.

I don't think—I act.

I pull hard on the mane, my horse shifting beneath me, gaining speed as I reach for my blade, every muscle in my body coiled and ready to strike.

Balancing on the back of the horse, sword in hand, I time my strike perfectly. As the hellhound launches itself at the youngling, I soar through the air, my sword arching with me.

I barely feel any resistance against the blade as it slices cleanly through the beast's thick neck.

Landing and tucking into a roll, I right myself directly in front of the child, now behind me.

My left arm shoots behind me, securing the babe to me as I ready for another attack.

Seeing it's clear, I turn, grab the child, and run across the wide dirt path, spotting a group of Fae huddled together.

A woman sees me coming, her eyes locked on the child as she bursts into tears. The young Fae responds the same, reaching for her. "Ma!" he cries. They must have been separated.

I slide to a stop, partially kneeling as I hand off the child.

"Get inside and stay quiet."

I don't wait for an answer.

I spin back to the side of the hut, pressing my back against the charred wood as I breathe.

One beat.

Two.

The sounds of battle rage on—metal on flesh, fire on bone, the thick, wet snaps of bodies breaking. I roll my shoulders, assessing.

The village is still burning, the air thick with heat and smoke, but the fight isn't lost.

Orion and the guards are pushing forward, cutting through the Cŵn Annwn in brutal flashes of steel and magic.

But it isn't enough. They are still losing ground.

I step out from the shelter of the hut, blades in hand. I run.

My feet barely touch the ground as I close the distance, my sword slicing through the nearest beast before it can react.

The blade bites deep, severing shadow and sinew, and the hound collapses with a vicious, garbled shriek.

Another lunges at me. I twist, my momentum carrying me forward as I drive my dagger into its throat, wrenching sideways.

Black ichor sprays across my arm, burning like ice where it touches my skin.

A flash of movement. Another beast charges—I pivot, ducking under its snapping jaws, and bury my blade into its side, twisting until it howls.

More.

I can still feel them. The hunger in their eyes. The endless, consuming dark.

I keep moving. Keep killing.

And then a sharp, burning snap of irritation slams into my skull, like an invisible fist curling around my mind.

Orion.

His voice—his fury—erupts through my thoughts, low and vicious as a winter storm.

"You're supposed to be at the castle."

I barely slow, dodging another beast as I snarl back into the void where his voice came from.

"Fuck off," I snap, unsure if he can hear me the way I can hear him.

Apparently, he can, because I feel his anger tighten, like talons digging in, trying to push deeper into my mind.

I shove back.

I imagine a wall slamming up between us, thick and solid as stone. A shield. One that he cannot pass.

And just like that—his presence vanishes.

Silence. I cut him out.

A savage, victorious grin cuts across my face as I turn back to the battlefield, blades dripping, heart thrumming like thunder in my chest.

He'll be furious.

Good. Because I'm fucking pissed.

The moment I block Orion from my mind, I see it—a large building standing at the edge of the village.

Dread coils in my gut as flames crawl hungrily up its sides, thick smoke rolling into the night.

The fire is bad enough, but it's the doors and windows that send a sharp, nauseating realization straight through me.

They're locked. From the outside.

Someone's inside. Sealed in a burning tomb. Someone meant for them to burn alive.

Everything else fades. The battle, the beasts, the bodies on the ground—none of it matters.

I whistle, the sharp sound cutting through the chaos, already pushing into a full sprint before the note has even faded.

The Duskbane answers my call like a shadow tearing through the night—powerful and relentless, a creature born for war. Born for havoc. A fitting name, I think.

I don't bother slowing down; instead, I reach for him, grabbing fistfuls of his thick mane and swinging onto his back midstride.

The instant I land, I drive my heels into his sides, urging him forward.

He explodes into motion, hooves pounding against the ground, the speed nearly tearing me off his back.

On either side, two more war beasts race with us, their dark forms streaking through the firelit haze, crushing any Cŵn Annwn that cross their path.

I barely register the snarls, the shattering of bones

beneath their hooves—my focus is locked on the burning structure ahead.

The heat thickens as we close in, blistering against my skin, the acrid scent of burning wood and scorched flesh choking the air.

My heart slams against my ribs, a frantic rhythm of urgency and fear.

I can't be too late.

Havoc surges forward, unrelenting, and the second we reach the doors, I jump.

The landing jars every bone in my body, but I don't stop moving.

A shadow lunges at me from the side—a beast, black-eyed and snarling—but I twist sharply, my blade flashing through the smoke before it has a chance to strike.

The creature crumples at my feet, but I'm already turning, breath ragged as I reach the heavy iron chains sealing the doors shut.

I pull at them, twisting, yanking with all the strength I have left. They don't budge.

From within, cries pour out of the cracks, rising over the roar of the fire around us.

They're still alive.

Desperation flares inside me, burning hotter than the flames consuming the building.

I shift my grip on my sword, lift the hilt high, and bring it crashing down against the lock.

The moment metal strikes metal, the world erupts.

A shockwave of energy explodes outward, raw and violent, slamming into my chest with bone-crushing force.

The ground disappears beneath me.

I'm airborne before I even realize what's happening, my body weightless for the briefest second—then I'm hurtling backward.

The impact when I hit the ground is brutal, pain splintering through me as I crash into the dirt, rolling across the debris-littered earth.

My lungs seize, struggling to drag in air, my limbs heavy and useless beneath the crushing ache now swallowing me whole.

I fight to lift my head. The fire rages on, hungry and merciless. The screams behind the locked doors still echo, raw and desperate.

And the doors remain shut.

The air shifts—an unnatural stillness creeping in, like the space between heartbeats. Cold dread prickles along my skin, not from the battle raging around me, but from the force I feel descending.

The darkness comes fast, a monstrous, crushing weight plummeting toward me like a fist straight from the void. It moves with purpose, with hunger, and I know—instinctively, undeniably—that I can't fight it.

I barely have time to react. My sword lies between me and the burning building, just out of reach. Useless to me now.

Panic flares sharp in my chest. I turn, trying to crawl away, but the darkness is already upon me.

It engulfs me in a suffocating wave, swallowing the light, dragging me into something far worse than the battlefield I just left.

This isn't just shadow.

It's something deeper. Something ancient and merciless.

A voice stirs within the abyss, soft and distant, a whisper threading through the void like a chant carried on the wind.

The words are unfamiliar, a language I have never heard, yet somehow, I understand them.

Come, Tana.

The voice is neither sharp nor cruel. It is gentle, laced with something soothing, something sweet and persuasive. It doesn't demand—it invites.

Let me in.

The words resonate through me, vibrating in the marrow of my bones as if they have always been waiting there, whispering beneath my skin.

It knows me.

It knows what I want.

A flicker of heat stirs deep in my chest, not from the fire outside, but from something far more dangerous. A promise. A temptation.

You don't have to fight anymore, the voice murmurs, coaxing, patient. Let go. Let us become one.

The darkness presses closer, curling into the hollows of my ribs, wrapping around my failing heart, offering something I've never allowed myself to dream of.

Strength.

Power.

A heart that does not fail.

The longing is immediate and vicious, sinking its claws into me before I can stop it.

A life without this weakness, without the constant

reminder that I am breakable, that my own body is my greatest enemy—God, what would that even feel like?

For a terrible moment, I hesitate.

The void surges forward, sensing my doubt, pushing deeper, wrapping tighter.

But something inside me snaps.

I dig my fingers into the dirt, clutching at the ground, at anything real.

No.

The darkness is relentless, but I fight back, the way I did when Orion tried to force his way into my mind.

I shove against it, forcing it out—but this isn't just a voice in my head.

This is everywhere.

It screams, writhing through me, refusing to let go.

I push harder, dragging myself forward, crawling blindly through the suffocating black. My hands scrape against the earth, my knees burn, but I keep moving, inch by agonizing inch.

And then—my fingers brush against metal. The familiar weight grounds me like an anchor in a storm.

I grip the hilt of my sword, wrapping my fingers around it with everything I have left.

The Obscura shifts. The whispers turn to wails, their voices rising, desperate now.

Then, the darkness twists, trying something new.

A figure takes shape in the void.

Tall. Familiar.

I know the way he stands—the sharpness in his gaze, the effortless way Orion commands space.

But I don't trust it.

The darkness has already tried to break me. Now, it wants to trick me.

Nice fucking try, bitch.

With a snarl, I tighten my grip and strike.

My sword slices through the illusion, the blade cutting fast and deep.

A burst of moonlight erupts through the darkness, searing away the shadows, burning through the void like a cleansing fire.

A furious, earsplitting scream shreds through my mind—

And then, just as suddenly, it is gone.

I collapse, my body folding under its own weight, my lungs heaving as I drag in air.

The ache is unbearable, my limbs trembling, but I can see again.

The world rushes back in sharp, blinding clarity.

And in front of me—

The lock on the hut's door falls away.

The chains snap, dropping into the dirt with a final, metallic clang. Then the doors burst open, and one by one, the Fae stumble out, covered in soot, coughing, gasping for breath.

But they are alive.

I exhale, my body shaking, exhaustion crashing over me like a tide.

Sitting back on my heels, I close my eyes and let my head fall back, releasing a deep sigh of relief.

I freed them. They're okay.

Looking around the field, I take in the devastation. The Cŵn Annwn are dead, mixed among the bodies of the Fae who lost their lives to this senseless attack.

The village still smolders, flames licking at what remains of the homes.

Orion scans between the buildings, his search frantic. He's looking for me.

Relief floods him the moment his gaze lands on me. I see his shoulders drop, the visible release of tension—the strain of believing, if only for a moment, that I had been harmed.

That I was gone.

But how could he?

How fucking could he?

I shake my head slowly, my eyes narrowing.

He knows. He knows why I'm so angry. The look in his eyes tells me he still thinks he did the right thing—that he'll use his duty as an excuse for what he did.

But he doesn't really understand.

It's not just the act of tricking me. Of locking me in my room.

It's that he underestimated me.

That he believed I couldn't do this. That despite the words he's said to me for the past two weeks, he never truly meant them.

A shadow shifts in the periphery of my vision.

The darkness around me seems to gather, a swirling vortex forming just behind me.

Is it back?

Has the dark cloud returned to try and consume me again?

Well, good fucking luck.

My fingers wrap around the hilt of my sword, and I grit my teeth, rage surging through me like a second heartbeat.

The power builds to an apex. I spin, my sword level with my shoulder, ready to drive it into whatever enemy approaches.

But I stop as I stare into the calculating, red eyes of Mor.

Bored indifference lingers on her pale face.

She must be close to her transition into The Morrigan— that higher power that shrouds her in obscurity and rot.

Behind her stands Hypnos, his piercing gaze locked onto my sword before a slow, knowing smile creeps across his face.

Mor surveys the battlefield with an air of detached amusement. She takes in the dead, the burning village, the carnage left in our wake.

And then, she pouts. Her shoulders drop, along with her brow as a sullen look takes over her face.

"You have taken all the fun and left us with no marks to kill?" she says, her tone as close to a reprimand as she can muster. "We have determined it is you who has become the party pooper."

I snort, the unexpectedness of it punching a nasally laugh from my nose.

Slowly, I reach behind me and slide my sword back into the scabbard at my back.

"How about I make it up to you with some cheeseburgers?" I raise my hands in surrender, surveying the wreckage around us.

The village will need our help before we return to the castle.

Mor cocks her head, considering. Then, with a regal nod, she declares, "We will accept this offering as your apology."

With that, she strides forward, shadows curling across the ground as she assesses the damage.

I watch her go, exhaling as the tension finally, finally begins to bleed from my body.

Then—my gaze drifts back to Orion.

He's still watching me.

Still searching my expression.

But my mind is silent. Free of his voice.

And I'm not sure if I'm thankful for that or not.

CHAPTER 56
Tana

The waves lap at the shore in a slow, steady rhythm, a gentle hush against the emerald sand.

The Misting Lake stretches out before me, its surface smooth as glass, reflecting the endless night sky.

Wisps of fog curl along the water's edge, moving like something alive, swirling and shifting with the breeze.

I dig my fingers into the cool sand, letting it slip between them, grounding myself in the sensation.

My arms ache, my legs burn, and exhaustion lingers in every part of me—but my mind refuses to be still.

The battle still clings to me, thick as smoke, seared into the backs of my eyelids every time I blink. The Cŵn Annwn, their molten eyes gleaming in the firelight.

The burning village, the screams, the scent of scorched flesh and blood. The darkness that tried to take me, whispering its poisoned promises, digging into my bones, offering me something I almost wanted.

And then there's the sword—my sword.

I glance at it now, lying in the sand beside me. The hilt gleams, the metal untouched by blood or battle, as if it didn't carve through the shadows like a blade of pure moonlight.

As if it didn't save me when I had nothing else left.

Everything is connected. I can feel it.

The sword, the missing courts, the beasts, the creeping sickness spreading through Avalon like rot beneath the surface.

There's a thread linking them all, something just beyond my reach, taunting me with half-formed answers I can't quite grasp.

I don't know what to do about it.

I tilt my head back, staring up at the eternal night sky, searching for something in the stars that I won't find.

A part of me wonders if I should leave.

The thought lodges itself deep in my chest, an uncomfortable weight pressing down, squeezing something raw and aching inside me.

I came here for answers, but all I have are more questions, more uncertainty, more reasons to wonder if staying is the right choice.

The courts are missing. The darkness is growing. And me?

I don't even know what the hell I'm supposed to be.

A protector? A warrior? A pawn in whatever game is being played between Avalon and its shadows?

I exhale, pressing my fingers deeper into the sand. The lake hums softly, the mist curling tighter around the shore. Everything feels quiet, waiting.

I don't know if I should stay.

But I don't know if I can leave.

I want to—purely to spite Orion and the stunt he pulled, locking me away when I would have been most helpful.

All his talk of believing in the realm's choice, like he believes in me, was fucking bullshit.

I haven't spoken to him since, and I don't plan on it.

What happened was clearly the first two trials of the ascension to the throne. The Trial of the Heart—a battle of wills with the realm until it gave me the sword I wouldn't leave without.

The Trial of Shadows—when the Obscura tried to consume me, when I stood on the edge of something terrible and chose to fight rather than become it.

And Orion locked me in my room like a liability. What would have happened if I had stayed?

Then, there were the Lesser Fae.

Even now, the memory of that moment stands out against the chaos of battle.

The way they bowed to me—not as a queen, not as a ruler, but as someone who had fought for them.

A woman with silver-streaked hair had stepped forward, pressing a small token into my palm—no words, just quiet reverence, gratitude written in every movement.

It was a stark contrast to the High Fae, who had spent centuries bickering, scheming, and clawing for power, caring more about their own ambitions than the realm crumbling around them.

They wanted thrones, titles, control—but the Lesser Fae wanted something far simpler.

They didn't crave power.

They needed someone to fight for them.

That realization sits uneasily within me, shifting something I don't quite have words for yet.

I've never thought of myself as a leader, never wanted the weight of responsibility that came with ruling.

But when I think of the High Fae, all I see is endless want—self-serving, desperate.

When I think of the Lesser Fae, I see need.

I draw my knees to my chest, staring out at the lake as the mist weaves across the water. The hush of the night is broken by the faint rustle of movement behind me.

I stiffen, my gaze tearing away from the water, my body tensing on instinct. But when I turn, the breath leaves my lungs in a slow, stunned exhale.

A beast stands at the edge of the trees, its form more myth than flesh—the kind of thing whispered about in old stories, the kind of creature no one truly expects to see with their own eyes.

It's the White Stag. It's not just white—it's radiant, glowing with a soft, ethereal light, as if it has been spun from the very fabric of the stars themselves.

Moonlight clings to it, rippling across its body in a way that seems almost alive.

Slowly, I push to my feet, careful not to make any sudden movements. My pulse is a steady drum in my ears, but I keep my breathing even, my eyes never leaving the magnificent creature before me.

The stag lowers its head, nibbling at the grass at the edge of the forest, utterly unbothered by my presence.

But then, as if sensing my gaze, it lifts its head once more, ears twitching, luminous eyes locking onto mine.

It sees me.

Truly sees me.

A breath shudders through me as it steps forward, nostrils flaring as it tests the air. The space between us shrinks, and yet I don't dare move, afraid that the smallest shift might break the fragile spell of this moment.

It walks with slow, deliberate grace, the light of its presence casting long, shifting shadows across the emerald sand.

I should bow. That's what the old legends say—to bow before the White Stag of Avalon is to show reverence, to be granted the chance to seek its guidance.

But I can't move, can't think of anything beyond the sheer, breathtaking wonder of what stands before me.

The stag stops only a few paces away. The night hums around us, the stars above seeming to burn brighter in its presence.

For the first time in days, I am not thinking about the battle.

Not the sword. Not Orion.

Only this.

The stag.

And the undeniable pull between us.

The moment my fingers graze the stag's luminous coat, the world fractures.

A force seizes me, a violent pull as if I've been wrenched from my body and thrust into something else—something wrong.

My breath vanishes, my stomach lurching as the earth shifts beneath me.

I blink, and suddenly, I am no longer on the emerald shores of the Misting Lake.

I stand at the center of nothingness.

It starts beneath my feet—a slow, insidious crack, like ice splintering across a frozen river. The emerald sand blackens, turning brittle, then crumbling away into dust.

The air thickens, heavy with an unnatural silence, pressing in on my chest.

Then, the world begins to die.

The lake—the vast, eternal waters that have always been here—begins to shrink.

The mist that drifts lazily across its surface is the first to go, evaporating like breath against glass.

The water darkens, twisting, boiling, before receding inward, exposing the cracked, lifeless earth beneath.

The edges collapse inward, dry and barren, until there is nothing left but an empty, gaping pit.

The trees surrounding the shore begin to wither, their leaves curling inward before turning black and flaking away like embers carried on the wind.

One by one, they collapse, their trunks splitting, their roots shriveling into dust.

The luminous flora—flowers that have glowed for centuries, vines that have pulsed with life even in the darkest nights—fade, their light flickering out, swallowed by the encroaching black.

The destruction doesn't stop.

It spreads outward, racing through the land, swallowing Avalon in an endless tide of nothingness.

I turn, heart hammering against my ribs, and see Starfall

—the village at the edge of the lake, its spires stretching toward the sky.

The lights flicker within its delicate towers, its streets still pulsing with life.

For a moment, it remains untouched.

For a moment, I think—hope—that it might survive.

And then, the first scream rips through the silence.

I watch, helpless, as the darkness reaches them.

It moves like ink spilling across parchment, slow at first, then relentless, curling through the streets, up the buildings, over the bridges, through the lantern-lit alleys.

The Fae don't understand at first. Some stare, frozen in place; others run—but there is nowhere to go.

The moment the darkness touches them, they break.

Not in a violent explosion of gore—no, this is something far worse. They flake away, their bodies crumbling like dried leaves caught in a storm, their skin peeling from their bones in delicate, weightless fragments.

Their wings dissolve into nothing, their voices cut short as they vanish into the wind.

I can feel it happening.

Not just see it, not just hear it—I feel it.

The shift in the air as the life is drained from the land. The sudden, unbearable silence where there was once laughter and song.

The whisper of ash brushing against my skin, sticking to me as it carries the remnants of the dead.

My breath stutters, my chest aching, my hands trembling at my sides. I try to move, try to run, to stop it, but I am frozen.

The darkness does not take me.

But it lets me watch.

Starfall is gone.

The forest is gone.

The Misting Lake is gone.

There is nothing left but the endless, crawling void.

And then, at the edges of the ruin, something moves.

A figure, standing just beyond the destruction. Waiting.

I can't see its face, can't define its shape, but I feel it watching me. It knows I am here. It knows I see what is coming.

The air around me shifts, warping, pulling inward as the darkness curls toward me.

"Join us," a voice murmurs, thick as smoke, deep as the void itself.

The shadows lunge, and I tear my hand away from the stag. In a blink, the world snaps back into place.

I stumble, my breath ragged, my body drenched in sweat. The lake is here. The trees are standing. The village is alive.

But my heart pounds with the certainty that if nothing changes, if I do nothing—

That vision will become real.

And I know now with every bit of certainty in my mind, I cannot let that happen.

The stag lingers for a moment longer, its luminous form glowing softly against the darkness before it turns, stepping gracefully into the woods.

Its radiant light fades with each step, absorbed by the

towering trees, until it is nothing more than a whisper of brilliance in the shadows.

But the stillness left behind does not feel empty.

It feels like a beginning.

I turn back to the water, my reflection rippling across its glassy surface.

For the first time, I don't see a mortal woman lost in a realm of magic. I see a warrior standing on the edge of something vast, something undeniable.

A woman with the chance to become more than she ever imagined—to fight not just for Avalon but for herself.

I inhale deeply, the crisp night air filling my lungs, steadying me as I allow myself the freedom to admit the truth I've kept from myself.

I'm not ready to die.

Not yet.

The stag's departure leaves behind a quiet acceptance, a realization that settles in my chest, warm and grounding. It was here because of me—because I have stopped running.

From Avalon.

From the trials.

From whatever fate is pulling me toward something greater.

The life I left behind on Earth feels like another world, another version of me that no longer fits.

This place needs me.

And maybe, just maybe… I need it too.

I release a deep breath, and it feels like the weight of a thousand lives has lifted from my shoulders. The charged stillness that follows leaves the air feeling electric, as if the realm itself is waiting for what comes next.

I sit with it, absorbing the weight of everything, when movement in the distance catches my eye.

Emerging from the path near Pandora's cave, I see three familiar figures.

Orion leads, his stride sure, his presence as steady as ever, but there's something different in his posture—something rigid.

Mor walks beside him, her crimson eyes glinting in the dim light, her usual smirk present as ever. Hypnos lingers behind them, his expression unreadable.

His steps falter, his gaze flickers to the place where the stag disappeared, and I wonder if he knows. If he can feel the energy of the White Stag.

When he looks back at me, his gait matching his companions, he wears a knowing grin, and it answers my question. He knows.

As the trio approaches, I push to my feet, brushing my hands absently against the leather of my pants, as if I can shake the weight of what just happened. Hypnos's smirk grows slightly, and I narrow my eyes.

"What?" I demand, half expecting him to tease me.

"Nothing," he replies smoothly, his voice laced with its usual vague wisdom.

But the moment I turn to Orion, I sense the shift. His silver eyes meet mine, unreadable, but the tension in his frame is impossible to miss. Something is wrong.

"What's going on?" My voice is low, firm.

He doesn't answer right away. He only holds my gaze

before finally tilting his head toward the path. "Come with me."

There's no hesitation.

I nod and fall into step beside him. Mor and Hypnos follow, their presence both reassuring and foreboding.

The unease I've carried since the battle sharpens with every step toward the cave.

The cavern entrance looms ahead, stirring memories I hadn't meant to revisit—the last time I stood here, I'd stabbed Orion with a fork and nearly escaped through a dormant portal.

But something is different now.

The air hums, a pulse of energy thrumming through the stone, vibrating beneath my feet.

Before I turn the dark corner, I already know what I'll see, and it feels like all the air in my lungs is torn from my chest.

The once-dark, lifeless portal is now alive, its surface gleaming with an eerie blue light.

The glow bounces off the walls, illuminating the cavern in shifting shades of sapphire, making the space feel both surreal and suffocating.

My breath catches.

"It's... working?" My voice comes out barely above a whisper.

Orion watches me carefully, his jaw tight. "It is."

I take a slow step forward, the glow pulling at me, its energy familiar yet foreign, like something that doesn't belong yet refuses to be ignored.

"How?" I glance at Orion, searching his face. "Why now?"

He exhales, his shoulders stiff as he speaks. "I made you a promise." His voice is quiet but heavy. "If a way back to Gaea ever presented itself, I would tell you."

The words settle over me, cold and sharp, and for a moment, I can't move.

The portal is a doorway. A lifeline. A tether to the world I once called home.

He kept his promise.

I stare at the glowing light, my pulse thudding against my ribs. I could walk through it. I could leave all of this behind—the trials, the throne, the danger.

But as I turn back to Orion, as I take in the weight in his eyes, something inside me twists painfully.

Leaving Avalon was all I wanted once.

Once... but now?

The air in Pandora's cave feels suffocating, thick with unspoken words, as though it holds the weight of every decision ever made within these walls.

Orion stands stiff, his gaze unreadable, but I feel it—the quiet bracing of someone expecting the worst.

He thinks I'll leave.

That I'll walk through that portal and disappear from Avalon's fate, from his fate.

The hum of the portal vibrates through my bones. I let the weight of the moment settle over me. Let the enormity of the choice sink in.

Then, without a word, I turn and walk out of the cave.

Behind me, I hear the shuffling of boots, and I can envision Mor and Hypnos exchanging a glance before following. Orion doesn't hesitate either, his presence steady at my back, but he says nothing.

No one does.

As we make our way back toward Starfall, my steps quicken, my pulse pounding not with doubt but with purpose.

The castle looms ahead, its spires cutting through the mist-heavy night, a monument to the power struggles that have plagued this realm for centuries.

The courtyard still hums with life, Fae lingering from the remnants of Bloomrise, their glittering robes a stark contrast to the secrets and schemes that lurk beneath their polished exteriors.

Their eyes follow us as we pass, curiosity and suspicion woven into their pointed stares.

Liora stands near the fountain, her golden skin glowing unnaturally bright, a sneer curling at her lips as she watches me approach.

I don't spare her a glance.

She doesn't matter. She never did.

We stride into the throne room, the vast space filled with hushed murmurs and watchful gazes. Fae from every court are gathered here, their quiet conversations laced with intrigue.

I keep walking.

"What is she doing?" Mor whispers, her tone sharp with intrigue.

I feel the shift in Orion's aura, from unsure to proud. He lengthens his spine as his hand moves to the hilt of his sword, his steps as purposeful as mine. "She is taking her throne."

My boots echo against the polished stone, my pace never faltering as I move straight toward the dais.

Orion remains at my side, his presence solid, while Mor steps to my left, a dark, watchful shadow.

Hypnos lingers behind, unreadable as ever, but I feel his steady eyes on me.

The throne of Avalon looms before me—empty, waiting.

It has remained untouched since Pandora. Even Demeter, for all her delusions of power, never dared to sit here.

A seat of legitimacy. Of destiny.

And it has been waiting—not for just anyone but for the next true queen.

I let my gaze sweep over the room, meeting the eyes of those who would doubt me, who would challenge me.

My voice is calm when I speak, but there is no hesitation, no uncertainty.

"It's time to prepare," I say as I lower myself to the seat, my hands resting on the ornate arms of Avalon's throne, "for the queen's coronation."

ACKNOWLEDGEMENTS

Well. Here we are.

Book one of my *second* fantasy series. If you'd told me back when I was writing my first book that people would actually read it—let alone that I'd be here, with seven published books and a growing fantasy multiverse—I probably would have laughed nervously and gone back to scrolling Booktok instead of editing.

And yet, here we are. Expanding this world, weaving threads that my readers don't even realize are tying everything together yet—yet. And when they finally connect the dots... I can't wait for the chaos that is sure to unfold after.

To My Kids

First and foremost, to my kids, who watch me live my dream while also witnessing me mumble about plot holes at 2 AM like a deranged goblin.

Being a single mom, working full-time, and still somehow managing to write entire books is a balancing act.

But it's all worth it. I hope seeing me chase my passion inspires you to do the same (minus the sleep deprivation).

To My Writing Besties, The Distracted Inklings

My dear Inklings—you know who you are (but let's be honest, you're already distracted and probably not reading this carefully anyway😊).

I don't know how I'd survive this writing life without our daily shenanigans, brainstorming sessions, and mutual avoidance of actual responsibilities. You make this whole process infinitely better.

To My Readers

And, of course, to my readers—without you, this would just be me yelling into the void.

The fact that you pick up my books, fall in love with my characters, and stick around for whatever madness I throw at you next is mind-blowing.

You're the reason this dream is real. Every message, every review, every time you rant about my plot twists? You motivate me to keep going.

So thank you. For being here. For reading. For trusting me to take you on this journey—even if you have no idea where it's all going yet. [insert evil giggle here]

Until our next adventure,

To stay informed on my upcoming releases, book signing events, and more, visit my website and sign up for my newsletter.

www.rebekahsinclairwrites.com

If you'd like to chat with other readers, join the Rebekah Sinclair Writes discord!

Welcome to
The Black Ledger

Where every desire has a price...
and every contract is final.

A new dark romance series
coming Summer 2025

The Black Ledger
Billionaires

Check Out www.RebekahSinclairWrites.com for more!